Herrick's Key

Book 3 of The Neath Trilogy

By

T.M. Blanchet

A Tiny Fox Press Book

Library of Congress Control Number: 2023952192
ISBN: 978-1-946501-68-4

Tiny Fox Press LLC
Parrish, FL

For Don and Ginger Blanchet

Prologue

The Neath
Midyear, 1698

Ellora's hair splayed like sunbeams, gold and voluminous, against the burlap pillows of the bed. The girl's blonde was no ordinary blonde, just as her magic was no ordinary magic. George Herrick knew this to be true.

He had known it from the moment he first spotted her, lingering at the edges of the group, lost in a tangle of her own musings. Younger than the rest, and clearly uninterested in the long-winded discussions of her elders. Fidgeting. Nearly bursting with accumulated kinetic energy. Herrick had been immediately struck by the girl's obvious beauty and power, each twisting around the other in a magnificent helix. But he had been more interested to observe that Ellora seemed somehow unaware that she possessed either one.

It was the opportunity he had been waiting for. An opportunity in the guise of a lovely, unsuspecting witch.

At that first meeting, Herrick had made a point to catch the girl's eye. To share a smile, then another, and then, finally, a conspiratorial wink. Ellora had reacted with shy delight. As expected. She had been as transparent to him as a slow-dripped icicle, even then. And now, just a few short months later, she was exactly where he had planned for her to be: Lying beside him in bed, staring up in wide-eyed adoration. Still lovely, still unsuspecting.

Herrick had melted the metal; now he had only to mold it into a blade.

He tasted the satisfaction, savoring it, until her voice floated like a phantom through the fog.

"What occupies your thoughts so, my love?" Ellora was asking. As she spoke, her finger traced a delicate path through the hair of his arm.

Herrick suppressed a snort. Why did females ask such questions? Did they imagine that men's brains were consumed only with thoughts of affection? If so, the world would be a half-formed place, indeed. Still, he knew what answer she expected, as clearly as he knew that her sliding finger would soon give rise to goosebumps on his skin.

He turned to her, smiling, and grasped her hand. "My thoughts in this moment are the same as they were upon awakening. And the same as they shall be when I close my eyes to sleep, and in every moment in between. I think only of you, my dear, sweet Ellora. How could it ever be otherwise?"

The young witch blushed with pleasure. "Surely you must have *some* other contemplations throughout your day."

"Of what?" he asked. "Of food? Of learning? Of daily chores? What need have I for such ordinary things when I am blessed with an angel in my midst?"

Ellora poked him gently on the arm. "You jest," she said. "It is kind of you. But you do not fool me. You are a very important man, George Herrick! The most important man in the Neath, I dare say."

Her voice was flush with pride. Not pride in his accomplishments, he knew—only pride in her acquisition of him. Herrick was not just any important man. He was *her* important man. And that, in the end, was what mattered.

"Oh, now I would not say so much as *that*," he said.

"Well, I most certainly would!" she countered. "Look at what you have created! What your ideas have spawned! It is nothing short of astounding. Everyone says so. An entire, wonderful, underground sanctuary. A place of respite and peace. And all of it, born from your own imaginings!"

Herrick waved a hand in false modesty. "I am only grateful that the witches entrusted me with the creation," he said. "As you know all too well, I am only a mortal. And a flawed one, at that. It is the magic of your kind that made this place possible."

She sat up straighter. Yellow ringlets fell from her shoulders. "Be that as it may, you are truly a friend to witches. And to me."

"Only a friend?" he asked with an exaggerated pout.

In response, she blushed again, then leaned forward to kiss his lips. After a moment of silence, she whispered, "You know, good Sir, that you are much more than a friend to me. I only wish—" She stopped midsentence.

"You wish what?" Herrick prodded. "Name your wish, and I shall render it true."

Ellora sighed. "Alas, you cannot. My fondest wish, my only wish, is that I did not have to hide my affections like some...some..." She floundered. "Like some common criminal!" she finally finished, indignant.

He nodded sympathetically. "Aye. Some days, I confess, I am near to bursting with this secret we must bear. Your name lingers on my tongue with each breath, and yet I am unable to speak it!"

Despondence settled onto her delicate features. "I fear it is impossible," she said. "The elders have forbidden it. They say I am too young, and that you are too..."

"Too human?" he finished.

Ellora gave an apologetic smile. "Perhaps, yes."

Herrick adopted his best look of chagrin and pulled her close. "They have only your best interests in mind, my darling. I am sure of it. And we must heed their wisdom. Still, it is a shame, is it not? That they cannot see what I see?"

"And what do you see?" She looked up at him, so hopeful, so credulous.

A fish begging for the hook.

It was almost too easy. Herrick paused for dramatic effect before continuing. "What do I see? I see a girl like no other. A girl who is so much more clever, and more capable, than her kind give her credit for. A girl who is young in years, perhaps, but old in wisdom." He kissed her knuckles. "How you would soar, my dear! How you would surpass us all! If only..."

"If only what?"

He gazed into her wide, mahogany eyes. "If only they did not hobble you so."

At this, Ellora flinched. "You believe the elders are hobbling me?"

Herrick shrugged. "Of course. How else to contain a spirited mare? After all, you are clearly the more talented, and beautiful. Not to mention the more powerful. I suppose it is only natural for them to be jealous."

"Jealous?" the girl scoffed. "Of me?" But the idea had taken hold, he could see. It unfurled from her consciousness like a freshly sprouted rhizer shoot, eager and searching. She reached up to run a hand through his thick hair. "Well, maybe Goody Hutchinson is a bit jealous," she allowed. "That wretched woman has never had a kind word for me. She told me more than once to stay away from you, did you know that? She thinks you are up to no good."

Herrick let his eyebrows climb. "Really? Well, one can hardly blame her, I suppose. After what I did..." His words dissolved into a pained grimace.

"That was a long time ago, before you knew better," the girl insisted. "You're different now. Look at all you've done for the witches! Building this beautiful place! Why can they not see that you've changed?"

"Ah, my dear. There is a lot, it seems, that they do not see. And yet, in some ways they are correct, are they not? There is so much more I wish I could do. When I think of the suffering that I helped to perpetuate, during those cursed trials in my beloved Salem..." He hung his head and shook it, slowly, back and forth.

It was no secret that he had served as the Deputy-Sheriff of Salem Village during the witch trials. No secret that he had been the one to drag the accused from their homes, toss them into fetid jail cells, and even carry them to the gallows to hang. He had not objected to the proceedings—what care did he have for such wretched people, after all? Still, the job was beneath him, as was the pay. George Herrick had been born a gentleman in Mother England, for heaven's sake. But here, in the colonies, things had been different. Crude, and ignoble. Nevertheless, he had persevered. He had done what was asked of him, and he had done it well. Was it his fault that the magistrates had gotten it wrong? That they had hung blameless villagers and let the real witches walk free?

In the end, however, it had made little difference. Everyone knew what role he had played. Especially the witches. And they intended to hold him accountable. The thought of such creatures—women, no less!—with such domination over him... It was insufferable. Humiliating beyond compare. Even now, the notion made bile rise in his throat. And yet, he'd had no choice but to acquiesce, feign remorse, and bide his time. To climb into bed with his enemy.

And so it had begun.

Herrick convinced the coven that he was penitent, and that he wanted to atone for his past misdeeds by creating a beautiful, magical, underground sanctuary. "The Neath," they would call it: a place where all persecuted people could at last be free from the witch hunts in the world above.

He spun his tales with practiced skill. When Ellora entered the picture, he told her of his yearning to help his fellow humans, especially those who suffer at the hands of others. And she believed him.

He regaled her with plans for a better, more just world. An expanded and improved Neath. A penitentiary, perhaps, designed only for peaceful rehabilitation. And she believed him.

He flattered, and pined, and professed grief for his past actions. Time and again, he dropped nuggets of ideas for her to pick up, examine, and accept as her own.

And finally, when Ellora's youthful, lovesick heart was at its ripest, Herrick took his bite.

"If I had but a fraction of your gifts, we could be together forever," he told her with a wistful smile. "But alas, it is not to be. You know it as well as I do, my darling. I hold no magic. I am not your equal. And so we are cursed to remain apart. Someday soon, this world shall tear you from my arms. And when it does, I swear to you, I shall never be whole again."

He dropped his head, staring down at his lap. Watching a single tear fall from his cheek and land soundlessly onto the blanket below.

Waiting.

After several seconds passed, Herrick began to wonder if he had miscalculated. Then, Ellora's voice broke into the heavy silence.

"There...might be a way," she said.

At that, he looked up. "A way for what?"

"A way for me to share my magic. With you. It is strictly forbidden, of course. And I would suffer grave consequences if..." Her sentence evaporated into nothingness.

Herrick could see the girl's anxiety calcifying. Quickly, he moved to soften it. "No, my dear. You cannot put yourself at risk. I am not worthy of such an honor."

"You are my love," Ellora replied. "And this is my magic. I should be able to do with it what I wish, should I not?"

"Of course you should. I only fear the wrath of those that would seek to hold you back—"

"To *hobble* me?" she interrupted, scornfully. "Let them try."

At that, a satisfied grin began to curl the edges of Herrick's lips. He squelched it.

Ellora reached for his hands, her eyes alight. "Yes. That is what I shall do. I shall share my magic with you, my love. And we shall determine our own fate. Together."

He shook his head. "No! I cannot! I say again, I am not worthy of such an honor!"

"Please, George. I see now... It is the only way. Tell me, will you take it? Will you do this for me?"

Herrick let his eyes travel her features. Let the seconds tick away. Let a shadow of worry cross her face. Then, and only then, did he answer in a gentle, solemn whisper: "For you, I will. Only for you."

Ellora shrieked in happiness and lunged toward him, wrapping her small arms around his neck. "Then let it begin! We will be together forever, and we shall change the tides of history! Centuries from now, they shall speak of us. I swear it will be so."

"You have already written our entry into the history books, I see!" he said, laughing.

"Our entry shall write itself," she countered. "Mark Antony and Cleopatra, Hadrian and Antinous, Helen and Paris—"

"George and Ellora," he finished for her, grinning.

She brushed his cheek. "The mortal made magic, and the witch who loved him evermore." When she leaned in to kiss him, she tasted raw and sweet.

Like innocence.

"You are going to change the world, George Herrick," Ellora whispered into his ear. "*We* shall change it. Together."

He pulled the young witch close and rested her head on his waiting shoulder. "Yes," he agreed. "Yes, I think we shall." Slowly, he began to stroke her thick, flaxen hair. And this time, when the satisfied grin curled once again at his lips, he did not attempt to stifle it.

Chapter One

Boston, Massachusetts
Present Day

Someone was watching.

That was Ollie's first coherent thought, after the shock wore off. After he had climbed out from among the dead at Copp's Hill Burying Ground, stepped into the astonishingly bright sunshine, and steadied himself on both feet.

Someone was definitely watching. The awareness squeezed him like a blood-pressure cuff, insistent and uncomfortable.

But who?

Ollie had just traveled up and out of the bowels of the earth—from a place so far below Boston that the subway tracks of the T rumbled, unheard, somewhere in the great distance above. Its denizens called it the Neath. If you knew where to look and who to ask, you could find it. But very few people did. The obscure, subterranean realm had been there, and not there, for more than 300 years, populated by witches, trogs, Nova Scotian water nymphs, hummingtails, worms with feet, hundreds of captured prisoners, clear-skinned humanoids, giant crows, affable mutants, and, until very recently, one Ollie Delgato. Visitor turned resident. Captive turned hero.

Hero turned stooge.

A strange set of circumstances had sucked Ollie into the Neath, and an even stranger set had kept him there. It was not, at first, a voluntary sort of stay. To put it mildly. Not long after arriving, he'd found himself languishing in a prison cell, staring at crumbling walls, clinging to madness, and dreaming of the day he might, impossibly, return to his city. Now, many months later, he had done exactly that. Ollie was back in Boston—or "the Brickside," as they called it in the Neath. Aboveground, at last. And unbelievably, all he could think about was how and when he could head back down.

That, and the creepy-crawly feel of someone's—some*thing's*?—focused gaze.

Finally, he said it out loud: "Someone is watching us."

Ollie was talking partly to himself and partly to the Lycra-suited man perched on a nearby crumbling tomb.

"Yes," the man agreed in a thick, Eastern European accent. "Is true."

They shared a moment of silent discomfort as their eyes darted in tandem around the graveyard's shadows.

When Ollie had surfaced, terrified, from the cemetery's depths, Laszlo Kravchenko had been waiting. His friend had looked into the darkness, held out a hand, and lifted Ollie into the light. As only true friends do. Six months ago, Ollie hadn't even met this strange, amiable acrobat. Today, he would trust him with his life. Come to think of it, he already had. More than once.

They were the unlikeliest of companions—the local kid and the hardened immigrant. Green versus seasoned. Plump versus lithe. Teenage versus...older, though Ollie couldn't quite get a handle on how old, exactly, Laszlo was. Twenties? Early thirties? Anywhere in that range seemed plausible.

Laszlo, as always, was a sight to behold: a peacock in full plume striding amongst the pigeons. He wore the shiny blue tights, belt, and tank top befitting a street performer of his stature, which, apparently, included a close familial relation with *the* famous Flying Kravchenko Brothers of Ukraine. He also had wavy dark hair that reached all the way to his shoulders, a hooked nose, bulbous muscles, and an almost constant demeanor of joviality that defied all rational explanation.

Even now, in this moment of uncertainty, with a shrouded threat lurking somewhere just beyond their sight, Laszlo was swinging one of his legs jauntily back and forth, back and forth, alongside the mossy tomb. Confident. Restless. Ready to meet whatever natural or supernatural challenges might lay in their path.

Ollie, on the other hand, felt as powerless and petrified as a million-year-old fossilized stump.

As a wave of heat flushed his face, he realized with a start that both winter and spring had passed in his absence. Of course they had. Did he think that the planet would stop its orbit the moment he slipped below its surface? On the day he had fallen through the Freedom Trail, its red line of bricks had been crusted with snow and ice. Today, no doubt, they were hot enough to fry eggs—and he would know, because he had once done that very thing, long ago, crouching to watch the sticky, yolky mess congeal on the sidewalk until his mother called him in for dinner.

Summertime in the city. It all came back to him, suddenly, in a tumble of childhood memories. Long, lazy days. Secondhand sneakers. Fire hydrants spraying. Chalk drawings on cement steps. Fish poles at the wharf. The sprint from Mrs. Locatelli's corner store after an accusation of shoplifting. Ollie hadn't stolen anything, of course; he'd merely been curious to find out if the rubber lizard would fit in his pocket. It did.

He'd been pudgy, even then, with pale skin and a thick mop of curly blond hair. Always the tallest—and the roundest—person in the classroom, or at the park, or on the street. Not much had changed.

Well, one thing had changed, down there in the Neath. The biggest and best change of his life.

Tera.

Thanks to her, Ollie no longer saw himself as a blanched, freakish giant. Tera, remarkably, seemed to love him exactly as he was, warts and all. Not that he had any warts. But if he did, she would love them. Or at least pretend not to notice them. That was just the kind of girl she was: kind and clever and beautiful and way, *way* tougher than him. Braver, too. Braver than anyone he had ever known.

Ollie took a deep breath, forcing himself back into the present. His body swayed on the uneven cemetery ground. He waited for his eyes to adjust to his new surroundings, but found that the sunlight remained blindingly radiant.

Mud to brick, dark to sun.

Words of prophesy, coming true. Again.

Someone had known he would make this journey. Someone had predicted it, warned him about it, and even helped to usher it along. Someone whose identity and motivations remained frustratingly murky.

This was where he'd been heading, all along. To this place, on this day. Of that, at least, he was certain, though the reasons still eluded him. Ollie shivered and inhaled it all: Mildewed gravestones. Window boxes bursting with color. Boats zipping through the harbor. Thumping beats from passing cars. Glossy, green leaves casting welcome patches of shade. Out-of-towners in flip-flops, tripping on the cobblestone paths. Bicycle bells chiming. An iced coffee in every hand.

The sights swam before him like a foggy, half-remembered dream. Was it real? Was he really here?

Yes.

Yes, he was here. But not, unfortunately, for a summer picnic.

Ollie shook his head, hard, struggling to regain focus. Her name floated again above the confusion.

Tera.

She was his everything. He had been forced to leave her behind in the Neath, and now she was in danger. Hideous, mind-bending danger.

Tera was depending on him. They all were. Ollie had much to do, and not much time to do it. He knew that. He remembered it all.

But now that he was actually back, standing in the long shadows of Boston's brownstones and red maples, things suddenly seemed a little less...clear. The Neath, so solid and real just hours ago, now seemed so terribly far away. So...nebulous. Church bells chimed somewhere down the hill. Glorious aromas wafted in from all directions. Bakery ovens. Sauces simmering beside opened kitchen windows. Burgers cooking on balcony grills. Ollie's mind, once so purposeful, went slack. And he realized with dismay what was happening: His brain was being hijacked by his rumbling stomach.

Pizza.

The sudden thought was all-consuming.

Pizza, pizza, pizza.

He looked at Laszlo, who nodded again. "You are thinking of food, yes?"

"Yes," Ollie whispered.

"Is normal, this," the Ukrainian explained. "You come back to Brickside from down below, you must have food. First thing."

Ollie nodded weakly. If anyone knew what was normal in this very abnormal situation, it would be Laszlo.

In his day job, the acrobat performed for tourists in Fanueil Hall, collecting ones and fives in his hat while juggling, balancing on tiny platforms, and bending his limbs into mind-boggling knots. But it was his second, more secretive occupation that had brought him into Ollie's orbit all those months ago. Laszlo worked as a "Runner" for the Women's Resource Center, or WRC, ferrying victims of abuse to sanctuary in the Neath. Anyone who found themselves in need of peaceful refuge could get it, thanks to Runners like Laz. It was much more than a job, of course. For Laszlo, it had become a calling.

The acrobat's WRC duties weren't always so rosy, however. In some cases, he'd been tasked with the far less pleasant chore of transporting the perpetrators of all those crimes—wife beaters, child abusers, and others who preyed on the innocent. Those passengers were bound for very different Neath accommodations: a decaying, grisly prison tower known as Herrick's End. There, the abusers had paid "only what they owed," which usually translated to torture, appalling conditions, and no hope of release. Ollie had learned all of that the hard way when he'd been mistaken for a perpetrator and condemned to a long, miserable life in a tiny, miserable cell.

Laszlo had been there to help Ollie and Tera escape the terrifying confines of Herrick's End. Later, he'd also stepped up to accompany them on their journey to reach a hidden laboratory beneath the Neath's deep, green lake. Now, Ollie found himself muddling through yet another perilous mission—a mission he'd expected to face alone. So he'd gone weak with relief to peer out from that burying ground portal and find Laszlo's angled, friendly face peering back.

Once again, Laszlo had come through for him. And once again, he was unspeakably grateful.

"We must get you food," the acrobat said now, studying Ollie with concern.

"But—"

"Yes, yes, we have much to do," Laszlo interrupted, holding up a hand. "And yes, someone..." He paused, darting his eyes again around the dappled sunlight of the graveyard and its surrounding streets. "Someone watches. I feel this, too. But you will not be thinking in the straight until you are done with the eating."

Ollie wanted to protest. Tera was waiting, after all. And Meatball, too. Plans had to be made and carried out; this was no time for lingering over lunch.

Pizza.

The thought intruded again, weakening his knees.

For months, now, Ollie had eaten only the most basic of foods. First, the repulsive slop served at Herrick's End. And then, the bland meals that his new friends had shared with him after welcoming him into their home. He'd been thankful for the nutrition—mostly blindfish from the lake and potato-like rhizers. It was sustenance, and it was fine. Sometimes, more than fine.

But it was no North End.

Then again, what was?

"Pizza?" Ollie said. The word had a desperate edge that shamed him.

Instead of answering, Laszlo swept an arm in a "lead the way" kind of gesture.

Ollie swallowed. Then he kicked dirt from his sneakers and rushed forward, his peripheral vision blurry with tipping gravestones and unmowed grass. He pushed past clumps of tourists on his way through the opened wrought-iron gate. Ollie doubted that any of these people had seen him emerge from the ground; the portals to and from the Neath seemed to be invisible to all but those who needed to find them.

He exited the cemetery and turned left, with Laszlo close on his tail.

All of the passersby seemed lost in their own musings and conversations. And yet, with each face, Ollie wondered: Him? Her? Was this the person who was watching? For what it was worth, no one caught his eye. No one stuck out a leg to trip him as he passed. No one grew horns and blocked his path with a menacing, fiery stare.

Pizza.

Ollie's steps quickened as he approached the end of Hull Street, knowing what he would find around the corner. The North End had been a primarily Italian enclave for more than a century; today, the small neighborhood was still crowded with close to one hundred bakeries, trattorias, cheese shops, cafes, and salumerias run by immigrants and their descendants from Milan, Naples, Rome, Genoa, and Sicily. For all of his nineteen years, Ollie had been enveloped by deliciousness. It had all seemed so...normal to him, then. So mundane. Now, he could not imagine how he could have ever taken it for granted.

He rushed down the hill and veered right at the Old North Church. Tripped over the feet of the elderly, chatty men lingering in apartment doorways. Dodged a baseball-hatted woman taking a photo. Stepped off the sidewalk to avoid a chihuahua on a long leash. The dog was wearing a bowtie, and its steps were sprightly, assured. The man walking him was engrossed in a cellphone conversation, jabbing his finger in the air for emphasis as he spoke. Ollie gaped at it all.

There, just ahead: Vona's Bakery. Eclairs beckoned in the window, their chocolate shells glistening with a sheen of moisture. Champagne cookies and cinnamon-swirled "elephant ears" sat alongside Panettone and almond macaroons. Colorful cakes with whipped-cream frosting spun in a rotating case. The line, as usual, stretched out the door.

And there, further down Salem Street: The Zesty Pesto, with its drooping awning. Bella Vita, a few doors down, and Venezia Trattoria after that. Each restaurant, Ollie knew, offered a full menu of dishes like Gnocchi Sorrentina, Pollo Parmigiana, Zuppa di Pesce, and Beef Carpaccio. His mouth watered as he imagined Caesar dressing, creamy and white, poured onto homemade croutons. Broccolini dusted with parmesan. Thick pork chops, perfectly seared, accompanied by a heaping pile of linguini.

He took a sharp turn at Vona's, then another. A red Volkswagen honked as he hurried blindly across the street.

"Ollie!" Laszlo shouted from behind. "Where we are going?"

And there it was, straight ahead. The one, the only. The original. The best.

Gianelli's Pizzeria.

Ollie had come to a full stop, staring at the door.

Laszlo stepped up next to him, panting. "Why so far?" he asked, jerking a thumb over his shoulder. "We pass five other pizza people on the way!"

"None like this one," Ollie said reverently. Saliva rushed like a river in his cheeks, threatening to dribble out.

"Mmm." Laszlo folded his arms. "And how do you think to pay for this feast?"

Ollie went still, then looked up at his friend in wide-eyed dismay. Well, shit. He slipped a hand into the right front pocket of his regulation Neath jumpsuit and pulled out a wad of square, brightly colored papers. Down below, it was money. And hard-earned money, at that. Up here, it was nothing more than confetti.

"I...don't have anything," Ollie said, the words slipping out in quiet panic. No cash, no clothes, no phone, no ID. He was, for all intents and purposes, an illegal alien in his own hometown. He froze in place and might have stayed that way indefinitely if not for the sudden, hard thump on his back.

"I kid you!" Laszlo boomed, thumping once more. "My friend, what do you think? This is my first riding of the rodeo? No." The acrobat laughed and gave Ollie's shoulder a firm squeeze. "Come, now. This is what I do, all the days. I take people where they need to go, and I get them what they need when they get there. I know all of this like front of my hand."

Ollie shifted and smiled. "The back of your hand, you mean."

"The what?"

"You know it like the *back* of your hand."

Laszlo furrowed his brow. "Why would I know back of hand better than front of hand?"

Ollie shrugged helplessly.

"Your English," the acrobat sighed, "is never making sense to me."

Ollie shrugged again.

"Well, front of hand, back of hand..." Laszlo lifted both into the air and waved them. "They are here, now, to do the paying for the pizza. And this is what matters, yes?"

"Yes," Ollie answered, the gratitude returning in a rush. "Thank you."

"Come." Laszlo pushed open the door. "We will eat, and then you will tell me all the things."

Ollie nodded hard and fast enough to pull a neck muscle as he followed his friend inside.

Barely one step across the threshold, he had to hold onto the wall for balance. The smell...*oh, sweet saint of all things holy*...the smell. It was like his late grandmother's kitchen, but better. Like St. Anthony's food festival, but better. Like a gentle breeze drifting off an actual angel's cloud in actual heaven, but better.

He stood there, dazed, while Laszlo ordered and paid. They sat down at a booth. Ollie found himself glancing nervously out the window while they waited. Someone was still watching, he was certain of it. But nothing—and no one—seemed particularly out of place.

And then, mere minutes later, there it was: On the table. In his reach. Paper-thin, slightly charred crust. Browned, bubbling cheese. Discs of pepperoni, curled up at the edges. Ollie's hands trembled as he reached forward to separate one slice from the pie. Lifted it into the air. Watched the oil drip, the cheese cascade, the crust flop, as he brought it to his mouth.

It was too much. Too perfect. Ollie felt lightheaded as he chewed. Slowly at first, then faster. And faster. Before he knew what had happened, that first slice was gone. Then another. He ate like a guy who'd recently been stranded on a desert island (which, actually, he had). Like a guy who had nearly drowned. (He'd done that, too). Like a guy who'd escaped a cursed cave, climbed a Salt Witch's jagged mountain, and found his way into a genuine, honest-to-God, mad scientist's laboratory. (Check, check, and check.) And he'd done all of it, every onerous thing, without a single slice of pizza to tide him over. Unthinkable.

He was moaning, he realized, but couldn't seem to stop.

"Ollie, my friend," Laszlo said, gently touching his arm as Ollie reached for a third—or was it a fourth?—slice. "Maybe you should slow down the eating, yes? Pizza will not run away, I promise you."

Ollie paused. Embarrassment colored his cheeks. "Right. Sorry. It's just so...good. And it's been so long."

Laszlo waggled his eyebrows. "That is what she said."

Ollie stared at his friend for a moment, then started to laugh. And laugh, and laugh, until his belly ached and tears pricked the edges of his eyes.

Laszlo leaned back in his seat, looking pleased that his joke had elicited such an enthusiastic response.

Ollie didn't have the heart to tell him that he wasn't laughing at the lame joke. He was laughing because the shocking wonder of it all had suddenly become too much to contain. The food, the city, the purple summer flowers poking out of terracotta pots... Despite all the terrible trials he'd been through, and the even worse trials that were undoubtedly still to come, here he was: healthy and whole, sitting in an air-conditioned restaurant, eating the world's best pizza with quite possibly the world's best friend. Didn't that make him lucky? Maybe it even meant that things were not quite as bad as they seemed. He clung to the thought like a life raft.

Ollie leaned back in his seat, exhaling the kind of happy sigh that only follows a much-needed laugh.

"Now you tell me everything, yes?" Laszlo said, tucking a strand of dark hair behind his ear. He took an enormous bite of his own slice and chewed. His mouth was still full when he asked: "What happened in lab?"

And just like that, the blissful reprieve evaporated. Reality descended. Ollie's stomach twisted. And the pizza, which had been so irresistible only seconds before, suddenly began to resemble nothing more than a cold, congealing pool of grease.

Heartburn was coming.

Heartache, too.

Luckily, Ollie was already an expert at both.

Two

Ollie, truly, didn't know where to start.

What *did* happen at the lab?

Not what he had expected to happen. And sure as hell not what he had wanted to happen. As for the rest, it was still smoldering in a bonfire of anger and confusion.

After thirty seconds of awkward silence, Laszlo dropped his pizza onto the paper plate with a wet thud. "Ollie," he said, his voice quiet. "You must tell me. Is Tera...?"

"She's alive," Ollie said quickly. "Sorry. I should have said that right away. She's alive, and Meatball, too. But he's got them trapped. It's this gooey stuff, really disgusting, in giant tanks. And there's some kind of a spell holding them in. I couldn't get them out." Now that he had started, Ollie couldn't seem to stop. "I tried! I really did! But I guess he has to say some specific words, or whatever. And he couldn't say them, because his face was all squished, because I made him kind of...blow up. You know, like a tick. It was really gross. I didn't mean to do it. I mean, I guess I did, but I didn't know that—"

"Ollie!" Laszlo interrupted, dropping a hand on his friend's arm. "You know I am not good at hearing when you do the talk, talk, talk so fast."

"Sorry," Ollie said. He steadied himself. "I know, sorry."

Above their heads, a row of cheaply framed photographs hung in a line—celebrities, mostly, posing with Gianelli's slices. Or with the Gianelli's themselves. The closest picture featured an actress whose name Ollie had forgotten; her face looked out of focus. Or maybe his vision was still wonky from the trip.

"Is okay," Laszlo said. "Just start with first things, yes? How did you get to here? How you are breathing?" Laszlo waved a few fingers in front of his own nose and mouth.

It was a valid question: Theoretically, Ollie shouldn't have been breathing at all. Once his lungs had adjusted to the Neath's atmosphere, he had been trapped there, unable to return to the Brickside—until he and Tera had found the Grimshawe Laboratory and the fabled breathing device hidden within.

Ollie glanced down at his forearm, where a bullet-sized bulge stretched the skin. "There was a peashooter kind of thing, in the lab," he said, pointing to the bump. "I used it to shoot a pellet, here."

"Pea...shooter?" Laszlo repeated, perplexed.

"Like, a gun. But instead of a bullet, it had a little...pill. Or something."

"And this...pill, it lets you to breathe?"

Ollie lifted his palms. "I'm not dead yet." He gave a weak laugh.

Laszlo didn't echo the amusement. Instead, he said, "Okay, next things. You say 'he.' He, he, he. Who is he? Who has Tera?"

Ollie took a deep breath, gripped the edge of the Formica table, and looked straight into his friend's eyes. "George Herrick," he answered.

Laszlo's head gave an almost imperceptible shake. "But... George Herrick is dead. You mean to be saying, you found another Herrick note?"

"No, I mean he's not dead."

The acrobat blinked slowly—so slowly that Ollie wondered for a moment if his eyes had sealed shut. When the lids finally parted, Laszlo spoke in a gentle, overly patient tone. "Ollie. My friend, you saw this man die. We buried him! In Neath! There is a stone of the head. How do you say...a headstone. With his name!"

Ollie didn't avert his gaze. "I saw somebody die," he agreed. "Somebody that we all thought was George Herrick because that's exactly what he wanted us to believe. But it was just...some guy. Some patsy, from Herrick's End. Floor Thirty-Two, apparently."

Laszlo's mouth hung open. He didn't reply.

"I know." Ollie held up his hands. "It's crazy. *He's* crazy. And he's up to some really bad shit down there. You should see that lab of his! All kinds of creatures, like the Unnatural Wonders, but worse. Way worse. And he's—" Ollie stopped.

"What?" Laszlo prodded.

"He's...stealing magic. From *people*. Witches. He's got them all hooked up to these weird...I don't know, machines, or something. They're floating in the goo, and it's like he's siphoning off their magic. Using it for himself."

"Using for what?" Laszlo asked. His face had paled.

"I don't know. Nothing good! He's planning something, and he needs them to do it. That's why I had to come back here. I need to figure out what's going on. I need to stop him, Laz. *We* need to stop him."

The acrobat nodded. Swallowed. "And our Tera... She is hooked up to machine, too?"

"No," Ollie said, gritting his teeth. "She's just...floating there. In a tank."

"But not dead?"

"No. Not dead." At least, that's what Herrick had told him. Not dead, not alive. Just some terrible place in between. He squeezed his eyes shut, trying not to remember. Trying not to picture her face, contorted into a silent scream. Her body, encased in the revolting gelatin. And Meatball beside her, his furry little torso and webbed feet frozen in a swim that might never resume.

Pain shot through his chest.

Ollie realized, suddenly, that he'd been picking at a tear in the plastic seat cover for several minutes. Making it worse. Now, the white padding was spilling out like pus from a wound. Hurriedly, he tried to stuff it back inside.

Laszlo had been absorbing the news, rubbing his forehead. Then he asked, "And why not you, in tank? Why did this bad man let you go?"

"He didn't. He—" Ollie paused. "He tried to capture me. He wanted to put me in some other tank, back by the witches and the weird machines. He said he needed me for something. I don't know what. He and the other guy, Carmichael... They came at me. They were going to grab me. To throw me into the other tank. And then..." Ollie furrowed his brow.

And then...what, exactly? Then, something had happened. Something he still couldn't explain.

"And then...you escaped?" Laszlo finished for him, looking confused.

"Yes," Ollie said. "Right. I...uh, fought them, and I escaped." It wasn't the whole truth, but it wasn't a lie, either. For now, it would have to do. What else could he possibly say? *Well, Laz, as it turns out, when I get pissed off enough, beams of light shoot through freckles on my skin and I'm suddenly able to move inanimate objects with my mind. So, I stabbed George Herrick in the neck with a poisonous quill pen without ever actually touching the thing, and then I made a break for it. Pass another slice of pepperoni, would you?*

It sounded absolutely absurd, even to him. Part of him wondered if he'd imagined the whole thing. He looked down at his forearms, checking for the telltale reddish blisters, but saw nothing.

Laszlo was tapping the table restlessly. "And what about missing women?"

Right. The missing staffers from the WRC. As if all the rest of it wasn't bad enough. Ollie rubbed his palms together. "Herrick did that, too," he answered morosely.

"But...women were taken here, on Brickside. How did Herrick do such thing from down there?"

"His henchmen, I guess. He must have had somebody kidnap the women, and then sent the ransom note to lure me to the lab. He knew I would take the bait."

SEND OLLIE UP OR THEY ALL DIE, the note had demanded. Shortly after, he and his friends had learned that someone had broken into the WRC offices and taken the staffers against their will. Straight-up kidnapping. They were still missing. The perpetrators had also roughed up Ollie's old boss, the wonderful, innocent Mr. Bonfiglio, and forced Ollie's friend Nell to pose with the ransom note.

And for what? What the hell was the end game, here?

"Wait," Laszlo said, holding up a palm. "Wait. I thought Herrick wanted to do the helping? Why would he send you the helping notes, if he did not want to do the helping?"

"That's the thing," Ollie said. He leaned forward and lowered his voice. "He didn't send the notes."

"But... they are Herrick notes," Laszlo protested.

That's what they had all called them, anyway. Those "Herrick notes" had guided them through prison tunnels, underwater caverns, spinning islands, mutant circuses, and every bewildering spot in between, prophesizing events to come and providing helpful hints for escaping said events. Sometimes they rhymed. Sometimes they didn't. Either way, the notes made very little sense until...well, until they suddenly did. It was all very weird, even when they thought Herrick had sent them. Now, it was even weirder.

"Trust me. When I mentioned them, he had no clue what I was talking about," Ollie said. "It wasn't him."

"If Herrick did not send the helping notes, then who did?" Laszlo asked.

Ollie had no idea. But he did know this: George Herrick had ruined Ollie's life. He had ruined many lives. And he seemed dead set on ruining many more. That's why Ollie was here—to find the missing women, to figure out how to rescue Tera and Meatball from their half-dead confinement, and to uncover Herrick's plan and thwart it. Life and death, here and now, do or die. And he had less than one week to make it happen.

As if reading his mind, Laszlo asked: "What to do next?"

"I'm...not sure."

Laszlo nodded, then nodded some more, wringing his long hands. "This is not good."

"No," Ollie agreed. As he let out a deep sigh, he felt it again: A prickle on the back of his neck. The watching. He spun, catching sight of a figure in the window. Army-green, hooded sweatshirt. Mostly shadowed face. The steam from the pizza ovens had obscured the glass, making a clear view impossible. The figure darted away.

A flicker of recognition drifted across Ollie's consciousness... then disappeared. Something...familiar. He furrowed his brow.

Laz had followed his gaze. The window was empty. "You are seeing something?"

"Yeah. I mean, no…" Ollie shook his head. "Probably nothing. Just somebody walking by." He cleared his throat. "Any updates on the missing women? Were you able to find anything out up here?"

Laszlo flashed a regretful frown. "Nothing yet."

"And what about Nell?" One of his only friends on the Brickside, Antonella "Nell" Cascone had spurred Ollie's trip to the Neath when she'd disappeared suddenly from their "Lighter Tomorrows" weight-loss support group. Ollie had gone searching for her and ended up trapped underground. Then, after Nell returned to Boston, Ollie saw her face again: This time, she was holding up the ransom note for the missing women. Ollie had yet to learn how, or why, she'd been forced to display the note, or what had happened to her afterward.

"Nell is not at her home," Laz said, sounding hesitant. "And she is not at meetings. Other things… I do not know."

They sat in uneasy silence. At the next table, an employee was folding pizza boxes and stacking them into a teetering pile. *Fold, fold, fold, close, thump. Fold, fold, fold, close, thump.* There had to be nearly twenty boxes already in the stack, but the guy showed no signs of slowing. Or of starting a new pile.

"I am thirsty," Laszlo finally said. "We did not get drinks. Drink for you?"

"Yes, thanks," Ollie said. He tried to smile, but the question brought back a flood of distressing memories of the last time someone had offered him a drink (that wasn't just a drink) and what that drink (that wasn't just a drink) had made him do. His gut churned.

Ollie watched Laszlo approach the counter. He slipped a hand into his pocket and ran a finger along the edge of the crunchy parchment. Then, he pulled it out, placed it on the table, and stared at it. The page was still folded neatly. Some of the ink had bled through, leaving black smudges.

Fold, fold, fold, close, thump. Fold, fold, fold, close, thump.

The parchment was real. Really real. Ollie had shoved it into his pocket in the Grimshawe Laboratory, carried it up and out of the Neath, and now it was here on a table next to the greasy paper plates at Gianelli's Pizzeria. And if the parchment was real, that meant that all of it had really happened. That the lab was real, the tanks were real, and Tera and his trog were really down there, right now. Maybe conscious. Maybe suffering.

He reached out to touch the dried, yellowed paper, hoping it might disappear.

It didn't.

Two paper cups landed on the table, making him jump.

Laszlo slid into the seat across the table. "Lemon limey," he said, pointing. "Is okay?"

"That's great, thanks."

The acrobat tossed a straw; it landed next to the folded piece of parchment.

"What is that?" he asked.

Good question. Ollie considered how to answer as he unwrapped his straw. "It's another note. Sort of."

"A Herrick note?" Laszlo asked, then remembered. "Or—"

"A not-Herrick note," Ollie corrected. "It's from the same...person, I think. The same sort of gobbledygook."

"Gobble...?" Laszlo stared at him suspiciously. "Like, with turkey?"

"It means, like, nonsense. Words that don't make sense."

"Ah. Like other notes, then."

Ollie nodded. "But this one was sort of...dictated. By the witches."

"Which witches?" Laszlo asked, then laughed. "Which witches!"

Ollie smiled. "A few different ones, actually." He thought about Bert, Elisha, and Lizbeth in their nest, and Weelichka in her salty fortress. "They said they had...messages for me. From 'the person who wanted me to have them.' And then they kind of went into, like, a trance, and said a bunch of...stuff."

Laszlo's eyes went wide. "Like old man at park. Old man who said words to you, and died."

Ollie nodded. The old man they had thought was Herrick. But wasn't.

"And these new words are...gobblybook?"

Ollie nodded again. "As I was leaving, I wrote them all down. I figured... I don't know. I figured they might be useful."

Laszlo slurped his soda and tapped the side of his head. "Is good thinking," he said. "That is what happened before, yes? The words helped you. Now they will help you again."

"Yeah," Ollie said. The straw squeaked as he slid it into the hole in the plastic lid. "Sure." That was true, in theory. He didn't mention that the first witch messenger seemed to be drunk off his ass, or that the second one had a maniacal, disgusting obsession with collecting salt from people's sweat.

He took a long, slow sip, savoring the sweetness and carbonation. Tera had once told him, "Don't look a gift horse in the mouth." Even if it wasn't perfect, the message was still a gift. And at the moment, it was the only one he had.

"Well?" Laszlo said, pointing. "What does all this gobbling say?"

Ollie sighed. He started to unfold the parchment, half expecting it to disintegrate in his fingers. When it didn't, his eyes scanned his scribbles. The black ink was smeared with red blood—Herrick's blood, which had spurted when Ollie yanked the sharp quill pen out of the man's distended neck.

Ollie flattened the paper on the table and spun it around, giving Laszlo a moment to read.

A message for you, from the one who wishes you to have it: Water, earth, air! He will need it, way up there!

Three points. One key. Water, earth, air. Three points make one key. Not here, but there. Not down, but up. Up and up and up.

Water first. The water of your youth. From Myrtle to Coral, and then further still.

Earth! Earth second. Herrick's home. The place of his sin. The remnants of the victims will guide you.

Air! Air third. Two-twenty-one, two-ninety-four. Climb to fly. Walk the sky.

Laszlo scrutinized the scribbles, then looked up. "This is lot of words," he said. "But not very much..."

"Sense?" Ollie finished for him.

"Well, yes. But also, not very much...how do you say...cutting the clear?"

"It's not clear-cut," Ollie smiled wearily. "No argument here."

"Still..." Laszlo read the words again, looking thoughtful. "I do see same words, over and over again. Like this 'up.' It says, 'way up there.' And, 'not down, but up. Up and up and up.'"

"I was thinking that must mean the Brickside," Ollie said. He grabbed a paper napkin and dabbed it against his neck. The air conditioning, so refreshing when they first entered, now felt like nothing more than a weak wheeze. No match for the blistering ovens behind the counter.

"Yes," Laszlo agreed, then pointed. "And this 'water, earth, air.' So many times."

Ollie nodded.

Rubbing his chin, the acrobat asked, "What is key? 'Three points make one key.' Is this what we need to be finding?"

Ollie lifted his palms. He had no idea. But he did find Laszlo's use of the word 'we' to be incredibly reassuring.

"So you do not know what any of this means." Laszlo said it as more of a statement than a question.

"Nope." And between the desert-island escape, the laboratory horror show, and the exhausting climb through the earth's crust, he hadn't had time to think about it, either.

"But the witches... They give us order, yes? They tell us where to start? First, second, third. Here, it says, 'Water first. The water of your youth.' And witch was talking to you, when she said this thing?"

Ollie sat back in his chair, fingering the crust on his plate. "Yes."

"Okay, then. So it is your youth we must think about!" Laszlo looked delighted. "That is what we need to know, first thing. What is water of Ollie's youth?"

Ollie took another sip of his soda, unsure where to begin. His youth had been surrounded by water: The North End perched on the edge of Boston Harbor like a scoop of vanilla in a root-beer float. He had sometimes ventured out on fishing boats with neighbors. He had spent plenty of time down at the docks. And his mother had also taken him to the local beaches from time to time: Revere. Nantasket. Spectacle Island.

Was he supposed to go looking for something out in the harbor, or the ocean? Again, that didn't narrow things down much.

He furrowed his brow. *The water of your youth.* The local BCYF pool, where he took swim lessons? Nothing special about that place. Nothing...magical. It was just a cement rectangle, doused with too much chlorine. The Greenway fountains? Maybe. Was he supposed to just go frolicking around down there and hope something appeared in the spray?

Water first. The water of your youth. From Myrtle to Coral, and then further still.

Who the hell were Myrtle and Coral? Neither name rang a bell.

Unless... they weren't people's names. Now that he thought about it, the capitalizations had been his. An assumption that they were names. But maybe...they were places? Myrtle Beach? Plenty of water there. But far away. Ollie had never been down south, as far as he knew. So unless someone had taken him there as a baby, it didn't seem to fit.

He looked at the other name. Coral. Coral was also a noun. What if the message was referring to just regular coral? Like, the stuff that grows in the ocean? The New England coastline, he assumed, must have its share, though he most associated coral with tropical locales. Barrier reefs and huge, colorful fish. The kind he used to see at—

Ollie looked up, wide-eyed. "The aquarium!"

Laszlo tipped his head.

"The water of my youth! We had a family pass. We went all the time, me and my mom. I think I even went a few times with my father, before..."

He let the sentence trail off, and Laszlo lowered his eyes respectfully.

Before. Such a loaded word. Especially in this case. And he didn't want to think about his father. Not now, not ever. Why bother? It never did any good. Thinking about Matteo Delgato usually only managed to leave Ollie feeling angry, nauseous, and muddled. A rage hangover, you might call it. And that was the last thing he needed now, when so much depended on him thinking clearly and moving quickly. Matteo had already ruined Ollie's past—he'd be damned if he was going to let the asshole ruin his present, too.

"Why aquarium?" Laszlo asked.

"It has tons of coral," Ollie continued, tapping his finger against the words. "And there's lots of water, of course."

"Water of your youth," Laszlo said.

"Right." Among others. But this one seemed to fit the bill the best. Or at least, that's what he'd suddenly decided to tell himself in an effort to avoid the crippling panic of indecision. Doing something was surely better than doing nothing, wasn't it? Better than wandering the sidewalks and tripping over chihuahuas with bowties, all the while imagining the details of Tera's ongoing anguish somewhere far below?

"Okay, then!" Laszlo said, looking pleased. "We have first thing first. And second thing... That is easy."

"It is?"

"Yes! Look here..." Laz leaned forward and pointed to the scrawled lines. "It says, 'Herrick's home. The place of his sin.' Is clear, yes? Only one place?"

They looked at each other and said it in unison: "Salem."

George Herrick was, undoubtedly, a man of many sins. But there was only one sin in particular that a witch would be whispering about in Ollie's ear.

Herrick had served as the Marshall and Deputy-Sheriff of Salem Village in 1692. His job description, such as it was, included rounding up accused witches during the infamous trials and dragging them to their deaths. His neighbors, acquaintances, and friends. They had all been innocent of the charges, of course—not witches at all, just ordinary, all-too-human villagers. But in the end, it hadn't mattered. Five victims had died in the jail, one unlucky man had been pressed to death with stones, and nineteen more had hung at the gallows. Twenty-five, in all. Death by hysteria.

Every American knew the shameful outcome. Very few, though, knew the truth hiding behind the tale.

No witches had hung in Salem. But that didn't mean that witches weren't there.

As the treacherous events of that spring and summer had unfolded, as screams filled the streets and death choked the air, the real witches had watched from a distance, aghast. When it was all over, they had punished Herrick for his sins. And then, somehow, he had managed to turn the tide. He had convinced the witches that he felt remorse, and that he wanted to atone for his sins. Herrick helped the witches create the Neath as a place of sanctuary for all victims of abuse and persecution. And they had celebrated him for it.

But George Herrick was full of shit—then, and now. He had never changed his ways or felt remorse. He had simply manipulated the witches, and their magic, for his own gain, though Ollie still didn't know how.

It all reminded Ollie of that old song about the kindly woman and the sickly snake. The woman takes in the snake, nurses it back to health, and then is surprised when it bites her. Fatally. But the creature is unrepentant, saying, in effect, "You knew I was a snake when you took me in!"

Once a snake, always a snake. Ollie's eyes narrowed as he thought about what that vile man had done to Tera. What he had done to everyone, and what, potentially, he was still planning to do.

"Yes," he said. "We have to go to Salem." *The remnants of the victims will guide you.* That part should be easy. Though much time had passed, Ollie imagined that many descendants—and long-lasting consequences—remained. And from what he had learned of the man so far, there were undoubtedly plenty of Herrick victims to go around.

Laszlo nodded and tapped his fingers against the table. "We will need car," he said. Salem was about an hour's drive north of Boston. "But we do that second, yes? 'Earth second,' it says."

Ollie nodded.

"Okay, then. Okay." Laszlo seemed to be mostly talking to himself. Ollie could see his wheels spinning. "You go to aquarium. First things. See what you can see. And I will go see about getting car. Second things."

"But...what about the missing women? And Nell? And Mr. B? I should go visit him in the hospital, shouldn't I?" Ollie also wanted to visit the scene of the crime—or scenes, as the case may be. The WRC, where the women were taken, and Bonfiglio's Caffe, where he used to work. Where Mr. B had suffered a beating at the hands of Herrick's minions. And all of it, every horrid thing, had been done in an effort to catch Ollie's attention.

And poor Nell... What had they done to her? Had she been taken with the other women? Where was she now? How would he find her?

He shivered as the guilt tripped down his spine.

Laszlo frowned. "How much time?"

"How much time, what?"

"How much time you have, here? On Brickside? With breathing...bullet?" He gestured toward Ollie's arm.

"Oh. I...don't know. Not exactly. Carmichael said I probably had about a week? But he didn't know. Or claimed to not to know, anyway. Who knows?" He paused. This was starting to sound like an Abbot and Costello routine. "Anyway, not much time. That's the short answer. At the very least, I have to get back down there before Herrick shrinks backs down enough to cause more trouble." Or to touch a hair on Tera's head. At the thought, Ollie's lips hardened into a line. As much as he wanted to linger in the bakeries and sunshine, he had to get moving. And keep moving. Whatever it took.

"If that is case, then I think, my friend, that you cannot visit hospital. Not yet. We must follow the words. The words will help us find the missing girls, yes? And help learn other things? We must do the first things first."

"Wait, what about the police, and the press?" Ollie asked. "This must have been on the news, right? About the break-ins, and the kidnapping?"

"No. But that does not surprise me," Laszlo said. "Neath...business has way of staying quiet here, on Brickside. They can make it so."

"Quiet, how?"

"Quiet, like invisible. Like things never happened. No questions, no seeing. Nothing."

"What are you saying? No one even noticed they're gone? That's impossible. Their families must be frantic."

A look of surprised amusement flashed across Laszlo's face. He stared at Ollie for a moment, as though considering his answer. Then he said, "You know what I do, yes? For WRC?"

Ollie felt a lecture coming on. He squirmed. "Yeah."

"All those days, I take abusers to the Neath. They just...poof! Disappear. So many, gone! And yet, you never see that on news, no? You never hear police ask, where are all those people?"

Ollie shook his head, slowly. Come to think of it, no. He'd never heard any news reports like that at all. And all the other people in the Neath...the survivors, who chose to escape. They were missing people, too, weren't they? Here on the Brickside? Hundreds of people, vanished. Yet he'd never seen so much as a flyer posted on a telephone pole.

"So the witches are...what? Controlling reality?" It was absurd. Wasn't it?

Laszlo's eyebrows rose—two spindly inchworms creeping up his forehead. "What is real?" he asked. "Real is only what you see. What you *think* you see. Your real is different from her real, and his." Laszlo gestured toward pizzeria patrons at the nearby counter, then tapped his own skull. "Is all here, your real. And if there is no one real, then real can change, yes?" He dropped his booming voice to a quieter rumble. "They can make it change. They can make you remember. And..." he paused, seemingly for effect, "they can make you forget."

Despite the sip of soda, Ollie's mouth went dry. Was that some kind of warning?

No. It was just...the truth. Ollie had seen it for himself, down in the Neath. Time and time again. He'd seen hard surfaces that looked like flowing water. He'd seen the Novas' beautiful, and dangerous, mirages. Those had certainly looked real. He'd even seen a wonky invention in Grimshawe Laboratory that was designed to implant false memories.

Reality, it seemed, was relative. Above the earth and below.

And now, someone was watching them. Or seemed to be watching them. Real or not, the sensation was strong enough to give him goosebumps.

"So no one is helping?" he finally asked. "No police, nothing? It's just us?"

Laszlo didn't bother to answer. His expression was almost apologetic.

And then, the inevitable happened: The pizza guy's precarious stack of boxes fell to the floor with a clatter. Not a particularly loud clatter—more like a dull, cardboardy resonance. But it was enough to make both Ollie and Laszlo jump in their seats. Seconds later, they looked at each other with embarrassed grins.

Ollie sighed. Laz was right: He'd have to wait. He'd follow the weird clues first and find what he needed to find. How long could it take? Then he'd circle back to check in on Mr. B and Nell. It's not that he was abandoning them, or ignoring them...It's just that he was postponing the check-in. A little tiny bit.

He gathered himself. "All right. No problem. We can do this. We've done harder stuff, right? This is just like...a scavenger hunt. Three stops. Piece of cake." With his Boston accent, the words came out sounding like "pisacake." He nodded firmly and added, "We'll divide and conquer."

Laszlo's forehead scrunched into a row of wrinkles.

"Piece of cake means easy," Ollie explained. "And divide and conquer is like...teamwork makes the dreamwork. Two heads are better than one."

"Two heads?"

"Two heads, baby." Ollie pointed at his own noggin, then Laszlo's. "One, two."

Laszlo sighed. "Sometimes I think is *your* words that are gobblybook."

"Forget all that," Ollie said, waving a hand and leaning forward with an intense stare. "It doesn't matter. All you need to know is this: We're going to get this son of a bitch, Laz. One way or the other."

"Ah," Laszlo grinned. "Now that, my friend, I understand."

Three

The aquarium was only a short walk from the North End. Ollie took the scenic route through Christopher Columbus Park, making sure to cross under the long, wisteria-wrapped trellis. The scents of fresh-cut grass, sausage vendors, and salt air tickled his nose.

Hundreds of locals and tourists lounged, strolled, and picnicked in the sunshine. They gazed out at the sparkling harbor while Ollie gazed at them. So many people. Young, old. Tall, short. Running, resting. And not a single one had the slightest inkling about the other world—magical, dangerous, and extraordinary—that existed right below their feet.

It made him feel lonely. And a little dizzy.

He missed Laszlo already.

Before setting off to find them a car, Laz had pulled a few more tricks out of his acrobat's bag: namely, a wad of twenties and a change of clothes. Ollie was now wearing an extra-extra-large "Wicked Smaht" t-shirt—probably bought from the nearest vendor cart at Faneuil Hall—and a pair of jeans. The last time he'd seen denim, he was peeling off his Levis for an embarrassing barter at Nikki and Floyd's Brickside Curiosities shop. This pair was stiff and new, and felt strangely confining after so many months in a loose jumpsuit.

His waistline, similarly, seemed too silent without his usual jangling toolbelt. And as for his shoulder...

Ollie felt a pang. He had grown so used to having Meatball perched there, snuffling and spinning and snorting in his ear. A comforting, weighted ball of fur and cuteness. Now, his shoulder was just...empty. No webbed feet clinging to his shirtsleeve. No platypus-like bill slurping up snacks.

Would he ever see his trog again?

Stop. Ollie glared down at the pavement and shoved the question away. He couldn't think about that now. If he thought about it, he might crumple. And if he crumpled, everything else would crumple, too.

Ollie heard his mother's voice in his head: *You must keep flapping if you want to fly, Passeroto.* Her little bird. Perhaps she had known, even then, that he would be flying on his own soon enough. That the cancer would take her long before he was ready to leave the nest.

I'm flapping now, Mama, he though with a grimace. Flapping, and tired. Would a little gliding be too much to ask? Maybe a nice, strong jet stream or Santa Ana wind? He wanted to pause on one of the benches, to steady his spinning head. To ponder the startling realization that his former life, his former home, now seemed so...foreign. Instead, he pushed on, furtively checking the faces as they passed. Looking over his shoulder.

Someone was watching. Still.

How was he so sure? Was it some kind of lingering ability or side effect of his newly acquired Neathian powers? Or maybe it was just some primal, hunt-or-be-hunted instinct inherited from his caveman ancestors on the savannah. He didn't know how he knew, only that he did. This surveillance was not paranoia. It was as real as the hard ground beneath his feet.

Minutes later, cement gave way to bricks as Ollie came upon the aquarium's main entrance. To his right, the towering theater annex loomed. Straight ahead, a roped-off, zigzagging queue led to a row of admissions windows. Ollie's feet moved past it all, almost of their own accord, toward the left. To the one aquarium exhibit that was still absolutely free to anyone who happened to wander by—no ticket required.

He rounded the corner and stopped short.

There they were, as always. Ollie's favorite Bostonians. He approached the glass and felt a spark of forgotten delight as the smooth, spotted bodies of the harbor seals swam into sight. They darted and spun, waving their flippers. Playful. Curious. Flexible as bendy straws. In quick succession, they brought their noses to the edge of the tank, then swerved away.

Except one. That particular seal, darker in color than the others, seemed to be lingering. Peering out through the glass. Ollie had never seen a seal go so still. It was unnerving. An odd tingle moved up his spine as he felt the unlikely, yet unmistakable, weight of the animal's gaze.

Someone was watching.

They observed each other, locked in a strange kind of staring contest, as Ollie shifted awkwardly from foot to foot.

Did the seal's eyes just...dilate? Ollie could swear that they did: two shiny black circles, growing bigger against the white rims. Nothing else moved except the animal's long, thick whiskers, which waved in the current.

Ollie felt himself stepping closer. Reaching up to touch the thick glass. And as he did, the present and past collided in a not-so-distant memory that made him convulse.

Tank.

His mind propelled him, suddenly, to that other tank. The one far below, where Tera and Meatball floated, helpless.

One tank among many, many others. Humans, witches, and terrifying mutant creatures, all suspended in gelatin. Frozen in time. Waiting.

But waiting for what?

Ollie shivered, returning to the present with a jolt. The harbor seal was still there. Still watching. Tilting its bulbous head. Then, slowly, it rolled itself upside down and right side up again in a perfect spiral—never once breaking eye contact.

The animal's strange behavior reminded Ollie of something he had seen—or thought he had seen—just a few blocks away, at the creature carousel. A lifetime ago, really, before he had fallen into the Neath. Ollie had been standing on the Greenway in front of the carousel, debating his choices: to go or not to go? Follow Nell's trail, or stay home? Neither option had struck him as particularly appealing. That was when the peregrine falcon sculpture had seemed, impossibly, to come to life, ruffling its feathers and shaking its head before fixing Ollie with a pointed stare. The same kind of stare he was getting now, from the seal.

It must be you, the falcon had said.

Different animal, same message. Or was that just another figment of his addled imagination?

Yessss. It must be you.

Ollie wobbled on his feet. "I have to go," he heard himself say. Out loud.

Next to him, a little girl looked up curiously. He hadn't noticed her until that moment. "Are you talking to him?" the girl asked, pointing at the seal.

He thought about her question, then answered, "I guess I am."

"Oh." She nodded as if this made perfect sense. "He seems to like you a lot."

Ollie didn't know how to respond. She wasn't wrong.

"Can you tell him I said hi?" the girl asked. He guessed she was about nine or ten years old. She had a cartoon character on her shirt that he didn't recognize and wore sunglasses shaped like hearts.

"Sure," he said. "What's your name?"

"Sadie."

Looking at the seal, he said, "Sadie says hello."

The creature flared its nostrils. Open, shut, open, shut, in a quick, repeatable pattern. It was like Morse code... Morse code that Ollie couldn't translate.

Finally, he tore his gaze away and glanced down at the girl. She reminded him, in a strange way, of Tera—spunky, observant, and unafraid. It made his heart clench.

"Who's that?" he asked, pointing to the character on her shirt. Some kind of superhero dog.

She glanced down as if she'd forgotten what she was wearing. Then she grinned widely. "That's Mack Attack."

"Oh," he nodded. "Cool. You and Mack keep an eye on this one for me, okay?" Ollie pointed to the seal, who was still watching them.

She gave an eager nod, her blond ponytail bouncing. "Okay. I come here a lot."

"Thanks."

An awkward silence descended as the girl continued to study him. She seemed to be memorizing the features of his face. Ollie squirmed under the weight of her stare, then finally let out a nervous laugh. "What's wrong?" he asked. "Am I uglier than the seal?"

"No. But you don't look like I thought," Sadie said.

"I...uh, what do you mean?"

"You don't look like I thought you would look," she clarified.

"But...we've never met," he answered, as gently as he could. He looked up and around. The girl seemed a little confused... Where were her parents?

"We've been waiting for you," she added. "I thought you'd come sooner. To do the searching."

"The searching?"

"For your three things," Sadie said matter-of-factly. "But you should be careful." She was holding a lollipop—the tall, twisty kind, with multicolored loops. Why had he not noticed the lollipop before? Where had it come from? After she spoke, she gave it a long lick from bottom to top.

Ollie looked down at the girl, so adorable and pink and blonde, and heard his heartbeat thudding louder than normal. "What...what three things?" he finally asked.

"You know," the girl shrugged. "Your stuff. Your list. Three things. You should be careful about that. About the searching."

His mouth went dry as chalk dust. When he spoke again, he tried to keep his voice light, but managed only a strangled kind of stutter. "Oh. Wow! Well. Huh. I'm not sure what..." He wiped a trickle of sweat from his forehead. "Why, uh...why do you think I should be careful?"

She licked the lollipop again, looking thoughtful. "Some people don't want you to find them."

He tried to speak, failed, and then finally managed to squeak out: "What people?"

"I dunno." Her answer had an amused, sing-song quality. "But that won't be good for you. So you should be careful."

Ollie's swallow took deliberate effort. Then he attempted a smile. "Well, that's... Wow. Aren't you... a funny kid. That's a funny thing to say."

The girl giggled. It should have sounded sweet. Instead, it sounded like a warning.

His eyes flicked to the space behind her, left and right. He saw nothing unusual. No leering men or women. No blur of green, like he had seen back at the pizzeria. Still, his palms had gone slick; he shoved them into his pockets. "Did someone...tell you to tell me that?" he asked lowering his voice. "Where are your parents? Who are you with?"

The girl named Sadie only smiled. Then she gave him a wave—five tiny fingers lifted and wiggling—before turning and disappearing into the throngs.

Ollie's feet felt heavy and stuck as he craned his neck, trying to follow the girl's path. But it was useless. The crowd was too thick, and she was too small. For one unhinged moment, he considered taking off after her—then realized just as quickly that chasing a nine-year-old through a public plaza was probably never a good idea. That would not end well.

No, there was nothing left to do but gape, perplexed, at the empty spot on the pavement where the strange little girl had stood just a minute before. What the hell was that?

He turned back to the tank. *What the hell was that?* he asked again, this time directing the question at the still-hovering seal.

The animal's nostrils flared.

Ollie, ridiculously, flared his own nose in response.

The seal seemed to consider this. Then it flipped over, spun around, and swam away into the murk.

Thanks for nothing, Ollie muttered in his head, glaring into the swirling eddies.

Who was she? What did she mean, *You should be careful?* How did she know what he was looking for? Her words still hung like sentence-fragment speech bubbles: *Your list. Three things.*

Had someone sent her? The same someone who had been watching him since he arrived back on the Brickside? Worse still, what if she was right?

The tank was still busy and bubbly; other seals flipped and swam into his line of sight. But not *his* seal. That one was gone. Just like the girl.

That won't be good for you. The sound of her giggle echoed in his skull.

Ollie pursed his lips, straightening. What was the matter with him? He had barely started on this journey, and already he was letting himself get sidetracked. She was just a kid, for God's sake. A babbling, confused third-grader wearing a superhero t-shirt and heart-shaped sunglasses.

Pull yourself together, idiot, he told himself.

In a daze, Ollie walked to the admissions line, where twenty or so people were already waiting. He used Laszlo's cash to buy a ticket before heading to the entrance. A pair of overly enthusiastic staffers tried to take his picture in front of a green screen; he declined, though they didn't make it easy. Finally, Ollie made it past the lockers, bathrooms, strollers, screaming toddlers, and hand-stampers and stepped into the main exhibit hall itself.

He inhaled. The air was briny and humid, with a hint of disinfectant. Bodies pressed all around. Parents and kids, mostly, along with a few summer camp field-trip groups in matching neon t-shirts. He looked across the sea of bobbing heads, searching for Sadie's blonde ponytail, but didn't see it.

Ollie pushed through the crowds to reach the nearest railing. Despite his mounting anxiety, he felt a tiny smile curl his lips as a small army of comical characters tottered into view. *Penguins.*

Their habitat weaved throughout the main hall, just below the maze of walkways. Visitors could peer down from almost any angle and see pools, water sprays, rock formations, and, of course, the stars themselves. Dozens of rockhopper and African penguins seemed oblivious to the attention from above as they preened, waddled, and swam. Depending on the time of day, visitors could also catch sight of the dinner show, when staffers appeared with buckets full of fish and tossed them into eager, open gullets. For now, though, all was quiet on the penguin front. The Africans tussled, the rockhoppers shook their yellow-trimmed heads, and the crowd drank it all in.

As popular as they were, the penguins were overshadowed in every sense of the word by the aquarium's enormous Ocean Tank, which towered in the center of the action. It was cylindrical, as tall as a North End apartment building, and encircled by a ramp that wound around its perimeter with ever-changing views of the myriad creatures living inside. Parrotfish. Barracuda. Sharks. Stingrays. Tiny chromis and gobies. And of course—coral.

Lots of coral.

Ranging from drab brown to yellow, teal, emerald, and every hue in between, the coral twisted throughout the tank in a complex and spreading web of colonies. They looked like plants, and Ollie always had to remind himself that they were actually animals. Hundreds and hundreds of hungry and probing little animals, stuck together to form mutually beneficial clumps.

As he contemplated the colorful hodgepodge from afar, he wondered: Was that the coral he was looking for? And even if it was, so what? What was he supposed to do, smash through the six-inch glass with his bare hands and grab some?

With a shake of his head, Ollie let go of the railing and kept moving. Maybe he'd see a hint, somewhere. A trail of bread crumbs. Or fish-food flakes. Or a guy in a yellow vest waving a couple of glowsticks and yelling, "Hey! Ollie! Over here!"

Sadly, he didn't see any of that as he wandered from one floor to the next. He did see pendulous sea jellies, a color-changing octopus, neon-striped sea dragons, and even something called a spotted ratfish. It was all just weird enough to make him think of the more fantastical underwater creatures he'd met in the Neath's deep green lake, not too long ago.

Ollie took a few minutes to watch the sea lions and their trainers, but skipped the IMAX theater shows. He peered at poison dart frogs, electric eels, baby lobsters, and pouty lionfish, all while winding around the knots of kids waiting their turns at interactive displays. He stayed on high alert for the approach of ominous nine-year-olds, and felt embarrassingly thankful when none materialized. Finally, he strolled the winding walkway that hugged the giant tank. Aquatic creatures of every size and color bobbed in and out of sight as he passed from one viewing window to the next.

No hints, though. No guy yelling his name. Just...fish. Lots and lots of fish.

The water of your youth. Did he get it wrong?

A green flash caught his attention in the crowd. Olive-green sweatshirt. Hood up, long, dark hair poking out from the bottom. The same one he had seen at the pizzeria? Inexplicably, the sight of it gave him goosebumps.

As before, a nagging sensation of familiarity swept over him. He knew that hooded figure. He knew that walk.

Was that...*Nell?*

No, it couldn't possibly be. Nell was kidnapped. She'd been taken, forced to hold that ransom note.

Hadn't she?

Was it possible his old friend was actually safe and sound? And...following him? That made no sense. Awash in a churn of confusion and excitement, Ollie took off running. The green hood bobbed just ahead, moving between the throng of bodies.

He called out as he ran: "Nell?"

The woman ahead was in earshot, but didn't turn.

"Nell!"

Just ahead, a camp counselor was gathering his field-trippers into a clump. He darted around them. "Nell? It's me! It's Ollie!"

He rounded the corner and saw strollers, harried parents, couples holding hands. Hypnotic jellyfish tanks. Emergency exit doors. But no green hoodie.

Ollie stood perfectly still in the center of the commotion, his hands hanging limply by his sides. His cheeks flushed. Maybe it wasn't her. There was more than one green sweatshirt in the world, after all. And there were lots of long-haired brunettes in Boston. It was entirely possible that he'd been mistaken. He'd wanted to see her, to believe that she was safe. And so he had.

That was the most logical explanation. But nothing about this day was logical, and something in him remained unconvinced. With a sigh, he continued his plodding search up, down, and around the aquarium's interior.

As the minutes passed, Ollie felt himself getting increasingly frustrated. And hot. And claustrophobic in the pressing crowds. What was he doing here? What had made him think this was the place? And why didn't any of these people wear deodorant? He'd walked every inch of the exhibits and seen nothing of use. He was on one of the straightaway ramps in the main hall, ready to give up, when he noticed a nondescript door. Staff-only, from the looks of it: metal, windowless, and probably locked. Black lettering near the top read:

New England
Oceanographic
Voyage
Association

Huh. It struck him as odd, the way the words were displayed one on top of the other. He'd never heard of that particular "association," though that wasn't surprising. Ollie wasn't exactly up-to-date on all the latest oceanographic voyage trends. Still, something about the name pecked at him. *New England Oceanographic Voyage Association.* Stacked, top to bottom.

Like you do when you're trying to emphasize an acronym.

Ollie looked at the sign again, this time paying attention to the first letter of each line.

N
O
V
A

He froze.

A coincidence?

In the Neath, Ollie had met a whole pod of Nova Scotian Water Nymphs—usually called Novas, for short. Not the friendliest of creatures. They were dangerously beautiful, highly territorial, and quite aggressive during mating season (as he and Laszlo had learned the hard way). But, to be fair, they had also helped Ollie on his quest to find the lab. And saved his life. So he might describe his experiences with them as a mixed bag.

N.O.V.A.

Could it be? Were there actually Novas here, on the Brickside?

Ollie glanced left and right. He turned and looked behind him, at the great, wide span of the main exhibit hall. He'd already looked everywhere else. Unless the penguins were hiding valuable secrets in all those splatters of white poop, he had run out of options.

Ollie turned back to the door. He took a deep breath, held it, and raised his hand to knock. But before his knuckles could hit the metal, the door swung open.

"Hello, handsome."

The woman staring back at him was not actually a woman at all. She had a tall shock of red hair, spindly limbs, and a dress made of dried kelp. Her head was overly large. Tiny scales shimmered all over her body.

Stunned, Ollie didn't respond.

The creature studied him a moment longer, looking pleased. Then she reached out one unnaturally long finger to touch his face. There was no fingernail on the tip, just a damp, webbed stump.

Ollie flinched and pulled away.

If she was offended by his response, or noticed it at all, she didn't show it. Instead, the Nova smirked and asked, "Coming in?"

Before he could answer, someone else piped in: "That's an easy yes, big guy. Unless you want to catch another sea lion show. But trust us: They don't get any more interesting." Ollie leaned to his left, peering around the first Nova to see a second. This one also had red hair, though the cut was shorter and the color was darker. More russet than crimson.

Then, a third voice: "Coming in means you actually have to come in." Yet another redhead, perched on top of a tall filing cabinet. Her scarlet braids were piled in a twist so high they almost reached the ceiling. "As in, move. Today. So we can close the door." She didn't add, *stupid human,* but he heard it in her tone.

Dumbstruck, Ollie shuffled forward, finding himself in a decent-sized room that looked like it might be an office. Three desks, three wooden chairs, three metal filing cabinets. He also saw a few non-officey items, including two large plastic kiddie pools (full) and an enormous tank of live goldfish (also full). The walls were covered in 70s-era wood paneling. The floor tile looked like it had been picked up at a closeout sale, with a matte finish and a color best described as puke-chartreuse.

But the Novas...ah, the Novas. They were every bit as cartoonishly gorgeous as he remembered. Huge, glimmering eyes. Full lips. Cherry-kissed hair. Stunning enough to lure sailors to their deaths on the rocks? Maybe. But also just menacing enough to make him want to run the other way.

The first Nova waited until he was fully inside, then swung the metal door shut. "I'm Isma," she said. "That's Fluvia, and that's Nyad."

"Hi," he answered.

"And you are?"

"Ollie. Ollie Delgato. I'm here to—"

"We know why you're here," Nyad said from her tall perch, sounding bored.

"How do you know that?"

"Because you saw the door."

"I—" he paused, flummoxed.

"Most people can't see the door," Fluvia explained. "Only the people who need to see it, see it. And you saw it, so..." She lifted one shoulder.

"I...don't know what that means."

"You know enough, I guess. And here you are." The shorter-haired Nova pushed past Isma, who huffed. Then she approached Ollie and pressed two grotesquely elongated hands against his chest. He was too surprised to react. "So...strapping," she said. "And meaty. Isn't he meaty, ladies?"

Ollie's eyes went wide. He wasn't sure if she wanted to slather him in barbecue sauce or tear off his clothes. Or both.

The other two murmured in agreement.

Uh oh. Was it still mating season for Novas? Maybe every season was mating season for Novas. He remembered Derrin's warning: *Whatever you do, don't call them mermaids. They hate that.* Ollie cleared his throat. "Thank you for, uh, opening the door."

"Mmm hmm." More murmurs.

"I know some of your friends," he added. "From the Neath."

"Let me guess. Eelia?" Nyad asked.

From her tone, Ollie couldn't guess if that was a good thing or a bad thing. "Uh, yep. And Crinni, and Nerida, and—"

Isma raised a hand, stopping him midsentence. "Whatever," she said. "State your business."

"My...business?"

"Duh, yes. Your business. Why are you here?"

Ollie cleared his throat. "I think...I'm supposed to find something."

"Says who?" Nyad jumped down from the filing cabinet; her large feet made a splatting sound when they hit the tile floor.

Wow. Tough crowd. "I don't know, exactly," Ollie answered, feeling more defensive by the minute. "The witches gave me a message. From...someone who, uh, wanted me to have it, apparently."

After a moment's silence, Fluvia asked, "Well? What's the message?" Her hands were still on his chest.

Timidly, he reached up to peel her fingers off his t-shirt. Her scales were surprisingly sharp, like tiny shards of glass. Fluvia didn't stop him; she just gave him a coy wink and backed away. "Look," he said. "I appreciate you opening the door and all. But...what is this place? Who are you?"

"We're Novas," Isma said.

"Yes, I know that. But what are you doing here? At the aquarium? Have you always been here?"

"Not *always.* Geez," Nyad said. "We're the Guardians. For now, anyway."

"The Guardians of what?"

"Well, handsome, that all depends on your message."

Right. The message. After a short internal debate—*Was it really a good idea to trust them? Did he really have a choice?*—Ollie decided to spill. "It's... short," he said, almost apologetically.

Nyad folded her arms. Isma rolled her hand in a "let's move this along" kind of gesture. And Fluvia continued to stare at him like he was the main course.

Ollie chewed the corner of his lip, then began to speak. "Water first," he recited. "The water of your youth. From Myrtle to coral, and then further still."

The three Novas glanced at each other.

"What?" he asked. "Do you know what that means?"

"We do."

"Can you help me?"

Isma sidled up beside him. Her freakish toes wrapped around his ankle; this time, he tried not to flinch. "We can," she said. "But first, we must wait."

"Wait for what?"

"For nightfall. What we have to do, we can't do while the crowds are about. You'll wait here, with us, until the aquarium closes. And then we'll see about that message of yours." She grinned, baring two rows of small, sharpened teeth. "How does that sound, big fella?"

Ollie gulped. How did it sound? Terrible. Time-consuming. And possibly lethal, if the gleam in Fluvia's eye was any indication.

It also sounded, unfortunately, like an offer he couldn't refuse.

Four

Ollie didn't remember seeing a cot, approaching a cot, or falling asleep on a cot. And yet, seven hours later, he woke, drooling, on a cot, with three giant-eyed redheads staring down into his bleary face.

He bolted upright.

In a muddled rush, it all came back to him: The aquarium. The Novas. The-office-that-wasn't-an-office for the Association-that-wasn't-an-Association. Ollie struggled to sit up. "What did you do to me?" he asked, relieved to see that he was still wearing clothes.

"You needed sleep. Obviously."

"So you...?"

"We helped you sleep," Nyad said with a shrug.

"What time is it?"

"Nightfall," said Fluvia, glancing down to straighten her short kelp skirt.

Since that wasn't, technically, a time, he waited for her to say more. She didn't.

"We can go now," Isma said.

Ollie was sweaty; he could feel the perspiration sticking his t-shirt to his back. When they turned, he surreptitiously sniffed his underarm. Not too bad. He wished he had a toothbrush. And maybe a pumpkin muffin with brown-sugar crumble. And a cappuccino. But none of that, sadly, seemed to be on the agenda.

With no further preamble, the trio of Novas led him out of the office-that-wasn't-an-office and back into the main exhibit hall. Ollie turned the corner and peered down, unsettled. Night had turned his once-familiar aquarium into an eerie, quiet stranger. He found himself walking gingerly, almost tip-toeing, through the shadows. The penguins were gone—perhaps sleeping in some kind of den?—and most of the lights had been dimmed to a soft, soothing glow. Nebulous shapes swam and slithered in nearby darkened enclosures. The interactive exhibits had fallen silent, their screens black. There were no other humans in sight.

"Where are we going?" he whispered.

Nyad pointed a finger in the air. *Up.*

They approached the ramp that encircled the central giant tank and started ascending. Ollie barely took notice of the circling, schooling creatures on the other side of the glass. How could he when the creatures on *this* side were so unnerving? And alarmingly close at hand? The Novas had an awkward, almost reluctant gait, as though their legs were protesting all the land-based locomotion. Why weren't these "Guardians" in the water, where they belonged? Moreover, why weren't they in the Neath?

A few minutes later, Ollie and his tour guides reached the terminus of the ramp. It ended at a viewing area overlooking the wide-open top of the massive tank. Above their heads, a ring of muted lights lent a quiet, almost moonlit sparkle to the water's surface.

"Here we are," Isma said. "This is your stop."

Ollie looked down. He saw blurred waves of color, branching coral outcrops, hundreds of fish, and a huge, speckled sea turtle swimming lazily below. "My...stop?"

"Yes. You were told to go from Myrtle to coral, and back again. Right?"

He nodded, perplexed.

"Ollie, meet Myrtle."

He followed Isma's gaze. "Myrtle...the Turtle?"

"The one and only."

Myrtle met his eye, briefly, before paddling away to continue her circular, seemingly perpetual journey around the tank's surface.

"She's the biggest thing in there," Nyad added. "Five hundred pounds, I think."

As if in response, the turtle changed direction. Ollie watched her hefty, domed shell dip in and out of the water as she moved at—well, at a turtle's pace.

"I don't understand. What am I supposed to do?"

"You have to ask her permission," Isma said.

"To do what?"

"To enter the tank."

Ollie's eye went wide. "Why would I want to do that?"

"To find what you're looking for." She pointed down. "Myrtle to coral."

Again, he peered over the edge. The clumps of coral stretched from the bottom of the tank all the way up to its surface, growing in every conceivable color and texture. Was he supposed to paddle along the top, like Myrtle? Was he supposed to dive deeper? He glanced at the back wall of the observation area, where wetsuits and SCUBA tanks hung on hooks. "I don't know how to use those," he said, panic making his voice go high.

The three Novas stared at him, arms folded. Waiting. Isma raised one eyebrow.

"Oh," he said, realization barreling into him like a linebacker. "You're going to give me the breathing thing, aren't you?"

Down in the Neath, the Novas had lent their underwater breathing abilities to Ollie and his friends, enabling the humans to search the depths of the lake for the hidden laboratory. The temporary gift had been nothing short of miraculous. Ollie, Tera, and Laszlo had nosedived, spun, and swam with ease, befriending the lake creatures and floating in a state of utter euphoria. It had been one of the most exquisite and wonderful experiences of his life—until it had transformed into one of the worst.

Ollie swallowed. "Okay, so how do I get permission?"

"Here," Nyad said. "She likes these." The nymph reached inside a darkened, nearby closet, pulled out a bucket, and handed it to him. Ollie recoiled at the sight, remembering similar buckets in the Neath that had been filled with chopped-up, still wriggling creepy-crawlies for Mrs. Paget's mealtimes. Reluctantly, he took the handle and peeked inside, expecting the worst. But all he saw was a small mound of greenish-brown lumps. Definitely not wriggling.

"Brussels sprouts?"

"Uh huh. They're her favorite." Nyad flicked her long fingers. "Go ahead."

Ollie lifted his eyebrows, then climbed out onto the staff-only ledge. Getting down on both knees, he plunged his hands into the bucket, pulled out a fistful of sprouts, and dangled his hand. *Here, turtle, turtle.*

Nothing happened.

"You have to *ask,*" Fluvia prodded.

"Right." Feeling foolish, he cleared his throat and said, "May I have permission to enter the tank?" He considered adding an honorific—something like *oh, wise Turtle Queen*—then thought better of it.

Myrtle paddled closer. She paused below his outstretched arm, studying his offering. Finally, she reached out her long neck, pulled two sprouts from his fingers, and began chewing slowly. Very, very slowly. So slowly that Ollie had to squint to observe any movement at all.

Isma hopped out onto the ledge beside him and pounded his back. "There you go! All set."

He coughed, startled at the thrumming, and nearly fell forward. "All set, what?"

"That was it. Permission," Nyad explained. "You're good to go." She reached up to adjust her high pile of braids, which had started to lean precariously. The style reminded Ollie of a wedding cake with too many tiers.

"Great," he said, though that wasn't the actual adjective he had in mind. "So now you....give me the breathing thing?" He wondered, briefly and nervously, if it would hurt. It hadn't, in the Neath, but things might work differently up here.

"We already did," said Fluvia. Then she winked and made a kissy face.

"Oh! Wow. Great," Ollie said again, though this time he meant it. Whatever they had done, and whenever they had done it, he hadn't felt a thing. "Okay, then. I guess I just...jump in?"

"Yep."

He looked down. Myrtle had meandered away, leaving a clear view into what had to be thousands of gallons of salt water. The faux moonlight on the ceiling illuminated shiny scales, waving fins, and countless permutations of marine animals. Sea life soup. And what did that make Ollie? The oyster cracker on top?

"Does that one have a name, too?" Ollie asked, pointing warily down at a bright green, menacing moray eel. The thing had to be five feet long. And maybe, probably, poisonous.

"Don't worry about them," Isma said, waving to indicate the entire tank population. "They know you're with us."

"All right. Great." That word, again. Ollie was embarrassed to hear his voice shaking. "How will I know where to go? And what I'm looking for?"

"Not our problem, handsome," Nyad said. This seemed to please her.

"But we do have something we're supposed to tell you," Fluvia added, sidling up beside him. Too close. Someone really needed to teach these Novas about personal space bubbles. Ollie tried not to grimace as she scraped a blunt fingertip against his ear lobe.

"Oh yeah? What's that?" If she told him he had to get naked, he was going to run screaming down the ramp.

"Two things, actually," Isma corrected, giving Fluvia a stern look. "The first thing is, you were wrong."

Ollie tilted his head. He was wrong? That's it? "Yeah, that happens a lot," he said. "Wrong about what, specifically?"

"About what you said." Isma recited the next part as though she'd memorized it: "The sword is mightier than the pen."

Isma's face blurred as Ollie felt himself reeling. Those words... How could she have known?

Only days—hours?—before, Ollie had stabbed George Herrick in the neck with a quill pen. Then, once the damage was done, he'd yanked it out. As the blood spurted and his anger mounted, Ollie had growled an admonition into Herrick's ear: *I guess the pen really is mightier than the sword.* Herrick, swollen and infected, had been unable to reply.

"Wh...what's that supposed to mean?"

"Don't shoot the messenger, big guy," Nyad said. "You were wrong. The sword is mightier than the pen. That's it. That's the message."

Ollie had already felt unsteady; now, he worried he might tip over. He fell back from his knees onto to his butt and thought back in astonishment to that other version of himself: the hissing, angry, powerful version that had overwhelmed George Herrick and sent objects flying through the air with nothing more than a simple thought. Who the hell was that guy? Where did he come from? And how could Ollie get him back? Right now, he barely seemed to have power over his own bowels.

You were wrong.

"What's the other thing?" he asked. *Please, sweet Jesus on a crumb cake, let it be instructions. A map. Better yet, GPS narration in a soothing Australian accent. "Descend twenty feet. Take a left at the brain coral. Your destination is ahead on the right."*

"Hmm?"

"You said there were two things."

"Oh, right," Isma nodded. She paused and looked up, as though concentrating. Then she said, "We're also supposed to tell you, 'Find the real among the false.'"

Ollie's arms hung limply by his sides. "The real among the false."

"Yep."

"The real *what?*" Frustration mounting, he held up a hand. "Wait, don't tell me. You don't know. You're only the messengers."

"Well, technically we're the Guardians," Fluvia corrected. "But, yes."

He stared at their three smiling, crudely oversized faces. A trio of bobbleheads, that's what they were. Bobbleheads who were about to send him down into 200,000 gallons of probable shark-infested water with nothing more than vague assurances and a nonsensical riddle to keep him safe.

"Well, that's just...great."

"You say that a lot," Nyad pointed out.

"Anyway," Isma interjected, "best to move this along. The staff gets here pretty early in the morning, so we don't have much time." She folded her bony fingers together.

Ollie gritted his teeth. He glanced again at the wetsuits hanging on the wall, then abandoned the thought. The Novas had come through for him in the Neath, hadn't they? Chances were, they would come through for him here. And if all else failed, at least he'd make the front page of the *Boston Globe* tomorrow. *"Body of local man found floating in aquarium tank."*

Or maybe: *"Pieces of local man found floating in aquarium tank. Questions mount as investigation continues."*

"Don't worry. Geez." Nyad rolled her eyes.

"We'll take care of you, big man," Fluvia added, practically purring.

Ollie took two steps back before she could wrap her elongated toes around his ankle. Again.

"So, I just...what? Drop in?" he asked.

"Like a tea bag," Isma nodded.

The irony wasn't lost on him, of course: He had fled terrifying tanks in the Neath only to arrive at another terrifying tank here on the Brickside. Would you call that full-circle? Or full-cylinder, maybe? The whole thing might be laughable if it wasn't so alarming.

You should be careful, the girl had warned him. *It won't be good for you.*

She might be right. But it wasn't himself he was worried about.

In his mind, Ollie quickly ran through all the reasons why he shouldn't lower himself into the teeming, cobalt water. The list was long. Then he thought about Tera, and Meatball, and a much worse tank far below, and did it anyway.

Five

This time, he didn't panic when the oxygen transformed into something wetter. His body fell, his lungs inflated, and he breathed. Miraculously and easily, he breathed.

Remembering his last experience with the Nova's subaquatic respiratory "loan," Ollie waited for the giddy intoxication to kick in—a high so perfect it would have put all of Woodstock to shame. But after several minutes, he was surprised to find that that he felt only like...himself. A waterlogged, confused version of himself, maybe, but nothing more. Brickside magic, it seemed, was a little duller than its Neath cousin.

Hands and feet waving, Ollie took stock of his surroundings. The Ocean Tank creatures might not have been magical, but they were beautiful nonetheless: All around him, the bodies and scales shimmered in a kaleidoscopic, floating parade. While he'd been submerged in the Neath's lake, the names of the creatures had just popped into his head, unbidden, like long-lost friends. Here, though, the tank's inhabitants remained nameless strangers. He saw white polka dots, orange zigzags, blue stripes, and yellow tails, but had no idea what each particular species might be called. Some of the fish traveled in rapid, spiraling schools; others plodded along in sullen isolation. None seemed to show the slightest interest in the pudgy, clothed human that had suddenly dropped into their midst.

Ollie rotated his body to face the bottom of the tank and started swimming. The animals veered out of his path, but the obstacle course of branching coral forced him to bend and twist into awkward poses as he made his way down into the depths.

Coral.

He studied the colorful clumps with squinting eyes. Fan shapes. Tubular shapes. Horn shapes. Clusters. Swirls. Sharp points. And still others that looked like tiny branching trees. Again, Ollie hoped for a guy with an orange vest to wave him in the right direction, and again, he was disappointed.

Myrtle appeared suddenly, making a leisurely pass above his head. From below, the turtle resembled an old woman who had lost her dentures. Maybe Myrtle knew what he was supposed to be looking for. Maybe she would offer a hint.

Instead, she paddled away.

Were the Novas watching from above, he wondered? Twittering at his ineptitude?

Nearby, a big, dark blue fish hovered, looking disappointed.

This was not going well, he knew. Nothing beckoned. Nothing blinked. Nothing looked like anything other than regular old critters that anyone could see, anytime, in any aquarium tank. It wasn't until he circled the bottom reaches for the second time that Ollie noticed something odd.

A series of tubes, snaking out from below a clump of pink polyps.

At first glance, he thought they might be another version of the tubular-shaped coral he had seen elsewhere in the tank. Then he realized: He wasn't looking at anything organic. He was looking at pipes. Ordinary, metal, Brickside pipes, cleverly hidden from visitors.

Ollie swam closer.

He reached out to touch the fuchsia skeleton of the coral that obscured the pipes. He expected the surface to feel fleshy. Or gauzy. Instead, it felt hard as stone. He pulled away, startled.

It was fake.

Ollie floated in momentary confusion. Then he kicked out his arms and feet, swimming in circles in a frenzied attempt to touch every coral cluster in the vicinity.

All of it, every last fleck and branch and polyp, was artificial. Shaped and colored cement, if he'd had to guess. How had he never realized this before? In all those years of aquarium visits, Ollie thought he'd been seeing actual coral in this tank. Living invertebrates. And all he'd been seeing were props on an underwater stage.

As the realization dawned, panic began to set in: He was supposed to find coral. Wasn't he? Not cement, coral-like sculptures, but actual coral.

The big blue fish glided past, giving Ollie a look of disinterest before swimming away again. As Ollie watched it go, he remembered, suddenly, the Novas' message.

Find the real among the false.

He'd identified the false, at least. Did that mean he now had to find some of the real stuff hidden somewhere in this maze of imposters?

Overhead light twinkled throughout the water as Ollie pushed off from the sandy bottom. He felt a little better, now, knowing he had at least a vague idea of what he might be looking for. As he began the search anew, he passed rocks—fake rocks?—and plenty of real fish, along with rays, eels, a few smaller turtles, and hundreds of tiny, floating flecks of algae. Or was it...feces? Ollie cringed at the thought. The view beyond the glass stayed dark in the evening stillness, but that, he knew, wouldn't last long. The aquarium would swing open its doors to staff and guests soon, and he didn't want to be here, splayed and sputtering, when it did.

He passed the entrance to a claustrophobic, bouldered cavity that he had ignored earlier. Ollie paused, waving his arms and feet while a school of orangey fish circled his head. He didn't want to go in there. It looked too small for a guy of his size. Still, he had to admit: As large as the Ocean Tank was, there were still only so many places to search.

He would have sighed, if breathing water into lungs didn't make that sort of thing difficult. Instead, he pursed his lips. Then he turned sideways, sucked in his gut, and squeezed his large body through the narrow crevice. Seconds later, he was in.

Whoever had designed the rock and coral habitat had done a masterful job; here in the enclosed area, Ollie could easily imagine himself lost deep inside some far-away, tropical reef. The human world all but disappeared as the fish darted in and out, back and forth, around and around and around. As Ollie watched them, mesmerized, his claustrophobia melted away. It was like a meditation, this place. A sanctuary. For the first time since he'd climbed up and out of the Neath, Ollie felt something close to serenity. His heartbeat slowed. The water pressure created a steady, hypnotic thud in his ears.

No one was watching him here. He was blissfully, finally alone.

That was when he saw it.

The tiny, purple polyp protruded from the edge of a nearby outcropping. It caught his eye because it looked, oddly enough, like Tera's hair: a violet wave that usually rose defiantly from the top of her head. The polyps moved like hair, too, waving slightly back-and-forth, up-and-down, with the currents of the water. Flexible and free. Ollie was no expert on fake cement coral, but he was pretty sure it couldn't do that.

Find the real among the false.

The purple cluster also seemed to be glowing. Not a blinding ray, but definitely a soft, welcoming gleam.

Ollie moved forward, his vision narrowing. This was it. The closer he got, the more confident he became. No yellow-vested guy necessary, no fish-flake trail. The polyp might as well be labeled with his name.

When he was near enough, he reached out to touch the waving strands and felt squishy, pliable tissue. *Alive.* Most definitely alive.

He felt a burst of excitement and pulled his face closer, until his nose was only inches away. Each undulating tendril had a tiny flower growing on its tip. The flowers were purple, too, though a slightly darker shade. Pretty. He smiled.

Wait, no.

One of the flowers was not a flower at all. It looked more like...a bubble. A plum-colored bubble, resting like an organic growth at the end of one of the polyps. It was transparent. Something—something very small—rested inside.

Ollie poked it, trying to pop it, but found that it was more solid than a bubble should be.

He squinted, trying to get a better look at the miniscule object encased within. It looked like a grain of brown rice. Or perhaps a seed? And it also seemed to be shaking, or jumping. The movement was subtle, but there.

Ollie pressed a finger against the bubble again, harder. Then he tried a fingernail. Neither attempt worked. The transparent skin remained stubbornly solid.

He ground his teeth in frustration. Whatever that thing was, he needed it. This was what he'd been searching for. He felt it as clearly as he felt the salt water stinging a fresh cut on his forearm. Tera's life—maybe everyone's life—depended on him getting this seed, or grain, or whatever the hell it was, and then getting his ass out of this tank.

And he was being defeated by a bubble.

He'd come all this way, followed the instructions, and found the thing. *The* thing. *This* thing. Here it was, right in front of him, and he wasn't going to leave without it.

He tried tugging on the bubble. It didn't release. He tried yanking it from side to side. Then he tried jabbing it with multiple fingers, to no effect.

Ollie narrowed his eyes. Fine. If he couldn't remove the piece he needed, then he'd just take the whole damn thing. His hand wrapped all the way around the purple clump. He yanked. Then yanked again. But no matter how hard he tugged, the lone little coral stayed rooted to the outcropping like a duct-taped fender.

Anger and acidity simmered beneath his skin. The last time Ollie had felt angry, he'd been able to do incredible, unthinkable things. Maybe he could do it again. He clenched his fists, letting the exasperation build. Waiting for the raised freckles to appear on his arms. For the light beams to illuminate the darkened water.

He waited. He concentrated. But...nothing happened.

As before, he stared at the object—in this case, the bubble—and gave the order in his mind. *Come to me.*

Nothing.

Pop, he said.

Nothing.

Ollie felt a growl deep in his throat. *Break open. Float to me. Explode.*

Nothing, nothing, nothing.

The Salt Witch had told him, *"Your rage will show you who you are."* Maybe simple anger wasn't enough. Maybe Ollie had to be in a *rage* in order for the power to manifest? *Krite on a kabob...* What good was a power if you had to be in a state of delusional, red-faced fury to even use it?

On the plus side, he was certainly getting madder with every passing second.

Ollie closed his eyes and dropped his head back in defeat. When he cracked them open again, despondent, he was looking through the opening in the boulders, out into the wider tank beyond. He saw the usual array of swirling stripes and spots...and one solid-colored fish, as well. It was gunmetal gray, and quite large, with fins on the bottom and top of its body. But the fish's most prominent feature was an astoundingly long, astoundingly sharp snout.

A swordfish.

The silvery-gray creature lingered at the opening, turning in small circles. Then it turned and looked directly at Ollie.

Ollie looked back.

The sword is mightier than the pen.

Ollie smiled and kept his gaze locked.

The pointy-nosed creature continued to stare, reminding him of the peculiar, peeping seal back at the aquarium's entrance. And the falcon at the carousel. *Hello, friend,* Ollie said. *I need your help.*

The swordfish rotated its fins, still hovering in its spot.

Would you mind? Ollie curled his fingers in a welcoming gesture.

A school of smaller fish passed through the water between them, temporarily obscuring his view. Seconds ticked by—a long enough time for Ollie to wonder if he had truly, finally lost his mind. *What am I doing? I'm talking to fish, now?*

When the school finally passed, Ollie watched the swordfish meander through the crevice towards him. Closer, then closer still, until it was hovering between Ollie's arm and the coral outcropping. Then it turned its beady eyes to Ollie. And waited.

Tentatively, Ollie pointed to the purple bubble.

He was wondering if he should explain, or describe exactly what he wanted. But before he could, the silvery fish edged closer, jabbed its point directly into the bubble, and burst the skin wide open. Suddenly freed, the tiny, oblong seed began to float up and away. Ollie reached out just in time to grab it before it drifted off into the murk.

Thank you, he thought, keeping his fist closed tight. *Thank you!*

But the swordfish had already turned to leave, sliding its narrow body through the crack in the boulders. Ollie caught once last glimpse of its tailfin, waving, before it disappeared into the open water beyond.

Six

"It lot of trouble to go through, for such small thing. No?"

Laszlo took his eyes off the road to scrutinize the brownish seed dubiously. It lay in the center of Ollie's opened palm, barely covering half-an-inch of skin.

Ollie couldn't disagree. He was sitting in the passenger seat of a mustard-yellow, decades-old Ford, which Laszlo had borrowed or rented or possibly stolen. Ollie hadn't asked, and didn't want to know. He'd just finished relaying the story of his after-hours fishing expedition as they barreled north in the fast lane on I-95.

"And it does shaking? All by itself?" Laszlo gave another nervous sideways glance.

"All by itself," Ollie confirmed. The seed had been bouncing around in his hand ever since he had freed it—or, more accurately, since the swordfish had freed it—from its underwater purple bubble. The jiggle was subtle, but definitely there. It reminded Ollie of the "jumping beans" his neighbor had once carried home from a trip to Mexico. From what Ollie remembered, those had been some kind of larvae encased in a pod; during metamorphosis, the larvae would move around and cause the pod to jitter. The other kids on the block had been fascinated. Ollie had been mostly grossed out.

This could be the same type of phenomenon, he supposed: nothing more than an ordinary, disgusting larva temporarily stuck inside a seed. But considering where, and how, he had come across the tiny pod, Ollie doubted that there was anything "ordinary" about it.

He curled his fist around the newfound treasure and turned his gaze to the window. As the trees and cars and big green signs flew past the window, Ollie marveled at the sight. It had been a long time since he'd moved so fast. In the Neath, he'd gotten used to traveling at the speed of crow boat. And even before that, when he'd lived on the Brickside, his city-kid lifestyle meant he'd rarely had a need for a car. This sudden, swift trip down the highway was starting to make him queasy—and it didn't help that Laszlo had apparently learned to drive at the Ukrainian Academy of Acrobatics and Drag Racing.

He closed his eyes. Pressure and anxiety weighed like dumbbells on his skull. He'd gotten some sleep on that aquarium-office cot, but not much. Not enough. The droning road noise and off-key humming from Laszlo lulled him into a drowsy stupor as his thoughts, as always, went to Tera.

What was she thinking right now? Was she thinking at all? Maybe she was, and she thought that he'd abandoned her. The possibility made him want to retch.

How could he possibly do all that he had to do and get back down there in time to save her and Meatball? What if Herrick shrunk down too fast? Or too slow? Either one might cause insurmountable problems. And what of Carmichael? Ollie had left that top-hatted buffoon with nothing but a whispered threat in his ear—would it be enough?

Absently, he ran a finger along his forearm. The pellet was still there, lodged under the skin, though the protrusion didn't feel quite as prominent as it had the day before. Was it...smaller? Was it withering? If the pellet had come pre-loaded, like a propane tank for a barbecue grill, then the supply was draining with every breath he took. Draining fast.

Don't think about it, he told himself, gripping the seed tighter. *One down, two to go. Keep your eyes on the prize.* Or on the...jumping seedpod. Was that what he was supposed to be looking for? More of those? And once he had all three, then what? Was he supposed to grow a goddamn jumping garden?

"Almost there," Laszlo said, moving the car one lane to the right, then another.

The North Shore town names had been popping up in regular succession on the highway signs. Peabody. Danvers. Beverly. And Salem.

As they took the exit and started to wind through the crowded back streets, Laszlo gripped the wheel with purpose. "Okay, my friend," he asked. "What is plan?"

He sounded so eager, so businesslike, that Ollie almost felt sorry to disappoint him. Didn't Laszlo realize there was no plan? There was only a scribbled bunch of lines on a crackly old parchment. The mutterings of a mad witch.

Herrick's home. The place of his sin.

The place of his infamy, really. That was what they needed to find. And considering the body count that George Herrick had left behind during the 1692 trials, this had to be the place. Of that, at least, Ollie was certain. Beyond that? He didn't have a clue.

"Um..." Ollie cleared his throat. "I think we should just, you know, look around."

Laszlo slowed for a red light, then sent a skeptical glance into the passenger seat. "Look around? Where?"

"At the sights. You know, all the...witchy sights."

The light turned green. "What does this mean, witchy sights?"

Ollie shrugged. "There's all kinds of stuff there. Museums, stores, cafes. You know. Tourist kind of stuff."

"But we are not tourists," Laszlo pointed out.

"I know," Ollie said, shifting uncomfortably. "Of course we're not. But I just thought... I don't know. I just thought it would be a good place to start." He wished his concentration was better. Something about the air...the unrelenting sun... It was all so... disconcerting. Returning aboveground was proving a little harder than he'd expected. Was this how the astronauts felt when they returned to Earth?

Laszlo paused, then lifted his shoulders. "You are boss."

Ollie gave an inward groan. That was exactly what he was afraid of.

They followed the signs to the Visitor Center, though the directions were largely unnecessary: The closer they got to the downtown area, the more crowded—and eclectic—the sidewalks became. Tall, pointed hats poked above the foot traffic. Some of the pedestrians wore t-shirts emblazoned with pentagrams. Others carried miniature, twiggy brooms. Most of the visitors walked with quick, excited steps, like concert-goers en route to a show with their favorite band. The air fairly crackled with commotion.

Ollie noticed a gap in the cars parked along the curb. "There! A spot!"

"See? Is our lucky day," Laszlo said jovially, cutting the wheel in a series of sudden jerks that left Ollie gripping the armrest in mild panic. Finally, the car came to a stop. The ancient Ford's doors opened with embarrassing squeals as they stepped out together into the hot summer air.

While Laszlo fumbled with the parking meter, muttering a string of Ukrainian swear words under his breath, Ollie took a moment to look around. To his left, he saw a long line of visitors gathered outside a gothic-looking, stone building. A former church, maybe. From this distance, Ollie could just make out the yellow letters on the building's sign: SALEM WITCH MUSEUM. A wide green expanse across the street looked like a typical New England town common, complete with gazebo. Next to that, Ollie saw a historic hotel and restaurant. And to his right, a busy street corner attracted another steady flow of pedestrians.

The place was hopping. If Ollie had hoped for a little solitude to gather his thoughts, he was going to be disappointed.

Worse, he could already feel it: the watching. Had someone, or something, followed them up from Boston? How? Why? He glanced left and right, looking for a green sweatshirt. Or a sinister face peering intently out of a bush. Or lollipop-licking tweens. All he saw were people chatting amiably and enjoying the sunshine.

"Okay, is all set," Laszlo said, returning to Ollie's side. "Many hours to park. So. Where to begin?"

Ollie looked again at the museum in the distance. They'd learn a lot of history there, to be sure. Maybe even about Herrick himself. But there were too many people in the queue. And a leisurely stroll through wax-figure exhibits didn't seem like the best use of their precious time. His gut was telling him to stay out and about. To keep moving.

"Let's, uh... Let's head that way." He twisted his head toward the other busy area, less than a block away. People were pouring in and out of the intersection; there had to be something of interest down there.

Wordlessly, they turned down Essex Street. The first thing they passed was a pub with a few outdoor tables. Then, a store selling "fine wizard wares."

"Are these...?" Laszlo paused, staring at the window display.

"They seem to be magic wands, yes," Ollie confirmed.

They looked at each other, shrugged, and kept walking. Before long, the pavement gave way to cobblestones and a pedestrian-only thoroughfare. Another museum, this one newer looking, loomed on the left. On the right, they passed a small park, the Visitor Center, and a courtyard with a water feature and a café. Sightseers strolled all around.

Laszlo had traded in his Lycra "work" clothes for black pants and a satin shirt, which meant that he, for a change, wasn't the most oddly dressed person around. Most of the visitors wore shorts and t-shirts, but some were bedecked in full, witchy regalia. Black lace. Purple silks. Tall, angled hats. Sparkling fingernails. Long skirts fluttering with each stride. It was like a Halloween costume party in the middle of summer. Ollie tried not to stare, but found it impossible.

"Do not look too close," Laszlo joked, poking him in the side. "They will put hex on you."

Ollie smiled weakly.

His mind raced as the colors, sounds, and heat swirled around him like a dust storm. *Concentrate, dammit. Look beyond the obvious.* Maybe the looming lampposts were important. Or the giant bell they had just passed, perched up on a cement slab? Or how about that guy dressed as a werewolf, playing the saxophone and posing for pictures? He glanced into the courtyard's water feature, half hoping to see a helpful pod of Novas frolicking in the shallows. But all he saw was refraction: a kaleidoscope of light and splash.

Ollie thought again about the second clue he'd been given: *Earth! Earth second. Herrick's home. The place of his sin.*

Not a waterfall, not a bell, not a werewolf with plastic fangs. Earth.

Meaning, the ground? Maybe he should walk back to the town common. Lots of earth there. Or right here, next to the Visitor

Center. The small park had plenty of trees and dirt. As for the rest of it... The path ahead was a long stretch of red brick and gray cobblestones, lined with shops and restaurants on both sides. The overhead sun burnished it all in a golden, hungry glow.

A giggling clan of women approached; the one in the center wore a white t-shirt that read, *This Witch is getting hitched!* All the others wore black shirts announcing themselves as *The Witch's Bitches.* As Laszlo parted the way through the center of the inebriated bachelorettes, Ollie couldn't help but stare down dizzily at the uneven clay bricks at his feet. *The Brickside.* Here, there, and everywhere.

The shop windows offered tantalizing glimpses of the wares inside: wooden spoons; healing potions; stuffed black cats; incense; travel mugs; crystal beads; pumpkin heads; horror books; pentacle pendants; movie-themed t-shirts; gemstones; chimes; scented pillar candles; and a seemingly bottomless supply of dried herbs and leaves. Spell-casting kits promised everything from "harmony with friends" and "financial abundance" to "rising above the patriarchy" and "re-enchanting the world."

Services abounded, as well: Tarot readings. Psychic readings. Closed-door sessions with mediums. Haunted houses. Monster museums, dungeon museums, and wax museums. One sign read simply, "Vampire. By appointment only." Ollie gave that one a wide berth as he hurried past.

Before long, the sun started to sink, leaving twinkling strings of bulbs and glowing storefront windows to light their way. Laszlo glanced at the sky worriedly. "Is getting dark," he said. "What to do next?"

Ollie wrung his hands, glancing up and down the busy thoroughfare. Instead of thinning the crowds, the approaching nightfall seemed to have only attracted more. And everyone, it seemed, was ready to party. This wasn't right. Something wasn't right. Time was slipping away with startling, frustrating speed, and they'd found exactly nothing of use. He could feel the tiny seed hopping around in the front pocket of his jeans.

Tera was waiting. Maybe dying. And he was doing what, exactly? Shopping for souvenirs? Putting on a show for his stalker? His teeth ground together in a distressed, side-to-side crunch.

Laszlo was standing with his hands on his narrow hips, looking at something over Ollie's shoulder. "How about this?" he asked, pointing.

Ollie turned. A few feet away, a bearded man was standing at a sidewalk podium, handing out pamphlets. A propped-up sign beside him read, *Salem's Best Ghost Tour! True tales of haunted history! Infamous sightings and lingering legends! Get your tickets here!*

Ollie gave Laszlo a skeptical look. "A ghost tour?"

"Why not?" his friend replied. "Is best way to learn fast about this place, no? Like history lesson. We walk, we listen...and maybe we hear something, or we see something, and we say, boom! Yes! That is thing! That is just thing we were looking for!"

Ollie glanced again at the sign, written in a jagged font and framed by swirling, black ghouls. "I don't know, man..." He heaved a sigh. They'd already wasted hours wandering aimlessly—they couldn't afford to waste any more. But Laszlo had a point. At the very least, a tour would give them a better lay of the land, and maybe provide information that they needed to start them heading in the right direction. A name, a story, a building. Anything.

"Fine," he said, his stomach churning. "Okay. Let's get tickets."

The man at the podium looked more preppy than goth. Ollie approached him warily, having had his fill of podiums down in the Neath. He half expected the clean-cut guy to ask them, "How many for entry?" Instead, he sold two tickets to Laszlo and pointed them in the right direction.

"Right down there, at the memorial," he said. "Tour starts in 10 minutes. Look for the lady in the black hat. Have fun!"

"The lady in the black hat. That should narrow it down," Ollie muttered.

They headed off down the small hill. If Ollie had any concerns about finding the right place or the right person, they were banished as soon as he turned the corner. He and Laz were not, apparently, the only ones seeking out a ghostly tour that evening: A crowd was already starting to gather around a lanky woman standing near a stone wall.

"Come on in!" she was saying. "Come on over. That's right. Here for the tour?"

Ollie gave a half-hearted wave and pushed through the throng. He nudged Laszlo.

The acrobat didn't move.

"Laz? C'mon. She needs the tickets."

Finally, Laszlo stepped forward slowly. Too slowly.

Ollie glanced over at his friend, who was looking, oddly enough, like he'd already seen a ghost. His jaw was slack. His eyes were wide. For the first time since Ollie had met him, Laszlo seemed to be stupefied.

The tour guide, too, appeared to be almost frozen in place as she returned Lazlo's stare.

Ollie looked from one to the other. What was going on here? Did they know each other?

The woman wore black pants, a black glittery sort of shirt, and extra-long feathered earrings. And a black hat, of course. Ollie had expected a pointy witch's hat, but this one was more like a bowler, with a turned-up rim. She was tall and thin, like Laszlo. Her hair was long and dark, like Laszlo's. And her skin was just as pale.

The acrobat took another step forward, then another, until the two of them were less than twelve inches apart. "My goodness," he said, pressing the tickets gently into her hand. "Now, I see."

The woman held his gaze. "See what?"

"Why the ghosts do the haunting of this place."

She blushed.

Ollie shifted uncomfortably. Was Laszlo hitting on their tour guide? No...it was more than that. His friend seemed genuinely enamored. This was no act, like the one he'd seen Laszlo perform with the Novas. This was something else entirely.

"My name is Laszlo Kravchenko," he said, his hand still resting on the paper tickets and, by extension, her hand. "You are wondering, of the famous Kravchenko Brothers of Ukraine? Yes. The very same."

The woman blinked.

"And you are...?" he prodded.

It took her a moment to answer. "Caroline," she said, almost in a whisper. Then she cleared her throat and looked up, as though suddenly remembering that the rest of us were standing there. "My name is Caroline," she said, louder. "I'm going to be your guide for this...for the, uh..."

Laszlo grinned.

Caroline took two steps away from him and gathered herself. "Thank you for joining me tonight," she said, flashing a practiced smile at the gathered crowd. "Such a great group! Who here wants to see a ghost?"

Two dozen hands shot into the air, along with the sound of good-natured laughter.

And with that, they were off.

Caroline began by telling them about the memorial park. The group strolled behind her in respectful silence as she pointed out the 20 stones around the perimeter, each protruding like a bench and carved with the name of one of the witch trial's victims. Most of the stones were scattered with fresh-cut flowers, coins, and other tokens.

"The trees in the center, here, represent the victims who died in jail," she explained. "The burying ground behind us does not contain the remains of any of the victims, but it does contain the burial sites of some figures from the era, including two of the judges from the trials."

Laszlo raised his hand.

"Yes? Question?" the guide asked, blushing again.

"Is haunted? The cemetery?"

Caroline rubbed a hand against her collarbone as she answered. "There have been more than 400 reported sightings of supernatural activity at the Charter Street Cemetery, including recorded voices, lights and orbs caught on videotape, and of course the famous Lady in White." She paused, looking away from Laszlo to address the entire group. "In one instance, a police officer on his shift came across a woman and a child wandering through the cemetery after-hours. He approached to tell them they had to leave, but as he got close, he noticed that they both appeared to have burns on their skin. Then, he says, they simply disappeared. This woman and child have been seen by others, as well, and they are believed to be victims of one of the many fires that have ravaged Salem through the years."

Her speech had its intended effect, with many people in the tour group peering anxiously at the shadowy, tipping gravestones over her shoulder.

"You must be very brave, to walk in such scary place every night," Laszlo told her, stepping closer.

Ollie groaned.

"The living need not fear the spirits," she responded with a shrug. Her earrings were so long they brushed her shoulders. "Unless, of course, you have wronged them. Have you wronged them, Mr. ...Laszlo, was it?"

He puffed out his chest, clearly pleased that she'd remembered. "Not that I am knowing of."

"Then neither of us have anything to worry about." She winked at him—Was it a twitch? No, definitely a wink—and took a few long strides forward. "Right this way, everyone! Lots more to see!"

Laszlo leaned in to Ollie's ear. "This is good tour," he said.

Ollie smiled wryly. "I'm so glad you're enjoying it."

For the next thirty minutes, they strode through the dark alleys, cobblestone walkways, and paved city streets of Ye Olde Salem Town, learning about all the haunts and happenings. The stories came in fast succession:

A man who was murdered by his own niece and nephew, now left to haunt the home where he died.

A local bar regularly visited by the specter of a young woman, known as the "Blue Lady," who had reportedly been strangled by a jealous husband.

Hidden tunnels under the streets, once used by pirates and smugglers, now the site of mysterious happenings.

A cursed seafood restaurant that was built on the site of an apple orchard once belonging to Bridget Bishop, the first victim to be tried and executed in 1692.

And more, and more, and more. All of it was fascinating. But none of it was useful.

Before long, Ollie's feet began to ache. He cracked his knuckles, then cracked them again. *Pop, pop, pop.* Maybe this hadn't been such a good idea, after all. And now they'd gone and wasted another hour. As Caroline launched into yet another story of unholy happenings, he sighed, glanced across the narrow street, and froze.

A child was there, sitting on a bench. Alone. Nothing unusual about that. Except this child, a young girl, was staring at him. And she looked a hell of a lot like the kid he'd talked to outside the aquarium. The one who had shared an eerie warning: *Your list. Three things. Some people don't want you to find them.*

Her name fluttered into his mind: *Sadie.*

She was wearing a different shirt—no superhero dog, this time. Just a plain black top. But the longer he looked, the more sure he became: It was definitely her. Blonde ponytail, swinging feet. Back at the aquarium, she'd been licking a swirled lollipop. This time, she was licking an ice cream cone. Strawberry, possibly. Or Peppermint Stick. Something pink. Her gaze never wavered from his face.

A shiver ran up his sweaty back. Unthinking, Ollie stepped forward. He would talk to her. He would ask her what she was doing here.

But a group of chattering pedestrians had chosen that moment to cross the street, blocking Ollie's path. He waited impatiently for the mass of shuffling bodies to pass, then stepped forward again.

The bench was empty. The girl had vanished.

Like a ghost. The thought tripped through his consciousness before he could stop it.

Ollie whipped his head from side to side. Okay, now he was really losing it. Was he getting heat stroke? Or hunger-fueled, lightheaded delusions? He leaned wearily against the nearest solid object to his right; it was lumpy, and slippery. He looked down.

An ice cream cone. Ollie's elbow was propped against a painted statue of a sugar cone topped with two scoops of vanilla. It stood as tall as his shoulder, chipped and cartoonish.

He pictured the now-missing little girl, licking her ice cream with purposeful progress. She had seemed so *real*. Her dessert had seemed so real, too. *Too* real. Melting in the humidity. Dripping down the side of the cone in slow, pink rivulets. Rich, and creamy, and...

Ollie's mouth began to water. He hadn't eaten in hours. They'd already passed a dozen cafes, pubs, and restaurants, but hadn't had time to stop at any of them. He probably just needed some food. Yes. That was it. A little nosh, and maybe a cold drink, and then he'd stop seeing ghosts.

"Pssst." He tapped Laszlo's arm.

The acrobat was casually juggling three small foam balls. "Hmm?"

"What do you say we grab a quick snack?" Ollie asked in a low voice, jerking a thumb over his shoulder toward the ice cream parlor's entrance. He decided it was probably best not to mention that he'd started hallucinating.

Laszlo's eyes followed the foam balls around, and around, and around. "What about tour?"

"We'll catch up."

His friend caught all three balls in one hand. Then his eyes went back to their guide, who was swinging her lantern and gesturing toward a nearby building as she spoke. She noticed Laz looking, and she smiled. Ollie wouldn't have thought it was possible that someone could swing a lantern suggestively, but he would have been wrong. *Swish, swish, swish, swish.*

"I think I will finish tour," Laszlo said. "Is very interesting."

Ollie rolled his eyes. "Fine," he said. "If I can't catch up, I'll meet you after, I guess."

Laszlo finally turned to face him. "We have room at old hotel. Hawthorne Hotel. Is under my name." Then he leaned forward and flashed a mischievous grin. "Do not stay awake to wait for me. I hope to give our guide a tour of Laszlo, if you know what I am meaning."

"Yeah, I think I've got it." Ollie grimaced and rubbed his scalp with his fingertips, as if to wipe the image clean. "But pay attention, okay? And maybe ask her a few questions while you're at it. You know, the reason we're here? Tera? Meatball? The rest?"

Laszlo gave a quick nod. "Yes. Yes. Of course. I will ask all of the questions. See you back at room, yes?"

Ollie gave a weary wave and watched Laszlo hurry back to the group. Or, more specifically, back to Caroline the Beguiling Tour Guide. He shook his head.

The ghost tour was a waste of time. Ice cream would be a waste of time, too. But at least it came with a fat-and-sugar high, which might just kick his brain into some kind of useful gear.

Or at least that's what he told himself. The truth, if he stopped to consider it, was something more curious: The funny little ice cream shop was calling to him. Granted, ice cream shops always called to him, no matter the time or circumstance, but this felt different, somehow. This *sounded* different, in an almost literal way. A quiet but insistent siren song rising above the street's already noisy symphony. Not just the pull of a growling stomach. Something more. The seed in his pocket was practically vibrating with it.

The sign above the ice cream parlor read, *Sweet Screams Ice Cream and Candy Emporium*. Sweet, sweet screams. The letters danced and spun. He stared up at it, mesmerized, and began to walk toward the door—then promptly collided with another person on the sidewalk.

"Oh, geez, sorry," Ollie muttered. He'd been so focused on the sign above, he hadn't been watching where he was going.

As he took a step back, his brain processed several things at once.

Green. The person standing in front of him was wearing an Army-green hooded sweatshirt.

Long, auburn hair.

A pale and pretty face, peering at him. Two feet away. Looking concerned. Looking like...

"Nell?" he gaped.

Unmistakably her, this time. Not running away, not darting past windows. Just...standing there. The tiniest of smiles tugged at her pink lips.

"Hey, Oll."

The last time he'd seen her in person, she'd been down in the Neath, begging him for an exit pass back to the Brickside. And not just any exit pass: she'd wanted his one and only exit pass, which translated to his one and only way to escape the underground world all those months ago. With time running out, Ollie had made a split-second decision—an easy one, and the right one, as it turned out. He had given Nell the canary-yellow ticket to freedom and stayed behind in the Neath to begin a new, underworld life with Tera.

The next time he saw Nell, she was only a projected image on a Mirrormoth's wings. A still picture from another, far-off place. She'd been holding up a piece of paper in front of her chest like a hostage: SEND OLLIE UP OR THEY ALL DIE, the message read. Herrick had used Nell, and the ransom note, to manipulate Ollie into searching for an underground lab. And the ploy had worked. Herrick had pulled the strings, and Ollie had danced like a stupid puppet right into his trap.

Since that time, he'd done nothing but worry and wonder: What had happened to Nell and the other kidnapped women? Were they still being held somewhere? Or worse?

And now, here she was. In the flesh. She was wearing denim shorts and a thin white tank top under the hoodie. Flip-flops. And, as always, hot-pink fingernails and lipstick.

"Nell!"

He threw himself at her, flinging his arms around her shoulders.

She laughed, the sound muffled into his chest. Then she pushed him away gently. "Oll, you need to listen to me."

He held her at arm's length, marveling. "What are you doing here? How did you find me? Jesus, it's so good to see you! Are you okay?"

She took in the barrage of questions with the same, small smile. Not answering.

He pressed on. "What happened to you? Where are the other women? When I saw that sign—"

"Ollie," she interrupted.

"I thought I saw you yesterday, at the aquari—"

"Ollie!"

He stopped.

"I don't have much time," Nell said. Her eyes were darting in zigzags around the sidewalk. "I need you to listen."

What was she looking at? He followed her flitting gaze, but saw nothing unusual. "Nell, what's going on? Are you okay?"

"Yes," she said, pushing the word out with forced patience. "Yes. I'm fine. Totally fine. You don't need to worry about me. Not anymore. I promise."

"But—"

She reached up to grip his forearms, stopping him midsentence. "Don't go inside here, okay?"

Puzzled, he looked up at the *Sweet Screams Ice Cream Parlor* sign. "Here?"

"Yes. Just don't. Don't go looking for things. You don't need to do that."

"What? Nell, what the hell are you—"

"Do you trust me?"

"Well, yeah. Of course." He'd known her for a while. Two years, at least. Ever since he started attending Lighter Tomorrows meetings. They'd commiserated about their weight-loss struggles together, and even went out for coffee once in a while. Ollie didn't have many friends on the Brickside, but Nell had always been nice to him. Nicer than most. "I don't understand... What are you talking about? What are you *doing* here?"

"You need to stop looking, Ollie. That's all. Just stop. Okay?"

Ollie took a step back. None of this made any sense. How did Nell know he was looking for something?

"Have you been following me?" he asked.

She didn't immediately answer.

"That *was* you at the aquarium, wasn't it? And at Gianelli's?"

"I'm here to help you," she said.

"That's not an answer."

Nell folded her arms.

"Still not an answer." Ollie's initial joy at seeing her was starting to morph into something else. Something more like confused annoyance. It was one thing to get riddles from witches, or from unknown parchment-scribbling sources. It was another thing altogether to get them from a friend.

"Look, just...just go home. Okay? For your own good."

A strange iciness stilled his limbs. He resisted the urge to reach out and pinch her, to make sure she was real. Another hallucination? But he'd already hugged her. Can you hug a ghost? Ollie tilted his head. "Did someone tell you to tell me that?" he asked, trying to keep his voice even.

"No! Jesus. Ollie, it's me, all right? You know me! I'm trying to give you some advice, that's all."

He nodded numbly. Something was very off, here. What, exactly, he couldn't say. If she wasn't an apparition, then maybe she was... an imposter? No, that was ridiculous. But what other explanation was there? The Nell he knew wouldn't follow him around, or spout befuddling "advice." The Nell he knew had never offered advice in her life. She was straightforward. Simple. Kind of shallow, and scatterbrained.

And *kidnapped.*

"What happened to you?" he pressed. "What was with that note? Where are the other women? I've been so worried!"

"Look, I have to go." She was glancing furtively, again.

"Why?"

"Because...I do. Just be careful, okay? Promise me." Nell gave his forearms a dual squeeze. Another quick smile, and then she scurried away.

Ollie looked down at his arms. He saw a red spot on the skin where she had squeezed and the sharp indents from her nails. It was real. Nell was alive, and she was fine. This should have made him feel better, he knew. But all he felt was unglued.

❦

Screw it.

He did consider listening to her. Maybe she knew what she was talking about. Maybe he was walking into a lion's den of disaster. But since Nell had declined to provide any specifics—or make any sense whatsoever—Ollie decided, instead, to listen to the seed, which was now dancing an impressive singleton samba in his pocket. *Go, go, go, go, go.*

Besides, he hadn't promised not to go in there. He'd only promised to "be careful." And he would.

Ollie gave himself a silent pep talk. Then he yanked the door open, stepped across the threshold, and stopped, momentarily startled.

"Good God," he murmured.

It looked like somebody threw up Halloween.

The parlor had two levels: the lower one, where he stood now, with a candy counter and gift shop, and the upper one, where the ice cream counter perched. And every inch of the place, from its creaky wood floor to its tall ceiling, was decked out in brassy autumn décor. Flying bats. Hanging spiders. Stacked pumpkins. Friendly skeletons. Cauldrons and scarecrows and wicker baskets. Orange and orange and black and black. And of course, witches. Witches on brooms, witches in coffee cups, witches every which way you looked.

Ollie walked cautiously through the spooktacular minefield and made his way to the stairs. The ice cream case beckoned with an alabaster glow.

80

His steps quickened. A chalkboard on the wall listed the flavors; eagerly, he began to scan.

Cookies and Scream
Pumpkin Patch
Red Rum Raisin
Spooky Strawberry
Bubble, Bubble, Toil and Bubble Gum

The man ahead of him ordered a scoop of "Cauldron Coffee" with chocolate jimmies.

Ollie felt crippled by the dilemma he always faced at ice-cream counters—too many wonderful choices. He kept reading, hoping one might jump out above the rest.

Chilling Chocolate Chip
Vampire Vanilla
The Mint Reaper
Freaky Fudge Ripple
Monster Mash
Egg Nog Fog
Poison Pufferpine

The overhead lights seemed to glare, suddenly, marring his vision. Ollie blinked, then read the last flavor in the list again. *Poison Pufferpine.*

What the...?

Ollie had first seen pufferpines in the Neath's vast, green lake. They were outlandish creatures, barbed and goofy and hairy, that he might describe as a cross between a porcupine and a pufferfish. As far as he knew, they didn't exist anywhere else.

Certainly not here, on the Brickside.

Pufferpines, despite their comical appearance, were poisonous. Ollie had learned that only moments after he had plunged one of their quills into George Herrick's neck. In a lab. In the Neath. Far, far away from the Sweet Screams Ice Cream and Candy Emporium in Salem, Massachusetts.

He swallowed thickly.

"You all set?"

A girl's voice had interrupted his thoughts.

Ollie looked up to see a bored-looking teenager watching him from behind the counter. She was chewing gum—plucked, probably, from the "Bubble, Bubble, Toil and Bubble Gum" ice cream tub nearby.

"Hmm?"

"You all set?" she asked again, more slowly this time. "To order?"

"Uh... I..." Ollie stammered, feeling a wave of unexplained dread. He pointed. "What's in that one?"

"What one?" She smacked her gum, not even bothering to follow his finger.

"That one. The...uh, Poison Pufferpine."

The girl stopped chewing as her mouth, and her entire body, went still. She stared at Ollie through a thick layer of mascara and eyeliner. She also wore maroon lipstick, a choppy hairstyle, and a t-shirt that read, *Familiar Veterinary Clinic of Salem,* complete with images of cats, bats, frogs, and hares in various states of illness or injury. A nametag pinned to the shirt identified her as *LUCY* in large block letters.

"You can see that?" the girl asked.

He nodded. What did she mean, see it? Of course he could see it. It was right there, on the sign. Literally in black-and-white.

Though the words did seem to be... glimmering. Fading in and out. Not unlike the sign he had once seen at the top of Henchman Street, back when this whole demented journey had begun.

"Huh." Her voice betrayed a pleased sort of curiosity. She looked at her counterpart behind the ice-cream case. "Cameron, you got this for a sec?"

The other teen looked up from his phone, shrugged, and nodded.

The girl dropped her scoop into a small tub full of water. "Come with me," she said to Ollie.

"What? Why?"

An exasperated sigh escaped her mouth as she wiped her hands on the apron. "Just come, all right?"

Ollie's thoughts swam. Not in formation like a synchronized Olympic team; more like hyper six-year-olds at a pool party. What the hell was going on? Nell's warning rang again in his head; this time, sounding more credible. *Don't go looking for things.*

The girl walked out from behind the case and toward the opposite wall, weaving through a smattering of unoccupied tables. Her rubber-heeled black boots made a clomping sound with each step. When she reached a door, Ollie narrowed his eyes. Had that door been there a minute ago? He didn't remember it.

She knocked and listened. She must have heard something because she swung it open.

"Go on in," she told Ollie. "They've been waiting for you."

"For me? Who?"

The girl observed him with an expression that fell somewhere between sympathy and disbelief. "The coven, dude," she answered. "Who else?" Then she blew a big, pink bubble. It hovered there for several seconds, wobbling, before it popped.

Seven

The room beyond the doorway looked dark. And smoky. Ollie took a few cautious steps forward, feeling sweat pool in his armpits.

The coven? Like, an actual coven? He flashed back to his experience with the "nesting" witches in the Neath. The things they had subjected him to. The horrible, terrifying sights they had forced him to see.

Surely the witches in this group were just as powerful, if not more so. Surely they were wise, and wizened, and "suffering no fools," as his grandmother used to say. Would the elders in the Salem coven want to teach him a lesson, as the others had? He wasn't sure he could face something like that again. And even if he did, he couldn't imagine emerging on the other side of it with all of his marbles intact.

The ice-cream girl, Lucy, was watching him. Her chestnut, shaggy hair covered half of her face; the other half looked increasingly irritated. She waved a hand, urging him forward.

Despite his trepidation, the pull of the mysterious room was undeniable. He heard the strange siren song, again. Felt the jittering seed urging him forward. Clearly, this was the place he'd been searching for. Now he just had to muster the courage to step inside.

One footfall, then another. He passed the girl and walked over the threshold. Thick yellow smoke swirled all around. As the outlines of figures came into view, Ollie shuddered and thought about all the underground witches he had come to know: Weelichka; Widow Hibbins; Bert; Elisha; Lizbeth. At turns worldly and eccentric, glassy-eyed and daft, bitter and reproachful.

He steeled himself for more of the same.

But as his vision began to focus in the murk, all he saw was...teenagers.

Regular, ordinary-looking teenagers. They were gathered around a circular table, playing cards. Muttering. Guffawing. Slurping loudly from soda cans. Even in the shadows, Ollie could make out patches of acne, overdrawn eye makeup, and lots of costume jewelry. Bass-heavy music thumped against the walls. Dozens of brass incense burners had saturated the room in an overpowering smell of patchouli and sandalwood.

Only one of them looked up when he entered. She was younger than the rest: black t-shirt. Blonde ponytail. Traces of pink ice cream smeared at the corners of her mouth. The girl gave him a wink and flashed a crooked smile before returning her attention to the cards in her hand.

"Sadie?" he heard himself ask. The room spun.

The girl didn't reply.

Lucy shut the door behind them with a thud. "He's here," she announced, lifting her voice above the music.

"Mmmm," one of the card players responded, sounding unimpressed. "About time."

Ollie bristled. *About time?* What was that supposed to mean?

The boy didn't elaborate. He looked to be about 17 or 18, at most, with partly-brown, partly-bleached hair. He wore one dangling earring, a purple bracelet, and a red shirt emblazoned with a black dragon. When he finally cast a glance at Ollie, his expression was decidedly neutral. Then the boy returned his focus to the table. "Three in, all players," he said to the group. In response, the other kids started tossing cards onto the felt surface.

Ollie stayed rooted to his spot. He counted ten kids around the table, including little Sadie: some light-skinned, some dark-skinned, some gangly, some stout. Take all of those, plus Lucy and the other kid from the ice-cream counter, and that made twelve.

Not a one of them looked old enough to order a drink. Was this the coven? That couldn't be right. Ollie knew precious little about witchy things, but even he knew that a coven was supposed have thirteen. And that they should probably be out of high school.

The card game continued to hold everyone's attention. Ollie had been so busy analyzing the players that he missed, at first, the freakish nature of the competition unfolding in front of him. These cards had not been pulled from a garden-variety Bicycle deck. Instead of Kings, Queens, Jacks, and Aces, they sported a variety of colorful, mythical beasts. What's more, all of the creatures seemed to be moving—writhing and reaching and clawing in three dimensions, up and out of the cards themselves.

The sight rendered him speechless.

"Three out, all players," said the boy with the dragon shirt. At his words, the players scrambled to retrieve new cards from the center of the table. When they added the new cards to their hands, the beasts on each face promptly began interacting: baring teeth, flicking out tongues, and thrashing with paws and hooves. Players shuffled their hands in a valiant effort to do...something. What that thing was, exactly, Ollie couldn't say. Perhaps the object of the game was to try to keep your cards from killing each other.

Lucy, who had been watching alongside Ollie, now folded her arms. "It's him," she said.

"How do you know?" the boy asked.

"You know how I know," she retorted. "It's him."

"Yeah, well, as Cardmaster, I am hereby—"

"Exactly," she interrupted. "You're Cardmaster, not Covenmaster. And I'm telling you, it's him."

The boy paused, then regarded Ollie with reluctant interest.

"Ian, what's the call?" asked a young girl to his left.

The boy she called Ian glanced around at the various warring hands. "Two in, all players," he said. At his words, the air was suddenly aflutter with tossed cards. One landed face up; its creature, a winged frog of some kind, started to fly away. Ian quickly reached out and flipped it over. "We'll have to wait for Damira," he said. "Nothing to be done 'till then."

Lucy sighed. "I'm telling you—"

"She has to be here," Ian insisted, fighting to reign in his cards. One of them bit the one next to it; he separated them with difficulty.

Ollie glanced around the room as mild panic started to build in his chest. What were they talking about? Nothing to be done? Until when? "I don't have time to wait!" he blurted. "Look, I don't know who you think I am, or what this is, but I have to—"

"Do not fear time, Oliver Delgato," a voice interrupted. The sound tinkled like a wind chime, high and sharp. "Like so much about this life, time is nothing but an illusion. Smoke and mirrors, meant to distract us from our truth."

He turned. A girl had emerged from the room's far shadows. How? He didn't see a door. Unlike his own entrance, this one did cause a stir. The teenage players at the table lowered their cards. Ian straightened in his seat. Even Lucy took a small step backward.

Questions tumbled into Ollie's mind. The biggest—*How do you know my name?*—seemed stuck to his tongue.

The girl advanced, floating with little effort along the ground. She looked impossibly young and also, somehow, impossibly old, with deep olive skin and white hair cut into a sharp bob with bangs. A pair of tortoiseshell glasses perched on her nose. The girl gave off an air of studiousness and gentility. But she also looked like she'd cut a bitch, as the kids said back home. And everyone in that room knew it.

Her status hung like an invisible sign around her neck. This, then, was the Covenmaster.

"How do I know your name? The same way you know mine," she told him with a dismissive wave.

Ollie cocked his head. Wait, had he asked that question out loud? He didn't think he had. But now, suddenly, he wasn't sure. "You're...Damira?"

"That's right. And I'm very happy to see you at last."

As usual, Ollie felt like he had arrived twenty minutes late for a movie and was frantically trying to catch up. Incense smoke swirled up his nose and down the back of his throat, making him cough. When the fit passed, he lifted his palms. "I'm looking for something," he hacked.

"Yes, I know," she answered.

In response, the small seed sped up its confined dance. Ollie glanced around the room; his eyes were still watering from the coughing fit, rendering everything blurry. "Is it here?"

"No, not here. But close." The music continued to thump on the back wall, its vibrations making a mirror wobble. Damira glanced at the mirror. She didn't say anything, but apparently she didn't have to: One of the kids jumped up to turn down the music. Then, slowly, they all returned to their game.

Was she bluffing? Pulling his leg? Ollie couldn't tell. How could she possibly know what he was looking for?

"Your eyes will clear in a moment," Damira said. "And I know what you are looking for because it was written. Because things are as they always were, as they always shall be, and we are each just cards in the game."

He startled.

"Yes, I can hear your thoughts." She waved a hand again, as though this was the least interesting part of their conversation. "What do you think, Lucy? Shall we tell our visitor what he needs to know?"

In response, the girl next to Ollie shoved her hands into the front pockets of her cargo pants and shrugged.

"I think he needs a test," called out Ian from the table, his eyes still on the squabbling cards. "Just to be sure."

"A test? What a fascinating idea. Yes, a test." Damira held out an arm, fingers spread as though expecting something. Seconds later, one of the players wordlessly picked up a can of cherry cola and passed it into her waiting fingers. She popped the top and took a long swallow. "What do you say, Ollie? Join us in a game?" She gestured toward the green felt, where clumps of snarling cards battled in the center of the table as players attempted to pull them apart.

"What? No! No games! Please," he begged. Visions of Moseby's not-so-distant drinking challenge swam into his mind... fizzing brew, chanting spectators, black-out delirium. Who knew what the Salem coven's games might entail? With his luck, he'd probably get his fingers chewed off by one of the card creatures before the first round was over. "I don't have time for games. I'm in a hurry. People are waiting for—" Ollie paused, remembering what she'd said about 'not fearing time,' then continued— "People are depending on me. Please! If you could just point me in the right direction, I'd—"

"Maybe a riddle, then," interrupted Cardmaster Ian. He pointed at the table. "Two out, Kaelyn only." As soon as he said it, the tallest girl at the table scrambled to comply, reaching to grab two of the scattered cards.

"Hmm." Damira scratched her chin with five long, painted fingernails. They looked like lighthouses: red and white stripes with black tips. "A riddle. Yes, all right. Ollie, do you have time for a riddle? Just so we can feel assured that you are who you say you are. You understand."

"I didn't *say* I was anybody," Ollie argued. "You're the ones who—"

"It's just one riddle," Lucy said, stepping closer again. Her kohl-rimmed eyes flashed with something that might have been amusement. "What's the matter? You scared?"

Why did he suddenly feel like he was the butt of some unfathomable joke? "Fine," he snapped. "Fine. If I solve your stupid riddle, will you tell me what I need to know?"

"Of course," Damira smiled. "Why don't we have a seat?" She was gesturing toward two rocking chairs perched on either side of a massive fireplace.

Ollie blinked. Until that very moment, he hadn't noticed the chairs. Or the fireplace. Which seemed all but impossible, considering their now very obvious presence in the room. The hearth—Colonial-era, from the looks of it—was charred and lined with bricks. It burrowed into the back-wall shadows, in the very spot that Damira had emerged from only moments before. Had she walked out of the fireplace itself?

He gave his head a sharp shake, then walked hesitantly toward one of the rocking chairs. It was wooden, with no pad. Possibly an antique. He sat.

Damira settled into the opposite chair, dropped her can of soda onto a nearby side table, and picked up two knitting needles and a skein of yarn. "Well then, does anyone have a riddle? If not, this is going to be a very short test."

One of the girls lifted a finger. "I've got one!" she said, adjusting a jangly necklace around her neck.

"All right, Chloe," the Covenmaster said with a short nod. "Go ahead."

The girl, who looked to be about twelve or thirteen, shuffled the cards in her hand and continued in a loud, authoritative voice. "I will never talk to you, but if you yell at me, I will yell back. Who am I?"

Ollie rubbed his forehead. "My seventh-grade gym teacher?" he muttered. No one laughed.

After a moment, he noticed that all eyes were trained on his face. Oh, shit. He was really supposed to solve this thing. Absently, he started to rock the chair.

"Um..." Ollie wracked his brain. *Talking...yelling...mouth... don't talk...won't talk...* What, or who, could yell but not talk? And more importantly, why had he let himself become separated from Laszlo? His clever friend would know the answer. Laz would have guessed it already.

"Give up?" the girl with the big necklace asked. Without waiting for a reply, she said, "It's a cave. Get it? Like, an echo."

"Wait a sec!" Ollie protested. "That's not fair! You have to give me a minute to think!"

"I don't know, man," Ian said, shaking his head with exaggerated sadness. "If you were the guy, you probably would have known that."

"I am the guy! I mean, I don't know if..." Ollie sputtered in frustration. "Give me another one. Go ahead."

Damira's eyes stayed on her knitting. She seemed to be making some kind of scarf. Silvery-white, like her hair. "Okay, let's call the first one practice," she said. "Does anyone else have a riddle for our new friend?"

Another girl looked up with a grin. "I know one," she said, fanning one of her playing cards to make a breeze against her cheek. The sentiment on her shirt read, *Devil may care...but I don't* in white letters on a black background.

"All right, let's hear it," Damira told her.

Ollie gripped the arms of the rocking chair and listened intently.

"Okay, here it is: To take you home, we start at eight and end at five," the girl said. "What are we?"

"Eight...and five?"

"Yep."

"You're, uh…" *Eight and five. Eight and five.* Ollie pictured a clock, spinning. Hands. Time. Train station, train tracks. Commuting. "You're, uh, a subway. No, wait. You're a…"

"Give up?" The girl asked, clearly delighted.

"No! Give me a second, will you? What is this, some kind of timed thing? Just let me think…"

More seconds passed. No answer appeared in his brain.

"Give up?" asked the girl again.

"No! I'm just—"

"Okay, here's another one," she interrupted. "Same sort of thing, but I'll make it easier." Barely suppressed snorts erupted around the table as Ollie's cheeks flushed pink. The Devil-May-Care girl stopped fanning the card against her face and returned it to her hand, where the gargoyle on its surface promptly began to claw at the adjacent card's centaur. "Ready? Here goes: To take you away, we start at 1 and end at 25. What are we?"

One and twenty-five.

Okay, he thought to himself. *One and twenty-five. To take you away…* The last riddle had said "to take you home," not "away." And the numbers were different. But the riddles sounded essentially the same, otherwise. So what was the difference between "home" and "away?" Maybe it was like, baseball teams? The home team and the away team? But what did that have to do with the numbers?

Think, you moron… The chair rocked beneath him in an increasingly frantic motion. Home, away. Eight and five. One and twenty-five.

Eighth and fifth? First and twenty-fifth? Something occurred to him, suddenly. He started mumbling and counting on his fingers.

"Letters!" he shouted, making Lucy jump. "They're letters! 'Away' starts with A, which is the first letter in the alphabet, and ends with Y, which is the twenty-fifth. And 'Home' starts with the eighth letter and ends with E, the fifth." He grinned and looked from face to face. "Right? Is that right?"

"You'd have to ask Riley," the Covenmaster demurred, pointing at the girl who had proposed the riddle.

"Yeah, he's right," Riley responded, sounding glum at the prospect.

"That was too easy," one of the boys protested.

Ian seemed to concur; he nodded twice before shouting, "Two in, Hailey only." As soon as he finished his proclamation, the girl sitting two seats down tossed a pair of creature cards with a whoop.

"To be fair, you did need a hint," Damira said, sounding thoughtful. Her knitting needles crossed and uncrossed in regular rhythm.

"What? That wasn't a hint. It was more of a...a..."

"It was another example of the same thing," Lucy interjected. "So basically, a hint."

Ollie stammered something unintelligible. He looked across the room at little ponytailed Sadie, hoping for...what? A little help, maybe? But she just smiled her sweet smile.

"Too bad, buddy," Cardmaster Ian said with a sorry-not-sorry shrug. "I guess you're not the guy, after all. Thanks for stopping by, though."

Ollie watched, dumbfounded, as the game resumed. Cards flew. Players whooped. He experienced a rapid tumble of emotions: surprise into anger, anger into panic, panic into embarrassment. But it wasn't until the seed went still in his pocket—still and quiet, like death—that all of them muddied together into a sad paste of despair.

Eight

The arms of the rocking chair were surprisingly soft and brittle; Ollie dug his fingernails into the wood.

So, that was it? Two stupid riddles, and he's tossed out on his ass? Whatever happened to three strikes? Nine lives? Med kits and health bars and level bosses? If this were a video game, he wouldn't be anywhere close to done.

"Wait!" he said. "No way. Wait a sec! This is bullshit! Give me one more!"

The demand elicited nothing more than a few lazy glances in his direction. Then, Damira released a small, reluctant sigh. "I'm afraid our Ian is right. We *did* give you two chances already." Her voice trailed off as she resumed her knitting. *Clackety, clackety, clack.* The sound was grating. And infuriating.

Ollie stared at her, his blood pressure thudding into a dull roar. Then he looked at Ian, and Lucy, and all the other bratty teenagers who suddenly held his life—and Tera's life, and Meatball's life—in their hands. Not to mention the kidnap victims, lingering God only knew where under God only knew what conditions. These witches, these *kids*, were toying with him, he could feel it. He was nothing more than a mouse in a room full of cats.

Then again, the mice at his old North End apartment always managed to escape his traps—and usually make off with the cheese in the process. So maybe mice had their share of tricks, too.

"You have to give me one more," he insisted. "I saw the sign, didn't I? The pufferpine flavor?" What had the Novas told him, back when he'd first arrived at their aquarium office-that-wasn't-an-office? *Only the people who need to see it, see it. And you saw it, so... You know enough.*

He straightened in his chair and parroted the words out to the room: "Only the people who need to see it, see it. And I saw it. So I must be the guy. You have to give me another chance."

Damira raised a single eyebrow.

The kids at the table started to mutter. She raised a hand to quiet them. "All right, young Ollie. Perhaps just one more. But no hints this time."

"Fine," he said quickly. He chewed the inside of his cheek as butterflies began to flap around his gut. "No hints."

She paused her knitting to push the glasses up the bridge of her nose. "All right, then. Last chance. Think carefully, now. Are you ready?"

No, he wasn't. But he nodded anyway.

Damira cleared her throat. Instead of asking for suggestions from the others, she surprised him by proposing a riddle of her own: "I am always part of your journey, but I will never travel with you. Who am I?"

Journey.

The word triggered something in his synapses. He'd been on his own journey for months now, hadn't he? A seemingly unending journey. And every time he thought he'd finally settled down to rest, *bam*—more journey. Wiseass kids in an ice cream shop. Aquarium swordfish. A climb through the corpses and headstones at Copp's Hill. And before that, Howerbout's cave. Angry clown guards. Bats sliced in half like bagels. Mirrormoths trapped under glass, carrying warnings on their wings.

Like a dying man, he watched all the scenes materialize, fade, and flicker. Ollie saw himself swinging at Dozer in the fighting pit. Tossing back grog at Moseby's. Holed up with Leonard in a birdcage. Bargaining with a blinking keychain. Riding a door like a sled down a spiraling staircase. Suffering through endless days in a Herrick's End cell, giving up all hope, until the day a petite, fearless, purple-haired rescuer had arrived to pull him out of the bowels of hell itself using nothing but her wits and her own two hands. *Tera.*

My God, Tera, what have we done? Bile rose in his throat.

And back, and back, and back. The memories continued to flash, all the way to Henchman Street. To Bonfiglio's Caffe. To Nell's mysteriously empty chair. To...

Ollie looked up. The hazy room swirled around him, thick with Patchouli smoke.

"The beginning," he whispered.

Damira's face betrayed nothing. "Is that your answer?"

"Yes," he said. A sense of calm had settled like pond sand around his nerves. "The beginning is always a part of your journey, but it will never travel with you."

Damira smiled and lay the knitting in her lap. "Very good. Every journey must have a beginning. It is, perhaps, the most important part. But that is where it must stay... Always behind you. Always in the past. So it was with George Herrick's journey down his dark path."

Ollie's eyes widened. "You know about Herrick?"

Her expression betrayed a flicker of wrath. Instead of answering, she said, "If you want to find 'Herrick's home, the place of his sin,' then that is where you must start. At the beginning."

Ollie tilted his head. How did she know Herrick? And how the hell did she know what the note in his pocket said? Probably the same way she had walked out of a nonexistent fireplace and read his mind. Wondering would get him nowhere, so he pushed the question aside. "But I did come back to the beginning!" he protested. "That's why we came here. 'The place of his sin.' Salem!"

A titter traveled through the room. Ollie looked around in confusion, but no one caught his eye.

The Covenmaster took another sip of her cherry cola. "Almost, but not quite," she said, wiping her mouth before reaching again for the needles. "The witch trials wound their way here to Salem Town, of course. The courts, the jail, the hangings. But they did not begin here."

"They didn't?"

"The first victims were accused, and the hysteria began, in Salem *Village*."

"And that's...a different place?"

She nodded. "In those days, it was a farming community. Unlike the merchants and wealthy residents of Salem Town, the neighboring villagers struggled. They struggled with subsistence, with gaining independence, and with each other. Jealousies, hostilities, and misunderstandings were rampant. It was there, in the fertile soil of rising tensions and religious tyranny, that that the seeds of the evil vine were planted. And once they were planted, there was no rooting them out. Not until—" Damira paused. A visible shudder passed through her torso. She didn't bother to finish the sentence.

Ollie nodded respectfully. After a beat, he asked, "So, the village is gone?"

"Not gone. Just called by a different name. Today, we know it as Danvers."

Danvers? Ollie had heard of it, of course, but not in any particular context. As far as he knew, it was just another North Shore suburban town with strip malls and Friday night football and traffic on 128. No wax museums, no tourists, no Halloween hysteria.

"You're telling me I need to go to Danvers?"

Damira didn't immediately answer. She seemed to be considering something. Finally, she set aside her lumpy tangle of yarn. Then she rose to her feet, walked to the green table, and picked up one of the scattered cards. When she tore a piece off the bottom, the card screamed.

"Hey!" Ian protested.

The Covenmaster rolled her eyes and lifted one of her lighthouse-striped fingernails; a moment later, the card had been restored to its original state, complete with an intact, four-legged, wolfish looking beast. She ignored its snarl, picked up a pen from the felt tabletop, and scribbled several lines of text onto the fragment she had torn.

"Here's the address," she said, walking to Ollie's chair and holding out the scrap of card. "It should be easy enough to find. Wait until first light, tomorrow. When you get there, be respectful of the neighbors and the history. And the ghosts."

He wasn't sure if she meant that last one literally. He hoped not.

"You'll need these when you arrive," Damira added. She flipped over the paper to reveal what looked like a set of numbers. Which was odd because Ollie hadn't seen her write any of those down.

The sweat in his armpits began to pool again. "And then what?"

"And then, you will find what you're looking for." She handed him the torn card. "Or you won't. Good luck." It was a dismissal.

"Yeah, but..." Ollie spluttered, looking down at the paper in his fingers. Address on one side, numbers on the other. "But...I need more information! What am I looking for? Why am I looking for it? What am I supposed to do with all these numbers?" His eyes flitted from face to face, though the gathered teens mostly seemed to be ignoring him. "This isn't a game! Krite! Don't you understand? She's in danger! All of us...all of *you*...might be in danger! If you know something about what's going on here, you have to tell me!"

Damira stepped closer. Reaching out, she curled his fingers over the card in his hand. "Find what you are looking for," she said, more softly this time, peering at him over her glasses. "Then bring it back here, to me. And we'll see what we see."

"No," he said, shaking his head. "No! That's not good enough! If you know something, you need to tell me now!"

Damira's expression was serene. And infuriatingly condescending. "All in good time," she said.

All in good time. Where had he heard that before? Then the blood rushed to his ears as he remembered: "The Doc" had used that exact phrase, repeatedly, down in the Grimshawe Laboratory. And Ollie had listened. He had been patient. He had shut his mouth and taken the stupid tour and drank the Kool-Aid. Literally. And where had that gotten him? Where had it gotten Tera? And his trog?

Ollie's jaw clamped. His hands gripped the arms of the wooden chair. He was done waiting. He was done playing by their schedules, playing by their rules, and playing their ridiculous cat-and-mouse games. Anger simmered in his throat, restricting his airflow. Ollie was no one's patsy. Not anymore. And if they thought he was going to sit here, in the smelly back room of some tourist-trap ice cream shop, pushed around by a bunch of surly teenagers, while the love of his life suffered and waited and choked on chunky, impenetrable, yellow goo—

His train of thought burned up in a furnace-blast of fury. His mind went suddenly, ominously blank.

He felt it, then: the familiar fever on his skin. Ollie looked down at his arms, which were suddenly covered in hundreds of inflamed, crimson freckles. Like an army of warriors, they began to rise. His epidermis started to thin. Light began to trickle through the surface of each small pock, sending bright beams out into the candlelit room.

In his mind, he saw Tera's anguished face behind the glass. Heard Herrick's snide chortle. Felt the unrelenting frustration of every setback, every puzzle, every barrier, every delay. Ollie was trapped in a waking nightmare, like so many he had suffered in his sleep: Calling for help, but the phone won't work. Trapped in a room, but the door won't open. Stuck in quicksand, but there's no rope to grab. Sinking, falling, vanquished.

Losing, losing, losing, *losing*.

The dark room grew lighter as his body illuminated everything around it. The rocking chair stopped rocking. Each sight, scent, and sound came into sharp focus: The muted rub of a sneaker's sole against the wood floor. The smell of charcoal, old and blistered, in the fireplace. Particles of dust. A bouncing knee. Termites skittering. Ancient layers of varnish on the wood planks. A slurp. A brewing strep-throat infection nearby. Sound waves from the speakers, now as visible as a rainbow. The ring of the cash register and the hum of outsiders beyond the walls.

The seed in his pocket, jumping. Agitated. Straining to burst through the fabric.

Ollie rose to his feet. He felt them lifting off the ground, buoyed by the light and heat. He could fly now, he knew. He could destroy them all with nothing more than a whim. The knowledge made him neither happy nor sad, just...assured. His jaw hardened.

And then—he felt pressure, gentle but firm. A hand on his arm. Ollie squinted, peering out through the luminous sheen. He saw Damira shaking her head. Her gray hair reflected his light, making it gleam like a silver crown. As he watched her, all else faded into dull unimportance.

"No," she said simply. "Not now."

Not now?

"Reign it in."

Reign it in. Her words cut through the fugue with urgent, entrancing power. Ollie imagined a mighty horse, galloping. With difficulty, he steadied it. Felt the powerful beast slow to a canter. He exhaled, watching a cloud of acrimony and resentment escape through his lips. The light, he noticed, was dimming. He glanced down at his arms: The bumps were fading from red to pink, and were nearly flat. The horse in his mind trotted, then walked, then, finally, pawed leisurely at the nonexistent dirt.

Every witch in the room was staring at him with wide, wary eyes. The game had come to a halt. The incense smoke churned in slow motion. Even the belligerent creatures on the cards had fallen quiet.

Lucy was the first to speak. "I told you it was him," she muttered.

Ollie stared at her, blinking his lids with effort. Then he looked around at the others. *What* was him? What did that *mean?* When his eyes fell on Sadie, he remembered the little girl's words at the aquarium: *You don't look like I thought you would look.* His limbs felt as loose as dangling ropes. "What's... What's happening to me?" he whimpered.

Damira smiled calmly. Whatever was happening, she didn't seem surprised by it. And it didn't seem to ruffle her in the least. "You, my dear, are a caretaker," she told him, sounding proud.

"Of...what?"

"You are a caretaker of all the hidden things." Damira's hand was still on his arm. "It is a lot to manage, I know. But now is not the time for tantrums. Now is the time for action, right?"

He wanted to focus on the first part of her answer—a caretaker of all the hidden things?—but instead, foolishly, found himself fixating on the second. *Tantrum?* Was that what she thought of him? The word made him think of a toddler. Or worse, of his father.

"Right?" she repeated, adding a squeeze.

Ollie cleared his throat. "Right," he said. *Action.*

"You have to go." Damira spoke with the overexaggerated patience of a Kindergarten teacher coaxing a five-year-old in from recess. Her tone annoyed him, but also soothed him. Now that the strange surge had come and gone, Ollie felt drained of...everything. Drained into emptiness.

And into that emptiness, suddenly, came a voice. His mother's voice.

Listen with more than just your ears, Bambino, she said. *Listen with all you have.*

His mother had told him that many times through the years—usually when she was trying to get him to focus on a task. Was she telling him again, now? Speaking from some far-off, unseen place? Or was he merely remembering?

Listen with all you have.

I am listening, Mama, he answered, though he wasn't entirely convinced it was true.

Ollie was out of his depth—more and more by the day, by the minute. So far out of his depth that he wasn't sure he'd ever see the shallows again. His body was changing. His mind was changing. The atoms in the air around him were changing, and there didn't seem to be a damn thing he could do about any of it.

But he had to assume he'd been sent here for a reason. This Salem coven, such as it was, had been waiting for him, just as the Novas at the aquarium had been waiting for him. He was on the right path. He had to be. The alternative was just too painful to consider.

Ollie steadied his sway. Then he looked at the spectacled, white-haired Covenmaster, and he nodded.

"Find what is yours, and return here," Damira said. "And then we shall see what there is to talk about. All right?"

"All right."

The grotesque card game had restarted. Throats cleared. Potato chip bags crinkled. Fingers tapped the table. And all eyes returned to the squabbling, brawling monsters in their hands.

"Three out, all players," Ian called. In a mad scramble, the witches flung their cards.

Lucy stepped closer, her boots clomping. "Come on," she said.

At first, Ollie wasn't sure she was talking to him.

"Come *on,*" she repeated. She was gesturing toward the door. Was he mistaken, or was her tone a little gentler than before? More friendly? It sounded less like an order and more like a helpful nudge.

Ollie shoved his hands into his pockets and followed. Yes. This felt right. *Right as rain,* as his old cellmate Dozer used to say. Thoughts tumbled in a weirdly sequential sort of daze: He would go to the hotel, get some sleep, and then he and Laz would set out in the morning. *First light.*

At the door, he paused, turning back. "Wait, I have a question," he said to Damira. "Two questions, actually."

"All right, let's hear them," she said pleasantly, settling back into her rocking chair.

Ollie folded his arms. "I didn't really have to answer any riddles, did I? You would have told me anyway."

Damira didn't immediately reply. Over at the table, quiet laughter spread. No one met his eye. Lucy looked down at her boots, but not before Ollie caught a glimpse of a suppressed grin.

"I plead the fifth," the Covenmaster finally said. "And? What's the second question?"

He jerked a thumb toward the door. "I'm getting a free ice cream, right?"

After all that, it was really the least they could do.

Nine

Danvers was exactly what Ollie had expected it to be: older houses, elementary schools, towering oak trees, and a steady stream of commuters on the busy, yellow-lined road. Modern Massachusetts in all its humdrum glory. For some reason, the sight depressed him. And worried him. Surely this couldn't be the place? They were looking for magic, after all, and this was all so...normal.

Laszlo, on the other hand, seemed to have no such compunctions. He was walking with a definite spring in his step, humming a tune that Ollie didn't recognize.

"I think that tour guide might have put a spell on you," Ollie said wryly.

A grin spread across the acrobat's face. "Is true, my friend," he answered. "Ah...Caroline. Caroline! I am...how do you say...bewitched?"

Laszlo hadn't returned to the hotel room until the wee hours, stumbling and whistling before falling into a snoring slumber. Ollie had watched with one eye open from his own bed, after tossing and turning for most of the night. Hadn't the tour guide mentioned this very hotel as one of the most haunted buildings in town? Dead former guests walking the halls, ghostly faces in the mirrors, objects flying through the air, and myriad other nightmarish reports? Once the possibilities had burrowed into his brain, any hope of a decent night's sleep had been lost.

So neither one of them had been particularly well-rested when he'd shaken Laszlo awake at "first light"—per Damira's instructions—to begin the next leg of their journey. Over pastries in the lobby, Ollie had filled him in on the details of his visit with the adolescent, card-shark coven and the odd visit he'd received from Nell. And Laszlo, in turn, had tried to regale Ollie with the details of his after-hours date with Tour Guide Caroline, until Ollie had raised a hand to stop him.

Thirty minutes later, they found themselves wandering down an ordinary sidewalk in an ordinary town, looking for something extraordinary. So far, they hadn't found it.

As they walked, Ollie glanced down at the pellet bump on his arm. Yesterday, he had wondered if it was shrinking. Today, there was no doubt. The lump was definitely smaller. He'd thought he had a week to get this all done, but what if he was wrong? He inhaled deeply, studying his lungs' reaction. Never had the simple act of breathing felt so valuable, and temporary, like a borrowed tool from the neighbor's garage.

He threw a sideways glance at Laszlo, who was still staring straight ahead. Still humming.

"Laz?"

"Mmm?"

"I have to tell you something."

"I am all the ears," the acrobat said, not slowing his pace.

"Remember how I said that I...fought Herrick, in the lab? And escaped? That wasn't entirely true. I mean, it was true, sort of. But it wasn't the whole truth."

At that, Laszlo did slow. He turned his head. "Oh?"

"Yeah. The whole truth, the weird truth, I guess, is that..." He cleared his throat. "Something happened to me. I got really mad. Like, *really* mad, after they did that to Tera and Meatball. I just lost it. And then the anger just kind of, uh, took over."

"Took over what?" Laszlo asked.

Ollie took a few steps before continuing. "Took over...me. I got these bumps, all over my skin. Like freckles, but red. And then a light started to glow. From, uh, from inside me. I think. And it's not the only time that's happened." Taking a deep breath, he plowed forward. "And the weirdest thing is—"

"That is not weirdest thing?" Laszlo interrupted, raising an eyebrow.

Ollie wasn't sure how to answer that, so he just kept going. "When it happened, I was able to make things move. Not with my hands, I mean. I was able to make things move by just...thinking about it. And I made the pufferpine quill pen move, and it stabbed Herrick in the neck, and he got all puffed up. By the poison. And that's how I got out."

Laszlo stopped. He turned to look at Ollie, pursed his lips thoughtfully, and resumed his steady pace along the sidewalk.

"I'm sorry I didn't tell you," Ollie said, rushing to catch up. "I just thought... I don't know. I thought maybe you wouldn't believe me."

Laszlo looked baffled, as though that was the most surprising statement he'd heard so far. "Why would I not believe you?"

It was a fair question, Ollie supposed. If they compiled a list of all the weirdness they'd witnessed in the past few months, glowing red freckles and possible telekinesis would probably fit right in with the rest. "But this is bad, right?" Ollie asked. "I mean, I don't even know what it is! Or why it's happening."

"Maybe bad, maybe not," Laszlo answered. A puddle had formed on the pavement ahead; he plowed straight through it with a splash. "Is power, yes? You might need such power, for what you are doing."

Ollie walked around the puddle. "Yeah, but I can't control it. And I only feel it when I'm really pissed off. What good is a power if you can only use it when you're mad? I mean, this is nuts. My whole life, I've been trying to—" He stopped.

Laszlo glanced at him curiously. "Trying to what?"

Ollie sighed. "All my life, I've been trying *not* to get angry. You know, because of..."

"Because what?"

Now it was Ollie's turn to stop walking. "Because of my dad."

"Ah," Laszlo nodded. They stood together in silence as a trash truck surged past with a thunderous clatter.

Ollie had grown up thinking that his destructive, jerkoff father had abandoned the family. Then he got to the Neath and learned that his mother, Francie, had actually condemned his dad to a life sentence at Herrick's End. No trial, no jury, no lawyers. Just imprisonment. On the one hand, the punishment wasn't entirely undeserved. Matteo Delgato was physically and mentally abusive toward his wife, and would have eventually turned his fists onto his growing son. Francie did what she did to protect Ollie, and for that, he would always be grateful. But he couldn't help but feel conflicted about how it had all come about.

Laszlo knew the whole story; he had even helped Ollie spring Matteo from the prison back when they made their daring escape. They had found Matteo drooling and semi-comatose in his cell—a direct result, perhaps, of the tower's brutal and torturous conditions. Ollie still didn't know why he had rescued his father. A sense of familial obligation, maybe. Matteo didn't deserve rescue. Hell, he didn't deserve the time of day. Now, he was living in a small, staffed care facility in the Neath. Still drooling and comatose, Ollie supposed. But since he never visited, he couldn't say for sure.

In the Neath, Matteo was helpless. Pathetic. But here on the Brickside, he had been a constant source of fear and instability. And now that Ollie was back above ground, all of his old childhood anxieties seemed sharper than ever.

When Ollie finally spoke again, he was staring down at the dappled sunlight on the cement. "My whole life, I've been trying not to get angry," he said softly. "Because I don't want to be like him."

Laszlo rested a hand on his friend's arm, then gently propelled him forward. As they resumed their walk, he commented, "Anger is not always bad thing, you know."

"What? Of course it is."

"Some kinds are very bad, is true," Laszlo said. "But some kinds are needed. Important, even."

Ollie snorted. "How the hell could anger be important?"

Laszlo lifted his palms. "Well, think about people in streets, holding the signs, yelling. Walking around and around in the circles."

"Like, protestors?" Ollie asked, furrowing his brow.

"Yes! This. Protestors. They are angry, yes? Because things are not always right. Some things need changing. And so, they feel mad, and this makes them do the protesting, and this makes the things change. No?"

Ollie shrugged. "I guess so…"

"And what about when someone is doing bad to you? If you do not feel the anger for yourself, this person will just do the walk, walk, walk all over you. And this is not good."

"Okay, yeah," Ollie said, holding up a hand. "Fine. Anger can be good in certain circumstances. But this anger…" He paused. "I don't know, Laz. It might be…dangerous."

At this, Laszlo grinned. "Sometimes, dangerous is good, too," he said with a wink. "Sometimes, is best thing you can be."

Ollie was considering this, feeling the weight of it, when he noticed a small blue sign ahead on the right, almost completely hidden in the overgrowth. Ollie pushed aside the vines and branches to read the orange lettering:

SAMUEL PARRIS ARCHEOLOGICAL SITE
1681-1784
VEHICLES EXCLUDED. PASS AT YOUR OWN RISK.

Below that sign he saw another, smaller placard. It featured, oddly enough, an illustration of a horse and carriage, moving away. A single driver held the reins.

Ollie stared at the silhouette of the man driving the carriage. A shiver ran up his spine. His breath stilled. What was he looking at, here? *Who* was he looking at?

Horse. Carriage. Surly driver. Trapped prisoners. All at once, like a soundtrack carried on centuries-old wind, he heard the clomping. The crack of the whip. The desperate women's cries echoing across a distant, faded hill: *By your own hands, you bring us to death, George Herrick! You bring us to hell!*

Ollie stumbled backwards.

Laszlo was leaning to his left, peering down the length of a nondescript, grassy walkway that ran between the two houses. "Is down here, I think," he said.

Ollie elbowed Laszlo's side, then pointed at the illustration.

Laszlo followed his finger. After a pause, he squinted. "Is our friend?" he asked. "Mr. Herrick?"

"I don't know," Ollie whispered.

Wordlessly, they both turned to look down the length of the shaded, fenced walkway. It appeared to be just wide enough for a few pedestrians.

Or maybe a horse and carriage.

In silent agreement, they started walking. Kids' toys, picnic tables, and other signs of normal habitation surrounded them on either side. "Guess it's just us and the chickens," Ollie said softly, passing a small coop in the nearby yard. Despite the abundance of scattered feed and hay, he heard no clucking. This place was starting to give him the creeps.

Someone was watching.

He turned to look over his shoulder, half-expecting to see Nell standing in the dappled shadows. Or a petulant nine-year-old girl. *Stop looking. It won't be good for you.* But he saw nothing but dirt and grass.

After about a hundred yards, they came upon a clearing. It contained a few trees, three signs, and a fenced-off area in the center. Upon closer inspection, Ollie realized that the fence surrounded the remains of a house—just a foundation, really, but a pretty significant one. Tightly packed stones created the clear, rectangular outlines of rooms.

"This is place, then," Laszlo said, planting his hands on his hips.

It certainly looked that way. And the jumping seed in his pocket seemed to agree: As soon as they had walked into the clearing, the seed's normal jitterbugging had accelerated to a frantic pace. Ollie began to wander and read the signs. The heftiest one was blue and metal; it carried the heading, "1681 SALEM VILLAGE PARSONAGE," followed by an all-caps description of the people who had once lived at the site. Another nearby sign, this one white, detailed the architecture of the original home and the more recent archeological dig in the 1970s. And a third sign, entitled "THE 1734 ADDITION," described another, smaller foundation nearby.

The entire site was shaded, well-kept, and eerily quiet. Ivy and moss encroached at the edges, creeping under the rustic, split-rail fence. Ollie craned his neck, looking for birds and squirrels, but saw none. On the ground, he spotted only dried patches of grass, one large, cleaved boulder, and two granite posts poking out of seemingly random locations.

"Is not much here," Laszlo said. His expression was starting to betray a hint of doubt.

Ollie ran his tongue over his front teeth. "Earth second," he said, recalling the Salt Witch's instructions. "The place of his sin. The remnants of the victims will guide you."

Laszlo leaned over the fence, looking down into the hole. "Is earth down there," he said.

"Yeah, but..." Ollie felt a jolt of discomfort. "I don't think we're supposed to go in there. Isn't that...sacrilegious or something?" Or at the very least, disrespectful. The fence was slight, and would be easy to climb. But there was a gate—and it was locked. Clearly, visitors were meant to stay outside of the archaeological dig.

Still, this was Tera's life they were talking about. And lots of other lives, too. Ollie couldn't let a little thing like propriety stand in his way. That damn second seed, or whatever it was, was here, and he needed it. But what was he supposed to do, just start digging? With what tools, exactly? And how far would he get before the neighbors called the cops?

He removed the torn card from his pocket. "Damira gave me a bunch of numbers, too. She said I would need to use them when I got here."

"Use for what?" Laz asked.

Ollie gave a helpless shrug. Flipping the card over, he stared down at the nonsensical sequence.

2nd, 17. 3rd, 7, 8, 9 and 45. 4th, 2 and 14. 6th, 27. 7th, 2

He started to read it out loud, then gave up and just handed the paper to Laszlo. The acrobat read the scribbles and looked up, his face blank.

"It must mean *something*," Ollie said.

Laszlo exhaled. "Let us read signs again. Maybe we will see numbers?"

Ollie nodded. The biggest sign, the blue one, seemed the most important. So he started there. Laszlo read beside him as they took in the history of the now-vanished home:

1681
SALEM VILLAGE PARSONAGE

In 1681 the Salem Village inhabitants built a home for their minister at this site. Ministers residing here were: George Burroughs (1681-83), accused in 1692 of being a witch and hanged; Deodat Lawson (1684-88), author of the first volume about Salem Village witchcraft; Samuel Parris (1689-96), minister during the witchcraft hysteria; Joseph Green (1698-1715), noted diarist and area peacemaker; Peter Clark (1717-68), famed theological author; and Benjamin Wadsworth (1772-1826), who tore down the old parsonage in 1784.

It was in this house in 1692 that Tituba, Rev. Parris' slave, told the girls of the household stories of witchcraft which nurtured the village witchcraft hysteria and resulted in the deaths of 23 persons. This house was the scene of many incidents during the hysteria, and is one of the most important sites in Colonial American history. Archaeological excavation began here in 1970. - Danvers Historical Commission 1974

Laszlo let out a low whistle.
"The beginning," Ollie murmured. "This is where it all started. Damira called it..." He paused, remembering. "She called it 'the fertile soil of rising tensions and religious tyranny.'"
Fertile soil. *Earth.*
"Lots of numbers," Laszlo said, sounding hopeful as he pointed to the various dates on the sign. "Maybe same numbers we are looking for?"
They did a quick scan, but were disappointed. Nothing seemed to match up.
"Let us check others," the acrobat said, and Ollie trailed behind.
The closest sign, at first, looked promising. It detailed the original measurements of the parsonage in the language of the time, using found documents.
"The Dementions of the House are as followeth," the text began. "42 feet long: twenty foot Broad: thirteen foot stude: Fouer chimleis no gable ends." None of which made much sense to Ollie.

The sign also explained that the home had two floors, four rooms, two bed chambers, and four chimneys. More dates. More numbers. One grainy photograph. He compared it all to Damira's scribbled numbers, but found nothing useful.

Dutifully, they moved to the last sign, where they learned about the Reverend Peter Clark's successful push to build an addition onto the home in 1734. More dates, two more pictures, and a lot of interesting tidbits that seemed to have nothing whatsoever to do with finding a missing, magical seed.

Ollie threw up his hands. "This is useless," he sputtered. Hours were passing. And passing, and passing, and passing, while he did what, exactly? Ate cinnamon scones for breakfast and took a leisurely Colonial-history tour? Why did everything have to be so difficult? So cryptic? Why couldn't someone just tell him: *Walk ten paces right, two paces straight, and there you have it!* Bingo. Seed found with plenty of time left for lunch. But no. They had to make this difficult. They had to test him. Challenge him, time and time again. Why? To what end? What exactly did they think he had to prove? And who was making him prove it? He'd been marching to somebody's orders for months now, with no idea about who, or what, was pulling the goddamn—

"These are bumps?"

Laszlo's voice knocked Ollie out of his internal rant. He looked up, dazed. "What?"

"Bumps," Laszlo repeated, pointing to Ollie's arm. "These are same ones as before?"

Ollie looked down, surprised to see the red freckles rising from his skin. "Oh," he said, feeling lightheaded. "Yeah. Those are them."

"You are getting worked up into tizzy," Laszlo said disapprovingly. "This is no good to us. We need to be thinking, no? Not making the angry bumps." He tapped his temple for emphasis.

Ollie took a deep, calming breath. "You're right," he said. Embarrassed, he rubbed a hand against his arm, as if to force the welts to recede. Then he stared back down at the line of numbers, hoping that something, anything, would occur to him. Nothing did.

"Let me see that," Laszlo said. He took the torn card from Ollie and read it again, running a hand through his long, dark hair. "Do you remember, my friend, the day of your leaving? At Freedom Trail?"

Ollie nodded. "Yeah, of course."

"There was code, in book." The acrobat continued to tug on his hair. "It told you how to find message in book, and to find hole in trail. Do you remember this code?"

Ollie nodded again, more slowly, as the details came back to him. Page numbers, line numbers, words in the line...

"The WRC people, and the witches, they like to use these codes. Is like passing secret notes, no? And these numbers, here, they remind me of the ones we use at trail. No book here, in this place, but—"

"But there are signs!" Ollie reached out to grab his friend's wrists. "Laz, you're a genius!"

"Well, maybe not say *genius,*" Laszlo shrugged, looking pleased. "Maybe we say my thinking is clear today, thanking to kiss of beautiful woman last night."

"Dude, I'll kiss you myself if we can figure this out," Ollie said, spinning back toward the "1734 ADDITION" sign. "Okay, let's see it." He read Damira's note from the beginning. "That's not 'two,' it's 'second.' Maybe the second line down, right? So the second line, then maybe the seventeenth word in the line?" He slid his hand over until he landed on the letter S. "Okay! Now we're getting somewhere! What's next?"

Laszlo looked down. "Third line, seventh, eighth, and ninth letters."

Ollie let his finger slide again. It landed on "T," "H," and "E."

"S...the?" Ollie asked, puzzled. They solved for the remaining letters, only to end up with an alphabet soup of confusion.

"This is not right sign," Laszlo concluded. "Next one, over there."

They walked over to the other white placard. After a few minutes of frantic finger-sliding, they ended up at the same, disappointing conclusion.

Ollie turned and trudged to the last remaining sign. The big blue one, cast in metal. Sending a long, rectangular shadow across the ground.

"Last one," he muttered. "Here goes nothing."

Laszlo called out the lines and numbers, again. Ollie's fingertips pressed against the metallic letters, somehow cold to the touch despite the day's oppressive heat. For once, he was glad to be freakishly tall. Slowly, miraculously, the words appeared.

O
THER
HA
L
F

Ollie took a step back. "Other half," he said.

"Yes!" Laszlo threw his arms into the air and performed what Ollie could only assume was a traditional Ukrainian happy dance. "Yes, yes, yes! We do it!"

"But... other half of what?" Ollie asked.

The question lingered in the humid summer air, bringing Laszlo's happy dance to a sudden and decidedly *un*happy end.

Ten

Ollie's eyes scanned the scene around him. *Other half... Other half...*

Other half of...the house? The foundation? It seemed already intact, and fairly symmetrical. The trees, likewise, appeared to be branching out in very normal, treelike ways. Other half of the...story? Like, a metaphorical thing? No, that didn't make any sense. He shook his head, hard. Those two granite posts. Randomly placed. Were they marking half of something? Half of another dig site, maybe?

His eyes fell on the closer post. It was perched near the fence corner, and one of the trees, and not far from the big rock Ollie had noticed when they first walked in.

The big, *cleaved* rock.

"That!" he shouted, pointing. "The boulder! It looks like it was cut in half, doesn't it?"

They hurried over to stand next to the triumvirate of fence post, tree, and rock.

Laszlo's hands perched once again on his hips, which had started to resume their giddy sway. "Yes," he announced. His voice boomed into the silence around them. "Yes! That is it!"

Jubilant, Ollie took a turn at his own happy dance. The seed in his pocket, likewise, seemed to speed its skitter.

"Now we just need to find other half," Laszlo added.

"Right," Ollie nodded. "Right. Well, it must be here, somewhere."

The small, wooded area behind the dig site seemed like the best bet. Thick with overgrowth and old, fallen leaves, it had to be chock full of rocks, too. And a big one like that would be hard to miss. But after several minutes of trampling through the brush, they saw nothing. The rest of the site was cleared and quite obviously devoid of giant boulders. And another examination of the house's two foundations didn't reveal any individual stones matching the size and shape they were looking for.

Ollie groaned and clenched his fists. Would they have to go somewhere else? No—that couldn't possibly be right. The Coven had sent him here for a reason. *Other half... Other half...* It had to be here. He was just about to ask Laszlo to swing himself up into the overhead canopy for a bird's-eye search when something caught his eye.

Something...sprouting. Sprouting at an unusually rapid pace.

First, a stem pushed itself up and out of the undergrowth. Then, multiple snaking shoots, poking out in all directions. As Ollie watched in amazement, the stem matured almost instantaneously into a sturdier, thicker trunk. The shoots morphed into branches. Delicate leaves unfurled into a crown of greenery. In less than a minute, the swiftly growing plant had taken its full form.

It looked like a pint-sized tree. Not a sapling, but a full-grown grown tree in miniature. A well-groomed bonsai, perhaps—a well-groomed bonsai that had somehow grown at breakneck speed in the middle of a deserted, wooded area. Its bright white bark and dazzling green leaves were vibrant enough to look unnatural. They reminded him more of Tera's luminous paintings than of actual organic matter.

It took a moment for Ollie to find his voice. When he did, he called out, "Over here! You've got to see this."

Laszlo ambled closer, scanning the ground. "What?"

"That." Ollie pointed at the bonsai.

"Is leaves," the acrobat said, sounding perplexed.

"No, not the leaves, the tree! The little tree, right there."

After several seconds of silence, Laszlo said, "Ollie, my friend, I see no tree."

"What do you mean? It's right there! Right—" he stopped, suddenly remembering the last ice-cream flavor on Sweet Screams' list. *"You can see that?"* the girl had asked him. As if no one else could.

"You don't see a tree?" Ollie asked. "White bark? Neon leaves?"

Laszlo shook his head.

"It's there," Ollie whispered. "I can see it." Not only that, but now he could also see a spectral, lime-green glow radiating from the leaves and branches. Everything nearby suddenly looked brighter, and more alive. It was mesmerizing. Ollie found himself unable to look away.

Laszlo inhaled. "If you see tree, then tree was meant for you," he said decisively. "You look for spot, tree looks for you. So, we dig here, no?"

Ollie nodded, feeling lightheaded. First a violet aquarium coral, then Poison Pufferpine ice cream, and now a dayglow bonsai. What was real? What was mirage? He remembered the Novas' vast and convincing illusions in the Neath, and realized with a twinge that he'd probably never know for sure.

Dropping to their knees, Ollie and Laszlo began to sweep away the thick layer of dead leaves and underbrush. Minutes later, there it was: one half of a hulking, gray-speckled rock, nestled into the dry ground. The tree glowed beside it, waving slightly in a nonexistent breeze.

Questions assembled in Ollie's mind like harried passengers at the airport check-in line. Who had cut this rock in half? And why? Why had the pieces been separated from each other? How long had they been apart? "C'mon, let's lift it," he said, feeling grateful, yet again, for Laszlo's company. Ollie never would have been able to move the heavy boulder on his own.

Grunting, the two men carried the stone out of the woods and back to the clearing, plunking it onto the ground next to its mirror image. Looking at the two pieces together, it was clear they had once formed a unified, oblong stone.

"Now, you push them together, yes?" Laszlo prodded.

Yes. Ollie lowered himself to his knees in slow motion, but couldn't bring himself to touch the stone.

"Go ahead," Laszlo said, pantomiming a push. "Rock will not bite. Unless you are seeing teeth like you see very small trees?" He smiled and waggled his eyebrows.

Ollie grimaced. No teeth. Just...unease. What the hell was going to happen when the two halves were reunited? Maybe they'd explode and scatter bits of Ollie and Laszlo all over the shaded clearing. More bones for the archeologists to discover. Maybe the Danvers Historical Commission would have to create another sign. HERE LIE THE REMAINS OF TWO TWENTY-FIRST CENTURY INTERLOPERS WHO DIDN'T HAVE THE COMMON SENSE GOD GAVE A MAYFLY TO LEAVE WELL ENOUGH ALONE. SERVES THEM RIGHT, VERILY AND MIGHTILY SO.

He steeled himself. Then, he rested both hands on the recovered half's cold surface, leaned forward, and started to push.

It was more difficult than he had expected. The ground, though hard and dry from the summer heat, seemed to resist his efforts. Finally, the two pieces touched. He adjusted a little to the left, a little to the right, and gave a final shove. He heard a click, not unlike the sound he'd heard when popping open the Freedom Trail portal to the Neath.

"Did you hear that?" he asked Laszlo.

Before the acrobat could answer, the seam of the two connecting pieces began to flare. Beams of light poured out like linear fireworks, popping and hissing, until the two sides were welded together. Just as suddenly, the sparks vanished. And all that was left was a rock: whole and smoothly integrated, as though the laceration had never existed at all.

Cautiously, Ollie reached out to poke it. The stone was still cold, but wobbly. And lighter? He grabbed both sides and lifted, astonished when the large boulder lifted into the air without any resistance at all. Like a fake, hide-a-key rock in a suburban garden.

They gazed at each other in bewilderment. Then, Laz tilted at the waist to peer into the rock's shadow. "I am seeing something," he said.

Ollie set the newly featherweight stone aside. In its place, he saw a hole. And inside the hole, he saw a square, wooden box. The container was clearly old. So old, it felt like it might disintegrate in his fingers as he lifted it from the pit and set it on the grass.

"Go ahead! Open!" Laszlo said, chopping his hands through the air in nervous impatience. "We do not come all this way to look at closed box!"

"Right, right. Okay. Here goes." Gingerly, Ollie lifted the lid, flinched, and scooted backwards, as though something might come crawling out. When nothing did, he leaned forward and saw a pile of drab-colored objects resting together in the darkness: Two metal thimbles, pockmarked with tiny indentations. Several long, bent needles. A wooden button sitting atop a bundle of cloth. A chipped earthenware bowl. Something that might have been a comb. And one small, silvery spoon.

Each item was delicate, hand-forged, and timeworn, like a smattering of artifacts he might see on display at museum.

Laszlo was rubbing his chin. "These things...they belong to people of this house?" he asked.

As Ollie considered this, the words on the parchment rose in his consciousness. "The remnants of the victims will guide you," he recited, looking up. "These must be the remnants!" According to the signs, the parsonage had housed numerous women and children, any number of whom would have logically owned 1600s-era needles, thimbles, fabric, and tableware. *Remnants.* Haunting vestiges of a now-vanished Colonial life.

Laszlo knelt down beside him and began to paw through the pile.

"Easy!" Ollie objected.

"Is fine, is fine," the acrobat replied. His hand reached the bottom of the box, then stopped.

"What? What is it?" Ollie asked.

Laz pulled out a soft, cloth object that had been hiding below the rest. "Is doll," he announced.

The small toy was clothed in a dress and bonnet, both originally white but yellowed with time. Its cheeks had been painted pink; its two black eyes stared up at them, unblinking. A row of tiny, brown buttons marched down the front of the dress.

"There," Ollie whispered, reaching out a finger.

One of the doll's buttons was not a button at all. It was a seed.

He plucked it, expecting resistance. Instead, the seed easily released into his hand as though it had been ready and waiting for the chance. Almost immediately, it started to wiggle.

Ollie reached his other hand into his jeans pocket, pulled out the first seed, and placed it beside the second. Together, they began to roll and shake in perfect unison on his opened palm.

Laszlo folded his arms with satisfaction. "What do I tell you? We do this! Did I tell you we do this? And we do!"

"Yes, you did," Ollie grinned. "You were right."

Laszlo dropped the doll back into the box and cupped his ear. "I am not hearing you. Say this again?"

"I said, you were right."

"Ah! This is the music to my ears! Now tell me, Ollie Delgato of the North End Delgatos. What is to do now?"

Ollie stared down at the dancing seedpods. "Now, we go get banana splits," he said. "And answers."

—⁓∞⁓—

The coven's round card table was gone. The teenagers were gone, too, as was the smoke. This time, Ollie stepped into Sweet Screams Ice Cream and Candy Emporium's clandestine back room to find only Damira, the fireplace, a smaller, rectangular table, and three chairs.

Damira did not seem surprised to see him. And he wasn't surprised that she wasn't surprised. The only surprised person in the room was Laszlo, who was cautiously licking a large cone of Cookies and Scream while surveying the room—and the Covenmaster—warily.

"Come in, please," Damira said. With one hand, she clutched something that looked like a stack of cardboard circles. Coasters? With the other, she gestured toward the two empty chairs.

"Thanks," Ollie said. "Uh, this is my friend, Laszlo."

The acrobat strode across the room, hand outstretched. "Pleased to be meeting you," he boomed. "Laszlo Kravchenko."

"Wait a minute," Damira said as they shook. "You're not one of the Famous Kravchenkos, are you? The Flying Kravchenko Brothers of Ukraine?"

A look of pure, mystified glee passed over Laszlo's features. "Why, yes!" he said. "Yes, I am! They are my uncles!"

"My goodness, how about that! That is a proud family legacy, to be sure." Damira smiled broadly before turning her gaze to Ollie. "How about that?" she repeated with the quickest flash of a wink.

"Yeah, it's...something." Ollie cleared his throat. "Anyway, we found what we were looking for in Danvers. You told me to come back here afterwards and—"

"What was yours to find," she interrupted. Her attention had turned to the pack of coasters in her hand, which she started shuffling.

"Hmm?"

"I said, you found what was yours to find. If you found it."

Ollie glanced at Laz. "Right," he said, lowering his cup of Mint Reaper—two scoops, marshmallow sauce, extra jimmies—onto the table. Cautiously, he reached into his pocket and pulled out the twin seeds. When he placed them on the table next to the ice cream, they shimmied in a harmonious dance.

Damira stared at the seedpods for a long, quiet moment. So long that Ollie worried he had done something wrong. Then, she gave a curt nod, hard enough to make her silver bob bounce. "I understand," she said. "You may put them away now."

"Away?"

"Back in your pocket," she hissed, then looked left and right furtively. "Hurry, now. These are for you alone."

Puzzled, Ollie scooped up the brown seeds.

"You helped him with this?" Damira asked Laszlo.

Mid-lick, the acrobat managed only to nod.

"Commendable job, both of you," she said.

Laszlo beamed once again.

Ollie grabbed his cup from the table and took an oversized bite. Marshmallow sauce dripped off the spoon and onto his shirt, making him swear under his breath. He was nervous. And when he was nervous, he ate too fast. Come to think of it, he also ate too fast when he was happy, or hungry, or...well, conscious. But still. Right now, he was definitely nervous enough to miss his mouth altogether and drop the entire gooey, melting concoction into his lap. He could only imagine what the unflappable Covenmaster would make of that.

What was he so anxious about, anyway? He'd been promised answers, and now he was about to get them. That was a good thing, right? A great thing. He'd wanted nothing more for months.

So why did he keep hearing Dozer's voice in his head? *Probably best not to know, that's my motto,* his old cellmate had warned him about the details of life in the Neath. *Less questions you ask down here, the better. That's lesson numero uno for you.*

And then, his mother's voice: *Be careful what you wish for, amore mio. Sometimes, what we have already is exactly what we need.*

And then, the image of his friend Nell, standing outside this very shop, warning him not to enter. Not to "look." But he had entered, and he had looked. Had he made a terrible mistake?

Ollie glanced around the strange little room, at the ancient fireplace that appeared and disappeared on command, at the table that grew, shrunk, and reshaped itself to meet the day's needs, and at the bespectacled Covenmaster who held his future in her deceivingly delicate-looking hands.

"Be careful what you witch for," he murmured.

Damira gave him a look of amusement. "What was that?"

"Nothing." Ollie shoved another large spoonful of green ice cream into his mouth.

"You have answers for our friend here, yes?" Laszlo asked.

"I do, if he is willing to hear them." She was staring at Ollie with curiosity.

"Oh yes, he is willing," Laszlo answered, dropping down into the empty chair with a thump. "He sees little baby trees, did you know that? Trees that grow up, up, up in very fast speed?"

Damira continued to shuffle the pile of coasters. Her smile was knowing, and crooked. "Oh, I imagine our boy here sees all kinds of things."

"All right, enough," Ollie said, his cheeks flushing red. "Do you know how to help Tera, or not? I've done what you asked. I found the...thing, I brought it here. Now I need to know what's going on here, or I swear, I'll... I'll..." As usual, he had no idea how to finish that sentence. The wishy-washy threat pressed against his throat, leaving an aftertaste of incompetence.

"Your Tera waits," the Covenmaster said casually. Too casually. "And she will continue to wait, until the right moment arrives." Her gaze traveled to his face. "Until the right person tells you the right information at the right time, setting the right cogwheels into motion."

"And you are right person?" Laszlo asked.

Damira nodded with self-satisfaction. "It would appear that I am. And this..." She held up the cardboard discs. "...is the information. And now..." She tapped the table. "...is the time."

Ollie swallowed another spoonful with a greedy, nervous gulp.

"Shall we begin?" she asked.

Mouth still full and frozen, he nodded.

"Wonderful." Damira began to lay the pieces of paper onto the table—*slap, slap, slap*—in a way that made him understand they were not coasters, but cards. Blank cards, from the looks of it. And round instead of rectangular. Despite what appeared to be a complete lack of suits, or numbers, or brawling mythical creatures, the Covenmaster nonetheless stared at each one with the concentration of someone reading Haiku in a foreign language.

In the silence, the two men glanced each other. Laszlo crunched off a bite of his cone.

Finally, Damira gathered up the cards again, took one from the top of the pile, and flipped it onto the surface of the table with a decisive snap. "Ollie, the cards would like to introduce you to your grandmother," she announced.

Warily, he looked down, but saw only a blank, white circle. Then, spot by spot, an image began to take shape. It looked like a grainy, coppery picture of a young woman in old-fashioned clothes and an old-fashioned hairstyle. She was blonde, with a closed-mouth smile. A beautiful woman, to be sure. But not his grandmother.

Ollie leaned back in his chair. "Nope, sorry," he said, feeling strangely relieved. Maybe this whole thing was a misunderstanding. Maybe they had the wrong guy, and now they could go find the *right* guy, and then he could get back to his life. "I knew both of my grandmothers. And neither one was her." He tapped the edge of the card.

Damira shook her head. "Sorry," she said. "I sometimes forget that you humans need more specificity. What I should have said is, the cards would like to introduce you to your great, great, great, great, great..." She paused with a smile and held up a hand. "Let's just say, however many greats it takes to get back to the seventeenth century."

Ollie restlessly shoved another spoonful of ice cream into his mouth and looked at the picture again. "Ooookaaaay," he answered, drawing out the syllables. He had no way of proving Damira wrong—or right. It seemed...not impossible. Though weird. And sort of beside the point. What did this great-, great-, great-times-whatever grandmother lady have to do with getting Tera out of that tank?

"I see resemblance," Laszlo piped in.

Ollie gave him a sidelong glance.

"What? I do. Yellow hair. Circle cheeks." He puffed out his own sunken cheeks, then touched Ollie's.

Ollie slapped his hand away and turned back toward Damira. "Okay, let's say you're right. That's my...very-great grandmother. So what?"

"Her name was Ellora," the Covenmaster said.

"All right."

"And she used to live right here, in Salem."

"All right."

"And she was a witch."

"All ri—" Ollie stopped mid-word.

Laszlo, who had been crunching his cone noisily, went still.

"And that means, young man, that you are a witch, too. Well, sort of."

"That's...that's ridiculous," he said. The words popped out like a reflex.

"Is it?" Damira asked, locking her eyes onto his.

Ollie felt the weight of her stare as a tingle began to rush to his extremities. Thoughts flashed in quick succession: Invisible objects made visible. Rage transforming into illumination and power. Cryptic messages, meant for only his ears. Prophetic notes, meant for only his eyes. All the whispers behind his back, from the moment he'd arrived in the Neath. "Is he...?" "Is that...?" Whispers that he'd willfully ignored.

Laszlo looked back and forth between their faces. "I am not understanding the English," he interjected. "What does this mean, 'sort-of' witch?"

Damira smiled. "What I mean to say is, you are *half* witch."

"Oh yeah? What's my other half?" Ollie snapped. Reflex again. He could feel his fear growing and morphing into unattractive snark. "Let me guess, Bigfoot? Hunchback of Notre Dame?" His palms grew clammy as a he recalled the message they'd just decoded in Danvers: *OTHER HALF.*

"No such luck," Damira said with a sigh. "I'm afraid your other half is very much human." She flipped another card onto the table and stared down at it, expectantly. She was waiting for another image to appear.

Be careful what you witch for.

He wanted, desperately, to close his eyes. To forget he ever came here. To forget he ever saw that message on a Mirrormoth's wings, or stumbled into that candelabra-lit laboratory, or climbed out from the depths of Copp's Hill Burying Ground into the harsh glare of a Brickside summer. He would close his eyes, and he would keep them closed, until oblivion fell. That oblivion, he was pretty sure, would be better than whatever he was about to see on that card.

Instead, Ollie looked down. The circle of white cardboard remained stubbornly blank. And then, like a Polaroid bleeding into view, the face of a man began to appear on its surface. Wire-rimmed glasses. Thick, wavy hair. Bushy eyebrows. Chapped lips, curled into a grin.

The card was silent, but Ollie could still hear the voice rumbling within. Young, then old. Past, then present. A harsh, gravelly voice, tinged with a British accent, simmering with venom.

The voice snarled on a Salem hillside, transporting doomed prisoners to their death: *"Cease with your tricks! You are mad, old woman. Mad, and cursed!"*

It rang out loud and confident in Grimshawe Laboratory: *"Names have great power, don't they? The power to change everything. Would you care for a tour?"*

It slithered into Ollie's head, giving orders, forcing him to do the unthinkable: *"Put them inside the tank."*

And finally, it hovered above all of its unholy creations, above Ollie's crumpled body, above all of the damage and darkness, sounding unmistakably amused: *"Your Tera is right where you left her. Don't you remember, Ollie? You did this. With your own two hands."*

The voice faded. And then, there was only the face on the card. It stared up at Ollie, smirking. The face of the man who wanted to destroy it all. Who very nearly already had.

Damira cleared her throat. "Ollie, the cards would like to introduce you to your—"

"No need," he interrupted with a croak. "We've already met." Then he turned his head and vomited green ice cream, marshmallow sauce, and extra jimmies all over the historic, hardwood floor.

Eleven

Ollie's brain pinged like a pinball machine, making his whole body vibrate. He felt himself tipping. Reeling. Struggling to make sense of the disparate thoughts bouncing and flying from one flipper to the next.

"It's a mistake," he finally managed to say. "They're wrong."

"The cards are never wrong," Damira answered. Her voice was firm, though shaded with sympathy.

"Well, this time they are," Ollie insisted. His stomach still roiled with nausea. "There's no way I'm descended from...that...that..." He caught the scent of the vomit on the ground and began to dry heave.

A blue handkerchief appeared in the Covenmaster's hand; she passed it across the table. As Ollie, now embarrassed, used it to wipe the corners of his mouth, she waved her lighthouse-striped fingernails and made the disgusting pile of regurgitated dessert disappear from the floor. As if it had never been there at all. Ollie ogled the suddenly clean, dry spot on the wood planks, his mind still trapped inside the pinball cacophony.

Lights, flashing. Silver balls, flying.

Ping, ping, ping.

Laszlo, who seemed entirely unaffected by the appearance *or* disappearance of the puke, was staring at the man's picture.

Ollie looked at Damira. "They're wrong," he said, tightening his lips. "Do it again."

"Ollie, as I said—"

"Do it again!"

Damira held up her palms in surrender. "All right. I'll do it again."

She was humoring him, but he didn't care. As Ollie held his breath, she flipped a new, white card onto the table's surface. As before, the image took several seconds to appear. When it did, he found himself staring at an older man in a black lab coat, wobbling on a cane.

Step, tap, lean. Step, tap, lean.

He trembled, then shook his head. "No. No way. Again!"

With a sigh, Damira flipped yet another card. This one revealed a closer shot of the same man. A streak of white meandered through his dark hair. A pair of hazel eyes peered out from behind his thick spectacles. The man's expression was misleadingly blank. Almost pleasant.

Ollie heard himself whimper: "Again."

Damira flipped another. The image came faster this time: A carriage driver spurring two horses along a rutted, dirt road. Behind him, three prisoners huddled and wailed in a makeshift cage. Accused witches, soon to meet their ends. Ollie could swear he heard one of them shout a warning to the driver, her words traveling across the centuries in a raspy shriek: *You cannot hide from this! They see all that you do. And they will know your name!*

Laszlo gaped. "Wait! Is...Herrick?" he asked. "*Our* Herrick? Very bad man Herrick?"

Ollie couldn't answer.

"It is," Damira confirmed.

"My friend, this is meaning that you are—?" Laszlo's query went unfinished.

Ollie slammed his eyes shut. *See no evil. See no evil. See no evil.*

Was this why Nell had been watching him? Why she had warned him to stop looking for answers? It had to be. She was trying to protect him. She knew what he would find. But...how?

"You wanted to know the truth, and this is it," Damira said. Her tone was irritatingly neutral, as though she were talking about the ingredients in a tub of Freaky Fudge Ripple. "It's hard to see the truth of things," she continued. "I get it. But we can't change what we can't see."

At this, his eyes flew open. Where had he heard those words before?

The witch called Lizbeth, in her nest.

We cannot change what we cannot see, Lizbeth had told him. *Hatred and ignorance persist, it is true. But the world is changing. We are changing it. You are changing it, one soul at a time.*

Then, as now, he did not understand.

Thoughts, impossible thoughts, rolled and flung themselves around his skull. *Ping, ping, ping.* It couldn't be true. It just couldn't be. The prospect of having George Herrick's blood running through his own veins made Ollie want to run out onto the Salem streets and hope for a speeding tour bus to knock him clean across the cobblestones.

The man who had hurt Tera—worse, who had forced Ollie to hurt Tera—was his...his...? No. It wasn't true.

And yet... He felt the truth pinching like a too-tight shoe. Which would explain the imaginary flashing lights of an imaginary pinball machine and the nausea that even now threatened to bring forth another round of marshmallowy vomit.

"But...why?" he finally asked. "If this man is my...my great-great-whatever grandfather, why would he do these things to me? *How* could he do these things?" Even as the words left his mouth, Ollie realized that he had asked the same questions countless times about his own father. Not an ancestor many times removed, but his own damn father, living in his own damn house, causing incalculable pain with his words and fists. *Of course it's possible,* he told himself bitterly. *It happens every fucking day.*

"The cards can tell you the story," Damira said, holding up the stack with a grim look on her face. "The whole story. But only if you're ready to hear it. Otherwise, they will not speak."

No. No, no, no. He didn't want any more of this. This was too much. Ollie pressed both palms against the table and pushed his chair backwards. Tears stung his eyes. He was halfway to his feet when Laszlo rested a big hand on his back.

"We do this together, my friend," the acrobat said, his voice low. "You are not alone in the listening. Cards will tell story, and we will see what we are needing to see. And then we will go, together, in ugly yellow car, and we will finish this."

Ollie looked at him, wavering.

"You can do this listening," Laszlo pressed. "You can. For Tera, and for your rodent friend. And cards cannot hurt, no? Is only listening. What is it they say, about the stones and sticks and the breaking bones?"

"Sticks and stones can break my bones," Ollie recited dully.

"Yes! This. The stones and the sticks are bad, but cards?" He gave a loud *psshhh* sound and waved his spindly fingers. "Cards are nothing. Just pictures. We see story, we leave, we do the rescuing. Is easy as the peas. Yes?"

Ollie didn't immediately answer.

"Yes?" Laszlo pressed.

"Yes," Ollie whispered.

"Good." The acrobat gave a decisive nod, then tapped the table. "He is ready. Let us see story." He kept his other hand on Ollie's back.

Damira threw a quizzical gaze at Ollie, who nodded. He didn't want to nod. He wanted to run screaming from the room, stop at the candy counter for a box of hazelnut truffles, and then disappear forevermore out the back door. But this wasn't about him. It was about Tera, and Meatball, and the captured Brickside women. If these cards could tell him what he was doing here and what he was supposed to do next, he had no choice but to listen. Even if the story was infuriating. Or disgusting. Or troubling. And if recent history had taught him anything, it was likely to be all three.

"All right, then," the Covenmaster said. "Let's begin."

With an expert swipe reminiscent of a Vegas dealer, she cleared away the cards they'd already seen and returned them to her hand. Then she shuffled the deck, muttered to it, and flipped three cards onto the table.

Three images appeared, one on each card: a ship; gusts of snow; and farmers toiling in narrow, hilly fields.

With that, Damira began to speak.

"Like so many, George Herrick came to the New World seeking a golden ticket of opportunity," she began, tapping the depiction of the tall-masted ship. "Instead, he found a harsh environment, a limiting social structure, and few creature comforts. In his old life, he had been aristocratic. But here in the Colonies, he was a simple villager, working very hard for very little reward. This, as you might imagine, did not sit well with dear old George."

Three more cards, three more pictures: Churchgoers, crowded into pews. Women in bulky, long skirts, trudging along a wooded path. And a young George Herrick, yanking a terrified, skinny man into a cell.

"In his mind, he deserved better," Damira continued. "He deserved more. And yet, at every turn, he was thwarted. Denied what was owed to him, by rights. His position as Deputy-Sherriff at least afforded him some power over his fellow villagers. He enjoyed that power, and abused it whenever possible. But when the witch trials began, the workload increased. The hours increased. The indignity increased. And Herrick's animosity welled by the day."

She flipped over three more cards, which slowly revealed the bleeding, bruised, and weeping faces of women and men, imprisoned. Transported. Doomed.

Ollie shrunk back.

"As you might expect, the Deputy took his anger out on the helpless prisoners in his custody," she said. "He was crueler than necessary. He took great pleasure in it, as abusers often do. Witnesses from the time described Herrick as having an 'eager zeal' for the prosecutions, and said that his "impatient activity' in the realm of examinations, torture, and incarcerations 'justly incurred the resentment of the sufferers and their friends.'"

"Is sounding like nice guy," Laszlo muttered sarcastically.

The next group of cards showed Herrick standing before a row of judges. Then, marching out into a snowy street. Then, surrounded by a group of cloaked women.

"And when it was over, what did Deputy Herrick do? Did he repent? Did he reflect on his actions? No. Instead, he approached the village council with a petition complaining about the 'hard times' he had suffered during the trials. 'For I have been bred a gentleman," he told them, 'and not much used to work.' The village, he insisted, now owed him additional 'supply' and 'plenty' for his troubles; today, we'd call his petition a demand for overtime pay. The court refused the request and tossed him out on his ear."

Damira took a deep breath before continuing. "In the end," she said, "one hundred and sixty people from around the region had been accused of witchcraft. Many of those were imprisoned, and many also lost all their property in the process. Five died while in jail, one was pressed to death, and nineteen eventually hung by their necks at Proctor's Ledge. Yet even after all this, Deputy Herrick, astoundingly, still believed himself to be the primary victim of the Salem hysteria."

Laszlo snorted and shook his head. Ollie just listened numbly.

"Not a single one of the executed victims was a witch, of course," she continued. "Not a one. But that does not mean there were no witches about. As it turns out, plenty of my kin had been watching the trials, and the Deputy's depravities, from a distance. The court's rebuff had humiliated him, they knew. They also knew that there are few things more dangerous than a humiliated, cruel man. The time had come to act. George Herrick, they decided, would cause no further harm to Salem. He would atone for his actions, and he would pay what he owed."

Only what you owe. The unofficial motto of Herrick's End. The words reverberated in Ollie's mind like a half-forgotten nightmare.

Damira lay down the next three cards. They depicted scolding witches, a cowering Herrick, and the woman that Ollie now recognized as his multi-great-grandmother, Ellora.

"You must understand that in the Deputy's mind, women were, by definition, inferior to men. To think that a group of women would have power over him—him! George Herrick!—was simply inconceivable. This was the greatest indignity of all. Still, he was wise enough to realize that he, as a mortal, was no match for this coven. He swallowed this knowledge as a child drinks down unpleasant medicine." Damira smiled ruefully. "Because he knew that he could not defeat them, Herrick decided to bide his time. He pretended to repent his sins. And eventually, he met a young, naïve, and uniquely powerful witch who seemed susceptible to his charms. Ellora. This witch, he knew, would finally change his fortunes for the better."

The Covenmaster attempted to lay more cards on the table, but the deck resisted. And then, with the force of a Boston Harbor gust, they blew out of her hand and scattered in all directions.

Ollie, Laszlo, and Damira all ducked as the cards flew past their heads, folding and flapping and chattering like agitated monkeys. Finally, they began to rearrange themselves on the table. Three upright, two across, forming a sort of platform. Then three more upright on top of that, and two more across. And again, and again, and again, until the cards formed a wobbly, teetering tower.

Ollie and Laszlo looked at the tall, cylindrical structure, and then at each other. There was no mistaking what it looked like.

Herrick's End.

Damira regained her composure and sat upright, once again, in her chair. When she resumed speaking, her voice was sharp and clear. "Herrick convinced the witches that he wanted to atone for his wrongdoing by helping them create a sanctuary," she said. "A safe haven where they could live in restful peace, far from the persecutions and witch hunts of the aboveground world. And together, they did exactly that. They called it the Neath, and in the beginning, it was a truly spectacular and magical place." Here, she paused and sighed. "But that was merely step one in Herrick's plan, of course. Not long after that, he convinced the beautiful and impressionable Ellora to help him achieve step two."

On the table, the card tower began to wobble and shake; they all leaned back in their seats until the quaking eased.

"Herrick told Ellora that the Neath could be used to provide safe haven for victimized mortal women, as well, and she agreed. Then he took it one step further, suggesting that the underground world could also serve a rehabilitative function. What if they created a facility where the offenders could live quietly, far from the temptations of society, and contemplate the error of their ways? If these mortal wrongdoers could be transformed, as he had been, then the world would truly become a better, and safer, place for all."

Damira reached out and touched the cards gently, as though patting a skittish dog. "Charming the young Ellora was one thing," she said. "The older, wiser witches presented another challenge entirely. Herrick knew they would see right thought his pretext, and would never agree to such a plan. And so he convinced Ellora that they must work in secret, together, to build the prison, fill it with inmates, and start them on the path to redemption. He told her that he was her soulmate. He told her that her fellow witches did not have her back, that they were jealous of her gifts, and that they were plotting against her. In short, this open and trusting girl, this beacon of beauty and innocence, was sucked entirely into George Herrick's ruse. And once that happened, she believed every one of his filthy, clever lies."

Ollie held up a hand. "Wait. You're saying that—"

"I'm not saying anything," Damira corrected. "The cards are."

"Fine. The *cards* are saying that George Herrick convinced Ellora to create Herrick's End? To build a prison, and to bring all those bad guys down there?"

"Yes. He used her, and her magic, to make it happen."

Laszlo and Ollie asked the next question in unison: "But why?"

The cards dispersed again. With dizzying speed, they spread themselves across the surface of the table, creating a series of symmetrical lines. In perfect formation, they began to march toward Laszlo and Ollie.

Tap, tap, tap. Tap, tap, tap.

The motion had an eerie, perfect cadence.

Damira answered in a hushed tone. "He was creating an army," she said grimly, staring down at the traveling legion.

Tap, tap, tap. Tap, tap, tap.

Ollie scooted his chair backward as the brigade advanced. The sound got louder, and more menacing.

TAP, TAP, TAP. TAP, TAP, TAP.

One by one, the orderly lines of cards reached the edge of the table and began falling onto the floor.

"An army?" Ollie yelped. "What the hell for?"

But Laszlo understood. "For Neath," the acrobat said with a frown, moving his feet aside to make room for the falling cards. "And then...for Brickside."

Ollie looked from one to the other, confused. "I don't understand."

"Laszlo is right," the Covenmaster confirmed. "George Herrick plans to get all the power and privilege he feels he was denied. He plans to make up for lost time—first in the Neath, and then..." She paused, swallowed heavily, and continued. "And then up here."

"Let me get this straight," Ollie said, rubbing his temples. "This asshole spends all these years collecting bad guys like baseball cards? Locking them up and throwing away the key? So they can...what? Become his personal soldiers?"

"Something like that, yes."

"And what if they don't want to?"

She gave him a wry smile. "If history is any indication, they won't exactly have a choice."

Ollie contemplated her words as he watched the last of the cards plummet off the edge of the table. It was genius, really, when you thought about it. Textbook evil genius. Herrick's plan managed to use people on both sides of the equation: the abusers *and* the abuse victims. First, he convinces the victims that their only real path to safety is to condemn their abusers to Herrick's End. Then, he forces the now-ensnared perpetrators to secure his reign as Dictator Extraordinaire. Genius. In the meantime, he works away in his lab to create a stockpile of horrifying, weaponized creatures— for back-up? For the front lines?

Reflexively, Ollie touched the bump on his arm. "That's why he's so bent on perfecting a breathing...thing," he murmured, his back vibrating with a shiver. "He needs to get all those soldiers back to the Brickside." And to keep them there for longer than a week. After all, it's pretty tough to subjugate Boston, and beyond, if you can't breathe.

"But how does this Herrick do all these things?" Laszlo asked. "He is only one man."

As if in response, the sad pile of cards on the floor rose into the air and swirled into a tornado above their heads. The chattering sounds returned, along with multicolored sparks.

Damira gazed up at the display. "It seems our George convinced Ellora to share her magic with him. 'Borrowing,' he called it."

"Which implies he was going to give it back," Ollie interjected. "I'm guessing that's not what happened?"

"You guess right," she answered flatly. "He did not give it back. Instead, he stole enough to weaken her, and then detained her somehow. Some...where."

"What does this mean, detained?" Laszlo asked. "What happened to witch girl? Where is she?"

"The cards don't know."

The floating twister slowed, then widened into a circular orbit over the table.

"I thought the cards knew everything," Ollie said.

"I didn't say that," Damira corrected. "I said, the cards are never wrong."

He let out a quaking sigh. "Great. Well, what *do* they know?"

"They know that Ellora needs to be found, if George Herrick is to be stopped. And that the only one who can find her," she added, "is you."

"Me?" Ollie said, his throat going dry.

Laszlo nodded as though this made perfect sense. "Because you are grandson," he said.

"Great, great, great-whatever grandson," Ollie objected, feeling a mounting torrent of dismay. Why were they talking about all this as though it was the tiniest bit plausible? As though he was actually the descendant of some seventeenth-century, frock-wearing sorceress? He swallowed, thinking back to his blur of a childhood. Trying to recall something, anything, that made this make sense. He supposed he always knew his mother had secrets. And that she was a few notches above and beyond the ordinary moms on the block. But a witch? He'd always assumed the only things she'd passed down to him was a penchant for knuckle-cracking and a kick-ass recipe for Steak Pizzaiola.

In a haze, he pulled the seeds out of his pocket. The cards above reacted by swooping closer, then hovering protectively over Ollie's outstretched hand. The little pods jiggled as if in greeting. "Is that what these are for?" he asked. "To find Ellora?"

"I believe so, yes," Damira answered, though she didn't sound sure.

Great. Time was ticking away, his very *breath* was ticking away, and the tasks seemed to be piling on by the second. He already had to find a third missing seed, not to mention a bunch of missing, kidnapped women. Now he had to find a missing ancestor, too?

All he wanted, all he desperately wanted, was to find a way to free Tera and return to his perfect, quiet, underground life. To snuggle beside her in their cozy, makeshift cottage. To watch her paint by the light of the wormwalkers' glow. To let Meatball nibble rhizers from his fingertips. To be young and safe and in love, and free from the threat of a monstrous army led by an all-powerful, narcissistic despot. Was that really too much to ask?

Damira was staring at him, a puzzled expression on her face. "Wait, what kidnapped women?" she asked.

Ollie looked up; she had read his thoughts, again. "They're here, somewhere, on the Brickside," he explained with a sigh. "A bunch of innocent staffers, from the WRC, taken because of me. To lure me to that stupid lab. Like a ransom. I take it you don't know where they are?"

She blinked, surprised. "Sorry, no."

Of course she didn't. Why should anything be easy, for once?

Laszlo straightened suddenly in his seat. "Maybe cards know," he said, pointing upward.

For a moment, no one spoke. Then Damira shrugged and said, "Let's ask."

She held out a hand; the round cards swirled down through the air like riders on a waterslide and landed in a neat pile on her palm. Damira shuffled the deck and mumbled something under her breath. Then, she held out a blank card to Ollie.

"First things first. They say you're going to need this. Not now, but soon."

"For what?" Ollie asked.

"That, I don't know," she replied, handing it across the table. "Keep it with you. Read it when you see swinging stars, and not before."

"Swinging...stars?"

She shrugged.

Alrightee, then. Tentatively, he reached out for the card, then slid it into his back pocket. "And the hostages...?" he pressed.

Damira nodded. She murmured again, squinted her eyes, and finally flipped a single card onto the table.

The image appeared slowly: a shape. Greyish-white. Straight edges. Wider at the bottom than the top.

Damira tilted her head. Listening. "They're calling it 'the Right Eulogy on the Wrong Hill,'" she said, looking perplexed. "That's where you'll find your missing women."

The Right Eulogy on the Wrong Hill. Ollie stared at the elongated, colorless shape. His heart began to skitter. His fingers pressed together into a steeple, then tapped against each other in frenzied rhythm.

"What is this...eulogy?" Laszlo asked, struggling with the pronunciation.

"It's like a remembrance," Ollie said. "A remembrance of the dead."

"Of dead?" Laz wrinkled his nose. He looked at Ollie, then back at the card. "Why does this make you smile?"

Ollie was surprised to discover that Laszlo was right. He was smiling. "Because I know where they are," he said in wonderment, gripping his friend's arm. "Laz, I know where they are!"

$\mathcal{T}$welve

Ollie and Laszlo craned their necks in the center of Monument Avenue, staring up. The steep hill forced them to bend their ankles at unnatural angles and lean forward like mimes. Parked cars lined both sides of the street.

Ollie, acutely aware that blocking traffic was a capital offense in Charlestown, nevertheless couldn't seem to move. They had walked here from the North End, crossing the bridge in a wet blanket of summer heat. He was quite proud that he'd only made one stop for a Raspberry-Lime Rickey along the way. Now, only ice cubes were left in the cup.

"Don't fire 'till you see the whites of their eyes," Ollie said. He made one last slurping effort on his straw, to no avail.

Laszlo turned to give him a puzzled look.

"Famous saying," Ollie explained. "Like, wait until they get close. A colonel said it right here, a long time ago, during the American Revolution. Supposedly. But it's probably just a myth. Like George Washington and his cherry tree." He shrugged.

Laszlo opened his mouth to speak, paused, then closed it again. After a shake of his head, he finally said, "You sure this is place?"

"I'm sure. 'Right eulogy, wrong hill.'"

The acrobat looked unconvinced. "I see hill," he acknowledged. "But why is *wrong* hill?"

In answer, Ollie pointed up at the gigantic obelisk looming in their field of vision. It stood alone in the center of an open, grassy park, as tall as a downtown high-rise. The sinking sun had transformed its white granite façade into a less impressive yellowish-gray. "That," Ollie said, "is the Bunker Hill Monument. But that," he added, lowering his finger to indicate the ground below it, "is not Bunker Hill."

"Is not?"

"Nope," Ollie said, feeling inordinately pleased with himself. "It's Breed's Hill."

The acrobat lowered his bushy eyebrows. "Why is wrong name?"

"Just a mix-up, I think."

"Why is mixed up?"

"One of history's great mysteries, I'm afraid," Ollie answered. The Bunker Hill Monument, as any Boston schoolkid could tell you, had been built to commemorate the 1775 Battle of Bunker Hill. Which was actually fought on Breed's Hill. Which was where the monument stood today. The two hills sat in close proximity to each other, and even went by still *other* names at one point or another. It was all a bit of a kerfuffle.

Ollie searched his history-class memory for some of the details. "It was one of the first battles in the Revolutionary War, right after Lexington and Concord, I think," he said. "The British thought it would be an easy rout. But the locals were pretty scrappy, and surprised everyone by holding their own. If I remember right, more Redcoats died in that battle than in any other during the entire war."

Laszlo nodded in approval. "So the colony fighters defend homeland. Win battle."

Ollie shifted. "Well, no. Not exactly." He opened the top of his plastic cup and shook an ice cube into his mouth.

"What does this mean?"

"The British ended up taking the hill, in the end." The words came out garbled as he crunched.

Laszlo turned to face him. "I am not understanding. The Americans build monument for battle that they... lose?"

"Well, yeah," Ollie said, suddenly squirming. "I mean, it showed their fighting spirit, right? And it was kind of a victory, really, when you think about it. It showed that the little guy can rise up against a bigger, more powerful army and still do pretty well."

"But not win," said Laszlo.

"Nope."

The acrobat gave a slow blink. "America is very strange place," he said.

"Mmm," Ollie agreed. "That must be why you fit right in."

Laszlo lifted one shoulder in acknowledgment.

Behind them, a horn honked, then honked again. They turned to see a car waiting to pass.

Laszlo touched Ollie's elbow and guided them to the side of the road. "We are going there?" he asked, glancing up. "To monument?"

"Yes," Ollie nodded. Of that one thing, at least, he felt certain. The card had depicted a tall, straight, whitish shape—not unlike an obelisk. There weren't too many of those around. This one also happened to be a sort of "eulogy" to the fallen that was located on the "wrong hill." If the cards were never wrong, as Damira insisted, then the kidnapped WRC women were definitely somewhere up on that rise. The question was, what kind of shape were they in? Had they been eating? Sleeping? Were they chained up like animals? Were they—

Ollie stopped mid-thought. He couldn't let himself finish that question. Not if he wanted to function like he needed to. He was here, now, and that was all that mattered. Even if the guilt was nibbling at his brain like a flesh-eating bacterial infection. Even if this mission was delaying his *other* mission to get back to Tera before his time, their time, ran out.

Ain't no sense in wearing your glasses on the back of your head, as Dozer used to say. Ollie was never quite sure what that particular Dozerism was supposed to mean, but he assumed it had something to do with looking forward, not back.

Gritting his teeth, he imagined moving a pair of glasses from the back of his head to the front, then began to climb the sloped sidewalk. Laszlo followed closely behind.

Nightfall had muted the hill's gloss, but not its charisma. All around them, postcard-ready brownstones lined Monument Ave in a charm offensive for the ages, complete with patriotic buntings, Victorian-style lampposts, and imposingly decorative front doors. Not quite as fancy as Beacon Hill, perhaps, but not too shabby, either. Once-sprightly window-box flowers had wilted in the day's heat. A few cars roamed about, headlights just starting to pop on; but for the most part, the local residents had found refuge from the evening's humidity inside air conditioned, cheerily lit homes.

At Monument Square, they followed the bricks of the Freedom Trail, crossed the street, and climbed the stairs into the park. This, finally, was the tippety-top of the hill. Laszlo pulled a handkerchief from his pocket and mopped sweat from the back of his neck. Ollie was panting. In what was becoming a habit, he ran his finger along the shrinking bump on his arm. He had used a hell of a lot of oxygen hoofing it across the bridge and up these slopes. Too much oxygen? Why didn't he think to take a cab?

"Not many people," Laszlo observed. "Is good, I think."

Ollie agreed. He still didn't know exactly what they were supposed to do here, but whatever it was, he was pretty sure they wouldn't want witnesses. He took in the small park with a sweeping glance: It was square, dotted with trees, and neatly intersected with paved pathways and grass. He'd been here before, of course, but mainly on school field trips where he'd been too focused on protecting his brown-bag lunch from Matty Peralta and his cronies to pay much attention to the scenery.

Near the stairs, the statue of a dapper Colonel William Prescott—he of the "whites of their eyes"—greeted visitors as they approached. And behind that, the guest of honor towered: A four-sided, granite block obelisk, reminiscent of the Washington Monument in D.C..

Though the Bunker Hill version was less than half the size of its Washington cousin, the structure was still mightily impressive. Especially when you were standing right below it. Ollie bent himself backward to gaze up in wonder. From his angle, the tip of the monument appeared to be poking into a fat, moonlit cloud.

"Is big," Laszlo observed.

Ollie laughed.

"What? Is big, yes?"

"C'mon," Ollie said, shaking his head with a smile. "Let's have a look around."

Their wanderings took them past a wheelchair ramp, numerous explanatory signs, and the base of the monument itself, which was comically "protected" by a puny wrought-iron fence. Beyond that, they approached the portico for the next small building, which, if Ollie remembered right, housed a bunch of statues and an information desk. A sign hanging on the door read: *Temporarily closed for repairs. We apologize for the inconvenience. Please visit nps.gov for updates.*

"Temporarily closed for a kidnapping, more like," Ollie muttered. What kind of magic-soup brainwashing did Herrick's henchmen have to conjure to pull this off? He tugged on the door for good measure. It was locked.

They followed the sidewalk around the back of the building, meandering in a big circle and finding nothing of obvious importance. A few teenagers hollered at each other as they raced their bikes along the nearby street. A couple canoodled on one of the benches but moved away once Ollie and Laszlo approached. All the day's tourists had probably retreated to bars and hotels for the evening. Cars traveled lazily past the square, but were mostly obscured by the trees. Ollie and Laszlo pretty much had the place to themselves.

But still ... someone was watching. As always. Just beyond his reach, just beyond his sight. Nell, again? Or someone else? Someone ... worse?

Ollie shivered in momentary discomfort. Then he turned back to look at the monument's base and propped his hands on his hips. *Glasses to the front, big guy,* he told himself. Out loud, he said, "The WRC women must be in there, somewhere. They have to be. But how do we get in?"

In answer, Laszlo hopped the fence to tug on the obelisk's one observable door, but it was unsurprisingly locked up tight. After that, they stood side-by-side to survey the imposing structure. Ollie saw a few narrow slits cut into the stone at even intervals, but they looked like nothing more than vent holes. A pigeon would be lucky to squeeze through one of those, let alone a person.

"There are windows, way up there," he said, craning his neck. "See? Observation windows."

The openings were relatively large. But they were also hundreds of feet in the air, at the very top of the monument.

Laszlo followed his gaze. "Ollie, my friend. I am good climber. Maybe best climber in all of city. You know this. But even my uncles could not climb this wrong-hill tower. Is like, how do you say ... Like cooking pan? Smooth."

"Like Teflon," Ollie answered morosely.

"Yes. Like this. Your Laszlo would slide off like frying egg."

Ollie sighed. Laz was right, of course. There was no possible way to climb the monument without getting inside to the stairs. He wished, suddenly, for the ropes-and-pulleys on Weelichka's salt mountain. Or the rusty rungs that had carried him up to the Mirrormoth's cave. Or even the claustrophobic, creeping elevator cage leading to "The Doc's" Grimshawe Laboratory. Where was a terrifying Neathian transport system when you needed one?

But this wasn't the Neath. This was the Brickside. The boring, normal, magically impaired Bricksi—

He paused.

Was that...? Yes, an opening. Definitely an opening. How had he not noticed it before? Big and wide, about halfway up. It looked like an entire granite block was missing.

"There!" he said, pointing. "There's a hole!"

Laszlo followed his finger, but didn't respond.

"See it?"

"See ... what?"

"That! Right there!" Ollie kept jabbing his finger into the air. "See? It's not as far. Like, halfway up! It's—" He paused, lowering his finger. "You can't see it, can you." It was more of a statement than a question.

Laszlo shot him a concerned look, then shook his head.

"It's there," Ollie said. "I'm telling you, it's right there."

The acrobat nodded slowly. "I believe you. If you see hole, then hole is there. But this does not help, does it? Even if hole is only half the way, I would have to be spider to get there. And I am no spider. I am only very handsome man. I am sorry to be telling this, but is true." His shrug was heavy with regret.

Ollie ran his fingers in frustration through his curls. This was another one of those things, then. Things that only he could see. Like the ice cream flavor and the miniature tree. But what was the use of seeing something if he couldn't use it? If he didn't even know what it meant? This strange new "gift" of his was starting to feel more like a hindrance.

As he stood, floundering with indecision, a sound traveled to his ear.

"Hey. You the guy?"

He spun, looking at Laszlo. "What did you say?"

His friend lifted his palms. "I said, I am sorry to be telling this, but is true."

"No, not that. The other thing."

"What other thing?"

"The other thing you just said!"

Laszlo's expression morphed back into worry. "Ollie, my friend, you are feeling good? Too hot? Maybe you are needing more to drink."

Ollie groaned and stooped to place his empty plastic cup on the ground. "I'm fine! I—" Still crouched, he caught site of something flickering in the low-cut grass. A moving light. Like a firefly, but bigger. More the size of a hummingbird. It darted back and forth, as if trying to catch his attention.

And then Ollie heard the voice again: "You the guy?"

"What guy?" he heard himself ask.

"The guy. The guy." The voice was louder now. Irritated. A deep, man's voice. "The guy with the job."

"I ... I don't ..." Slowly, Ollie stood. The light followed, moving upward. Ollie squinted into the murky air. He saw ... tiny wings, attached to a tiny body. From this distance, it looked almost like a human body. A trick of the nighttime shadows?

He moved closer, just as the flying creature did likewise. Seconds later, he found himself nose-to-nose with something that looked like a three-inch-tall, full-grown, flying person. More specifically, a man, complete with a five o'clock shadow, a pair of drab-brown wings, and a disturbingly hairy chest. Above his wings, a nodule glowed with amber light. The tiny man wore nothing but a tangle of grass blades, which, Ollie was relieved to see, stretched just far enough to cover his crotch.

The winged creature looked him up and down. "Yeah, you're the guy," he muttered. His voice was raspy, like a pack-a-day smoker, but easy enough to understand.

Ollie struggled for a response. After a few awkward seconds, he managed, "I ... I'm ... How do you know?"

The diminutive man buzzed closer, then lowered his voice and looked around. "I was told you needed help with a job."

"A ... job?"

"Yeah. You need somebody tuned up, or what?"

Ollie took a step back. "What? No!"

"Just sayin', I can do that." His tiny eyes darted left and right, then landed on Laszlo. "Who's that one? He with you?"

Instead of answering, Ollie froze in place, trying to absorb the bizarre sight before him. This man, or whatever he was, looked like a mostly-naked trucker from Teamsters Local 29. A mostly-naked trucker that was no bigger than a Lego figurine. With wings.

"Are you ... a fairy?" Ollie whispered.

"A *fairy?*" The suggestion left the creature aghast. And insulted. "For Chrissakes, ain't you never seen a Wicket?"

Ollie shook his head.

"Well, now you have," the little man said. "One Sticky Wicket, right here in the flesh. You're friggin' welcome." He puffed out his hairy chest.

"My friend, why you are talking to bug?" Laszlo asked. He was staring at Ollie with a tilted head, looking concerned again.

"It's, uh, not a bug," Ollie said. "It's ... a Sticky Wicket."

"A what?" Laszlo moved closer. When he was close enough to make out the details of their tiny visitor, he froze in place.

As they watched, the Wicket pulled a tiny stick-shaped object from his green-grass loincloth, lit the tip, and took a drag. A barely visible trail of smoke floated above the creature's head, illuminated by the light bulb on his back. Then he turned his hand in an impatient, circular motion. "How's about we move this along, fellas."

Ollie glanced at Laszlo, who shrugged helplessly.

"Someone told you I needed help?" Ollie asked.

"What'd I just say? Yeah." As the grumpy man threw his arms in the air, Ollie noticed that they were covered in dozens of miniscule, detailed tattoos. "Am I talking to myself, here? You got a job or not? I ain't got all night!"

This made Ollie wonder what else, exactly, a Sticky Wicket would do with his evening if he wasn't here. "Who sent you?" he finally asked.

The tiny man took another drag. "What's with all the questions? None of Your Business sent me, that's who."

"To help the women?" Ollie asked.

At this, the Wicket looked confused. "I don't know from no women. I just know I was supposed to wait here, for the guy. That's you." He flicked the smoking stick onto the ground and folded his tattooed arms. "Now, am I staying, or am I going? 'Cause I can do either one."

Laszlo dared a step closer. Then, he dared a question. "What is your name?"

"Why, you gonna send me a Christmas card?" The creature harrumphed. "You don't need my name, and I don't need yours. Let's just do what we came here to do, okay?"

"Which is ... what, exactly?" Ollie asked.

"How the fuck should I know? You tell me!"

Ollie wobbled. Why did he suddenly feel like he was stuck in a leprechaun drug deal gone wrong? Seconds elapsed. Maybe full minutes. Passing cars' headlights swept through the trees and sent shadows skittering all around them. He looked at Laszlo, who seemed uncharacteristically hapless. Then he gaped at the bad-tempered, yellow-toothed, miniaturized, buzzing being, and he thought about what could have possibly brought this creature into his life. *Who* could have possibly brought this creature into his life. A very strange creature with an even stranger name.

A Sticky Wicket.

Far-off ambulance sirens jolted Ollie back to the present. He leaned closer, narrowing his eyes. Watching the wings vibrate. "How sticky are you, exactly?" he asked.

"How sticky? Wicked sticky. It's in the name, bro."

Ollie nodded slowly. He looked at the irritated little flying man, then at Laszlo, then at the gaping hole located halfway up the monument. The hole that only he, apparently, could see. He rubbed his lower lip. "You have friends?"

"Yeah, I got friends," the Wicket replied with a shrug.

"Good," Ollie said. "We're gonna need 'em."

"What for?"

"For a job, *bro.*"

The creature considered this. "Yeah, okay. When?"

"Right now," Ollie answered grimly. "I can see the whites of their eyes."

Thirteen

Laszlo's shoes and socks sat together in a neat pile on the sidewalk. Above them, the acrobat's body splayed like a black-clad gecko against the side of the monument. His hands and bare feet stuck fast to the smooth wall, thanks to a small army of clumping, grumbling Sticky Wickets that had somehow adhered themselves to both surfaces. Each of his fingers and toes glowed.

"Are you okay?" Ollie whisper-shouted.

Laszlo twisted his neck, trying—and failing—to get a look at his friend on the ground. "I am … sticking," he said in answer.

"How does it feel?"

"Feels like slugs. On fingers," Laz replied, a note of disgust in his voice.

At this, the Wickets buzzed in collective complaint. The bulbs on their backs glowed brighter as they absorbed the insult.

"Jesus, Laz, don't piss them off! They're holding you up there!"

"Sorry, sorry." The acrobat squirmed, or tried to squirm, but only his butt had free movement. The result was a strange sort of mid-air twerk. "This is feeling good. Yes? Very good. I am thanking Wickets."

Ollie pressed his hands against his lips, trying to squelch a smile. He looked left and right, saw no one coming, and cleared his throat. "You look great up there! You ready to start?"

"No time like the now," Laszlo answered, though he sounded less than his usual enthusiastic self. Had Ollie finally found the limits of his friend's exuberance? Was forced climbing up a 200-foot monument with angry, tiny creatures squishing between your fingers and toes finally a bridge too far? If so, Ollie could hardly blame him. Laz was operating on blind faith—faith that these invisible beings could actually help him reach the access point, and faith that the access point actually existed. Oh, and also faith that they wouldn't arbitrarily decide to drop him halfway up.

Whatever wrongs Laszlo had committed against Ollie in the past—namely, luring him down to the Neath and plunging his life into utter chaos—he had more than made up for since. Laszlo was, quite simply, the best friend Ollie had ever had. And probably ever would. The kind of friend who would close his eyes, stick his entire body against a sheer rock face, and do what needed to be done. Even if what needed to be done was completely, head-shakingly bonkers.

"Okay, coast is clear!" Ollie called up as loudly as he dared. "Up and at 'em!"

But as they soon discovered, it wouldn't be as easy as all that. The Wickets had to first work out some kind of coordination system: Only one of Laszlo's hands could be unstuck at a time, while the other three limbs stayed fast against the wall. Then one foot unstuck, and then the other hand, foot, and so forth. All it would take was one wrong move at the wrong time, and bam—the park rangers would arrive for work the next morning to find whatever remained of Laz splattered all over their nice, neat sidewalk.

Ollie could only hear snippets of the ongoing Wicket conversations above him, which seemed to consist mostly of grunts, accusations, and apologies. Every few minutes he would call out directions to the entire, disordered crew—*a little to the left! Straight up, right there!*—trying to guide them toward a large hole in the wall that none of them could actually see. When he wasn't giving instructions, he was pacing in nervous circles and cracking his knuckles.

Pop, pop, pop.
This is a terrible, terrible idea.
Pop, pop, pop, pop, pop.

Laszlo's body continued to lurch upward and sideways in a series of awkward fits and starts that reminded Ollie of Frogger crossing the street. But he was not falling. Thank God and gorgonzola, he was not falling. Finally, after what seemed like hours, the acrobat reached the right spot.

"There!" Ollie said. His neck had developed a crick that felt like it might be permanent. "Right above you! Can you feel it?"

Laszlo tapped his free hand up, down, left, and right, against the solid wall of the monument. Then, suddenly, the hand fell forward. Not against stone, but into open air. "Is hole!" he shouted.

"Yes, that's it!" Ollie felt himself hopping. "Can you get through?"

After a few more minutes of muddled sticking-and-unsticking coordination with the Wickets, the acrobat managed to pull himself up and through the opening. Once his body disappeared, the Wickets scattered, their lights casting a brief glow above Ollie's head before buzzing out of sight entirely.

So much for farewells.

Now he couldn't see any of them—not the Sticky Wickets, and not his friend. Panic clenched his stomach. "Laz?" he called. *"Laz! Where are you?"*

Laszlo's head popped through the opening. He waved cheerily. "I am here! Is stairs."

Ollie exhaled in relief. He remembered the stairs, vaguely: They wound around in a spiral, with painted markers to let you know when you'd reached stair 100, stair 150, and so on. He didn't know exactly how many stairs there were, mainly because he'd never made it all the way up. While his classmates had shoved past him on their way to the overlook, he'd panted and wheezed against the railing until a teacher had snapped at him to "keep moving or get out of the way." Ollie had chosen the latter. He never saw the view from the top—which, he realized now, might actually be an apt epigram for his entire life on the Brickside.

"Get down to the door and try to let me in!" he called up.

Laszlo flashed a thumbs-up and vanished once more.

Ollie cast a few furtive glances into the shadows and was reassured to see that the park was still empty of loiterers. He hopped the little fence, hustled around to the door at the base, cracked his knuckles some more, and waited. *Pop, pop, pop.* A few short minutes later, he heard a clacking, squealing sound—like a heavy latch being moved—and the door began to open.

Laszlo's face, and dangling hair, emerged through the widening gap.

"Dude, you're amazing!" Ollie gushed. "We're in!" He reached for the door. "C'mon, let's take a look around. They've got to be here somewhere. Maybe there's some kind of basement level or someth—"

He stopped, finally taking stock of his friend's odd expression. "What? What's wrong?"

"No need for the looking," Laszlo answered, his voice solemn. "They are right here."

The words made Ollie's heart pound in an unnaturally heavy beat. Fingers still on the door, he pulled, then pulled again. At first, he saw nothing but inky obscurity. The smell of cold, damp cement, like an old wine cellar, wafted to his nose. As his eyes began to adjust, he saw what looked like a miniature reproduction of the monument, encased in a crevice behind protective bars, and the beginnings of the spiral staircase. The steps themselves were oddly lumpy. Uneven.

No. Not lumpy. They were...covered. With something. With...

Laszlo pulled a flashlight from his pocket and flipped the switch. As a beam of light swept across the vestibule, Ollie's blood ran frigid.

Bodies.

Each step was covered with a recumbent, human body.

They had been laid out on their backs, arranged in an orderly display. Hands clasped together on stomachs. Eyelids closed. Clothing straightened. Hair tucked behind ears. One on the bottom step, another on the next step, and so on, up and around the winding corner. Like pastries set out for a macabre afternoon tea.

"Jesus," Ollie breathed. "Is it—?"

"Is WRC women, yes," Laszlo managed, though his voice sounded strangled. "I had to step over them to ... to ... get to door."

The scene was revolting. Hideous. Ollie could feel bile rising in his throat as he took a reluctant step forward. Kneeling down, he leaned in closer to the woman on the lowest step. She had curly black hair, thick lashes, and freckled, dark skin. She wore a short-sleeved shirt and cargo pants. Her body rested in abhorrent, almost restful repose, reminiscent of a deceased monarch laid out for public viewing. Who could have done such a thing? And why just leave the bodies here?

But he knew exactly who could have done such a thing, didn't he? *Closed for repairs,* the sign had said. Evil had bubbled up from the Neath like an overflowing laboratory beaker, brainwashing and corrupting everything it touched.

Trembling, Ollie reached out to touch the young woman's arm, which was resting on her abdomen.

His head snapped around. "She's warm!"

An expression of cautious hope tripped across Laszlo's features.

Tentatively, Ollie moved his hand, holding it under the woman's nose. He kept it there, afraid to speak or move. Then he spun around again. "She's breathing! Laz, I think they're still alive!"

Instead of replying, Laszlo jumped into action. He mimicked Ollie's motions, touching the skin and checking the respiration of each woman on the stairs. Six in total: All breathing. All warm. And all as still as death.

"They are all...sleeping?"

"I don't know," Ollie said. They had returned to the base of the alcove. "It seems like something more."

The acrobat nodded somberly.

"What are we supposed to do now?" Ollie asked.

Laszlo thought for a moment, then said, "We must get them out of this place. We must take them home."

"But we don't even know where they live."

"So we take them back to office? To WRC?"

Ollie pressed his lips together. Maybe. But how? They couldn't exactly traipse through the streets of Charlestown carrying six unconscious women. The BPD tended to frown on that sort of thing. But they couldn't leave them here, either. "Let's try to wake them," he suggested.

Even as the words left his mouth, he knew it was a fruitless proposition. And just as he suspected, none of their efforts—from shaking to prodding to whispered pleas—managed to rouse the women from what was clearly a magically induced slumber.

"Six sleeping beauties," Ollie murmured. "Maybe we should kiss them."

Laz threw him a concerned and confused sideways glance.

Ollie opened his mouth to explain the fairy-tale connection. But before he got the chance, a graveled voice near the doorway erupted with anger: "What the hell is going on in here?"

Ollie spun. At first, he saw nothing. Then he narrowed in on the soft light and hovering body of the tattooed, as-yet-unnamed Sticky Wicket he had spoken with earlier. Mr. "None of Your Business." Mr. "Christmas Card."

"You hurt these women?" the Wicket asked, furious. If he'd had sleeves, he probably would have pushed them up in preparation for the ass-whooping he clearly thought was needed.

"What? No! Of course not!" Ollie yelped. He raised his hands in a gesture of surrender. "It's not what it looks like, all right? Somebody else put them here. That's why we had to get in. We were looking for them. We're here to rescue them. But they won't ... wake up."

Laszlo gave a strenuous nod of agreement, sending his black hair jouncing up and down.

The Wicket harrumphed. It was, Ollie decided, the creature's signature sound. He cast a suspicious glance at Ollie, then at Laszlo, then at the motionless women. "They dead?"

"No! Not dead. Just ... sleeping, I think. But not a normal kind of sleep. I don't know what it is. I don't know ... what to do." Ollie's hands fell to his sides in defeat.

After a moment of indecision, the Wicket flew forward. He hovered near the first woman's face, then the second. After examining each sleeper in turn, he rubbed his stubbled chin, grunted, and nodded. Then he buzzed back to Ollie. "You two. Get out of the way."

"What?"

"Get. Out. Of. The. Way." The Wicket swept his tiny arms in an outward thrust. "Move it. Now."

"Uh ..." Ollie looked at Laz. "Move ... where?"

"Over there, over there." In his thick Boston accent, the Wicket's words came out sounding like *ovah theyah, ovah theyah.* His beer belly jiggled as he thrust his arms again, gesturing toward the far wall.

Ollie and Laz had barely taken three steps backward when a startling sound filled the alcove around them. It was a high-pitched whine, loud enough to make dogs howl, and it was coming from the Wicket. They stooped and covered their ears in unison.

Weirdly, the creature's mouth remained closed, which made Ollie wonder how, and why, he was emitting the piercing sound. Ollie never did figure out the "how." But the "why" became clear soon enough.

The whine was a summons. Within seconds, the swarm of grumbling Sticky Wickets had returned, crowding the doorway and eventually swooping inside. Dozens at first, then more. Hundreds? With all the bobbing and weaving and buzzing, it was hard for Ollie to say with any certainty. Their little bulbs collectively lit the dark space with blazing, painful brilliance.

The two men stopped shielding their ears and started shielding their eyes.

Laszlo said something else, but the loud buzzing drowned out his voice.

"What?" Ollie shouted.

"I said, what they are doing?"

Ollie had no answer.

The flock, or swarm, or gang, or whatever you called a group of flying Wickets, was hovering near the tattooed man, who seemed to be communicating something to the group. Then, they moved together as one. Up, over, and around, whizzing through the vestibule in a traveling, glowing orb.

Ollie watched helplessly as the clump of Sticky Wickets approached the sleeping woman on the bottom step. Hovering. Observing. What the hell were they doing? They looked like hummingbirds darting around a sugary feeder. His fascination turned to revulsion when they descended in an aggregate cloud and settled onto her body. From his angle, it resembled a lustrous, pulsating blanket.

Still shielding his eyes, Ollie backed up all the way to the stone wall. His knees felt locked into place. Should he try to stop this? Should he shout?

The gleaming wrap grew ever-tighter around the young woman's face, torso, and limbs, looking less like a blanket and more like a glow-in-the-dark mummy's shroud. The stone walls continued to echo with the Wickets' noisy vibrations.

The scene was horrific. Worse than any horror movie he'd ever watched through parted fingers. Were they ... stinging her? Were they draining her life away before his eyes? Whatever they were doing, he couldn't just stand there and watch it.

Ollie rushed forward, ready to scatter the creatures into the air, or to pluck them off her body one-by-one if he had to. But before he could reach the bottom stair, the Wickets were on the move again. They had unstuck themselves from the first woman and traveled up to the second, where they settled onto the motionless body with the same kind of all-encompassing embrace.

As Laszlo grabbed his arm, Ollie forced himself to look back at the first woman, who seemed ... unharmed. She seemed peaceful, as before. She seemed ...

Awake.

Awake?

The freckled woman on the bottom step gave a small, almost unnoticeable stretch. Then she rolled over onto her side.

Laszlo pointed excitedly. "She moves!" he said. "She is waking!"

Awestruck, they watched the procedure repeat on each of the six stairs, on each of the six women. First, the swarm of Wickets would descend, stick, and depart. Then, each sleeping woman would show signs of slowly emerging consciousness.

The glowing creatures made their way back to the doorway, where their tattooed leader seemed to give them another set of garbled, unintelligible instructions. Less than a minute later, the group flew outside in a collective throng, plunging the interior of the stairwell back into quiet darkness.

Mr. None of Your Business stayed behind. He flew toward Ollie, pausing only when the two were face-to-tiny face. "They're up," he said, jerking a thumb toward the waking women. "They should be okay."

Ollie nodded, mute. He followed Laszlo's flashlight beam to see the women sighing, stretching, and rolling in various stages of wakefulness.

"So, you good?" the Wicket asked.

"Huh?"

"You're good now, right? I can go?"

"I, uh …"

"We are good." The acrobat interjected, looking pleased. "Very good."

Ollie was still awestruck. And tongue-tied. Finally, he found his voice. "Thank you," he said to the Wicket, meaning it. "Thank you for everything."

"Eh," the little man said, waving a hand. He seemed genuinely uninterested in gratitude. Then he looked over his tiny shoulder, as though hearing a call. "Listen, we're done here, you understand? I got shit to do. You're on your own."

Ollie didn't love the sound of that, but nodded anyway.

The creature paused to light another tiny smoking stick. "If I was you boys, I'd get a move on," he added, blowing a skinny stream of smoke into the air. He jerked his head toward the door. "Before whoever put these ladies here comes back to check on things, you know what I'm sayin'?"

Ollie gulped and nodded again. He did know. All too well.

"Alright, then. See ya around, kid," the Wicket said. The last Ollie saw of him was a brief blur of brown, dirty wings.

Fourteen

The heavy door, like Ollie's mouth, was still slightly ajar. Had that actually just happened? He and Laszlo stared at each other in momentary inertia.

"What's going on?" asked a nearby voice.

Startled, they turned to see the woman on the lowest step sitting upright. She was rubbing the back of her neck, peering into the darkness around her. Looking confused.

"Laszlo? Is that you?"

"Yes, Sara. Is me." The acrobat sounded overjoyed. And exhausted. "I am sorry it was taking me so long to get here. But I am here now, and we are going to get you home."

As Ollie looked from one to the other, observing his friend's slumped shoulders, wringing hands, and hanging head, he finally recognized the full extent of the burden Laszlo had been carrying in these past weeks. His job as a Runner for the WRC meant he was also the muscle. The protector. Laz knew each of these women, probably pretty well. He cared for them. When they had gone missing, he had felt personally responsible. Just as Ollie had. And now that they had the missing women in their sights at last, awake and apparently unharmed, the sense of relief was like an overstuffed cloud suddenly releasing its rain on their heads—drenching, wondrous, and somehow paralyzing.

The others had also begun to stir. All of them looked dazed.

"Where are we?" asked the woman on third step, propping up on one elbow. "Laz, what the hell is going on?"

"Who's that guy?" asked another, peering around from one of the upper stairs. She was staring at Ollie, and their dank surroundings, with bewilderment and apprehension.

"Hey, I remember him!" said the woman on the second step. She had dark-blonde hair, matted down on one side. "He came to the center a while back. Looking for someone." Her eyes narrowed.

Ollie remembered her, too. How could he forget? He had met her shortly after Nell had gone missing, back in the North End. He had followed the trail to Nell's last known whereabouts: Henchman Street, a nondescript cut-through lined with brick buildings and parked cars. Once there, he had seen only one sign of interest. *Women's Resource Center*, the sign had read. *Open 24 Hours*. Ollie had knocked, and this blonde woman had answered. Suspicious. Cold. Looking like she'd happily douse his eyes with pepper spray at first provocation. The other women inside had followed suit, turning him away without ceremony. The encounter had left him shaken and confused.

Nell had been there, at the WRC. He'd been sure of it. But the staffers had refused to help him find her.

At the time, Ollie hadn't realized that the blandly named "Center" was actually a reprieve for victims fleeing domestic-violence situations, or that abusers often banged on the door with nefarious intent. The women at the WRC were used to dealing with aggressors and jerks, and they had assumed Ollie was just one more of the same. Even now, the memory of their misplaced hostility was jarring.

Ollie nodded and spoke quietly. "I was looking for my friend, Nell."

The woman lifted her palms and eyebrows in reply, as if to say, *And?*

"And ... I found her." He thought it best to tell the short version, since the long version—descent into a magical underground world, mistaken identity, various prison breaks, food-cart employment, trog adoption, entrapment in a crab-hybrid's underwater cave, portrait-painting sessions, laboratory visits, ransom notes, aquarium dives, Salem history tours—would have kept them all there until morning. "I'm a friend of Laszlo's," he added sheepishly.

"Laz, seriously. What the hell is going on? How did we get here?"

The acrobat raked his fingers through his long, dark hair, pushing it from his face. "You ladies ... You are remembering nothing?"

"Nothing about what?" another of the women asked. Ollie recognized her as one of the "employees" he had met at the Boston Common Visitor Center, back when this whole, strange journey had begun. She had talked briefly with Laszlo in some kind of coded language, then handed him a guidebook—a guidebook hiding an open-sesame password that had allowed Ollie to disappear through a portal in the Freedom Trail. Clearly, these women were used to dealing with seriously weird shit. Which might make the coming explanations a little easier.

"What's the last thing you remember?" Ollie asked.

They looked at each other.

"We were at work," one said.

Nods all around.

"And then ..." Her sentence trailed off, unfinished.

"How long have we been here?" another asked. She was running a tongue over her teeth in disgust. Her clothes were rumpled. Her brown hair was noticeably snarled and greasy.

"Wait a second," said a woman behind her, glancing around at the cement-staired interior in astonishment. "Is this ... the Bunker Hill Monument? What the hell are we doing at the Bunker Hill Monument?"

One by one, they began to pepper Laszlo with questions.

"What is this?"

"How did you find us?"

"Were we drugged? I think we were drugged!"

The queries started overlapping in an increasing frenzy; Laszlo raised a hand.

"I promise, I will tell you all the things, while we are doing the walking," he said. "Yes? You can walk now? You are okay?"

The women murmured in cautious assent.

"Good. Is very good. Later, we do all the talking. Right now, we must do the moving. Moving, moving, moving." He waved an arm. "Or people who put you here, they might ..."

He didn't have to finish the thought: The women seemed to understand. Quickly, they began to rise to their feet and move down the staircase.

Ollie wasn't sure if he should offer a hand or stay out of the way. Considering the women's understandable suspicion of him, he opted for hovering at safe distance. Or as distant as the tiny alcove would allow. As he shrunk backwards, trying to make his big, bulky body as inconspicuous and unthreatening as possible, his eyes fell on a stack of posterboards leaning up against the stone wall. Children's school projects, from the looks of it, perhaps left behind from a recent display in the museum. Most included cartoonish drawings of the monument. Lists of historical facts. Sparkly stickers. Block lettering. Stick figures marching into battle.

Staring down at the closest posterboard, Ollie read a few lines of a child's adorably uneven handwriting. And stiffened.

With rigid steps, he approached Laszlo, who was helping one of the women through the doorway. "Can I borrow that for a sec?" he asked, pointing to the flashlight.

Laz handed it over without comment.

Ollie carried the light back to the far wall, where he crouched to examine the student project more closely. It featured a not-quite-symmetrical, magic-markered image of the monument, along with a bullet-point list of statistical facts about its construction. Mostly numbers:

- 6,700 tons of granite
- 30 feet square at the base
- 15.4 feet square at the top

And so forth. But it was two particular stats, highlighted in yellow, that made him catch his breath:

- 221 feet tall
- 294 steps to the top

Ollie swayed backward in a rush of recognition.

Air! Air third. Two-twenty-one, two-ninety-four. Climb to fly. Walk the sky. The note, folded in his pocket.

The final seed.

He turned, pivoting on his heel. "Uh, Laz?"

The acrobat, still busy escorting his disoriented colleagues to the exit, didn't reply.

"Laz!" Ollie said again, waving the flashlight like a beacon. "Dude! This is the place!"

His friend gave him a dismissive glance. "Yes, this is place." The "duh" remained unspoken as he gestured toward the stumbling women.

"No, I mean, this is the *other* place. Well, the same place, but also ..." He paused, shook his head, and pointed at the marked-up posterboard. "Look! Two hundred and twenty-one feet tall. Two hundred and ninety-four steps to the top."

Laszlo's palms lifted in impatient confusion.

"Two-twenty-one. Two-ninety-four. Air third! The note!"

At that, his friend's eyes widened. "Walking sky?"

"Climb to fly, walk the sky," Ollie confirmed.

As they stared at each other, the conundrum became immediately apparent.

"I have to stay," Ollie said. "I have to find the last seed."

Laszlo rubbed his lower lip, then turned to watch the sixth sleeping beauty gather her skirt and slide out the door. "And I must get them home."

Both things were true. And mutually exclusive.

"I guess ... I guess we'll have to split up," Ollie said hesitantly. But they couldn't do that, could they? More specifically, *he* couldn't do that. The thought of staying behind, alone, in the dark and dreary monument's interior, was enough to make his stomach lurch. What if he got locked inside? What if it was a trap? Without Laszlo at his side, he'd be screwed. By almost any mishap or attack. What if there was something awful waiting at the top? Ollie had never been particularly afraid of heights, but this height ... This was something else altogether. This was nice-knowing-you, no-second-chances kind of height.

Laz twisted his mouth sideways, perhaps wondering about the same things.

"Can you get all of them back by yourself?" Ollie asked. Part of him hoped the answer was no.

"Of course." Laszlo straightened and pushed out his chest.

"Okay, then." Ollie nodded. "Then, I guess ... you go, and I'll get the seed."

"Is last one," Laz pointed out.

"Right." That should have made him feel better, but didn't. If anything, it made him more worried. More than one person had already warned him to stop looking. And here he was, not only still looking, but ready to wrap up the search. And once he had the last seed, what would happen? Would some kind of Brickside magic alarm bell go off, alerting the evil-powers-that-be to his presence?

His very vulnerable presence at the top of a terrifyingly tall obelisk?

Ollie resisted the urge to slap himself on the cheek. *Get yourself together,* he told himself. This was not the time for hesitation. Tera was waiting. The pellet in his arm was shrinking. And this was almost, *almost* done.

"Where will I meet you after?" he asked. He tried to keep his voice light, like a guy momentarily separating from his buddy at the mall.

Laszlo thought for a minute. "We meet for late dinner. At Fioretti's?"

"Okay. Sounds good." Fioretti's always sounded good to Ollie. But tonight, it would taste especially sweet. The WRC women, freed. All three seeds, found. With any luck, he'd even have time to check up on Mr. B's recouperation and figure out what was going on with Nell. And then, one last plate of eggplant parmigiana before heading back down to free Tera and Meatball. *Perfetta,* as his mom would say, usually while kissing her own fingertips.

Of course, he still didn't know how all that would happen, exactly. Maybe he'd have to head back down through the Freedom Trail. Maybe once he had all three seeds, the answer would just ... appear. Another handwritten note, perhaps, carried over by a Fioretti's waiter on a silver tray. Or tucked inside an arancini ball with the rice and sausage. Or ferried down to Boston by the underage Salem Ice Cream Coven on a fleet of flying Schwinns. He didn't really care how the instructions came, as long as they came. Soon.

Laszlo was stealing glances the now-empty doorway, clearly not thrilled to let the women out of his sight.

"Go," Ollie said. Then, on a whim, he stepped closer and gave his friend a tight hug. "You did it," he said, a lump suddenly forming in his throat. "You found them."

Laszlo returned the squeeze, then pushed Ollie out to arm's length. *"We* did this," he corrected. Ollie was surprised to see that his eyes, too, were misting up. "We are good team, yes?"

"Like tacos and Tuesdays," Ollie smiled.

Laszlo gave him a quizzical look.

"Like ... uh, lock and key," Ollie added. Then he held up a finger: "Like a trapeze and a net!"

"Ah," the acrobat nodded, pleased. "I understand. We go together like these things."

"Right."

"Like the peanut butter and the jelly!"

"Yes. Just like that," Ollie laughed.

Laz gave his shoulder a final, friendly thump. "Well, mister peanut butter, this jelly will be seeing you at Fioretti's. If you get there first, order me glass of red."

"Will do," Ollie replied, not bothering to point out that he wasn't old enough to order any such thing.

Fifteen

The exit door closed with a heavy thunk. Ollie's heart thunked right along with it.

Laszlo was gone. The women were gone. And even Mr. None of Your Business Sticky Wicket was finally, definitely gone, or so it seemed. That meant Ollie was now very much alone in the hollow guts of a National Park monument with nothing but the bright beam of a flashlight to keep him company.

Scratch that—more like a sickly beam. The batteries were dying. *Dammit.* He tapped the flashlight desperately against his leg. "C'mon," he muttered. "C'mon!" The light wavered, then resumed its dreary ray.

Ollie waved it toward the stairs. There was, obviously, only one direction to head. *Climb to fly. Walk the sky.* And the sooner he started, the more likely he was to have a functioning flashlight for the entire journey.

He took one step, then another, then another. The staircase started to spiral, and he was on his way.

Two hundred and ninety-four steps. Good God. As intimidating as that sounded, it didn't worry him nearly so much as what might be waiting at the top: Walk the sky? What was that supposed to mean? If his journey to this point was any indication, he was pretty sure it wouldn't be anything easy. Or normal. Or OSHA-approved.

It didn't take long for him to get winded. Within five minutes, the wheezing and flashbacks started: Ollie had climbed another spiral staircase like this one not too long ago, in Herrick's End. Then, he had been terrified, exhausted, and bewildered. Now, he was—well, he was still all those things, he supposed. But at least this time he wasn't a prisoner. He knew where he was. And he wouldn't, God willing, be judged guilty by an ancient and imperious "Reader" witch when he got there.

A familiar, burning pain began to heat up his thighs, shins, and buttocks. His breath was coming in short gasps. Ollie took three breaks before even reaching the step painted with the number "50." *Holy ghost on a giblet*. He was only at 50? How was that even possible? He reached instinctively for the bump on his arm. Definitely smaller. Definitely, definitely smaller. But how much smaller? And what did that even mean? He desperately wished for countdown clock scrawled across his forearm: TWELVE HOURS, SIX MINUTES, TWENTY-THREE SECONDS ... TWELVE HOURS, SIX MINUTES, TWENTY-TWO SECONDS ... TWELVE HOURS, SIX MINUTES, TWENTY-ONE SECONDS.

Without it, he was only guessing. Badly. As far as he knew, he only had ten minutes left on this crazy, borrowed-breathing timer. And every taxing step, every gasp for air, was making it drain faster. And once the air was gone ... so was he.

Don't think about it, he told himself. *Keep climbing. One foot in front of the other. Think about something else.*

What came to him was a memory, thundering back like a herd of white horses through his jangled mind.

Tera had been teaching him to fish off the Tea Party docks. His first task had been to bait the hook with a wriggling wormwalker, which was exactly as difficult and gross as he thought it might be. The first wormwalker successfully resisted Ollie's efforts and slid itself off the hook, only to be slurped up by Meatball. The second waved its little legs in frantic resistance, freaking Ollie out to the point that he dropped it with an embarrassing shriek. Another snack for the trog, another empty hook for Ollie.

Finally, Tera had stepped in to help.

"Is this a Tom Sawyer situation?" she had asked, her long eyelashes lowered in a knowing glance.

"A what?"

"You know, Tom Sawyer painting the fence?"

He didn't know.

Tera explained: "Tom Sawyer's aunt told him to paint the fence. But he didn't want to. So instead, he managed to get everyone else to paint the fence for him."

"How'd he do that?"

"He pretended it was tons of fun, and convinced all the other kids that they were missing out."

"I'm not pretending to have fun," Ollie pointed out.

Tera considered this. "True. But you might be doing a variation on the theme. You know, pretending to be incompetent so that others step in and do the job."

"Oh, but I *am* completely incompetent," he said with a wide, unapologetic smile. "No pretending necessary."

She punched his arm and pointed at the jar of wriggling wormwalkers. "Give me that."

"So my evil plan is working?" he asked.

"No," she corrected. "I'm only holding it still. You're doing the rest."

He groaned in complaint.

Tera wore a stern expression as she fiddled with the wobbly hook. "Tough luck, buddy. You know what they say: Give a Brickside boy a fish, you feed him for a day. Teach a Brickside boy to fish, and his girlfriend is very happy that she doesn't have to do all the fishing anymore."

It was the first time she'd called herself his girlfriend. At the sound of it, he stilled, then felt a rush of adrenaline coursing through his synapses. Was this what it was like to have an EpiPen needle jammed into your thigh? The sudden jolt? The all-encompassing bliss?

Overcome, he dropped the fishing pole and tackled her in a bear hug.

"Hey!" Tera shouted, laughing.

They rolled on top of one of the poles, snapping it in half. They also knocked over the bucket of bait. Ollie barely noticed. As

Meatball took advantage of the sudden spilled feast, Ollie spun Tera onto her back and lifted himself above her.

"We're supposed to be getting dinner," she said. Her mouth was curled into a sly grin.

"I don't need dinner," he said. And it was true. The only thing he'd ever need for the rest of his life was right there, right then. Ollie bent his elbows, leaned down, and kissed her. Again, and again, and again.

They did manage to catch a few fish, after that. Well, Tera did. Ollie had mostly just watched in admiration.

The only other thing he remembered from that day was Meatball getting sick back at the house. When Ajanta asked how the trog had managed to eat so many wormwalkers, Tera had blushed, Ollie had cleared his throat, and the subject, thankfully, had been dropped.

Ollie replayed the memory over and over as he climbed. The poles. The lake. The wriggling bait. The sound of her laugh. The taste of something earthy and spicy as he pressed his lips against hers. He was so engrossed that the next stair marker—100—came as a pleasant surprise. Nearly halfway! He could do this. Though a part of him, a big part, wished he could somehow Tom Sawyer his way out of it.

He tried conjuring other pleasant memories, but found it harder and harder to do as each grueling minute passed. His lungs burned. His legs screamed. *Almost there,* he told himself, and it quickly became a mantra. *Almost*—next step—*there. Almost*—next step—*there.* The sound of his sluggish, sliding footsteps echoed against the stone walls: *Shlump. Shlump. Shlump.*

The mantra and the spiraling and the ceaseless pain dragged him into a state of forced meditation.

Shlump. Schlump. Schlump.

Before long, he could see nothing but gray. He could feel nothing but exhaustion. And each time he stopped to rest, it took a herculean effort to spur his feet back into motion.

Ollie's chest was a raging furnace when he rounded yet another turn to see the most beautiful, spray-painted marker he had ever laid eyes on: STEP 294. And beyond that...no more stairs. Just a miraculous, flat, empty landing.

He could swear he heard angels singing. Or maybe that was just his own pathetic whine of relief.

He had done it. Miracle of miracles, he had made it all the way up. Panting, Ollie climbed onto the landing and leaned pitifully against the wall, turning his head to look out of the nearest observation window.

The first thing he noticed was the Zakim Bridge, all lit up in its two-tone, nighttime splendor. And next to it, the Garden, where the Celtics and Bruins played. His city was aglow with summery splendor—inbound traffic, outbound traffic, low-rise apartment windows, high-rise office windows, billboards, bridges, tunnels, and boats, all pieced together in an ever-spinning polychrome of urban motion and beauty. Moonlight glinted on the Charles River, its stillness almost shocking by comparison.

Was that really his Boston? From up here, it all seemed so ... small. So quaint. Even the noises had a more harmonious, muted quality.

Ollie moved to another window. This one faced north, with views of myriad streets, apartments, factories, churches, and schools. The east-facing opening overlooked the Mystic River. And at the fourth window, he peered out at the U.S.S Constitution, bobbing at its dock, along with row-house neighborhoods, Logan Airport, and a wide stretch of harbor leading out to the sea.

Dumbstruck by the unexpected beauty, Ollie marveled at it all. Everything twinkled. He half expected a train to start circling through the scenery, as though the city and everything in it were merely props on a model-railroad set.

Finally, he turned his attention back to the interior of the monument. Nothing much to see there, by comparison: just granite-block walls, mooncast shadows, and a large, metal grate in the center of the floor. Ollie remembered learning about that grate during his school visits; it covered a deep, dark void that had originally been used for an elevator—conveying workers and equipment during construction, and also carrying early visitors before the park service switched to a "walk your own ass to the top" method of delivery. Now, the elevator was gone, but the shaft remained. And incredibly, the only thing stopping anyone from falling down that shaft was one round, and relatively thin, metal grate.

The grate.

At the sight of it, Ollie felt an uncomfortable pull deep in his chest.

He stepped forward warily, hoping he was wrong. But he knew he wasn't. And sure enough, as soon as he got close enough to peer down into the spaces between the bars, he saw a violet-tinged bubble, floating deep in the darkness of the shaft. Barely visible.

The two seeds in his pocket ricocheted against the constraints of the fabric.

The third tiny pod was down there, inside the bubble. The seeds knew it, and he knew it. Unfortunately, he also knew that the damn bubble was hovering above a 250-foot death drop, just far enough down to be out of reach, and covered by a protective metal grate.

Ollie crouched. He examined the grate's edge, not surprised to find it secured by heavy-duty screws. If he wanted to try to reach the bubble, he had to somehow get past the grate. He sighed, wishing he had one of Tera's fishing poles handy. Or one of those miniature, multi-tool things his asshole father had always carried around on his keyring. Everyone once in a while, the old man did manage to make himself useful, Ollie acknowledged begrudgingly. Not that it was any help to him now. In typical Matteo fashion, he was nowhere in sight when Ollie needed him most.

On closer inspection, Ollie noticed that the holes at center of each screw had a strange, bulbous shape. What sort of screwdriver would turn those? Not a flat-head or a Phillips. Maybe a weird sort of Allen wrench?

He straightened, still on his knees.

Huh.

His hand slid into his pocket and pulled out one of the brown seeds. Ollie looked at the curvilinear shape of the screw holes, then at the seed. They matched. The seedpod, meanwhile, had ceased its jiggling and fallen perfectly still in Ollie's palm. Ready for duty.

The tugging pain in his chest eased. His breath came in long, even bursts. He heard his mother's voice in his head: *"Oh, Bambino. Sometimes, you just have to stop thinking and do."*

And so, he did.

Gripping the wrinkled skin of the seedpod as tightly as he could, Ollie inserted it into the cavity at the center of the closest screw's head. He turned.

Nothing happened.

He turned again. This time, he felt the slightest give beneath his fingers. And then ... some more. Slowly but surely, the screw spun, as though it had been squirted with a generous spray of WD-40. Finally, it was loose enough for Ollie to pry out the remaining grooved thread with his fingers.

He repeated the motion seven more times, until all eight screws had been released from their holes and lay on a pile on the cement floor. Carefully, he slid the seed back into his pocket. Now it was only a matter of lifting the heavy grate from its resting spot. In the end, Ollie did more dragging and grunting than actual lifting, but nevertheless managed to move the metal grate out of the way.

He had done it. Ollie felt a quick flash of pride and self-satisfaction until he looked down into the yawning chasm of the shaft and wondered: *Now what?* The seed was in the bubble. The bubble was floating in the shaft, just far enough to be out of reach. He didn't have a rope. Or a ladder. Or a Laszlo.

Maybe he could call the Wicket again? Ollie dug his fingers into his flopping hair, remembering the little man's last words: *We're done here, understand? You're on your own.*

No. The Wickets weren't coming back. He had to figure this out alone.

Maybe he could go back down into the park and find ... something. A stick? But then, of course, he risked popping the bubble and watching the seed tumble down into the dark, never to be seen again. A net? A net would work great, but he wouldn't find one of those in the park. Maybe he could use his weird new power to retrieve the bubble. He could get really mad and ... and send out light from the freckles, and ...uh ... And what, exactly? Explode the seed into a hundred pieces? Make things worse?

Ollie clenched his fists.

He'd have to wait. If he stayed here long enough, Laszlo would come looking for him. Then Laz could help. But if Ollie waited too long, the sun would rise. The monument would reopen. The sightseers would arrive. And they'd all climb the winding staircase to find Ollie sitting in the middle of the observation-room floor beside a wide-open, treacherous shaft. Did the park rangers carry handcuffs in those uniforms? If so, they'd probably use them to perp-walk him down those stairs into Boston infamy. Trespass. Vandalism. Maybe an Attempted Murder of Tourists charge to boot.

What the actual hell was he supposed to do? He was so close! So, so, so close! The damn thing was right there, mere inches from his reach! There had to be a way. There just *had* to be a way!

Ollie buried his fists into his eye sockets. He felt like he was riding a roller coaster up a never-ending hill. *Tinkety-tinkety-tinkety-tinkety-tinkety.* Up and up and up: strapped in, no escape, with no peak in sight.

He could practically hear the chains rattling as they pulled him further into the sky.

Tinkety-tinkety-tinkety.

He could also hear something else. Something real.

A voice.

It was calling out a name ... His name.

He dropped his hands. Opened his eyes.

There it was, again: "Ollie!"

The voice was coming from the ground, outside. Cautiously, Ollie walked to the window. He looked down to see a figure waving. A young woman. Brown hair, green hoodie. Bewilderment made him sway. "Nell?" he asked out loud, though she was much too far away to hear him.

"Ollie! It's me!" She was shouting and swinging her arms in wide swoops. Despite the great height—and the thick pane of window glass—that separated them, he nonetheless managed to make out her words.

Nell pointed to her own chest, then pointed up. She wanted to come up to join him.

What was going on? What was she doing here? How did she know he was here? Was she still following him? Reflexively, Ollie curled his arm and hand in a "come on up" gesture.

Nell nodded and darted out of sight. She was moving, he assumed, toward the still-open door at the base of monument that Laszlo and the women had scurried through only a few minutes before.

Nell was here?

Nell was here. And she was on her way up. Why? He didn't know, and in that moment, he didn't particularly care. A friend was coming. He wasn't alone.

Tinkety-tinkety-tinkety—

A precipitous surge of hope pushed him up, up, up and finally over the imaginary summit. And suddenly, the view didn't seem so bad.

Sixteen

It took Nell less than ten minutes to reach the top. She had always been in better shape than Ollie, both physically and mentally. It was one of the reasons he had looked up to her. And now, here she was, winded but intact, standing just a few feet away with her back bent and her hands resting on her knees.

"Jesus, that's a bitch," she gasped.

Ollie stared at her, mute.

"I mean, seriously. No elevator?"

He watched her for several more seconds, waiting for an explanation. A normal hello. An expression of concern or friendly wisdom. Anything. Instead, she just continued to pant. Finally, he threw up his hands and asked, as calmly as he could manage, "Are you going to tell me what you're doing here?"

She straightened and pushed hair out of her face. "Whooo. Damn. Okay, better now."

"Nell."

"All right, all right! Geez. I'm here to help you, you big dumb dork."

"Help me how?"

"With ... whatever. Whatever you need help with." Her pale cheeks were flushed, matching the pink lipstick.

"How did you even know I was here? Have you been following me?"

"Duh. Yes. I already told you to stop looking, didn't I? But noooo. You just kept right on with your little, I don't know, hunt, or whatever." She looked down, suddenly noticing the enormous, exposed hole in the floor. "Whoa. Why is that open?"

"I'm asking the questions, here." Ollie folded his arms, trying to look stern. Nell's sudden appearance had left him grappling with unexpected ambivalence: On the one hand, pleased as cherry punch to have an ally; on the other, increasingly annoyed and confused by that ally's strange behavior. The pendulum swung back and forth, back and forth, in wide, nauseating arcs. "I want to know why you've been following me. And while we're at it, why did you hold up that sign in the park? Why did you tell me to stop looking for shit? Who told you to tell me that?"

She smirked. "That's a lot of questions. I'm going to have to write them down."

"Nell!"

The smirk disappeared, replaced by a look of regret. She held up a hand. "I can't, okay? I can't tell you that."

"What part?"

"All the parts. All you need to know is, I'm here to help you."

Ollie's sigh was so deep, and so sustained, that it could have blown a pigeon off its perch had there been any nearby. "For the love of God, Nell, are you serious right now? I went all the way down to the *Neath* to save you, and now you won't even—"

"And as we established, I didn't need saving," she interrupted.

"Fine. Yes. You didn't need saving. I get it. Nonetheless, I did travel to a hideous underground to find you. *And* I gave you my exit pass so you could get out, which meant I was stuck down there—"

She interrupted again. "From what I hear, that didn't work out so bad for you, lover boy." The smirk had returned.

His eyebrows shot up. How did she know about Tera? Who the hell had she been talking to? Laszlo? The witches? Someone else? There weren't many people who could communicate freely between the Neath and the Brickside. Whoever it was, it was probably the same person who had told her to watch him. "Look, that's ... That has nothing to do with anything," he said, flummoxed. "The point is—"

"The point is, I'm on your side. As always. Just like the old days. You trust me, right?"

Why did she keep asking him that? "Yes, for God's sakes. I trust you! But I need to know what's going on here."

"But you don't. That's the thing. I've been told to keep an eye on you. To help you. And right now, that's all you need to know." She tugged on the hood of her sweatshirt as she spoke, covering part of her face. A nervous gesture. As if she was unconsciously trying to hide.

Back at Sweet Screams in Salem, Ollie had wondered, momentarily, if she was a ghost. Or some kind of masterful Neathian imposter. Now, those weird, unwelcome thoughts surfaced again. He pushed them away. "Nell, I—"

"Do you need help, or not? If not, I can just go." She jerked a thumb over her shoulder. "It's a hell of a lot easier to go down that thing than it is to go up."

Ollie gritted his teeth. The stonewalling, the infuriating word play... It made his stomach roil. But it was clear he was getting nowhere with his line of questioning. And the plain fact was, he *did* need help. Now. And Nell was the only person who could offer it. She had appeared just when he'd needed her. Weird? Yes. Suspicious? Definitely. But as Dozer would say, *When you got no paddle, the creek's in charge.*

"Fine," he growled. "But later, when we're done here, I'm getting some answers, okay?"

"Okay."

"I'm serious!"

"I know!" She held out her palms defensively. "Damn. You really found yourself a backbone down there, didn't you?"

He gave a half-shrug.

"And despite the fact that you are *yelling* at me, may I assume you are actually grateful for my help today?"

"Yes," he mumbled.

"Sorry? I didn't quite catch that."

"Yes," Ollie said, louder. "I am very grateful for your help today. All right? Can we get started?"

"Absolutely," Nell said, shoving her hands into her front pockets. She looked pleased with herself. The hood had fallen away from her face. "So. What are we doing?"

In answer, he pointed to the gaping, black shaft.

Her brow furrowed. "The hole? What about it?"

"I'm going in it."

"Like, *in* it, in it?"

"Yes."

"But ... why?"

"It's, uh, a long story," he said.

She rocked from one hip to the other. "I've got time."

"A *really* long story," he amended. Starting and ending on the Brickside, with a whole lot of Neath in between. "I'll tell you later, okay?"

"Wait a second," Nell said, flashing him a bemused look. "Wait. You get mad at me because I can't tell you stuff, and then you say that *you* can't tell *me* stuff?"

"This is different," he insisted.

"Different, how?"

Ollie spluttered. It was different in more ways than he could verbalize. It was as different as name-brand and store-brand cotton swabs: one fluffy and comfortable, the other a hard stick in your ear.

The seeds were jumping again in his pocket. He placed a hand over them and pressed down firmly. "You keep asking if I trust you," he said. "Do you trust *me*?"

She raised one shoulder. "Well, yeah. Of course."

"Okay, then. Trust me when I say, it's very important that I dangle upside-down into that pit. And it's even more important that you don't let me fall in."

Nell's pink lips popped open into an oval, looking remarkably like a strawberry-frosted donut. For once, she seemed to be at a loss for words.

———————⌬———————

It was a simple problem of physics.

The bubble was floating, serene and purple, down in the chasm, just close enough to the top enough to catch glints of moonlight on its surface. Ollie could reach it—or at least he hoped he could reach it—if he stretched.

But he was a big guy. An unusually big-and-tall guy. And his top half was a hell of a lot heavier than his bottom half. If he tried to lie on the floor and reach into the hole, he knew with certainty that the heft of his belly alone would flip him down to his doom faster than a selfie-taking moron can trip and fall to the bottom of the Grand Canyon.

What he needed was a stabilizer.

Luckily, Nell wasn't slight. Though not nearly as tall or as heavy as Ollie, she was nonetheless strong and sizable enough to perch on his legs and hold him in place while he reached into the abyss.

She had looked doubtful as he explained the plan. Then, terrified. Then, finally, reluctantly acquiescent. Now, they were attached together into a single zigzagging shape: Ollie bent backward at the waist, hanging head-first into the unfathomably deep shaft, and Nell sitting on his legs.

"Ready?" he called out. His voice echoed back at him in a taunt.

Nell gripped his ankles with a fierce crush, then called back: "This is a bad idea!"

Yeah, yeah. He already knew that. Of all the bad ideas he'd had since this misadventure started, it might be one of the worst. "Ready?" he said again, this time giving the word an edge.

"Fine! Ready." Nell sounded scared.

Ollie wasn't scared. He was absolutely, positively petrified. Even just a few feet from the top, the darkness of the hole was nearly total. The depth was incomprehensible. Ollie thought back to all those winding stairs he had climbed. Now, he was at the top, contemplating a much, *much* quicker trip down.

If he fell now, if Nell let go or shifted, that was it. Plunge and splat. Game over. They'd probably never even find his body until construction workers in some future renovation project stumbled over a skeleton and launched a true-crime podcast. *Who was the Monument Shaft Man?* Meanwhile, Laszlo would wonder why he never showed up for dinner. The last seed would never be recovered. And Tera and Meatball would languish, forever, in their yellow-Jell-O hell.

Timidly, Ollie reached out toward the glowing purple orb. He was still several inches short.

Somewhere below, a faint howl escaped from the depths. Wind whipping around the narrow cavity? Or something worse? Gritting his teeth, Ollie tried to push the howl from his mind—along with thoughts about his imminent death—and reached again. A bit further, this time.

He heard Nell shout something succinct, but couldn't quite make out her words. It was probably something along the lines of "Be careful!" or "What the hell are we doing?" or "Hang on a sec, I'm losing my grip, you fat load of lard!" Whatever it was, he ignored her.

A little further...

His fingers waved and wiggled in the darkness.

So... close ...

The sharp edge of the shaft opening scraped Ollie's back as he slid. Nell's hands gripped and regripped his ankles, his shins, his feet. Her weight pressed hard against his knees and thighs.

Blood rushed to his head. He stretched, then stretched again. He was close enough to see the little seed clearly, now, hopping around in its protective case.

Just ... a ... little ...further ...

Nell's weight shifted. Too much.

Ollie dropped in a sudden, short plunge—he gasped, reaching out for the walls, his fingers desperate for something to cling to and finding nothing but smooth rock. Blackness and purple blurred together in a vision of terrible finality.

And then, her body moved again. Rested with authoritative plunk on his legs. He wasn't falling. Not yet.

Krite almighty!

Ollie forced his breath to slow—*in and out, in and out*—and his shaking fingers to still. For the first time, he noticed cold air snaking up the shaft. Surrounding him. He reached, and reached, and reached, until... His index finger, finally, impossibly, tapped the bubble. It popped immediately—faster than he was expecting. The seed was already free. *Shit! No, no, no...* Ollie lunged, not with his fingers this time, but with his whole hand. His whole body. He lurched forward and opened his palm, face up, only a fraction of a second before the seedpod fell into it. His hand closed around it in a tight, desperate fist.

He had it. He had it! The thought made him giddy with relief.

His next thought was not so joyous: He was slipping. He had lunged too far. Nell was in a tug-of-war with gravity, and gravity was winning. He could hear her voice, frantic, echoing in the empty observation room above.

No time to pocket the seed; instead, Ollie used his closed fist, his other open hand, and whatever stomach and leg muscles he could summon to push against the curved walls, wiggling and sliding and lurching his oversized torso in a northerly direction. His yelps traveled down into the cavernous space below, disappearing into the dark, cold air.

Somewhere above, Nell tugged and hollered. Time itself seemed to skitter.

And then, miraculously, Ollie's back, shoulders, and head slid up and around the lip. He was out. All of him, every last limb, was resting on the solid floor. Nell flopped off his legs with a grunt, and the two of them lay beside each other in a heaving, whimpering lump.

"You..." She started, then stopped, then started again. "... are a fucking lunatic."

Ollie nodded. Wearily, he lifted his arm, willing his eyes to convince his brain of what he hoped was true ... Yes. There it was. His fingers were still curled into a tight fist. Inside, something jittered.

Nell was right. He *was* a fucking lunatic. A lunatic who now had not one, not two, but three seeds in his possession.

Water, earth, air. Three points make one key.

The key to what?

Ollie let his head drop back onto the cement with a hard thump. Maybe, at long last, he was about to find out.

Seventeen

Ollie climbed with difficulty to his feet, then helped Nell do the same. Once he felt steady enough, he reunited the seeds in the palm of his hand.

All three, identical. Each smaller than a coffee bean. They seemed happy to see each other, if such a thing were possible. *Jiggle, jiggle, jiggle.* They performed the strange little dance in unison, as if they were three parts of a whole: Magical triplets. Rings in a binder. Musketeers. Blind mice.

See how they run.

Ollie closed his hand, squeezing gently. When he reopened it, he half-expected to see a key in his palm. Brass, or silver. Probably old-fashioned looking, with elaborate twists and curves. What would he do with it? What would it open? But as he curled back his fingers, all he saw were the same three kernels, dancing the same tango.

Huh.

"What are they?"

Nell's voice jerked him back to reality.

"Hmm?"

"What are they?" she asked again, pointing. "They look like flower seeds."

"Yeah, they're ... I'm not sure, exactly," he admitted.

She looked unimpressed. "Is that what you went down there to get?"

He nodded.

"Do they always dance around like that?"

"Usually. Well, sometimes."

Nell's mouth went sideways. She seemed to be chewing the inside of her cheek. Wondering, perhaps, why he would risk his life—and hers—for something as mundane as those three, drab-brown pellets.

"It's, uh, it's a long story," he said.

"Mmm hmm. You mentioned that." Nell straightened her rumpled hoodie and pushed the hair out of her face. "So that's what you've been looking around for, this whole time?"

He nodded again, though more slowly. Her question struck him as odd. Didn't she already know what he'd been looking for? She was the one who'd warned him to stop, after all.

As he moved to slip the seeds back into his pocket, Nell shot out a hand. "Can I see them?"

He paused, confused. "You just saw them."

"I mean, can I hold them? Just for a sec."

Ollie felt his fingers curl protectively back into a fist. "Why?"

"I don't know. Geez. They're just kind of cool. I've never seen dancing seeds before." Her head tilted. "What's the problem?"

"There's no problem," he countered defensively.

"So why can't I see them?" After a long pause, she added, "I just helped you get one, didn't I? The least you can do it let me see it." Now she was pouting.

Ollie's hand stilled in midair. She had a point. He wouldn't even have the final seed if not for Nell. Nell, who had been keeping tabs on him for days. Who somehow knew all about Tera, and about his screwy scavenger hunt. Who had shown up at the exact minute he needed her most. Not before, not after ... at just the right, perfect minute.

Her hand was outstretched. Her pink lips sparkled. Her gaze remained fixed on his hand. Eager.

Ollie reached out his arm. Then he stopped, feeling a numbness travel through the limb. Hearing his mother's voice. *Listen with more than just your ears, Bambino. Listen with all you have.*

The numbness turned to sadness, deep and wretched. Deeper than the shaft at their feet.

"How long?" he asked.

"How long, what?"

"How long have you been working for him?"

Nell's brow furrowed into an expression of puzzlement. "Working for who?"

That was the moment he knew for sure. It was something about the way her hazel eyes blinked too quickly. "For George Herrick," he said quietly.

"What?" *Blink, blink, blink.* "Who's that?"

It all zipped together, suddenly, like a coat closing tight against a December wind. Nell, holding the sign: SEND OLLIE UP OR THEY ALL DIE. Nell, following him around. Watching him. Warning him. Nell, his friend, his confidante, leading him on a wild goose chase into an unseen world. A world where someone had been waiting. *Send Ollie up. Send Ollie down.*

Don't you trust me?

He did trust her. Completely. Which was exactly why they had used her against him, from the very start.

When Ollie spoke again, his voice caught. "What did they offer you?"

"What? Oll, I don't know what—"

"Cut the crap, Nell," he interrupted. The betrayal was sharp enough to sever his vocal chords, but somehow he kept talking. "What did they offer you? You might as well tell me."

"Ollie, this is ..." And then, midsentence, she gave up. Her entire countenance slumped, as though she'd been held tall and straight by a plywood board that had suddenly snapped. "Look, you don't understand."

He snorted.

"You don't understand what it's been like for me! You know I had those student loans. Right? You remember that. And nobody was helping me, Oll! Nobody! I was drowning. I couldn't pay the rent. I couldn't even get groceries! What was I supposed to do?" She stepped closer; he stepped back. "They said no one would get hurt. And no one did, right? You're fine!"

He snorted again, though it came out more like a sob.

"I just needed a little bit of money! Look, I'm sorry, okay! I had no choice. I really didn't. I was desperate. I'm *still* desperate. It was ... I shouldn't have done it, okay? I know that. I'm sorry."

"Well, as long as you're *sorry.*" His sarcasm sliced the open air.

"I didn't know any names. Who they were. They wouldn't tell me anything. They still won't! But you know I wouldn't hurt you, Oll. That's why they promised me—no one would get hurt."

Oh, the bitter joke. He might have laughed if the punchline wasn't so tragic. Ollie used his free hand to rub his temples. "Jesus, Nell."

Did she have any idea what she'd done? What she'd played a part in? He remembered her, suddenly, as she had been: Giggling and winking at Lighter Tomorrows meetings. Patting his leg to cheer him. Affectionate hugs and shoulder punches. Puckered lipstick stains on white cappuccino cups. So pretty, so kind. A friend.

What parts of it had been real? Maybe none. The humiliation boiled in his throat.

She stammered nervously—vowels and consonants and sentence fragments rolling one after another. None of them made any sense.

"Stop," he said. "Just stop. Just tell me what they told you to do,"

She flipped the hood onto her head, chagrined. "Uh, what part?"

"Why did you follow me? Why did you tell me to stop looking, back at the ice cream shop?"

Nell swallowed heavily before answering. "I was supposed to keep an eye on you. To prevent you from finding ... whatever. Finding those, I guess." She gestured at his closed fist. "And then, when that didn't work ..."

He finished for her: "When that didn't work, they told you to take them from me. Is that right?"

She was chewing her lip again. Then she nodded, curtly.

"Well, you can't have them."

"Ollie, c'mon. I need them. If I show up without them, they won't pay me!"

He stared at her, astounded. "You think I give a shit if they *pay* you?"

Nell tried again. "You don't understand—"

"No, *you* don't understand," he snarled back. *"I* need them. For something a hell of lot more important than your goddamn student loans. If you want these seeds, you're going to have to kill me to get them."

"Oll, don't be ridiculous. I'm not going to kill you, for Chrissakes!" She paused for a semi-hysterical laugh. "C'mon, we're friends, right? Friends help each other. Just hand them over, and—"

She lunged, startling him. A blur of green and brown. He hadn't yet dropped the seeds safely inside his pocket; Nell knocked into his side like a linebacker, sending him sprawling. They tussled and shoved, moving in lurches around the small room. Before he knew what was happening, the seeds had fallen from his hand, scattering in three different directions.

Ollie had barely had time to process the loss, or Nell's sudden offensive, when he realized that their traveling scuffle had taken them close—too close—to the center of the room. To the hole.

Nell was muttering something, pleading and frenzied, when it happened. The heel of her sneaker dropped over the lip, sending her off-balance. Almost instantly, the rest of her body followed suit. She stood on the edge for a desperately long moment, arms swaying wildly. Her eyes met Ollie's. And both of them knew what was coming.

Backwards, she fell.

He reached out to grab her, but missed. Nell's head disappeared from view like a bobber tugged under by a big fish— quick and sudden.

Her fingers caught the edge. In a moment that was both agonizingly long and agonizingly short, she clung there, skin and knuckles turning white from the pressure. Ollie lunged again, trying to grab her hands, but couldn't make it in time. All he could do was watch, sickened, as ten glitter-pink fingernails clawed, then flailed, and then, finally, vanished down the shaft.

The empty room spun around him.

Olie didn't digest it. He didn't stop to contemplate the horror of what had just happened. His body moved mechanically, sliding forward. In the milliseconds that followed, he felt his skin open and expand. He saw beams of great light emitting from somewhere deep inside of him, lighting up the chasm. He saw his arm extend and his fingers spread. He felt his eyes close. Saw the deep, cataclysmic hole in his mind. Watched her body falling to its gruesome end.

Stop.

Nell had almost reached the bottom. Her terror was like a flavor in his mouth.

Stop.

In his mind, he watched her body yank to a sudden halt, mere inches from the dank, hard ground. Nell's limbs dangled above, nearly but not quite touching. Eyes still closed, he saw it all.

Up.

At his command, Nell began to rise. Ten feet, then fifty, then two hundred. He didn't think or struggle. He lifted her with nothing more than light and breath.

She was whimpering when she emerged from the shaft. Trembling with a visible quake.

Ollie set her gently onto the ground. Then he, too, collapsed. The light evaporated as quickly as it had appeared. Strength and certainty melted into utter exhaustion. His head throbbed with a migraine of colossal dimensions. *Whoomp, whoomp, whoomp.* His vision was filmy.

When his eyesight finally cleared, he saw that Nell was looking at him in fear. And confusion. But mostly fear. She had backed herself up against the wall, as if to get as far away from the open hole—and him—as possible.

His pulsing migraine was thick with disorientation. As before, the mystifying power had felt entirely natural and yet entirely foreign, as though he'd woken up after a bump on the head with a sudden, new knowledge of how to play concert piano or fluently speak an obscure language. He had no idea how he'd managed to pull that off, and was pretty sure he couldn't do it again right now if he tried.

But Nell didn't need to know that.

For several long minutes, neither spoke. The sound of their heavy breathing echoed against the walls of the empty room.

About ten feet separated them. And in the space between, three seeds sat scattered on the floor, the dark brown of their pods contrasted against the whitish cement. They were not dancing. That seemed like a bad sign.

He and Nell noticed the seeds at the same time. Her eyes brushed over them, then looked back up at Ollie.

She wouldn't dare. Would she?

He didn't wait to find out. Ollie narrowed his eyes, gathered his strength, and crawled toward the disbursed seeds. One by one, he picked them up and dropped them into his front pocket.

Nell remained pressed against the wall, watching him. Still trembling. Her hair was a wild tangle.

He stood, towering over her.

"Just go," he said.

"Ollie, I—"

"Just go! Now!"

Nell snapped her mouth shut. She slid her back up along the smooth wall until she was upright. Without another word, she darted for the stairs.

The hoodie stayed behind: a sad, green heap in the corner.

Ollie stared down at the sweatshirt. He listened to her footfalls on the steps, imagining the numbers counting down. *Two-ninety-four, two-ninety-three, two-ninety-two, two-ninety-one...* He stopped at 290. He had wasted enough time, and enough worries, on Nell Cascone.

Eighteen

Ollie returned the protective grate to its normal position and used one of the seeds to twist each screw back into place. The chore was welcome, allowing him to focus on something real. Something tangible. He checked, double-checked, and triple-checked each screw's stability. Then he climbed back to his feet and assessed his situation.

His skin felt normal—no blisters, no beams of light. He was hungry, hot, and tired. The headache was still pounding, but had diminished somewhat. The seeds were recovered and secure. The night sky was somber. The air inside the observation room was still musty and stale. The four windows were—

Wait.

Not four. Five.

He was sure there had been only four when he'd arrived: north, south, east, and west. Evenly spaced, one on each side. Now, however, he saw a fifth. Unlike the others, this new opening seemed to have no glass or frame...just a gaping, hazardous void. Definitely not child-proof. Definitely not permitted by the city Board of Building Regulations and Standards.

As Ollie's eyes widened, so did the cavity. He watched it grow, inch by inch, until it was bigger than the windows on either side. Then, much bigger. Then, as tall as a door. A blast of hot evening air swept through the void and hit Ollie in the face. He staggered backward.

Climb to fly. Walk the sky.

The voice tingled through his consciousness like a seltzer. The sound propelled him into action, and he obeyed.

One step forward. Two steps. Three, four.

He should have resisted, he supposed, considering what had happened the last time a voice in his head had spurred him to act. The Doc, the laboratory, the grisly tank. He should have felt frightened. This voice, though, sounded nothing like that one—less vile, more benevolent. A whispering cheerleader on the sidelines. Ollie felt entirely in control of his own actions, yet also inclined to follow the directions as given.

In his pockets, the seeds cavorted energetically.

Climb to fly.

Climb.

More stairs, new stairs, appeared in the doorway. They were flat, rectangular, and twisted up into a winding pattern, not unlike the 294 that had led him here. But these newer steps were less...opaque. The closer he got, the more Ollie realized that he could see right through them to catch a glimpse of the trees, paved walkways, and moving headlights of distant traffic far below.

Air, third. Climb to fly. Walk the sky. The words continued to ring in his head. He knew who the voice belonged to. Not by name, perhaps, but he knew enough. This was the voice of the person who had sent him to collect the seeds. Who had guided his journey to this place, who had spoken to him through witches, and Novas, and aquatic animals, and decks of white, round cards.

Ollie needed this person—he knew that, now. He needed this voice. If he had any hope of freeing Tera and thwarting Herrick's plans, he needed to follow these disembodied, seemingly sage words wherever they led. And if that meant stepping out onto a transparent staircase floating 221 feet in the air, then that's what it meant.

Ollie walked to the edge. All that was missing was a podium and an annoyed Neath attendant: *How many for entry?* Strangely, he didn't feel afraid. As crazy as this was, it didn't feel crazy. It felt ... inevitable. Had the reunited seeds infected him with some kind of idiot virus? Had they lulled him into a gullible stupor?

Maybe. But he didn't think so. In fact, for the first time in a long time, Ollie didn't want to think at all. And even if he'd wanted to, he probably couldn't hear his own thoughts over the cacophony of all the voices that had suddenly crowded into his head.

"You show your insides on your outsides, Ollie Delgato. You cannot help it. You are clear, like vodka." Laszlo.

"Rule number two is, sometimes you got to forget rule number one." Dozer.

"This might surprise you, young man, but you're not here to make googly eyes at the ladies all day." Ajanta.

"Those who have nothing to hide have nothing to fear." Kuyu.

"An Aristotle promise is an Aristotle promise." Derrin.

"Be brave, bambino." His mother.

"I like a whole lot of things better since you've been here." Tera.

Snuffle, snort, snorgle. Meatball.

The words and sounds enveloped him in a wash of illogical, wonderful reason. He wasn't alone here, at the top of the city. They were all with him. If the stairs couldn't hold him, those voices definitely would. Of course they would. Ollie raised one foot, stepped. Lifted the other, stepped. And smiled.

Solid.

The translucent stair was firm as rock, yet flimsy as gossamer lace. Whatever it was, it held his weight.

Below his feet, he could see the straight lines of pathways through the park. The wide swaths of grass. Small, dark shapes—squirrels?—scampering. It felt like standing inside a floating, slightly dirty, glass-bottomed boat. Not perfectly see-through, but pretty close.

Ollie took another step, then another. Up and up. *Be brave, Bambino.* Was this bravery, or something else?

Tera would probably love this wacky, winding, possibly nonexistent staircase, he realized. Laszlo, too. And the ragtag Salem coven. He could just picture all the gangly teens bolting up the stairs, laughing and unafraid, pushing each other aside in a race to the top. Black boots stomping, dyed hair flopping. Had they been here already? Did they know about this place? Maybe the magic staircase at the top of the Bunker Hill Monument was old news to the Brickside witches. Or maybe he was the first—and last?—to ever climb it.

The staircase itself wasn't talking. Instead, it wound itself around the ever-narrowing top of the monument, and Ollie followed. The spiral grew tighter and tighter, the steps smaller and smaller, as the obelisk's width decreased. After only nine stairs, he could almost reach out and touch the apex itself, which looked almost exactly like the tip of a giant, sharpened pencil. And by the time he reached the last stair, his size-14 feet were a tight fit, loping off the edges. Ollie wobbled.

He looked down, caught his breath, and shut his eyes. The strange, delicious courage was starting to ebb. The distance between him and the ground—and the ghostly nature of the stairs holding him up—was becoming rapidly more apparent. Ollie reached out to wrap his arms around the monument's narrowed pinnacle. It was, thank God, just the right size for a hug.

The panic passed. Or mostly passed. Ollie cracked open his eyes and loosened his grip on the stone, face-to-face with the monument's pointy terminus. And balanced on that point, he saw something small. Terracotta.

It looked like a pot. Just a regular clay pot, about the size of a teacup. Ollie's mother used to have dozens just like it scattered around their apartment balcony in the summer, overflowing with geraniums, petunias, and begonias. This pot had no flowers—but it did, he realized on closer inspection, have dirt.

A slow smile spread across his face.

How lucky, to find a pot, when he happened to have three seeds in his pocket. How very convenient. He felt like a child being led by the hand through a crowded department store. Not that way, *this* way. Not there, *here*.

The pot was too wide to balance on the narrow point, yet balance it did. Ollie knew better than to dwell on the impossible specifics. His next steps were obvious: He had found the seeds, and now he had found a pot to plant them in. Never mind the fact that the pot was barely stable, and he was barely stable, and this whole bizarre situation was barely stable. Never mind that a chain-smoking Sticky Wicket had gotten him here, or that his only Brickside friend had betrayed him, or that he was hearing voices. Again.

This was it. He was almost finished. He had climbed his last hurdle, metaphorically and literally. He had done everything that anyone had asked of him—even when he didn't always know who those askers were. He was standing at the top of the world, hugging a famous monument, staring into the abyss. And all he had to do now was plant three little seeds into an adorably pint-sized terracotta pot.

Easy as stealing a tail feather from a one-legged goose, as Dozer would say.

Ollie freed an arm from its stony embrace and reached into his pocket. The seeds nearly jumped into his hand, apparently as eager to be done with this as he was. He kept his fist closed around them as he slowly... *slowly...* reached for the pot. That was all he needed, after all this, for the damn seeds to jitterbug themselves out of his grip and fall to the ground. Not today. He clenched his jaw. His fingers hit the dirt: It was cool, and damp. Perfect conditions for planting.

Slowly... *slowly...* Ollie spread his fingers. The seeds dropped—one, two, three—onto the soil. They rolled and danced, as usual. Using his most gentle touch, he pressed each one down. Lower, then lower still, until they had all disappeared under the dirt. *You have to make them feel comfortable,* his mother had always said while planting. *Nice and secure.* Gingerly, Ollie tapped the surface flat.

Then he held his breath.

Would it be instantaneous, the growing? And what kind of greenery would three magically scattered-then-reunited seeds grow, exactly? He thought about the fast-sprouting Bonsai back in Danvers. He thought about Weelichka's words: *Water, earth, air. Three points make one key.* Maybe the seeds would sprout a tiny Key Tree, dangling with toothy metal. That would certainly be something. That would be a great story to tell Tera when he saw her.

His heart leaped. *When he saw her.* Soon, soon, soon.

I'm coming, T! he thought. *Don't give up!* Maybe she would hear it. Maybe someone, or something, would carry his words to her ears. Given all that he'd seen and experienced, he could imagine something like that happening. He could even dare to feel some hope that it would.

As if in response, the small clay pot began to rattle on the monument's tip. Ollie held out a hand, panicked, to catch it, but soon found there was no need. Despite its precarious position, the pot managed to stay put. Seconds later, Ollie's breath caught as he noticed the first burst of green—a tiny tendril, poking out of the dirt. That was followed by another, and then a third. Like the seeds that bore them, the shoots seemed to be wobbling, dancing. One, two, and three. Up, up, and up.

As Ollie watched in fascination, the tendrils grew wider and taller, stretching toward the dark sky. Finally, when each was about as long as a ruler, they began to wind themselves together. It looked to him like a braid, each wrapping around the next in a perfectly coordinated, entwined ballet. It was astonishing. It was beautiful.

It was art and nature and magic, all curled up into one green, glowing helix.

Tears sprung to his eyes. He had done it. He had really done it. He still didn't know what, exactly, he had done, but he knew it was something magnificent. He would take this delicate, braided plant with him when he left, holding the pot carefully while he wound his way back down the stairs. He would carry it down the hill, across the bridge, and back into the North End. He would show it to Laszlo, and they would marvel at it together while they enjoyed a last, hearty meal at Fioretti's before heading back down to rescue Tera. Maybe the key would be hidden in the bottom of the pot. Or maybe the plant would sprout another note complete with sing-songy guidelines. Or suggestions. Or step-by-step instructions for defeating Herrick and his minions once and for all.

This was it. This was the moment his prolonged, ghastly nightmare would come to an end at last. Ollie felt so many emotions burbling. He felt proud. He felt surprised that he had managed to pull it off.

He felt ... the stairs slipping.

Instinctively, he gripped the stone. The movement was subtle, but there. The step he was standing on had definitely dropped by an inch or so. Maybe more.

Ollie looked down, muscles tensed. Why did the staircase suddenly look more transparent? Like someone had hosed it down with glass cleaner?

And then, another jerk. Another inch, lost.

Shit. Shit, shit, shit.

Ollie thrust his arms out to grab the pot. His heart thudded. His mind reeled with one, urgent thought: *Get the plant and get out of here. Now.*

But before his hands reached the clay, he noticed with a jolt that something else had changed, too. The three stalks had stopped braiding themselves and started sprouting out in opposite directions. With increasing speed, they grew up and over the edge of the pot, creating perfect curves that looked like handles on a mug. The shoots then reached down, gripped the stone of the monument, and overturned the little pot. Just flipped it, bottoms-up, hard and fast. Ollie watched in confused alarm as clumps of dirt gave way to gravity, falling all the way down to the ground far below.

The plant was still growing. Upside down. It wore the pot like a little hat as its stalks multiplied, curled, and spread like greedy limbs. Ollie tried to take a step back, to lean away from the breakneck germination, but found that he couldn't. The stair was too small. And still dropping.

It fell another inch, then another. Ollie searched frantically for something to hold onto, but all he found was smooth stone and clawing, gluttonous vines.

One of them wrapped his wrist like a bracelet, clamping tight. He tried to tear it off. Another wrapped his torso. The pot was now out of his reach, lost in the green maze. The stairs were sinking, and also growing more translucent. In a fit of panic, he decided to make a break for it. To race down the staircase before it disappeared altogether. But the tendrils wrapping his body held fast, preventing escape.

He was trapped. The doorway to the observation room, to safety, was so close—mere steps away—and he couldn't reach it.

Then it happened: the stairs flickered, and were gone. The only thing holding him aloft was the grip of dozens of coiled and possessive vines. Ollie clawed the air, trying to shout, but terror had clamped his vocal chords shut.

With each blink, the plant grew thicker, greener, stronger. The stone had all but disappeared below the vegetation. Or had it ... actually disappeared? Yes. With a whimper, Ollie looked down into the shamrock-hued tangle and saw a hole. A hole where the point of the monument used to be. The crevice widened and spread, accommodating the insatiable hunger of the upside-down, rapidly growing plant, which had now coalesced into something that looked more like a tree. White bark was sprouting on its trunk. Branches burst out in all directions. The tree grew not up, but down, crashing through what remained of the obelisk's top, through the observation room, through the metal grate, and down into the old elevator shaft.

Earthward it plunged, taking Ollie with it.

The tendrils wrapped his shoulders, his ankles, even his throat. Ollie gasped as his airway constricted. Blackness came, then went, then came again, leaving him with an erratic slideshow of disconnected memories.

Nova Scotian Water Nymphs. Nesting witches. Clown guards and mutants at the House of Unnatural Wonders.

Howerbout in his cave. *Wishes only work when they're true.*

Derrin facing off with Moseby. And with Eelia. And with him.

Kuyu bursting through the doorway in a panic: *We've got Reds! Two houses down! They're making the rounds!*

Meatball licking fish-sauce from the tip of Ollie's finger, his tongue rough and probing.

Salt mountains and prison cells.

Ajanta's long braid, swinging. *Order up!*

Mrs. Paget shaking her feathers. Spreading her giant crow wings. Staring at him with stern displeasure.

Dozer gnawing on a stick of loosemeat. *Howdy, Roomie.*

Michael Carmichael's ridiculous top hat, set at an angle.

His best friend strutting for the ladies in a spandex suit. *No fighting over Laszlo! Is enough Laszlo for all!*

Tera tossing wadded-up laundry, laughing, darting out of sight behind the hanging clothes on the line. Tera screaming and kicking as the guards dragged her away. Tera at the water trough, holding out her hand: *Do you want to get out of here or not?*

George Herrick, dead. Then, not dead. Then, standing near a crimson door, tilting his head in smug amusement. *Names have great power, don't they? The power to change everything.*

As the white tree dragged him downward, Ollie stared up at the open, blue-gray sky. He saw twinkling stars, a passing plane, the luminous moon. *The man on the Brickside moon,* he thought dreamily as he fell. And fell, and fell, and fell...through the shaft, through the floor and foundation, through the deep, rocky soil of the earth.

The tree was planting him. For just a moment, Ollie saw the irony. And then he saw nothing at all.

Nineteen

Ollie's head was throbbing. Again. Not like "honey, I have a headache" kind of throbbing. More like "honey, someone smashed my skull with a two-by-four." Unless he was mistaken, the actual flesh of his brain was expanding and contracting in time with his heartbeat. His face, similarly, seemed too big, too hot, and too bulgy.

He felt himself swaying. Left, then right. Left, then right. The blood pools in his brain followed suit. He could almost hear them sloshing.

Ollie cracked open his eyes, which were caked with something crumbly. Dirt? After a few blinks to clear them, he was able to make out a large shape in front of him. Onyx, and feathery. It looked like a huge bird. A huge crow, specifically. More specifically, it looked like Mrs. Paget.

But she was upside-down.

Caw!

His thoughts tumbled like Tetris blocks trying, and failing, to fall into place. Where was he? Why was Mrs. Paget upside down?

His arms, he now realized, were dangling. Below him. His legs and feet were somewhere above.

Mrs. Paget wasn't inverted. He was.

Ollie coughed. His pounding brain rattled. Blood had rushed to his head, and stayed there. His concentration and his vision seemed equally obscured by a thin film of fog. How had he gotten here? And how long had he been strung up like a plucked chicken at a butcher shop?

Caw!

Mrs. Paget was giving him a familiar look of disapproval. Or possibly disappointment. He could never tell with her, but it was usually one or the other. After a quick shake of her head, the massive crow lifted herself off the ground, flew up to his feet, and started pecking at something near his ankles. Ollie fought a swell of motion sickness as her efforts sent him pendulating back and forth. Finally, she managed to snap him free of his bindings, and Ollie fell to the ground with an inelegant thud.

Krite almighty. Now, the pain in his head was matched by the sting of abrasions on his elbows. Ollie rose to his feet with difficulty. He rubbed the back of his neck, wiped the remaining flecks of dirt from his eyes, and looked around.

Stalagmites. Distant, greenish water, dotted with islands. Above him, a glowing, blue ceiling.

Ollie swayed, off balance. He knew what he would see if he walked in either direction, or took a crow-boat ride along the lake's misleadingly calm surface.

People, swathed in beige jumpsuits. Regular people, and not-so-regular people. Headlamps. Toolbelts. Never-ending coat racks, hung with coats that would never be reclaimed. Podiums and attendants. Sacred guano mounds, underwater labs, fizzing grog. Witches, Reds, and Nova mirages. Wormwalkers. Ramshackle houses. Rickety bridges and floating markets. Dried lakestars. Nikki and Floyd's Brickside Curiosities shop. Hummingtail songs. Lovable, hideous mutants.

Long falls and painful landings.

His friends. His new family.

And of course, a terrible prison tower, looming over it all. A dungeon that had been created by a lie, and sustained by many more.

Ollie was back in the Neath.

But ...how?

His peripheral vision began to sharpen as his heart rate increased. Wait, was this the plan? What *was* the plan, exactly? Had he screwed up, again? Frantically, he tried to piece together the last few bits of memory. Bunker Hill Monument. *Climb to fly, walk the sky.* See-through stairs. Clay pot. Three seeds. He had planted them, and then ... what? The stalks had sprouted, braided themselves together, and morphed into something monstrous. A tree. An entire tree, grown to full-size in seconds. And instead of growing up, like a normal tree, it had grown downward. Right into the ground. And it had somehow taken Ollie with it.

Caw! Caw!

Mrs. Paget toddled over to stand beside him, looking impatient.

Ollie was shockingly glad to see her familiar face, no matter how annoyed its expression. Mrs. Paget was Tera's crow. *Tera.* The connection made him straighten and focus his thoughts.

Ollie looked into the bird's beady eyes, searching. "What are you doing here?" he asked her. He didn't expect an answer, of course. But he got one anyway.

"I called her," said a nearby voice.

Ollie's felt his heart skitter. Tera? But when he spun, he didn't see her. His eyes darted desperately, eagerly. No Tera.

Instead, he found himself looking at an upside-down tree. *The* tree. *His* tree. The one that had dragged him down here. It had peeling, white bark, emerald leaves, and a definite gleam. The glow was strong, and green, as though hundreds of traffic lights had been mounted and rigged to say *go, go, go.* The leaves waved in a wind he couldn't feel. Shoots sprouted in all directions, curling and uncurling themselves in easy, nonchalant oscillation. Tiny seedpods—not unlike the three he had planted—hung and danced from the branches like happy tambourines. *Shake, shake, shake. Shake, shake, shake.*

And all of it, every last rattling, waving, and glowing bit, was bottoms-up. The roots and base were somewhere up at the cavern's ceiling, hundreds of feet above, while the outermost branches and shoots spread almost all the way to the rocky ground.

That's what had been holding him aloft, Ollie realized with a start. The winding stems. They had wrapped his ankles. That's what Mrs. Paget had pecked to free him.

I called her, the voice had said.

He swallowed. Was the tree ... talking?

"No, the tree is not talking, love," the voice said, sounding amused. "I am."

Ollie peered through the curlicue shoots, past the branches and leaves. He looked more closely at the white trunk beyond. Something was there, he now saw, in a hole. Peeking out like an owl. But this was no owl. This was a person. A young woman.

Long, golden hair. Apple cheeks. Knowing smile.

His first thought, coated with disappointment: *Not Tera.*

His second thought: *I know you.*

"Yes, you do," the young witch agreed. "In a manner of speaking."

"You're ... Ellora," he said. Though he supposed he could have just thought it, since she seemed to be reading his mind. Just like Damira had, back in Salem.

"I am." She seemed pleased that he remembered her name.

"My great, great, great ... uh ..."

From her hidey-hole in the bark, Ellora gave a quiet laugh. "Let's just say grandmother, for the sake of ease, shall we?" She had a subtle British accent. He supposed most settlers did, back in 1600s Colonial America. Where she had lived. Three hundred and fifty years ago. And yet here she was, young as a cherry blossom. Beautiful as a bride.

His own ancestor, right here, in the flesh. Ollie's throat went dry. He had seen her face in Damira's cards. She looked exactly the same. When he spoke, it took him two tries to form the words. "You did this, didn't you? You led me here."

Ellora nodded pleasantly.

"You passed along the messages. All that stuff about 'the water of your youth,' and 'the place of his sin,' and 'walk the sky.' That was you." *A message for you, from the one who wishes you to have it.* Ellora was the one who wanted him to have the information, to solve the riddles, to find the Brickside seeds.

She nodded again.

Only one word came to his mind: "Why?"

Ellora seemed to consider the question—then, apparently, decided to not answer it. Instead, she said, "Help me out of here, would you?"

He stepped forward, awkwardly, until he realized that she was talking to the crow. With a mighty flap, Mrs. Paget flew to the trunk's hollow and settled on a nearby branch, waiting patiently as Ellora climbed out and onto her feathery back. Moments later, they were both on the ground. Ollie was shocked to discover that the witch was tall—as tall as he. Six-foot-six, at least. He was able to look directly into her eyes without bending his head. He couldn't remember the last time he had done that.

She wore a simple, off-white frock, loose and flowy. A ribbon held a swath of thick hair away from her face.

"I suppose now you know where you got all that height," Ellora said, lifting her brows mischievously. "And that blond hair." She reached out to tousle the top of his head, and Ollie felt a shiver of recognition. And affection. When she pulled her hand away, he had to fight the urge to pull it back. Looking at this woman, this witch, he knew for sure: It was all true. Everything that Damira had told him, everything the cards had depicted—it was all remarkably true.

"Well, of course it is true," Ellora said, sounding surprised. "The cards are never wrong."

"Right," Ollie said, mostly because he couldn't think of anything better to say. And even that bit of idiocy came out garbled: His tongue seemed to be tied in a knot. As the woman's unexpected, grandmotherly essence surrounded him, a single thought hit with thunderous force: *Mama.* Goddamn, he missed his mother. He always missed his mother, but here, now ... The sudden burst of grief stole his breath and buckled his knees.

Ellora nodded and took his hand. "She is with you," the witch said softly. "Always."

Tears stung Ollie's eyes.

"I know you are missing your mother, dear Oliver. And your Tera. But for now, I'm afraid, I will have to do."

Caw!

"Well, myself and our lovely Mrs. Paget, of course." She laughed again and rumpled the crow's feathers.

"How... how did you...? I mean, why ...?" Ollie was at a loss.

"I shall tell you all, my nug. As we move. From what I understand, time is of the essence?"

Nug? He nodded.

"Well then, let us not waste any more of it. Much as we might like to be circumbendibus, I'm afraid we'd fare better with swifter feet. Yes?"

Yes. He nodded again, still trying to translate.

"Brilliant. Just one thing, before we go." Ellora held out a hand and closed her eyes.

Ollie looked down at her opened palm. One more thing? What was she waiting for? Was he supposed to give her something? He hadn't brought anyth—

His questions fell away as he felt it: a rush of outward-flowing energy, like a vacuum sucking out his insides. He gasped. The freckles on his skin rose, then flattened. Beams of light erupted, then disappeared. The rage boiled for just a moment across his consciousness, skidding out of all the dark corners, then dissolved.

Ollie's eyes went wide as he watched all of it—the light, the power, the fury—travel into the empty space between them. And then, with the velocity of a condensed nor'easter, it flew into Ellora. Her pale skin shone with the brilliant sheen of hundreds of glowing blisters. She stared up at the cavern's ceiling, her face awash in relief and euphoria, her arms outstretched. Whatever this thing was, she seemed to be swallowing it whole.

Almost as soon as it had appeared, the illumination was gone. Ellora took a deep, cleansing breath. She looked, he thought, like a woman who had just pushed back her chair after a particularly satisfying slice of chocolate torte at Bonfiglio's Caffe.

And Ollie felt suddenly, disturbingly, empty.

"Thank you for holding it for me," Ellora said, straightening her skirt. "I know it could not have been easy. But an unfortunate necessity, considering the circumstances." She waved an arm in the direction of the tree.

"Holding it?" He looked down at the skin wrapping his forearms. Smooth. Chicken-white. Inert. Whatever had been there, simmering beneath the surface ... It had deserted him. Just pulled up stakes and decamped for a different, better host.

Her smile pushed her rosy cheeks higher.

"You mean ... it wasn't ... mine?" Ollie asked. The knowledge fell like a blow. Like he was about to lose a friend he didn't even realize he had liked all that much.

What had Damira called him? A caretaker.

You are a caretaker of all the hidden things.

Of course it wasn't his. Hadn't he suspected as much all along? Still ... that power, that seething, surging, fiery power ... It was all he'd had. All that had made him strong. The power of a half-witch, or so he'd thought. And now, even that was gone.

The helplessness mocked him, tugging down his limbs and stooping his shoulders. *Hello, old friend,* he told it bitterly. *Together again.*

Ellora touched his wrist, and he could still feel the force there, pulsing between them. A delicious aftertaste of what had been.

"Do not fret, young one," she said. "Your gift is not so common as this one—of that, you can be certain. Your gift ... Well, let's just say I've traveled a long way to ensure that your gift does not go fallow." Her face darkened. "Or fall into the wrong hands."

Ollie pursed his lips. He didn't know how to break it to her— to tell this woman, this grandmother, who had traveled through time and space and white-barked trees, that she was mistaken. And she was on her own.

He opened his mouth and paused, unsure what to call her. Grandma? Granny? She-Witch of the Glowing Green Tree? Nothing felt right. Finally, he just settled on her name.

"Ellora, listen. I'm sorry. I know you've been through a lot, but... you've got the wrong guy. The wrong grandson. Maybe the wrong generation, I don't know. I don't have a gift."

"Of course you do."

He flashed her a look that was part sympathy, part skepticism. "So, what is it, then?"

"That is not for me to tell you."

"Why not?"

In answer, she gave him only a slow, wistful smile.

He tried again. "All right. Fine. If I have this great ... power, or whatever, then why haven't I seen it before now?"

"Because nighttime has no colors, silly boy."

Ollie stared at her. He tried to keep his expression neutral, even as the disquiet swirled. Was she mad? Were they all mad? A half-remembered vision surfaced ... Bert the Witch, spouting nonsense: *The burn of metamorphosis-o-sis! Transmutification. Inflammereria!* And Weelichka, the Salt Collector, red-eyed and blathering: *You have received your answers in fair barter.* And a dead man sprouting to life in Blackstone Park, his jaw unhinging to croak gibberish into the humid air: *All will be mended. The waiting is done.*

And now, Ellora. *Because nighttime has no colors.*

Was this what it had come down to? All the hopes of his underground and aboveground worlds, hung on the shoulders of insanity? Ollie thought of Tera, still trapped, still waiting for him, and shivered with dread.

Too late, he remembered that Ellora could read his thoughts.

She flicked her long locks impatiently behind her shoulder. "It is not madness, young man. Only common enough sense. On the Brickside, while the sun sleeps, all things appear to be the same, yes? Inky, flat, and dark. Uncomplicated. Of course, that is not the truth of it at all. In reality, the goldfinches are gold, the blue jays are blue, and the cardinals are five different shades of crimson. Even at night. Do the birds suddenly change color when the sun rises? No. Of course not. But it is only the rising of the sun that allows us to see them as they really are."

"I ..." He floundered for a response.

Cardinals, sunrise, gifts wrapped in ribbons ...

Maybe it wasn't madness. But it wasn't useful, either. Ollie knew what was coming, and all the pretty metaphors in the world weren't going to make a damn bit of difference.

Damira's cards had shown him the future back in Salem, marching across the table in formation. *Stomp, stomp, stomp.* Prisoners, Reds, and the mutant creatures from the tanks—all soon to be free and unleashed upon the Neath. If they weren't already. All of it, created and fed by one diseased mind. A megalomaniac with grandiose delusions, hell-bent on crowning himself King of a nightmarish future—in this sunken world as well as the one above.

The visions made a tremor run between his shoulder blades.

Ellora, for her part, seemed unconcerned. She gathered her long skirt in her arms. "All right, then. Now that all that's settled, shall we go?"

"Go...where?"

She tilted her head. "To get your Tera, of course."

Caw! Caw!

"Thank you, Mrs. Paget, but I think I'd rather walk," Ellora said. "I've been sitting down for... Well, let's just say for quite a long while." She winked at Ollie. "I think it will do us both a world of good to stretch our legs."

Twenty

Ollie's sneakers crunched along the hard-packed, narrow road. He glanced down as he walked, marveling at the tattered laces, worn rubber soles, and layers of grime. These sneakers had carried him to unimaginable places: from the summit of a briny mountain to the depths of a pea-soup lake, not to mention every prison kitchen, shadowy tunnel, tourist trap, and fighting pit in between. It was incredible that they had lasted this long.

Ellora, by contrast, walked in bare feet. She seemed to feel no pain, despite the scattered rocks and stalagmite chips along their path. She also seemed to know exactly where she was going, so Ollie didn't question their direction as they hurried along.

"I should tell you," he began, cautiously. "Warn you, I guess. Herrick built a shell around the place. The lab. According to Carmichael, anyway." Did he need to explain who Carmichael was? What the lab was? He glanced at her steely expression and decided: Nope. Probably not.

The young witch snorted. "Shell?"

"Yeah. To keep witches out, apparently. To keep them from finding him, and figuring out he was still alive. And seeing what he was up to. It's supposed to be, uh...impenetrable."

Ellora rolled her eyes. "Maybe for the others."

"Oh," Ollie nodded. "But you think you can...get through it?"

"Get through it?" She looked amused. "That useless lubberwort used *my* magic to build it."

"Right," Ollie said, trying to look as though he understood. As thought he had these sorts of walk-and-talks with spell-casting ancestors all the time. He cleared his throat. "So, Herrick, uh... He stole it, then? Your magic?"

The witch's smugness disappeared, replaced by a sigh. "Most sadly, no. He did not have to. I gave it away, as carelessly as a well gives away its water. I was young, and foolish, and, worst of all, in love. Or at least, I thought I was in love. I suppose it is all too easy at any age to mistake flattery and carnal interest for something more substantial. And to be taken in by those who wish to deceive."

She paused, leaving only the sound of Ollie's crunching steps between them. He didn't reply.

When she continued, her voice was quieter. "By the time I awoke to the treachery, alas, it was too late. My folly was total. George Herrick had tasted great power, and, like so many others before him, he developed an unquenchable thirst for more. And so, I was left with nothing but the nothings."

When she paused again, he prodded: "The nothings?"

"Nothing and nothing and nothing," Ellora spat. "He would stop at nothing to get what he wanted, and yet there was nothing I could do to stop him. Not anymore. My only option was to prevent him from taking more from me than he already had. To become...nothing. I used the last remaining vestiges of my abilities to scatter the seeds, plant the messages, and disappear."

"Into...the tree?"

She lifted one shoulder. "In a manner of speaking, yes. Into a place where no one could find me, and most importantly, where no one could find what was left of my power. I had a child of my own, by then—my child, and George Herrick's." A cloud passed over her face. She stopped, gathered herself, and continued. "I passed my power down through the generations. And I waited." Ellora turned to smile at him. "I waited for you. And here you are, at last."

Ollie didn't answer.

"My goodness, how you blanche!" she said, taking in his stricken expression. "There is no need for alarm. Your time is come, my boy. And whatever we face, we shall face it together."

"You don't understand," Ollie told her. And she didn't. She couldn't possibly. All this time, Ellora had been holed up waiting for a hero to emerge. Imagining, perhaps, that her descendant would be as skillful and confident as she was. How could she possibly have predicted that all those generations of pent-up magical power would result in nothing more than a pale, tall, and pudgy 19-year-old whose greatest talent was transforming rhizers into something reasonably appetizing and selling them at a small profit? "I can't do this, Ellora. I don't know how."

"You will know," she said with a shrug. "When the time comes."

He fought the urge to growl his frustration. Why did everyone keep saying that? "No, I won't. I'm not capable."

"Oh, tosh. Of course you are! You share my blood, do you not?" Ellora sounded mildly insulted.

"Yes, but—"

"And you know what I am capable of?"

"Yes! Of course. But—"

"My goodness, dear boy, look what you have already accomplished! Far beyond what you could have dreamed on the Brickside. You have escaped from prison, twice. You have rescued friends in this world, and in the one above. You found a soul mate for that strange crab creature, which was no easy task, to be sure. You breathed underwater, for heaven's sake! And now you have even managed to free me from three centuries of solitude. What makes you think you cannot face what lies ahead?"

Ollie slowed. "You don't understand," he said quietly. "It's not...that. It's not that at all."

"What, then?" Ellora turned.

He balled his fists. "It's that I'm...afraid." There. He'd said it. His apprehension had nothing to do with ability or strength or even magical powers. It had to do with pure, bald-faced cowardice.

"Now, Oliver—"

"Don't!" he interrupted, holding up a hand. "Please. Don't give me the whole, 'courage is being afraid and doing it anyway' line of crap. I get it, okay? I know I should be courageous. Who doesn't want to be courageous? But we're not all built that way, you know? We're just not. I'm not."

"My heavens. If it is Herrick's magic you're afraid of, I have—"

He interrupted her again. "You don't get it. I'm not afraid of Herrick, okay? I'm not afraid of facing him. I'm not even afraid of dying."

Ellora looked puzzled. "Then what, exactly, are you afraid of?"

Ollie hung his head. He could feel the shame spreading all the way down to his fingertips.

"Oliver?"

He sighed. "I'm afraid of losing them, okay?"

"Losing who?"

"Losing…everyone. My friends. Tera. Everyone."

"You mean, you are afraid they will die?"

"No. Well, yeah, of course, that would be horrible. But mostly, I don't want them to see."

"See what?"

When he answered, his voice was the barest whisper. "Who I really am."

Ellora dropped a hand onto his arm. "Surely, they already know?" she said gently.

"They *think* they know," he countered. "But that won't last forever. Especially when this all goes south." He pushed out a sigh of defeat. "Once they figure it out, once they see that I'm just a useless shmuck from Hanover Street, they'll change their minds. I mean, not Kuyu, because she never liked me much, anyway." He gave a short, hard laugh, then looked at her imploringly. "I never had friends up on the Brickside, you know. Not really. Some kids were nice to me, but only…to be nice. Not because they wanted to. Later on, I had Nell. And I suppose you already know how *that* turned out."

She did know. He could tell by the way her eyes dropped and her expression veered into pity.

"Anyway, mostly I just had my mom. And then she died, and it was just…me."

Here, in the Neath, he had done the impossible: He had found a place to belong, surrounded each day by a group of people who genuinely seemed to like him for who he was. Or at least, for who they thought he was.

But all that was about to change. Courage or no courage, the odds were stacked too high against him now. Ollie couldn't fight a magical despot and a bunch of terrifying mutant beasts with nothing but good intentions. He had brought this trouble to their doorstep, and everyone knew it. And when the chips fell, as they unequivocally would, he'd be left alone. Again.

Ellora resumed walking, her long hair swinging against her back. He followed, reluctantly. He waited for her to argue, to tell him he was wrong. Instead, she asked a question: "Oliver, have you heard of the sailing stones of Death Valley?"

"The...what?"

"Death Valley is a desert. As you can probably guess from the name." Ellora stared straight ahead as she sauntered. "There is not much there, of course. Just sand, cacti, jackrabbits, lizards, and the like. All common enough, for a desert. But this particular desert, as it turns out, also has stones that slide. 'Sailing,' the humans call it."

His eyebrows dropped. "Like, all by themselves?"

"So it would seem. They leave trails behind them, in the sand. Some weigh hundreds of pounds. The Bricksiders have been puzzled by the strange phenomenon for millennia. Earlier generations blamed ghosts, alien life forms, and even magic." She wiggled her fingertips with a mischievous expression. "In your time, however, scientists have used something I believe you call 'time-lapse photography' to observe the stones' movement, and to observe the forces of the natural world around them."

"And?" Ollie asked.

"And, the scientists learned what we always learn: That nothing, not even a stone, exists alone in this world. The sailing stones appear to move on their own power, but of course, they do not. Like all of us, like everything, they are merely part of an intricate web of the natural and unnatural world. Forces act upon the stones, and change them. And the stones, inevitably, change those forces in turn."

Ollie gave her a sidelong glance. "Let me guess. I'm the stone in this story?"

"I don't know, Oliver," she said, grinning. "Are you?"

"No one calls me Oliver."

Ellora gave an exaggerated pout. "Not even your grandmother?"

"Not even my great-, great-, great-, great-whatever grandmother."

"All right, then, *Ollie*," she laughed, gathering her skirts and picking up her pace. "Have it your way. Storytime is done, and it is just as well. Let us see what stones we can slide, shall we? The day gets no younger, and I have scores to settle."

Scores to settle.

For some reason, Ellora's words made his stomach clench. He thought about the Reader, Widow Hibbins, passing judgement in her clean, white room: *Only what you owe.* About hundreds of prisoners languishing in tiny, filthy cells. About torture. Fighting pits. Swinging cages. About his own father, punished to the point of drooling unconsciousness.

So many scores, so much settling. When did it end?

Death Valley. He shivered. Of all places she could have referenced in that particular moment, he would have hoped for something a little less grim. Ollie watched his ancestor stride away, momentarily picturing stark sand dunes, cactus thorns, and rattlesnakes before hurrying to catch up.

———————— ⌒⌒ ————————

They walked until they reached the water's edge; from there, Mrs. Paget carried them over the lake to reach the island with two stumps. As Ollie had predicted, they encountered a protective shell preventing Ellora from landing. And as she had predicted, it took only a few moments of concentration for her to dissolve it.

Ollie was embarrassingly eager to share the story of his last visit here, and to show off his prowess at solving the stump-turning mystery and gaining them entry to the hidden staircase. Ellora humored him, though he suspected she didn't need his help.

When the narrow doorway appeared at the base of the freakishly large fern, Ellora gave him a withering look.

"Another tree? Really?"

"Sorry. It's just for a minute," he assured her.

Caw!

"You wait here," Ellora told Mrs. Paget, who ruffled her feathers amiably and settled onto the sand.

Once inside, they descended the stairs and approached the tiny attendant holding a tiny clipboard at the tiny podium. It was the same miniature man Ollie had encountered on his last trip.

"How many for entry?" the attendant asked. He gave no sign of recognizing or remembering Ollie.

"Two," Ellora answered.

As before, the claustrophobic, painfully slow cage elevator made its descent into the depths. As before, another attendant at the bottom yanked open the sliding accordion grate to grant them entry into the long, salty hallway, which was still lined with doorways on both sides leading to eerily empty rooms. And as before, Ollie walked straight down the hall to reach the towering, wooden door at the end. He was moving like a horse with blinders, his heart hammering, with one thought repeating in a manic loop:

Tera. Tera. Tera.

She was there, behind that door. Or at least, she had been there when he had left. What would he find there now? Had Michael Carmichael kept his promise? Was Herrick still there, puffed up and pissed off? Had he shrunk down enough to say whatever words he needed to say to free Tera and Meatball from their yellow-goo confinement? What if, what if, what if...

"What ifs" won't buy you groceries, his mother used to say. Whatever the hell that meant.

Ellora was standing behind him, though he barely noticed her. He was fixated on the door itself.

Grimshawe Laboratory.

The last time he was here, he had stared at the big, round knob and wrestled with an internal alarm of foreboding. He should have heeded his body's warning. Not long after, the unthinkable had happened: Herrick had crawled into Ollie's mind like a parasite and forced him to throw both Tera and Meatball into the vat of suffocating goo.

I'm not going to hurt your paramour—or your strange little pet. And neither is Mr. Carmichael, Herrick had said, a nasty smile slithering across his face. *You're going to do it for us.*

Ollie curled his lip. Then he lifted his foot and kicked open the door with a thunderous, wood-splitting crash.

Tera.

He ran.

Single-minded, he darted through the cluttered aisle of gizmos, bubbling pots, and parchment scrolls. He banged his hips and shins repeatedly against the tables as he navigated the turns, sweeping away impediments, barely noticing the clatter and breaking glass as the beakers, jars, and utensils hit the floor. His vision was a tunnel. *Tera. Tera. Tera.* If the lab techs were there, watching him, he didn't notice them. He didn't care.

The red door.

It loomed, ominous and enormous. Ollie did what he had watched Carmichael do, on that fateful day: He yanked on the door's handle with all of his weight, sliding it open, while the facing door slid in the opposite direction.

A ray of caustic radiation burst through the crack, brightening as the opening widened. Ellora shielded her eyes; Ollie did not. Instead, he plowed forward through the doorway, running, slipping, then running again.

Tera!

His body seemed to move without any help from his brain, pulling him in the right direction. He forgot about Carmichael, forgot even about Herrick, as he stumbled and sprinted.

There. There!

The tank was sitting right where he'd left it, still full of the yellow, bubbly goop. Two figures floated lifelessly below the surface.

Ollie fell against the glass, his hands slapping the surface.

A cry of overpowering relief escaped his throat. *Tera!* Her body was positioned exactly as it had been before: arms extended, face contorted into a frozen grimace, hands reaching toward the wall of glass. Behind her, Meatball floated like a matted, brown bowling ball, his platypus-like bill open and immobile.

"They're still here!" he shouted, spinning to face Ellora. "Holy shit! They're still here!" *Thank God thank God thank God.* His leaving hadn't hurt them. Or at least, it hadn't made things worse.

"Mmm," Ellora responded thoughtfully. She approached the tank, then turned to gaze around the room. "Yet it seems they are the only ones."

For the first time, Ollie took a measure of his surroundings. The cavernous, dark ceiling, the dripping candelabras, the work tables, the weirdly jutting angles of the walls.

The other tanks.

They were all empty.

A week ago, the massive vessels had enclosed dozens of indescribably horrible, mutant beasts: a wasp as big as a man, its head covered with hundreds of beady eyes; an entire school of piranha fused into one murderous machine; a two-headed hyena; a scorpion that was large enough to swallow a tricycle. Worse still, some of the tanks had contained humans. Witches, specifically, strapped to dialysis-like machines that had enabled George Herrick to drain and steal their magic.

Now, though, the tanks contained nothing. Nothing but gelatinous, lemon-colored goo.

Ollie's eyes darted. Where was Herrick? And Carmichael? He saw long shadows, spilled pools of mysterious liquids, and a back wall lined with empty cages. The Bunsen-burner fires on the work tables were long-since snuffed, leaving behind only dry, cold piles of ash. In the corner, he saw the small chest that had held the pea-shooter he'd used to inject the breathing-pellet into his arm.

But no men, puffed-up or otherwise.

"Krite!" he shouted, slamming his palm against the glass. "They're gone. They're both gone! Now what are we supposed to do?"

Ellora seemed startled at his outburst. "About what?" she asked.

"About getting them out!" Ollie sputtered, waving a frantic arm at Tera and the trog. "Herrick has to be here. He has to say the words. Some particular, stupid, friggin' words. It was a spell. That's what Carmichael said. He said Herrick locked them in there with a spell, and only Herrick can get them out. But he has to *be here.*" He pressed his closed fists over his eyes. "I stabbed him with the quill. The pufferpine quill. It was poison, and it made him puff all up, and then he couldn't say the words. So I...I told Carmichael. I told him...I threatened him. I told him I was going to the Brickside, and that I'd be back soon, and that he had to—"

"Ollie," Ellora interrupted, pressing a hand against his shoulder.

"I told him!" Ollie wailed. The panic mounted faster than he could reign it. His hands shook. "I told him he had to keep Herrick here, or else... Or else I'd...I'd... But now what are we going to—"

"Ollie!" she said again, louder. "Stop."

"You don't understand! They're stuck now! Like, really stuck! How are we going to get him back here? What are we going to go?" Ollie slid down to the floor, staring at his hands. His useless hands. They were shaking.

Ellora abandoned her efforts to calm him. Instead, she walked to the stairs that wrapped around the backside of the enormous, cylindrical tank. When she reached the top, she leaned forward to touch the invisible, yet solid, casing that enclosed it.

"Huh," she said, nodding. "Very impressive."

"Impressive?" Ollie retorted. The admiration in her voice was infuriating. What did she mean, *impressive?*

"Surprisingly so," Ellora replied. She remained stoic and calm—too calm for his liking—as she walked back down the stairway and joined him next to the base of the tank. Then she ran her hands along its surface, barely grazing the curved, thick glass.

Ollie watched from his slump on the ground, mute. Despondent.

Ellora pressed her fingertips together into a steeple. "Step back," she said.

"What?"

"Step back!"

The words snapped him out of his stupor, reminding him of the Sticky Wicket's similarly thundering command back at the Bunker Hill Monument. *Get out of the way!* He scrambled to his feet.

"Step. Back." Ellora's tone had morphed from businesslike to impatient.

Ollie did.

"Further."

Ollie did that, too.

As he watched, Ellora moved closer to the tank. She reached out her arm, slowly, and tapped one dirty and thoroughly chewed fingernail against the glass. A single, quiet tap.

Nothing happened.

Ollie held his breath. Then, when he thought his face might turn blue, a crack appeared. The fracturing was difficult to see, but not to hear: *Craaaaaaack.* Like the drawn-out snap of a whip.

He exhaled in time to see more cracks spreading across the tank's outer wall. Thin, at first, then wider. Faster. Louder. They spread and multiplied and burst with the noisy boom of Fourth of July fireworks until, finally, it all gave way: The entire seemingly indestructible pane of glass shattered into thousands of pieces, sending a spray of shards across the room.

Ollie and Ellora ducked, shielding their heads.

Seconds later, he peeked through his arms in time to watch waves of thick gelatin pour out onto the dirt floor. The sea of goop covered his feet, his shins, his knees.

And there, in the middle, two bodies—both now exposed to the air.

"Tera!" The force of the scream chafed his throat.

Ollie waded through the muck, pushing his legs with the useless force of a dreamer stuck in a recurring nightmare. *Can't...move...* She seemed miles away, until suddenly she wasn't. Suddenly, she was right there, at his feet.

Limp. Silent. Slimed.

Beside her, Meatball also sat motionless, his fur matted.

"Tera! It's me! Wake up! Please, please, please, wake up!" He dropped to his knees, making a splatting sound in the ooze. As he cradled her, her arms flopped hideously. Her head lolled to the side. Ollie looked up at Ellora with a tear-soaked face. "Help her!" he begged. "Please! You have to do something!"

"No need," Ellora answered, pointing.

He followed her finger and saw Tera's hand, moving slightly at the wrist. Then, her head lifted. Then, a cough.

Ollie's mouth dropped open.

A few feet away, more movement on the ground: The trog was shifting. His flippers seemed to be waving, slightly, though the motion was so meager that it was almost imperceptible.

The rush of relief was so sudden, so all-consuming, that Ollie had to fight the urge to vomit. *Holy shit. Holy shit!* She was moving! His heartbeat thrummed in his ear. "Babe, it's me! It's me! It's Ollie! Can you hear me?"

She tried to speak, failed, and coughed again.

"Tera! Are you okay?"

She stared up at him, then found her voice. "That depends," she croaked. "Are you going to try to kill me again?"

His laugh came out as choking sob. "I don't think so."

"Then, yeah, I guess I'll be all right."

Twenty-One

Ollie squeezed her torso too tightly, as though she might float away. He had not dared to imagine this moment—even now, he could scarcely believe it was anything other than a technicolor hallucination. He would have pinched himself if he had a free hand.

Tera Martinez. Holy shit, did she look good. Disgusting and goopy, but so, so good.

Her beautiful, tawny skin was hidden beneath a thick layer of yellowy tank mucus. Her hair, shaved at the sides and normally swooped up into a purple, gravity-defying wave, was flattened. He could sort of see the irises of her deep brown eyes, though those, too, were mostly obscured by the mess; Ollie tried to use his t-shirt to clear them.

"Here. Use this." Ellora was holding out a clean, white handkerchief.

"Thanks," Ollie said.

That was better. He managed to wipe most of Tera's face clean; she blinked repeatedly, still looking dazed.

To his left, Meatball was making strange hacking sounds. Ollie turned to see the trog floundering on his back like an upturned turtle. All four flippers waved uselessly in the air.

"You okay?" he asked Tera.

"I'm fine," she nodded, reaching for the handkerchief and gesturing toward the trog. "Go."

Ollie rose to his feet. His big sneakers slapped through the puddles of goo, which were starting to disperse. "Hey, there, buddy," he said, crouching down. With his fingers slipping like squeegees through the sopping fur, Ollie flipped Meatball over and set him gently on his feet. "There you go."

The trog blinked, stared, then shook. Hard. Clumped gelatin sprayed in all directions, though most of it seemed to splat directly onto Ollie's face.

He spluttered, trying to wipe the gunk with the back of his hands but only succeeding in smearing it everywhere. "Okay, I guess I deserved that," he said. "I'm sorry, all right?"

Meatball looked like he was poised to shake again; Ollie reached out to stop him. "I'm sorry," he repeated, his tone more somber. He tried to make eye contact, but couldn't quite seem to find the creature's eyes behind all the wet fur. Instead, he focused on the general area above his beak. "Buddy, you know I would never hurt you on purpose, right?"

When he got no reaction, he asked again: "Right?"

This time, Meatball shook more gently. Then he toddled closer and leaned against Ollie's ankle. He seemed too exhausted to make his usual leg-and-torso climb, so Ollie picked him up and held him like a football.

"Here, use this," Ellora said again. As before, she was holding out a crisp, clean handkerchief.

For the first time, Ollie stopped to wonder where all these handkerchiefs were coming from. She was like a dinner-show magician. "You going to pull a rabbit out of that pocket next?" he asked.

"A hare?" Ellora tilted her head. "Why would I do that?"

"It's—" Ollie lifted a hand. "Nothing. Forget it."

From the ground, Tera watched the exchange. Her eyes narrowed. "Who are you?" she asked Ellora. And not in a friendly way.

The young witch linked arms with Ollie. "I am Ellora," she answered, sounding pleased to be sharing the news.

Tera, on the other hand, did not seem pleased. Not pleased at all. As her gaze dropped to their intertwined arms, she looked suddenly angry enough to bite clean through a jumbo Jawbreaker. "Ollie, what's going on?"

It took him a minute to recognize the obvious: Tera was jealous. She saw Ollie linking arms with a young, beautiful woman and she didn't like it. This realization made Ollie feel inappropriately happy. *Very* inappropriately, considering the circumstances. He let himself enjoy the feeling for just a moment before jumping in to clarify. "She's...uh..." He looked at Ellora.

"She's what?" Tera asked, her voice hard.

"She's... I mean, we're...related."

Tera's brow furrowed. "Related, how?"

While Ollie tried to formulate an answer, Ellora let go of his arm and stepped forward. "I am Ollie's great-, great-, great-, great-, great-, great-, great-, great-, great-, great-, great-, great, great-grandmother." She smiled. "I think that's all of them. And you must be Tera. I have heard so many wonderful things about you."

Tera sat perfectly still in her puddle. She looked from one to the other. Finally, she said, "I think I must still have some goop in my ears."

Ollie sighed. "It's true. I know she doesn't look it, but..."

At that, Ellora swept a swath of lustrous hair from her shoulder and shrugged immodestly.

"It's true," he said again. "She's my...ancestor."

Meatball interrupted the awkwardness with a noisy sneeze—once, then twice—sending a spray of small globs all over Ollie's already soaked shirt. Tera had not taken her eyes off of Ellora; finally, understanding dawned in her expression. She tilted to lean on one elbow.

"You're a witch," Tera said, still staring.

"I am."

"One of the originals? Who made this place?"

"In a manner of speaking, yes."

Tera nodded. She looked thoughtful, then startled, then confused. "Wait. Wait a sec. If she's a witch, and you're her...descendant, then that makes you..." Her voice trailed off as she turned her line of sight to Ollie. Her expression flickered into something unreadable. Something...fearful?

"Not a witch!" Ollie blurted, jumping forward.

"He's a half-witch," Ellora clarified helpfully.

"What the hell is a half-witch?" Tera asked.

"In this case, my dear, it means that he is half-witch and half-human."

Ollie lifted his palms sheepishly.

"I see," Tera said. Her voice was frighteningly neutral. "So, there's a human...dad?"

"Not my dad!" Ollie yelped. "Just my great-, great-whatever. Way, way, way removed." He was waving a hand, pushing this theoretical person far, far into the past. As far away from the here and now as he could get him. Maybe, he thought, this would be the end of it. Maybe someone would change the subject.

No such luck. If anything, his excessive arm waving seemed only to stoke Tera's suspicions. "And who was this great- great-whatever?" she asked.

No one answered.

"Ollie?" Tera's tone held a warning.

Unable to say the words out loud, he finally just gestured vaguely, apologetically, at their surroundings. Herrick's tanks. Herrick's lab. Herrick's blood on the quill pen. Herrick's sick mind, and sick plans, and sick, cruel squander.

"Oh, no. Oh, you've got to be kidding me." Tera's face went pale. She scrambled to her feet and held out a hand, as though warning them to stay back. "George *Herrick?* George Herrick is your—"

"Far, far removed!" Ollie interrupted, waving the hand again. "So far!"

"Blame me, my dear," Ellora said, stepping in between the two of them. "Please. I made the lapse, in my youth, of falling for the wrong man. As young girls often do. In this case, however, the man happened to hornswoggle me, steal my magic, live for centuries, create a penitentiary where he could collect and store future soldiers, fool everyone into thinking he was dead, and spend all his time plotting the eventual overthrow of the underground and aboveground worlds." She grimaced. "Did I forget anything?"

"He also made mutants. And was really mean to them," Ollie muttered.

"Yes, and that."

"And forced Ollie to try to kill me and Meatball," Tera pointed out.

"Ah yes, and there was that, too."

An uneasy silence settled around them.

Finally, Tera folded her arms. "How did you two find each other?" she asked. Ollie was relieved to notice that her tone had softened somewhat. She looked at Ellora. "How did you know he was here, in the lab?"

Ollie cleared his throat. "I, uh, wasn't."

"Wasn't what?"

"I wasn't here. I...went to the Brickside."

"You went—? Wait. *What?*"

He nodded grimly.

"Why? How?"

Ollie held out his arm, stepping closer to show her the pellet protrusion under his skin.

"What the hell is that?"

He sighed and gestured to the nearby worktable and chairs. "Let's sit, huh?"

They did—all of them, with Meatball settled into Ollie's lap. And then, he told her the story. The whole story, starting with Carmichael's handy-dandy pellet gun and ending with the eruption of a monstrous, upside-down tree: Copp's Hill Burying Ground; the Novas at the aquarium; Laszlo's newest girlfriend; the teenage Salem coven; the Danvers homestead; the chain-smoking Sticky Wicket at the Bunker Hill Monument; Nell's betrayals; the seeds; the riddles; the terracotta pot; and, finally, Ellora, poking her head out of the tree's hollow like an overeager blonde raccoon.

"And then...we came here," he finished. "And Ellora got you out."

"So the WRC women—?" Tera's face flushed with relief.

"All home safe," he nodded. "As far as I know. Laz was taking them."

"Thank God," she said, clutching his hand. "You did it, Oll!"

He chewed his lip, not quite ready to celebrate. "I wasn't able to see Mr. B. It all happened too fast. And Nell... Krite. Who knows what else she—"

"Screw Nell," Tera interrupted fiercely, squeezing his fingers. "And I'm sure Mr. B is just fine. I'm sure Laz took care of it."

"I hope so." But unease gnawed at him; he would have liked to know for sure.

Tera sat back in her chair. "So, now what?" she asked.

"Now, we end this," Ellora said, rising to her feet. "We fight back."

"With what?"

"With these," the witch answered, holding up her hands, palms-out. Then she pointed at Ollie. "And with him."

When Tera threw him a questioning look, Ollie rolled his eyes. "She seems to think I have some kind of power. Which I don't."

"You do," Ellora corrected.

"Then why can't you tell me what it is?"

"Because I don't know. Not exactly. That's not how it works, my boy," she said. "Each of us must discover it for ourselves, when the time is right."

He snorted, thinking of all the near-misses and disasters he'd already encountered—and only narrowly escaped. If none of those times had been the "right time," then he couldn't imagine what was. "I don't have a gift," he insisted. "Apparently I borrowed yours for a while, but that's about it. Trust me."

Tera cocked her head. "Wait. Say that again."

"Say what? Trust me?"

"No, no... before that. You said, 'I don't have a gift.'"

"Yeah, so?"

"That's just..." She blinked rapidly. "I just..."

"What is it, dear girl?" Ellora pressed.

"It's just, when I was...in there..." Tera glanced over at the space where the tank used to be. "I didn't really see anything, or feel anything. It was just...blank, you know? Not bad or good. But every once in a while, I would hear something. Like, a weird poem. Repeated over and over. It was kind of like one of the Herrick notes. Well, not-Herrick notes, I guess."

Ellora looked at each of them in turn. "What is a not-Herrick note?"

"They're like hints, or clues. Someone leaves them for us, when—" Ollie stopped midsentence. "Wait! That was you, wasn't it? You left the notes!"

The young witch widened her eyes. "I'm afraid not. I do not know of which notes you speak."

"It was her!" Ollie said to Tera, excited. "It had to be!" He turned back to Ellora. "You left me all those clues on the Brickside, so I could find the seeds. Water, earth, air. Blah, blah, blah."

"That I did," she nodded.

"So you must have left the other notes, too! 'Lion's feet will dig! Good is bad, beast will bite! Hows and abouts, souls and mates!' All that stuff!"

"Lion's feet will dig?" Ellora asked. She looked perplexed.

"You didn't write the notes?" Tera asked.

The witch gave a small shrug. "I'm sorry. I would tell you if I did." She did appear to be genuinely sorry. And confused.

"And you didn't...talk to me? In my head? While I was in the tank?" Tera pressed.

Ellora shook her head.

Ollie gave a frustrated sigh. "If it wasn't Herrick, and it wasn't you, then who was it?"

"I don't know," Ellora admitted. "Perhaps if your Tera will tell us the message she received, we can learn more."

Together, they turned to look at Tera; even Meatball seemed to direct his beak in her direction.

Tera nodded and closed her eyes. She paused in concentration, then began to speak:

"The root of all evil
Is planted in pain,
watered by tears,
and tied with a chain.

A gift he will need,
an answer he seeks.
He will find both complete
where the sleeping one sleeps."

She shrugged as she finished. "That's it."

"You heard this, like, in your head?" Ollie asked.

Tera nodded. "Every once in a while, yeah."

"But nothing else?"

"Nope. That was it."

Ellora looked thoughtful. "A gift he will need, an answer he seeks," she said slowly, as though tasting each word.

"That must be Ollie, right?" Tera asked. "You just said he had a gift. Or he needs to find his gift, or whatever. So this must be a message for him."

"Mmm." Ellora seemed to agree.

Ollie leaned back in his seat, discomfort starting to grumble in his gut. He pursed his lips.

"What?" Tera asked him. "Is that ringing any bells?"

Instead of answering, Ollie chewed the inside of his cheek. It rang some bells, all right. Bells he didn't want rung.

"Oll?" Tera was touching his arm.

He blew out a gust of air. "The sleeping one?" he said pointedly. "The root of all evil?" There was only one person he could think of who met that description.

"Who? I don't—" Tera stopped, straightened. "Oh."

"Oh, what?" Ellora asked, looking at each of them in turn.

Tera cleared her throat. "It's, uh, Ollie's father. Matteo. He's in kind of a...sleeping state. Like a coma or something. No one really knows for sure."

"Oh!" Ellora's hands came together in a clap. "Well, this is wonderful news, is it not? Ollie can visit his father and learn what he needs to learn. He can find his gift at last."

Ollie folded his arms, noncommittal.

Again, Ellora glanced back and forth between them. "This is not wonderful news?"

"It's kind of...complicated," Tera said.

"Ah," Ellora nodded. "Well, most of the best things are."

Ollie gave a hard laugh that wasn't a laugh at all.

"In any case, it's not like Matteo can tell us anything," Tera added. "The guy can't talk. He's unconscious."

"Huh," Ellora said, rising to her feet with a determined hop. "Well, maybe he does not have to talk. The message says only that the answer will be found *where* the sleeping one sleeps, yes? Perhaps the location is all that you need." When her beam of enthusiasm was not returned, the witch pressed on. "I suppose we will soon find out, either way. Here is what I propose: You two, and the trog, will go to visit this place where the sleeping father sleeps, and learn what you can."

Ollie's mouth twisted at the thought. "And what are you going to do?"

"I'm going to see old friends," she answered cryptically. "And some others, too. We have many preparations to make."

"And scores to settle?" he said.

"Something like that, yes." Ellora's expression was sweetly, purposely, vacuous. She gripped his arms with sudden firmness. "But Ollie, you must promise to remember one thing, when you get there."

"What?" he asked, fighting the urge to pull away. Her abrupt intensity was disquieting.

"When you discover your gift, you must remember: It starts with you. Always, our power must start here." She let go of his arm to press a hand against her own chest. "And sometimes, it must end there, too. Do you understand?"

"Sure, yeah," Ollie said. He didn't, of course. But that hardly ever seemed to matter.

"Repeat it back."

"It starts with me," he recited.

The witch touched his chest and smiled.

"Uh, guys?" Tera interrupted, holding out her arms. Drips of yellow goo fell to the ground below. "Before we do all that...I don't suppose there's a bathtub in here?"

"Unlikely. But there is a lovely lake up top," Ellora said. She pointed toward the ceiling, then turned her finger to tap Tera's nose with an affectionate boop. "And there is also a lovely, overlarge crow who is going to be very happy to see you."

Twenty-Two

Something was dripping nearby. In another room, maybe. Ollie concentrated on the uneven sound: *Drip, drip-drip, drip, drip-splatter-drip.* Was it a leak in the ceiling? The splattering wasn't important, of course. Not right now. But he fixated on it anyway.

Next to him, Tera cleared her throat. "You okay?" she asked quietly.

Okay. Such a funny word. Was he okay? No, probably not. He was sitting next to his abusive, comatose father's bed, watching the man drool on himself, and he felt nothing. Nothing at all. Not anger, not pity, not disdain. Just...nothing. So no, he was probably not okay.

Drip. Splatter-splatter, drip.

The care center had a nauseating smell: *eau de* abandoned litterbox and mildewed basement, with a splash of cider vinegar. Ollie squirmed in his narrow seat. He had Tera's head resting on one shoulder and Meatball's entire body on the other: two comforting weights. They were both waiting for him to do something. But what was he supposed to do? Talk to the guy? And say what, exactly? *Hey, Pop. Long time no see. Thanks for beating the crap out of my mom. You're welcome, by the way, for rescuing you from Herrick's End. Not that you deserved it.*

Finally, he plunged ahead: "Well, Papa, I'm here. It's me. It's Ollie." As soon as he said it, he rolled his eyes. *Genius. Practically Shakespearian.*

Matteo, unsurprisingly, didn't respond. His watery blue eyes stared straight ahead, rimmed by sparse lashes, seeing nothing. He was not a handsome man, even before taking into account the cauliflower ear, bent nose, and pocked skin. Most of his body was covered by a burlap blanket; only his shoulders and arms were exposed to the air. *Hairy arms.* The sight of them spurred a Pavlovian, tightening response in Ollie's stomach and throat. He remembered those arms. Remembered those calloused hands, too. It might have been a long time ago, but Ollie could easily recall every last, awful thing they had done.

And that mouth... Here, today, it had settled into a loose droop. But back then, it was usually curled into a snarl. Smelling of cheap beer. Spewing spittle and cruelty.

For just a moment, Ollie forgot to concentrate on the dripping sound and let himself relive it all; the screams; the smashing glass; the blood; the hiding in closets and under beds. The deep insecurities spawned by a childhood on the run. He was glad his mother had dragged the asshole down here. Glad he had suffered. Glad he was suffering, still. The flashbacks settled in like a thick, choking fog.

He didn't realize he was trembling until the tickle of trog fur snapped him back to the present; Meatball was pressing his body, hard, against Ollie's neck.

He exhaled, pushing the murk away. "I'm all right, buddy," he said, scratching Meatball's head. "I'm all right."

Tera rested her hand on his thigh.

The *drip-drip-splatter* continued to emanate from somewhere beyond the door. Matteo gave a sleeping snort, which made them jump, but then fell back into his usual stupor. The long, uncomfortable lull dragged on.

Krite. Ollie bent his neck back and stared at the patchwork ceiling. What was he doing here? This was ridiculous. Maybe Matteo wasn't "the sleeping one" they were looking for. The cavern was a big place, after all. For all he knew, dozens of other evil, permanently comatose people were snoozing all over the islands. Maybe the message had been referring to the Warden. He was sort of sleeping, if you could call a Black Heart Powder perma-freeze a sleep.

Ollie sighed. His gaze swept across the floor, the surfaces, and the grimy nooks and crannies of the room. He was looking, he suddenly realized, for the key. The damn missing key. He was always doing that, lately. As if it might suddenly appear on a shelf. Gold and sharp, or silver and ornate, or studded with decorative stones. He would know it when he saw it, he supposed.

He hoped.

Three points make one key. So where was it?

Maybe if he found it, all this running would finally end. Maybe it would open a box labeled "ANSWERS!" He would insert the key in the lock, pop open the box, and fling the contents into the air joyously. Problems, solved. Just like that. He and Tera would embrace each other, jump up and down, and live Neathily ever after.

But there was no key. Not here, anyway.

Ollie rubbed his temples. This place made his skin crawl, from the smell to the noises to the weird, dangling, trinkets in the open window. What was that, a wind chime? It wasn't making any noise, pleasant or otherwise. It looked like a bunch of dried lakestars—the same kind that Derrin had collected to present as an offering to the Novas, way back when. The stars were studded with sparkly bits of metal and hung with twine, each swinging at a different length.

Dried lakestars. Dangling.

Something stuttered in his mind. Something...familiar.

"Look at that," he said to Tera, pointing. "What do you think that is?"

She glanced over and shrugged. "I don't know. A wind chime, I guess? Or just a decoration. Why?"

His eyeballs felt dry; he blinked rapidly. For some reason, Ollie found himself suddenly thinking about Damira. How strange. Why would he be thinking about the Salem Covenmaster now? He conjured her image: Silver hair. Lighthouse fingernails. Young, but also somehow old.

He saw her sitting at her transmogrifying table in Sweet Screams' secret back room. Watched her share bad news with an apologetic expression. Watched her shuffle the round, white cards, lay them onto the table, and scoot out of the way as they marched and fell off the end of the table.

And then…what? She had stopped him, when he rose to leave. She had handed him one of the blank cards. *They say you're going to need this,* Damira had told him. *Not now, but soon.*

Ollie snapped back to the present. He looked at Tera, eyes widening. "Remember how I told you I went to Salem?"

She nodded.

"When I was there, the Covenmaster gave me a card. Just a blank card. She said I would need it, eventually."

"Eventually?"

He turned his face toward the ceiling, trying again to recall Damira's exact words. "She said, 'You're going to need this, not now, but soon.' And then she said, 'Read the card when you see swinging stars, and not before.'" He pointed. "Swinging stars!"

In unison, they both turned to stare at the non-chiming wind chimes.

"That must be them, right?" he asked.

He watched Tera as she considered the question. Her dip in the lake had removed all traces of tank gunk and restored her usual, exceptional beauty: The purple swoop of hair had resumed its flounce, and her now-clean jumpsuit was just tight enough to compliment the curves of her petite, muscled body. She touched a finger to her lips. "Well, those *are* stars, sort of. And they're sort of swinging. Do you still have the card?"

Luckily, Ollie hadn't yet changed out of his Brickside clothes. "I had kind of forgotten about it, actually," he said, shifting to reach into his back pocket. His fingers latched onto something flat. He pulled the card out and held it up; as before, it was round, alabaster, and completely blank. They squinted at it, together.

"What are you supposed to do with it?" she asked.

"I have no idea."

"Huh."

He waved it back and forth a few times, like a Polaroid. Nothing happened.

"Try it over there," Tera suggested.

Ollie got up and approached the dangling lakestars. He held the card near them, under them, and over them. Then he waved it around some more.

"Nothing," he reported.

"Uh, Oll?"

He turned around. Tera was still sitting by the bed, staring at Matteo. "He's doing something," she said.

At first glance, Ollie didn't understand what she meant. His father was still supine, still dribbling saliva. But then he heard it: A puffing sound. Matteo was blowing air out of his mouth in rapid whiffs.

"What's happening?" Tera asked, sounding alarmed. "Is he waking up?"

Ollie squinted. "I don't think so. He's just...breathing louder."

And louder, and louder, with every passing minute. Matteo's strange exhalations were starting to remind Ollie of a pregnant woman in the throes of labor. *Whooo, whooo, whooo, whooo.* Even Meatball seemed to notice, spinning on Ollie's shoulder restlessly as the huffing continued.

"Should we get a nurse or something?" Tera asked, rising to her feet.

"I...I don't know."

"Why is he blowing like that?"

"I don't know!"

"Maybe he's reacting to the card?"

Ollie held it closer to the window for better light. "No, I don't think—" He stopped.

"What?" Tera prodded from across the room.

"I..."

"What is it? Do you see something?"

Ollie tried to respond, but found that he couldn't speak. He did see something. He saw...himself. The round card had turned glossy, and bright, and then, reflective. It almost perfectly resembled the makeup mirror his mom had carried in her purse all those years ago. Befuddled, Ollie scrutinized his own face: pale skin, light-brown eyes, round cheeks. He stared at his reflection...and then the reflection began to talk.

A quiet murmur. Flashes of teeth. Lips moving so fast they created a blur.

"Do you...hear that?" he whispered.

"Hear what?" Tera asked. She walked closer.

On his shoulder, Meatball leaned forward, reaching out with his two front flippers. Was he waving? Trying to reach Ollie's reflection?

The Ollie-doppelganger was still talking. Murmuring. The sounds and sentences hit Ollie's ears with pinpoint precision. His own face, his own voice, his own nouns and verbs and adjectives, traveling from somewhere else, some*when* else, to this very particular place and time. One word echoed more than the others.

One word.

One ridiculous, nonsensical word.

Ollie struggled to understand. Until, finally, he did. Like an oil field ruptured by a drilling well, the knowledge gushed its way into his consciousness with one messy, greasy spurt. He staggered backwards.

Matteo kept puffing. The other Ollie stopped talking. And the card emptied again into nothingness as Ollie let it fall from his fingers.

———————❧———————

That couldn't be right. Could it?

No. It couldn't be right.

"Ollie? What is it? What happened?"

"It...it talked," he managed.

"The card? The card talked? What did it say?"

"It told me...what my gift is."

"Oh?" Tera leaned forward, eager. "What is it?"

One word. But he couldn't bring himself to say it.

"Oll?"

He pressed his lips, chewed his lips, twisted his lips. Then, with effort, he opened them and pushed out all three syllables.

"Empathy." His voice was a flat whisper.

For a moment, Tera didn't reply. Then she asked, cautiously, "What about it?"

"That's my gift. My *power*." He gave that last word a hard edge. "Empathy."

"Oh!" Tera said, sounding surprised. And a little confused. "Like, you feel a lot of empathy?"

229

"No." The awareness had rushed in, and all of his energy had drained out. He turned to face her. "Like, I can force others to feel empathy."

"You can force—?" Tera stopped, scrunched her eyebrows. "I don't understand."

"That makes two of us."

And yet, there was no mistaking what his own reflection had told him. Nothing had been lost in translation. The message had been short, simple, and crystal clear: Ollie Delgato of the North End Delgatos possessed the rare ability to force others to feel *empathy.*

Which was the stupidest goddamn thing he had ever heard.

What kind of a power was that? He was a half-witch, for Krite sake! He wanted to shoot lasers from his fingertips! He wanted to levitate! Or breathe fire, or read minds, or make his enemies wither and die with a glance! At the very least, he wanted to feel a fraction of the swelling, thunderous power he had felt while wielding Ellora's borrowed ability. Just a few days ago, he had moved a poison pufferpine quill with his mind. With *his mind!* He had stopped Nell's freefall and lifted her hundreds of feet in the air using nothing but heat from his skin. Immense heat. Extraordinary heat.

Now, he'd be lucky to melt fish fat at a fire pit. But he could, apparently, make people feel bad for the fish? Abra-freaking-cadabra.

Tera reached out to touch his arm. "Look, Oll, it's okay. This is fine. It's—"

"Fine?" he interrupted, embarrassed to feel the sting of emerging tears. "Tera, this isn't fine. This is a disaster. We're screwed. *Empathy?* What the hell?"

"There must be an explanation," she said. Her voice sounded firm, but her expression betrayed her concern. "Maybe there's, like, a thing, or a person, that we'll have to—"

"Right." He bobbed his head maniacally. "Sure. Of course. You remember that story about the kid who defeated a psychopath's entire army using nothing but his trusty *empathy* strapped in his holster, right? No? Me, neither." He threw his hands in the air, defeated. "Jesus, I don't think I even know what it is!"

"What *what* is?"

"Friggin' empathy!"

"Oh." Tera thought for a minute, then replied: "It's kind of like sympathy. But sympathy is more of a distant thing, like when you feel bad for somebody because they went bankrupt, or got cancer, or whatever. You understand that it sucks, and you sympathize. And that's where it ends. Like pity, right? But with empathy, I think, you're going one step further. You're trying to put yourself in their shoes, to understand what they're really going through. Someone is feeling pain, or behaving badly, or whatever, and you're trying to understand why. Instead of keeping their pain at arm's length, you're, like, voluntarily choosing to feel it, too."

He stared at her, perplexed. "Why would someone want to do that?"

She shrugged. "To share the burden, I guess? To understand."

Ollie didn't reply. He still didn't get what any of this had to do with him, or with the impossible task at hand.

"Here," Tera said, turning his body to face hers. "Let's try. Try it on me."

"Try what?"

"Try your gift! Go head, make me feel empathy." She lifted her chin expectantly.

"What? No. Tera, this is ridiculous."

"C'mon," she prodded. "What else are we doing here? Might as well try. I'm going to think of someone I don't like."

"Like who?"

She gave him a sardonic look. "Take your pick."

He thought about it, then said, "Carmichael."

"Fine," she nodded. "I'm going to think about Carmichael, and I'm going to try to find some way *not* to hate him with every fiber of my being." She smiled sweetly. "Ready?"

"I guess so."

"Okay, here we go." Tera closed her eyes.

For a minute, Ollie just stared, as he so often did when he found himself able to observe her unnoticed. She was so pretty. So unpretentious. So fiery and brave and smart. "Finer than a frog's hair split four ways," as Dozer would have said. Gingerly, he reached out to touch her shoulder. Now what?

Feel empathy, he thought.

He waited for a spark to travel through his skin, or for a cartoony bulb to illuminate over her head. But nothing happened. Tera didn't move.

Ollie tried again, this time giving the thought a more commanding tone. *FEEL EMPATHY.*

He watched her, looking for anything out of the ordinary. Then he tried to send a few other, related thoughts into her mind: *Carmichael's not such a bad guy. He has good taste in clothes. He's a hard worker.* All lies.

If Tera heard him or felt a change of heart, she gave no sign. Finally, she cracked one eye open. "Did you do it yet?" she asked.

"I...I think so. Did you feel anything?"

She gave an apologetic half-shrug. "Sorry. I still hate the guy."

Ollie sighed. Of course she did. Carmichael was an inhumane moron and coward, and perfectly deserving of her spite. And Ollie's so-called "gift" hadn't done a damn thing to change that. What had Ellora been thinking with this wacko errand? Why did she send him here? Maybe she wasn't as clever or capable as he thought. He hated to admit it of his own great-, great-, great-whatever grandmother, but for a supposedly all-powerful witch, she sometimes seemed a little daft.

Her face shimmered into his mind unexpectedly, along with her words: *When you discover your gift, you must remember: It starts with you. Always, our power must start here. And sometimes, it must end there, too.* Then she had hovered a hand over her heart. *Repeat it back!*

And he had parroted her directive: *It starts with me.*

He must have been wearing an odd expression, because Tera shifted and asked, "What?"

"Ellora..." he began, haltingly. "She told me, 'It starts with you.' Remember? She said, 'When you discover your gift, you must remember, it starts with you.'"

Tera nodded.

A peculiar annoyance was making him squirm. What was with all these witches, always burrowing into his thoughts? Always making him flounder, and wonder, and summon all their scattered bits and pieces? The recollections were coming particularly fast and furious today. So fast and so furious that he felt like a drowning man getting pelted by too many life preservers as he splashed and flopped. Man overboard. Still, he had to admit: A life preserver was still a life preserver, even if it smacked you in the face.

It starts with you.

"Maybe she meant, like, a jumpstart," he heard himself say. "Like, I have to start with myself, to get the gift going." *The stupid, useless gift,* he chided himself, then pushed the thought aside.

"You mean, someone has to feel empathy for you?"

"Maybe. Or maybe...it's the other way around. I think I have to feel it. To force myself to feel it."

"Oh." Tera nodded. "Worth a try."

Ollie straightened, resigned. "All right. So I'll do the same thing. I'll think of someone I don't like, and then try to make myself...like them? Or feel bad for them?"

"I guess so, yeah."

"Who should I pick?"

Tera didn't answer. Instead, she flashed him a bemused expression with one raised eyebrow.

"What?"

"Seriously, dude?"

"What?"

Tera gave her head a slight shake. Then she thrust her arms out toward the bed.

"What? No! No way. I'm not doing that."

"Ollie, c'mon."

"No! It's...too much. Pick someone else."

"Babe, there *is* no one else."

"Of course there is! There are dozens of people I don't like. Hundreds!"

"Maybe. But is there anyone you hate more than him?"

He ran a hand through his curls, churlish. "No."

"Exactly. So what better way to jumpstart an empathy force?"

Ollie lowered his eyelids into slits. "Jumpstart a what, now?"

"That's what I'm calling it," she grinned. "Ollie's Empathy Force. Dun, dun, dun. Sounds cool, right?"

"Nothing can make this sound cool."

"Well, it certainly can't hurt." She pushed him gently toward the sleeping figure in the bed. "And neither can this. Go ahead. Just try."

Matteo was still huffing and puffing, though less forcefully. His breath smelled awful. Truly awful, like no one had brushed his teeth in weeks.

"Fine," Ollie muttered, grimacing. He lifted the trog off his shoulder and passed him into her waiting arms. "Here, take him for a sec." For Tera, he would try. Only for Tera. He was still muttering to himself, thinking vaguely about the concept of empathy and the unlikely possibility that he would ever feel anything like it for this horrible, hateful man, when he felt himself shudder.

All at once, his father, and the bed, were closer than they should have been. Tera was further away. He reached for her, touching nothing. The world was moving around him, readjusting, quickly and illogically. His hand brushed against the burlap blanket, but he could not feel it. His fingertips might as well have traveled through the open air.

He tried to pull away, to free himself, but found it was useless: He was like a paper clip fighting the pull of a magnet. Whatever this was, there was no stopping it—like the plunging upside-down tree, or the nesting witches' shove into the past, or the Reader's numbered tunnels at Herrick's End, or the original, all-consuming portal that had sucked him below the Freedom Trail all those months ago. He was falling. Then, as now, as always.

No.

Ollie gritted his teeth. His body came to an abrupt halt in midair, sudden enough to snap a neck.

No falling. Not anymore.

Frustration rose like acid reflux in his throat. This was it, then? The gateway to his "gift?" Fine. So be it. He might have the world's most pointless ability, but it was still *his* ability, dammit. His to control or reject. He was done being pushed over edges, tumbling and flailing and landing hard enough, often enough, to suffer semi-permanent bruises on his butt. Screw that. *You get what you get and you don't get upset,* his mother had chided when he was a child.

But he wasn't a child anymore.

Ollie concentrated, struggling against the dislocation. With effort, he pulled the spinning world into focus. His father's room was gone. Gravity was gone. He found his target on the horizon;

there, just on the other side of the luminous, swirling vapor. He didn't know what he was aiming for, exactly—only that his aim was true. He felt weightless, fearless. Extraordinarily certain.

No more falling.

Ollie fixed his gaze on the distant spot, and he began to fly.

Twenty-Three

Ollie managed to land on his feet, though he suspected it didn't really matter. This wasn't a real place, and those weren't even his real feet. But still. It was something.

As he took in his nebulous surroundings, he was bizarrely reminded of the Foucault Pendulum exhibit at the Museum of Science: a circular Aztec calendar on the ground, with a pointy pendulum swinging above it. Every once in a while, the pendulum tip would travel just far enough to knock over one of the metal bits that had been placed at even intervals around the circle—a precise visual representation of the earth's rotation. If you stood there all day, you could watch them topple in perfectly timed, perfectly even succession. Ollie had never stood there *all* day, but he had stood there long enough to find himself mesmerized by the pendulum's soothing, even swings. Like a giant hypnotist's watch.

Here, in this in-between place, he felt like that pendulum, standing and slightly swaying inside a circle. Instead of an Aztec calendar, he saw an amorphous cloud below his feet. And instead of metal bits, he saw a random assortment of objects floating in a ring all around him. The objects were not life-sized, but instead more like scale models, or toys.

One was shaped like a sandwich. Another, a door. Another, a small, orange tent. He scanned the shapes for a key, but didn't find one.

Somehow, Ollie understood that these things, these shapes, belonged to his father. They were his father's...what? Memories? Secrets? In truth, he knew next to nothing about the man, which he had always thought was for the best. But now, here... He wondered.

We cannot change what we cannot see, the witch Lizbeth had told him. And, he supposed, we cannot see what we refuse to look at.

Fine. Ollie steeled himself and studied the various objects. Perhaps not surprisingly, he decided to start with the one shaped like a sandwich: Two slices of bread with something indistinguishable squashed in the middle. It fell easily into his palm, releasing itself from whatever pressure had been holding it aloft. Ollie stared down at his outstretched hands, wondering if he was supposed to do something in particular.

The sandwich shimmered. It made a quiet noise that sounded remarkably like a sigh. And then, just like that, Ollie found himself looking up at the world from a small, young body. His father's body—though he wasn't a father yet. He was maybe five or six years old, with hands the size of maple leaves. Seconds later, Matteo's little-boy observations barged into Ollie's consciousness in a disconnected, crackling jumble.

Fluffernutter sandwiches. He liked them at first, all peanut-buttery and marshmallowy, like a day at the fair. But then, there were so many. Day after day after day: Fluffernutters. Some days he had them for lunch and dinner. Other days, he didn't get any dinner at all. So he learned, quickly, not to complain. And to peel off the crusts and save those for when he needed them. In the beginning, he hid the crusts under the mattress on the floor, but then the mice sometimes got to them first. So he started stashing them inside his grandfather's old beer bottles, instead, and wrapping the whole thing in a plastic bag.

Without warning, the sandwich zapped Ollie's hand, like a burst of static electricity. Startled, he dropped it. *Krite.* Instead of falling to the ground, the blocky shape floated back into its place in the circle, beside the other objects. Hands shaking, Ollie reached for another. A miniature door, complete with a tiny knob and framed, rectangular windows.

His parents were gone. No one told him where they went. He lived with his grandparents in a duplex on a busy street. Every once in a while he caught a glimpse of his mother, usually when she appeared at the front door. She always started out quiet, talking and begging, but then started yelling. Her hair looked all tangled and matted, like it hadn't been washed in a very long time. Her skin had red splotches. Her teeth were no good—kind of cracked, and black in spots. She twitched. Sometimes, Matteo's mother asked about him. Not often, though. It never mattered, in the end. No matter what she said or did, his grandparents would always send her away. Then his grandmother would cry.

Zap.

Again, the unpleasant sensation shocked Ollie enough to make him drop the offending shape, which seemed to be the idea. The door fell, floated, returned to the circle. Ollie watched it warily. Then he grasped the object beside it: a threadbare coat, small enough to fit on a mouse. Its zipper was unzipped.

At first glance, the coat was kind of cute. Ollie found himself hoping it might evoke a more pleasant memory—toys? a beloved pet? a winter adventure?—but had a strong suspicion he was going to be disappointed.

The other kids at school didn't like him. He didn't blame them. He never knew what to say, and his clothes were weird. Cast-offs from some bin his grandmother had found. Sometimes they had logos for out-of-town sports teams, which always made things worse. The one time Matteo wore a Yankees t-shirt he came home with a split lip. His grandmother tried to get the smell out them, but it didn't always work. The other kids didn't like him, and he didn't care. He hated them all, anyway.

Zap.

Next: a bottle. Ollie found himself hesitating. The memories were worse than the zaps, but both made him want to keep his hands to himself. Resolutely, he pulled the shape from its spot in the circle.

His grandfather was old, but also strong. Too strong, sometimes. Especially when he'd had a lot of beer and that other stuff in the glass bottles. That's usually when Matteo would hear stories about his parents. None of them made much sense, but they always ended the same way: With his grandfather yelling that he'd gotten "stuck" with Matteo. Sometimes, he slammed the bottles into the side of Matteo's head as he finished each one. Matteo learned to grow his hair long, to cover the—

This time, Ollie anticipated the electric shock, and dropped the bottle prematurely. Probably just as well. He wasn't dying to see how that one ended.

Next: a reclining chair. Like the other objects, it seemed so...ordinary. Still, just the sight of it gave Ollie a cramp in the pit of his stomach. He wrapped his fingers around it and let the hideous images flow.

His grandfather died first. Matteo wasn't surprised, and didn't miss him. But when his grandmother died, that felt a lot worse. And more scary. Even thought he was teenager by then, Matteo didn't know what to do. So he just left her body there, in the green recliner. He went to school, and he came home, and then he did it again. Maybe if he left her there, if he didn't tell anybody, then it wouldn't be true. But then one of the neighbors smelled it, and lots of people in uniforms came to the house. They took his grandmother out of the green chair, and they took Matteo away to live somewhere else.

Zap.

Ollie felt the vomit rise. It burned his esophagus as he forced it back down.

Next: A single-story ranch house, not much bigger than a Monopoly game piece.

The first house he went to had seven other kids, all crammed into two bedrooms. There weren't seven beds, though, so Matteo slept on the floor. He never thought he would miss his old mattress at his grandparents' house, but he did. The food was okay. There was usually enough. Not always, but usually. He would have stayed there. He wouldn't have complained—he would have just minded his own business, kept out of the way of the other kids, and stayed until he was eighteen. It was the best he could have hoped for. Then, the thing happened, and Matteo had to leave.

Zap.

The image faded to black.

Wait. What thing? Ollie searched the house shape, squinting, but heard nothing else. Brow furrowed, he reached for the next image: Another house, this time a two-story Colonial. Painted white, with black shutters.

It was eerily quiet. Ollie concentrated on the Colonial, examining the windows, the siding, the crudely depicted chimney at the top. But he heard nothing except hissing white noise. A firewall. Whatever was there, Matteo refused to remember. The realization made Ollie's blood run cold. This time, there was no zap. With shaking hands, he returned the two-story house to the circle and lifted the next object from its floating perch.

The orange tent.

Finally, eighteen. Free. Matteo worked under-the-table bussing restaurant tables and lived on the street at Mass-and-Cass with all the addicts. He wasn't an addict, but he liked that they never noticed him. He could sneak right up inside somebody's tent, stay the whole night, and leave the next day. A lot of times, he'd even find food, and beer, and he could take it right out from under their noses. That's how he saved up the money to pay for trucker school. He'd seen a billboard advertising Northeast Professional Tractor Trailer Driving School, and decided to go.

Zap.

Ollie was getting better, now. Each zap felt less like a punishing jolt and more like the matter-of-fact buzz of an oven timer.

The next object was shaped like an eighteen-wheeler.

He got angry, a lot. He didn't know why. And sometimes when he got angry, he did things that got him into lots of trouble. That's how he lost the first trucker job. But then he got another, and another one after that. Luckily, they needed truckers bad enough that they didn't ask too many questions. Living on the road was okay. He was always alone, racing down the highway, which made him feel like he was flying. Like Superman. Then the bad thing happened, so bad that Matteo couldn't get another trucker job—even after all that trucker school. He'd have to find something else to do, some other way to live. This made him feel scared, which he didn't like. So he just felt mad, instead.

Zap.

Ollie released the truck and watched it fly back to its spot. There were more objects, as yet untouched. They started to spin around him—or was he the one spinning? Either way, the shapes and colors blurred together, smearing into a kind of khaki smudge. He felt dizzy, sick. He suspected if he kept going, he'd soon enough find Matteo's memories of his mom in there. And of their marriage. And, eventually, of Ollie himself.

No more.

He had to get out of there.

Ollie closed his eyes, shutting out the murky circle. He thought about the real world, where his real body still stood beside a real bed. Where Tera waited and dried lakestars hung in a window and Meatball was no doubt snuffling around the floor looking for crumbs. He thought about that place, and he jumped.

Puffs of fog raced past his ears.

Fever tingled his fingertips.

He heard a voice, calling his name. So far away, then...closer. When he landed, he realized he had never actually left. Not physically, anyway. His tattered sneakers were still pigeon-toed on the dirt floor. The place still smelled like wormwalker urine and mildew.

"Ollie!"

Tera was shaking him. Her voice was sharp with alarm.

He blinked. Reached out to grab the bed's dilapidated, wooden headboard. Matteo was lying right where Ollie had left him, inert as a still-life painting. He seemed altogether unaffected by his son's intrusion into his mind.

"Ollie!"

"I'm okay," he said, holding up a hand. "I'm...okay."

"Jesus, where did you go? You looked like a zombie or something." She pointed down at Matteo's drooling face. "You looked like him!"

"No, no... It was just...temporary." *Thank God.*

Tera collapsed into one of the chairs, clearly relieved. "Don't do that to me!"

"I'm sorry," he said, meaning it. "I didn't know that would happen."

"What *did* happen?"

"I don't... It was..." Ollie stopped, shook his head. He looked down at Matteo in wonder. "I think I was inside his head. His memories."

"Oh!" Tera said. "With...your ability?"

He shrugged helplessly.

"Well? What did you see in there?"

Ollie felt his mouth twist. What *did* he see? Stinking, old clothes. Beer-soaked sandwich crusts stuffed into empty bottles. Split lips. A two-day-old—or three-day-old?—dead body, rotting in a green recliner. His stomach churned. "Nothing good," he answered dully. "He had a pretty rough go of it."

"Of what?"

"Of...life." That was the best way he could think to explain it.

Tera nodded slowly. She picked Meatball up from the floor and dropped him into her lap. "Empathy," she said, still bobbing her head. "That must be how you do it. You see what the person has been through. Not seeing from the outside, like sympathy, but *really* seeing it. From the inside."

Ollie shrugged again.

She was staring at him with a curious expression. "How do you feel?"

"I feel fine," he answered, surprised to learn that it was true. He shook his arms as if to check for damage. "It didn't hurt or anything."

"No, I mean, how do you feel...about your father? Now that you've seen that stuff?"

Oh. That.

Ollie considered the question. "I guess...I guess I feel bad for him. He had a really shitty life, like, from the get-go. All kinds of terrible stuff." Images flashed through his mind again: a screaming, abusive old man; a coked-up mom at the door; a cold and crowded homeless encampment; scurrying mice; inhospitable foster homes. He shivered. Still, none of those, he knew, were as bad as the blank spots. The things that even Matteo himself refused to remember.

Tera leaned back in her seat. She stroked Meatball's fur absently. "Huh. So, do you..." She paused, then plowed forward: "...forgive him?"

At this, Ollie snapped to attention. "What? No. No way."

She held up a hand. "Sorry! Sorry. I was just wondering."

"No way," he said again, shaking his head. "I feel bad for the guy, sure. Like I said, he had a shitty life. But my mom and I had a shitty life, too, when he was around. And it was all because of him."

And now his mother was dead, and Ollie would never have the chance to make things right. To give her the good life, the easy and happy life, that she should have had in the first place. His voice hardened. "Sometimes people deserve what they get."

Tera didn't reply. She continued petting Meatball's back until the trog jumped to the ground, approached Ollie's leg, and started to climb. Thirty seconds later, he flopped onto Ollie's shoulder with a grunt.

Ollie grinned, reaching out to tousle the creature's fuzz. "I think that's our cue," he said.

"Our cue to what?"

"To get out of here." As soon as he said it out loud, the urge to run, to flee this depressing place, became overwhelming. His skin was practically crawling with it. *Must. Get. Out.*

Tera looked unsure. "I don't know, Oll. I feel like we're missing something. You know?"

He did know. The damn key, for one.

But as Ollie stood there, woozy, the collective impact of the previous days caught up to him with the jolt of a fender-bender. He saw all of it, all at once: Crawling out between the graves. Skulking around the dark aquarium. Tossing and turning in a haunted Salem hotel. Enduring the full weight of Nell's betrayal, hundreds of feet in the air. Waiting, then searching, then rushing. Floating inside the miasma of his father's head. Puzzles and riddles and word play, again and again and again.

And of course, the tank. Shattering glass. Tera's body floating, flopping...then coming to a stop, perfectly still. The terrible, endless moment before she opened her eyes—when everything had hung in the balance, and the worst was still possible. Ollie suspected he would relive those agonizing sixteen seconds on a loop for the rest of his life.

Exhaustion buckled his knees.

What was he still doing here, in this disgusting room? He turned to face her, to marvel, again, at his good fortune. Tera was free, and unharmed. She was, miraculously, standing by his side once again. That was all that mattered.

Ollie reached for her hands. "Damn, I love you," he said.

She smiled. "I love you, too."

"I love you to the Brickside and back."

This made her laugh. "Yes, you certainly did."

He pulled her in tight, enveloping her body inside his oversized embrace. With a happy sigh, Ollie rested his chin on the top of her head. Then he uttered his second-favorite string of three little words: "Let's go home."

Twenty-Four

When Ollie had suggested they "go home," he wasn't referring to their literal home, and they both knew it. Technically, Ollie and Tera lived together—along with Meatball and Mrs. Paget—at her former artist's studio, which they had expanded into a cozy abode. But that wasn't where they were heading now.

"Home," in this case, meant Ajanta's house: the ramshackle, cobbled-together, leaky cottage where Ollie had found shelter during his time of most dire need, made his first Neathian friends, and, most importantly, whiled away countless hours getting to know, and fall madly in love with, Tera Martinez. Ajanta's place was as much a home to Ollie as the old North End apartment he had shared with his mom.

They approached the curtained doorway together, holding hands.

Ollie felt the flop sweat starting to trickle. He had a lot to explain about what had transpired since he'd seen them all last. None of them would appreciate learning about the life-threatening peril Tera had been in, down in that lab. And all of them were likely to blame Ollie for every bit of it. As they should.

Still, he had to tell them. He had to spell it all out, every preposterous and frightening detail, and enlist their help in what was to come. But where to start?

"Ready?" Tera asked.

He wiped his palms on his pantleg and blew out a gust of air. "Yeah, I guess—"

Ollie was interrupted by the sweep of the curtain in the doorway. A head popped out. And screamed.

It took him a minute to realize it was a scream of joy.

"You're back!" Kuyu jumped through the doorway and leaped at Tera, throwing out her arms.

Tera laughed and allowed herself to be tackled.

"Hey, Kuyu," Ollie said.

The girl's dark eyes flitted over to him. "Hey," she said. Her tone wasn't hostile, exactly, but it wasn't overly chummy, either. Kuyu was short, even shorter than Tera, with East Asian features and a thick crop of black curls.

Ollie shifted from foot to foot awkwardly. Kuyu had never liked him, right from the start. He supposed it didn't help that his arrival in the Neath had been the catalyst for Tera to inadvertently place herself in mortal danger—not once, but twice. Kuyu loved Tera like a sister. The guy who kept dragging her "sister" into calamity? Not so much.

Kuyu held Tera at arm's length, appraising. Then she swung an arm. "Well, c'mon in! Lots to do, right?" She turned and jumped back through the doorway.

Ollie and Tera gave each other curious looks, then followed.

Tera walked into the house first and was immediately mobbed.

First up was Derrin, Kuyu's girlfriend. Derrin was part of an underworld faction that Ollie had come to think of as "native Neathians:" Instead of arriving as a refugee from the Brickside, she had been born here—as had her parents, and many sets of parents before that. Her appearance reflected that long period of underground adaptations, including pale, nearly translucent skin, lanky limbs, and eyes that seemed much too big and wide for her face.

Ajanta swooped in right behind Derrin, throwing her arms around both women. Hovering somewhere in late-middle age, Ajanta had taken on a surrogate-mother role for many of the younger locals. Ollie liked to think he was one of them. She had an Indian accent, warm brown skin, and a long, signature braid that usually hung down her back. She was also an excellent cook and

Ollie's business partner: He and Ajanta shared a food cart in the Tea Party market that they had named "Ollanta's" in a mashup of their two names.

Ollie marveled at the sight in front of him. Just a few days ago, he wasn't sure if he'd ever see these women again. And here they all were: safe, together, and jubilant. But how long would it last? His friends didn't even realize they were living on borrowed time. And now, he had to be the one to tell them. Ollie swallowed past the lump in his throat. Then, he heard a voice to his left.

"Ah. All together again, yes?"

Ollie's neck swiveled. "Laz!?" Surprise and confusion made his mouth go slack.

The acrobat gave a dramatic bow with an outstretched, muscular, Lycra-wrapped arm. When he straightened, he pointed a finger. "You do the standing up of me! I am very upset."

"I do the...what?"

"The standing up of me. You tell me to wait for you at Fioretti's. So I wait, and I wait, and I wait, but..." Laszlo held up his palms with an accusatory expression. "No Ollie."

"Oh! I stood you up! Yeah, I'm...sorry about that. That was, uh—"

"Ah, is okay," the acrobat boomed, slapping a big hand against Ollie's arm. "Is okay! Was not your fault. Was tree's fault! Big, big tree!" Laszlo laughed.

Ollie cocked his head. "Wait, how do you know about—"

"Your very great grandmother tells me!" Laszlo interrupted, looking delighted. "She tells us all of the things."

Laszlo stepped aside to reveal a tall blonde witch standing behind him. Ellora smiled and shrugged.

"She is most beautiful woman, your very great grandmother," Laszlo added.

Ollie paused, his eyes narrowing. "Don't even think about it."

"What?" The acrobat held up his hands again. "I am just saying. She is beautiful, yes?"

Ollie started to reply, but only managed an "oof" as someone tackled him from the side. Derrin, then Ajanta. The sudden rush of affection made his face flush. They were happy to see him—really, genuinely happy. Not as happy as they were to see Tera, perhaps, but he'd take it.

They began to talk over each other.

"'Bout time, you big idiot."

"Did you bring us any food?"

"Mister Meatball! How've you been, little guy?"

All the jostling threw the trog off-balance; he dug his claws into Ollie's shoulder and emitted a series of deep grunts.

Unlike the others, Kuyu said nothing, and she kept her hands to herself. But Ollie could swear he detected a reluctant admiration in her gaze.

He stepped back, glancing at Ellora. "So, you told them everything?"

"I did."

"Like...*everything*, everything?"

She pinched his cheek and winked. "Everything, everything."

Ollie and Tera exchanged surprised glances. *Well, damn,* he thought. Since no one had yet attempted to strangle him or toss his half-witch ass into the fire, he had to assume they were taking it well. Either way, he was exceedingly grateful that he didn't have to be the one to spill the beans.

Laszlo stepped forward. "I have good news," he told Ollie. "Is about your friend. Your Mr. B."

Ollie's stomach clenched. "You saw him?"

"I did. He is doing good. Fine. Your Mr. B is back, selling the coffee and the cakes. He is doing the limping, but not too much." Laszlo demonstrated with a slightly wobbly couple of steps.

Mr. Bonfiglio, back on his feet? Doling out lattes and greeting the neighborhood with his usual, sunny smile? The relief sent Ollie staggering. He reached out to the wall for balance.

When Ellora spoke, all heads turned in her direction. "Did you find it?" she asked. "What you were searching for?"

Then all heads turned back to him. Everyone, it seemed, wanted to know the same thing.

He shifted uncomfortably in the glare of their attention. "Sort of, yeah."

"You have a power?' Kuyu asked, sounding skeptical.

The answer, technically, was yes. So he nodded.

"And?" Ajanta asked. "Can we use it? Against Herrick?"

Embarrassed, Ollie had no idea how to answer. When an awkward silence descended, Tera broke it with a confident reply.

"Of course we can," she told the group. "He's just trying to...figure out the details, that's all."

He cringed. Having a lame gift, he decided, was worse than having no gift at all. And having Tera lie on his behalf was worse than both.

"What is this power?" Ajanta pressed.

It was a good question. A great question. Ollie could only wish he had an equally great answer. How was he supposed to describe this newly acquired, semi-ridiculous ability in a way that would make any sense? "It's...uh, kind of hard to explain," he said.

Another clumsy silence followed.

Ellora threw him a quizzical look, but didn't press.

"He just needs a little time, that's all," Tera interjected. Again.

This, clearly, was not the news the gathered group had been hoping for. Ollie could almost hear the waves of concern and disappointment in the silence that followed. Seconds later, they all began talking at once. Ollie could only make out snippets.

"What's the timeline in the—"

"Yeah, but I think we should—"

"What about Nikki? Has anyone asked—"

"...two more times, max."

"Well, you would say that. There's no—"

"...if they're coming, they're coming, right?"

"She told you it was—"

Ollie's head swiveled from face to face. And then, bizarrely, he began to laugh. He tried to fight it, at first, but then gave in. Harder and harder he laughed, belly jiggling, until tears had started running down his cheeks and everyone in the room had turned to stare.

"What's with him?"

"Maybe we should let him rest."

"You okay, big man?"

Ollie wiped a cheek and held up a hand. "I'm fine," he said. "I'm sorry. I know it's not... I just..." He threw an arm over Tera's shoulder. "It's just really good to see you guys, that's all. Really, really good."

⸺⸺⸺◦∞◦⸺⸺⸺

After a full meal, a change of clothes, and a quick conversational catch-up, Ollie retreated to the small yard behind the house. Despite the welcoming warm-and-fuzzies of the reunion, he needed a few minutes to himself.

He needed to think.

The ground beckoned; he flopped onto his back and stared up at the cavern's glowing blue ceiling. As always, the longer you looked at it, the more it seemed to undulate. When he'd first arrived in the Neath, Ollie had assumed that the dome above his head was one solid, gleaming chunk, only to learn later that he was actually looking at millions of slimy, phosphorescent invertebrates known as wormwalkers.

How easy it was to be fooled.

Laszlo had told him so, right from the start. He'd sent Ollie down the Freedom Trail with one piece of advice: "*You must trust this, and this,*" the acrobat had said, tapping Ollie's head and heart. "*Only those. Forget your eyes. Your eyes do not know as much as those. Yes? All right?*"

Still, reality had intruded—time and time again. Three-dimensional, physical, undeniable reality.

Ollie couldn't deny that his eyes had seen the massive mutants in Grimshawe Laboratory. Terrifying and ready for battle. Paranormal weapons of mass destruction.

His ears had heard the thinly veiled threats. *George Herrick, of the Salem Village Herricks. That is my name. And soon, the whole world shall speak it.*

He had touched the blood spurting out of the old man's neck. Smelled the stench of inhumanity in every laboratory tank. Tasted the danger in every rolling cloud of deep-cavern fog, all of it as bitter as a bite of raw ginger root. There was no mistaking the threat they all faced now, today, or the very real possibility that it would swallow them whole.

His senses were screaming. *Give up,* they told him. *It's already over.*

Shut the hell up, he answered, fists clenched.

Hadn't there been something better, all along? Something more reliable? His mother had called it a "bone-gut feeling," which had always sounded a little creepy to him but now sounded just about right. It was there, ever-simmering, in the marrow. Mute and relentless. It was every part of himself that he tried to ignore.

Like a marionette lifted by a string, Ollie stood.

Earlier, he had rummaged through Ajanta's shelves to find a piece of parchment and some charcoal pencils. Now, he pulled them out of his jumpsuit pockets and carried them to the yard's small, wooden picnic table. He sat down. He thought about the vast, empty cavern thrumming all around him. He made a map in his mind of all the dark corners he had visited. Remembered, one by one, all the unlikely people—and unlikelier creatures—he had met. It all came together like a mental scrapbook, or an outline for a first-day-of-school assignment: *My Deranged Summer Vacation*. The faces and places tumbled.

He thought about seedpods and shadows and promises and regrets, all the way back to a tiny, round window in a cell at Herrick's End.

Ollie quieted the screaming.

He let his bone-gut feeling lay him low.

And then, he began to write.

Twenty-Five

Ollie was still scribbling—and mumbling—when Tera and Ellora found him there, at the table, some untold amount of time later. Charcoal-pencil smudges covered his hands and face.

When he noticed their approach, he reached up to wipe his cheek with a sleeve.

"You're only making it worse," Tera said, smiling. She used her thumb to make her own effort at cleaning the residue from his skin. Then she looked down at the parchment. "Whatcha doing?"

"Thinking," he said.

"Ah." She exchanged a worried glance with Ellora and sat down beside him. "Listen, Babe, your grandmother and I were thinking..."

"Great-, great-, great-," he said, distracted, looking back down at the paper.

"Right." Tera flattened her hands onto the wooden planks of the tabletop. She seemed to be gathering her patience. "Your great-, great-, great-whatever grandmother and I were thinking, maybe you should come back inside. Everyone's getting a little bit, uh..."

Ellora seated herself across from them. "Everyone wants to know the plan," she said, fixing Ollie with a pointed stare.

"Mmm," he nodded.

At this, Ellora sighed. "Ollie, I need to know what happened. When you went to see your father, I mean."

He looked up. "Tera didn't tell you?"

"Not my place," Tera responded, holding up her hands.

"Was it made clear to you? Your gift?" Ellora asked.

He felt a scowl forming and tried to neutralize his expression. "Yeah, it was clear, all right."

"And?"

He answered only after a prompting leg pat from Tera. Even then, the word was barely audible. "Empathy," he muttered.

Ellora blinked. "Empathy?"

"Yep."

She looked at each of them in turn. "What about empathy?"

"That's it. That's my power." He used finger quotes around the word. "I can force people to feel empathy."

"Oh!" Ollie's very-great grandmother leaned backwards, clearly searching for an appropriate response. "Well, that's... My goodness. I've never heard of that one."

"That's a great sign," he said sarcastically, looking at Tera as if to say I-told-you-so. "You really didn't know?"

Ellora shook her head. "Only that it was extraordinary. And that it was yours alone. So it is when a farm goes fallow, and the seasons blend into stories. As we know, the soil does not—"

"Please." Ollie interrupted, pressing his temples. "Stop. No metaphors. I can't take it."

The young witched popped her mouth closed, abashed. Then she asked, "This gift of yours... You tried it? It works?"

Ollie really didn't want to talk about this. Not now. Well, not ever, but especially not now. But since he seemed to have no choice, he answered in a moping monotone. "I tried it on Tera, but nothing happened, and then I remembered you said that thing about 'it starts with me,' so I did that, and it worked."

Ellora was listening carefully, nodding. "You felt empathy for...?"

The sulking continued. "For my deadbeat dad. Oh, joy. I saw things in his past that made me feel bad for him, okay? End of story. It's a useless, stupid power, and it's not going to help us at all, so can we just move on?"

Ellora ran a hand through her long hair, looking thoughtful. "We don't know that it's not going to help. At this point, we don't—"

"I know, okay?" Ollie interrupted again. He was being rude, but didn't care. "It's pretty freakin' obvious. If we want to get through this, we're going to have to focus on...other things."

The witch drummed her fingers on the wood tabletop, which didn't make much of a sound. Finally, she pointed at Tera. "Let's try it again," she said.

"Try what again?"

"Your gift. I suspect you jumpstarted it adequately with your own...experience. Now we must see if you can wield it against others."

Ollie's mouth fell open. "I'm not going to 'wield' anything against Tera! Krite! Are you out of your mind?"

"I am sorry," Ellora corrected, holding up a hand. "That was a poor choice of words. What I meant to say is, let us see if you are able to manifest your gift in other ways. *For* other people. I'm sure Tera would agree to be our first *cavia porcellus*, as they say." She looked across the table with a pleasant, questioning expression.

"Cavia...what?" he asked.

"Sure," Tera shrugged. Her knee was bouncing. "Whatever will move this along."

"No," Ollie said. "This is a waste of time, I'm telling you. There's no point."

"Even the most winding river has points if you know where to look," the witch responded, flashing her usual knowing smile.

Ollie threw up his hands. "What does that even mean?"

"It means, let's get this show on the road," Tera said, turning to face him. She lifted one leg and flung it over the picnic table's bench, straddling it. "C'mon."

Momentarily speechless, Ollie blew out a gust of air. "Fine," he said. "Fine." He spun sideways, mirroring her body position on the bench. For a few awkward seconds, they stared at each other.

"Go ahead," Ellora prodded.

"All right, all right." Ollie wiped his palms on his pantlegs and cleared his throat. Go ahead, *what?* What exactly was he supposed to do? Stare intently into her eyes? Shoot "empathy force" out of his fingertips? He suddenly wished fervently for his trog's comforting presence on his shoulder, but Meatball was still in the house with the others.

"What am I looking for?" Tera asked. If she was nervous, it didn't show.

"Uh, you'll probably see...objects. Floating. You'll pick them up, one at a time, and see stuff."

Her eyebrows lifted. "What kind of stuff?"

"Like, the person's memories. Experiences. That kind of thing. You'll feel a little zap when it's done, and then you'll move on to the next."

She nodded. "Will you be with me?"

Ollie lifted one shoulder. "I don't know." He hoped so.

"Welp, I guess we'll find out." Tera wiggled her fingers in a "gimme" gesture and blew a lock of purple hair away from her eyes.

He nodded. "All right. So, I think you need to think about Carmichael."

"Do I have to?" she quipped.

He gave her a stern glare.

"Okay, okay, fine." Tera smiled and closed her eyes. "I am now thinking about Michael Carmichael. Lucky me."

Ollie looked across the table at his very-great grandmother, who nodded in encouragement. He reached out to touch Tera's arm, then realized to his surprise that it wasn't necessary. His physical body had nothing to do with the process at all. He wasn't sure how he knew that, but he definitely, suddenly did.

Instead, he concentrated on her breathing. Watched her chest rise and fall. He fell into the pattern with her, then rode it like an ocean wave into her consciousness. The wave crashed, and there he was.

In her head.

He was standing right beside her in the same soupy, nebulous place he'd been before. But she couldn't see him. Tera was squinting at her surroundings, at her own hands. She looked right through him as though he wasn't there.

Ollie spied the circle of hovering shapes in the distance, looking remarkably like the one he had stumbled across in his father's consciousness. Were all consciousnesses the same, then? Or was this just Ollie's brain's interpretation of what was actually there? He watched Tera look left and right before she, too, seemed to notice the floating objects. She walked toward the circle, then stepped inside. She appeared to be more curious than afraid.

One by one, Tera reached out to hold and study the objects—Carmichael's objects?—just as Ollie had done with his father's. From this distance, he could just barely make out the shapes—a coffee mug? A horse? Maybe...a lawn mower? He couldn't see what she was seeing, or gauge her reactions. After an indeterminate amount of time, Tera left the circle and walked back toward him. Could she sense him there? He wasn't sure. He did know that her journey was finished. She was ready to leave. And so...he studied her breathing pattern again...dove inside of it...and pulled her out.

They both gasped, as though they'd been underwater.

They were still sitting face-to-face, straddling the bench. Ellora was still seated across from them. The ceiling above still cast an indigo glow on the cavern below. The air still smelled vaguely of wet soil and pan-fried fish. Nothing, and everything, had changed.

Ollie reached out for her hands. "Are you okay?" He studied her for signs of injury or distress.

"I'm fine! That was...pretty cool, actually." Tera shrugged and grinned.

He looked at Ellora. "How long were we gone?"

"You were not gone at all. Your body remained just as it was. But I would say you seemed to be...entranced for perhaps a few seconds."

"A few *seconds?*" Ollie responded. He and Tera looked at each other in bewilderment. "That can't be right!" Tera said.

"Ah, but it is." The witch looked at her curiously. "What did you see, my dear?"

"Umm..." Tera searched her memory. "I saw a lot of bad things, basically. Things that he had been through. It was rough. All that stuff he does? The fancy clothes and all the...?" She waved her hands around to indicate razzle-dazzle. "He's just compensating, I think. For all the things that were taken from him."

Ollie nodded. That made a strange sort of sense.

Tera looked at Ellora. "So is that how it's supposed to work? Like, you only see bad stuff about the person's life?"

"I honestly do not know," the witch admitted, her British accent slowing to a ruminative crawl. "I suspect you see only what you need to see, whether good or bad." She tilted her head. "Did it work? Do you feel...empathetic?"

Tera considered this. "You know, I actually do. More than I did before, anyway. Don't get me wrong: I still think Carmichael is a total ass. But now I get *why* he's an ass. So that's something, right?"

Ellora brought her hands together. "That *is* something," she agreed. "Something wonderful!"

Tera gave an enthusiastic nod of agreement.

"Uh, no," Ollie broke in. "Not wonderful. Mildly interesting, maybe. A parlor trick, at best." A parlor trick that nobody wanted or needed and would forget about as soon as they left the parlor.

"On the contrary, dear Ollie," Ellora said, her eyes sparkling. "This is transformative."

He couldn't help but snort. "Transformative? So she feels bad for the guy? Who cares? What difference does it make? How does it help us now?" The questions, of course, were rhetorical. He knew as well as anyone that the answers were "none" and "it won't."

Ellora reached across the table to grasp his forearm. "Every gift has two sides, my boy. You are only seeing one."

He threw each of them a skeptical glance, then said, "Okay, I'll bite. What's the other one?"

"Empathy goes both ways, does it not?" the witch asked. "We can feel empathy for someone who has wronged us, it is true. But we can also feel empathy for someone we have wronged."

Ollie was still baffled. "And?"

Ellora folded her hands together and took a deep breath. "My dears," she began. "It is simple, really. Let us take the example of an abuser. Any random, unrepentant prisoner at Herrick's End. Imagine for a moment that you could force that person to feel empathy for their victim. Force them to understand the pain that they had inflicted."

"But that's what the Reds used to do, at the prison," Tera interrupted. "All that eye-for-an-eye crap. The torture. We got rid of all that."

The witch nodded. "Of course. In this case, however, we are not talking about the physical world. We are talking about a deeper consciousness, in which the body itself is not harmed. Instead, the abuser would be compelled to comprehend the exact experiences and feelings that their victims suffered at their hand. To truly absorb it. What do you suppose that kind of power could do?"

"I...I don't know," Ollie said.

"But you do know, don't you?" Ellora asked. She studied his face. "If perpetrators could understand, really understand, the painful results of their actions, if they were forced to metaphysically live through the experiences in exactly the same ways that their victims did, I imagine that those perpetrators might...perpetrate a little less. Don't you think? Maybe they would even stop committing heinous acts altogether."

"I guess so," he replied, shifting on the bench.

"Now, imagine that you could affect that change not with just one or two offenders, but with whole groups of them," Ellora said.

"Maybe with a whole prison-full!" Tera added, leaning forward.

Their eyes slid to the horizon, where the Herrick's End tower loomed in the distance.

"Yes," the witch said, tapping the tabletop. "Exactly. That is a tremendous power, Ollie. In the normal course of things, people are generally unwilling to admit wrongdoing, or to see the truth. It is human nature, I suppose. But you, my boy, could *force* them to see it. To feel it. To understand the effects that their actions have on the people around them. That is bound to transform their actions, but it is also bound to transform their hearts. How could it not?"

"Oll, this is incredible," Tera said. Her voice was weirdly breathy. "It's like a...a reverse Blackheart Powder! This could change everything. *You* could change everything!"

Ellora was studying him like a specimen, which made him squirm. Then she said, "I think I am starting to understand why George Herrick feels that you are the only one who can stop him."

Ollie furrowed his brow. "Why's that?"

"Because our friend is in the revenge business, is he not? And what is the one thing that is sure to snuff the fires of vengeful thoughts?"

Tera sat up straighter. "Empathy!"

Ellora nodded, pleased.

They were both looking at him in the strangest way. Ollie struggled to read the expressions on their faces. Caution, maybe, and admiration? Yes. Cautious admiration. It was giving him the creeps.

Instead of replying, he focused his attention on a glowbug that had drifted into the air above the picnic table. The insect's light changed colors every few milliseconds, creating a blurred, zigzagging line of varied hues as it darted up, down, and around in circles. Ollie found himself temporarily mesmerized by the rainbow gleam.

It reminded him, of course, of his fluttering Sticky Wicket friend. Minus the grouchiness and hairy chest.

For one brief, illogical moment, Ollie could swear the glowbug was...looking directly at him. It had paused its flight, hovering still and silent. Its spindly antennae waved. And then, the tiny creature turned itself upside down and right-side up again, all the while keeping its miniscule eyes locked onto Ollie's face.

Just like the seal had done, at the aquarium.

Ollie shivered.

A raspy voice intruded, suddenly, from somewhere far away.

It must be you.

The memory rose with surprising strength: A peregrine falcon on Boston's Greenway Carousel, speaking. To him. It had been a delusion; a side effect of exhaustion and unease. Hadn't it? An inanimate statue, coming to life. Ruffling its feathers. Convincing Ollie to go in search of his missing friend. To leave his old world behind.

Yessss. It must be you.

The sound ricocheted down his ear canal, making him dizzy.

Finally, the bug meandered away, leaving a trail of light and color.

Ollie shook his head. This was getting out of hand.

"Look," he said, folding up his handiwork and stuffing it into his pocket. "That's great. It's all well and good. And maybe you're right, for the future, or whatever. But we aren't going to *have* a future if we can't stop Herrick from destroying this place and enslaving every last one of us. I saw the mutants he was keeping in those tanks. Most of them were as big as a goddamn Chevy. With teeth. And claws. And worse. Trust me, when those things come marching around the corner, the power of *empathy* isn't going to do shit."

When Ellora started to respond, he held up a finger to stop her. "Uh, uh, uh. Don't even say it. Do *not* talk to me about winding rivers, okay? I don't care about winding rivers. I am so sick of riddles and...and...and *psychobabble.* It's all just—"

His rant was interrupted by a loud noise behind him. A crash, followed by a hubbub of raised voices inside the house.

Without speaking, all three of them jumped up from the table and ran across the yard.

Twenty-Six

Ollie was last through the door. As he stepped inside the one-room shack, the first thing he noticed was a toppled shelving unit in the kitchen area. Several glass jars had smashed in the fall, leaving Meatball to slurp up all the spilled and scattered seasonings. Two other trogs, one black and one white, had joined him.

The second thing Ollie noticed was that the room was more crowded than it had been when he left.

He felt a surge of elation—and disorientation—at the sight of his former cellmate, Dozer, standing near the spilled mess. A self-described "Southern Black redneck," Dozer was smart, funny, and tougher than a two-dollar steak, as the man himself might say. Without Dozer, Ollie never would have survived his time in Herrick's End. That was just the plain truth of it. And then Dozer had saved his neck yet again when they'd had to navigate their way through the shadowy underbelly of Carmichael's House of Unnatural Wonders.

What was Dozer doing here?

Ollie barely had time to finish the thought before he noticed a looming shape in his peripheral vision. Turning, he peered over the group to see a huge man standing near the back wall. Though the room was dark, there was no mistaking that silhouette: It could only be Leonard. But what was *he* doing here?

The brawny man waved over the others' heads, a slow grin spreading across his face. Dazedly, Ollie waved back.

Ollie had first met Leonard, a.k.a. "The Mallet," in the fighting pits at Herrick's End, where the Warden had matched the biggest and angriest convicts against each other in cruel, and often rigged, bouts. Leonard was certainly big, but he was hardly ever angry: On the contrary, his ominous appearance belied an unusually kind and gentle temperament. After Ollie and his friends had ousted the Warden, Leonard took over as the facility's new "Superintendent of Operations" and didn't waste any time making Herrick's End a better, more humane place. And now, he was…here? In Ajanta's house?

"What are you guys—" Ollie began to ask the obvious question, then stopped. His mouth went limp as he clocked the other new arrival in the shack. This man was shortish. Smooth-skinned. Bedazzled and posh. He wore a ridiculously tiny top hat on his head and an expression of abject terror.

Michael Carmichael.

Michael friggin' Carmichael?

Tera had noticed him, too. With the ferocity of a crocodile, she lunged.

Panic ensued. Tera's hands were already around Carmichael's neck before the shouting and shoving could start. One by one, the others tried to pull her away as the simpering man struggled and choked. Tera's words were mostly lost in the uproar, though Ollie was able to make out phrases like "tear you in half" and "weaselly little piece of bat shit" and "son of a" something or other.

So much for empathy, Ollie thought. Anger and astonishment roiled through his limbs, rendering him all but useless to do anything but watch Tera give Carmichael the assault he most definitely deserved.

With difficulty, the others managed to unpeel her hands and pull her away, kicking and screaming.

"Please!" Ajanta was saying. "Please! Calm down!"

"Calm down?" Ollie asked, still stunned. *"Calm down?* What the hell is he doing here? That monster tried to kill us!"

Meekly, Carmichael coughed and raised a finger. "Well, technically, I—"

"Do *not!*" Tera hollered at him. "Do *not* speak! You understand me?"

The group separated the three of them like boxers in a ring: Ollie and Tera in one corner; Carmichael in the other. Slowly and clumsily, they managed to explain that Carmichael had fled Herrick's clutches once and for all and was now trying to reform his ways. While Ollie had been on the Brickside, Carmichael been working with Ajanta and the others to try to come up with a way to free Tera from the tank. He'd been unsuccessful, of course. But he had tried.

Tera snorted and struggled. Leonard stood behind her, maintaining a strong grip on her arms.

Ajanta gave Carmichael a pointed look. "Michael, is there something you wanted to say to Tera and Ollie?"

"And Meatball," Ellora added, her smile placid.

"And Meatball," Ajanta agreed.

Carmichael shifted. He took the jaunty top hat off his head and held it in his hands. Staring at the ground, he mumbled, "I'm sorry."

"You're sorry?" Ollie gave a sarcastic laugh. "You're *sorry?*"

"I really am," Carmichael said, a little louder. Finally, he raised his eyes. "It was a shitty thing to do. I mean, yeah, I was pissed. And you *did* steal all my Unnatural Wonders. Just saying. And Tera *did* trick me with all that grog and—"

With a strangled cry, Tera tried to advance; Leonard held her in place.

"Is this supposed to be an apology?" Ollie asked, looking from face to face in irate stupefaction.

"Sorry, sorry!" Carmichael held up his hands and the hat. "What I'm trying to say is, it was a shitty thing to do, to help Herrick, and I'm sorry. He's an asshole, and I was an asshole for helping him. Okay?"

Neither Ollie nor Tera replied.

Ellora laid a hand on Tera's arm. "Remember what you saw, out there," she said quietly, gesturing toward the back yard and the picnic table. "Remember what you know."

Tera grunted.

Ollie folded his arms into a tight pretzel.

The others looked on in confusion, not understanding Ellora's instruction. Finally, Dozer draped an arm around Olie's shoulder and fixed Carmichael with a stern stare. "Never you mind, Roomie," he interjected in a drawl. "We're helping this here fella see the error of his ways."

"He's even starting a new refuge, for the lab creatures," Kuyu said.

When Tera's face erupted in fresh fury, Derrin added: "A nicer one! Not like the other place. No cages. This one is open and, like, lush. Green. Lots of room to roam and swim. Like a...sanctuary, I think they call them on the Brickside. We're helping him make it." She folded her arms in satisfaction.

"I'll keep an eye on him, Tera," Leonard told her, his huge biceps twitching as he glanced at the cowering Carmichael. "You don't have to worry about that."

At that, Tera's body reluctantly relaxed. She looked at Ollie, who shrugged, though his jaw was still clenched tight.

"Fine," she spat. "Fine. But I swear to God, one slip-up, and—"

Carmichael waved his hands in surrender again. "I understand."

"Do you?" Tera asked. "Because if this is some kind of trick, or if you hurt those animals again, you're gonna need a jar to hold all the body parts I'm gonna carve off you. And you won't like the part I cut off first. You get me?"

Ollie's eyebrows shot up.

"Damn, girl," Kuyu said approvingly.

Carmichael took in her expression, and the looming figure of Leonard behind her, and swallowed. "Yes. I understand."

Ollie's ears were still roaring. As the room's conversation floated around him, he heard something else, too. Not-so-distant words, in a not-so-distant laboratory. *"Wakey, wakey!"* Carmichael had said. He'd been poking Ollie, prodding him awake. Smiling his slimy little henchman smile as Ollie realized what horror had befallen Tera and Meatball in the hideous tank. Then, he'd tried to force Ollie into a tank of his own. *"Let's go,"* Carmichael had growled. A small, small man, drunk with temporary power.

And now, here he was. Right here. Just a few feet away. And the others expected Ollie to do what, exactly? To just...forgive him? Not a chance.

Ollie stared at Michael Carmichael, imagining the terrible things he might do to him. (After Tera got there first, of course.) The vengeance already tasted sweet and tart, like the tang from a perfectly baked batch of lemon Anginetti. He thought and he thought, and he stared and he stared, until something incredibly odd began to happen. Carmichael seemed to be...growing. Getting taller. Was he just standing up straighter? Standing on his tiptoes?

No, he was definitely *bigger*. Like, by inches.

Startled, Ollie squeezed his lids shut. The spell was broken. What was the matter with him? Seeing things, again? He stumbled a few steps back, resolving to ignore Carmichael—at least for the moment. Revenge, unfortunately, would have to wait.

Dozer's voice broke through the fog. "From the sound of it, you been busier than a long-tailed cat on a porch full of rocking chairs," his friend said. "What do you need us to do?"

Ollie lifted his chin to gaze around the room. It was the most remarkable sight. All of his friends, gathered. Watching him. Waiting, presumably, for him to say something. "So, you're all here...to help?" he finally asked.

Heads bobbed.

"Duh," Derrin said, tucking a chunk of stringy, fair hair behind her ear.

"Whatever you need, Oll," added Leonard. His deep voice boomed against the walls.

Even Carmichael nodded, though not as emphatically.

Kuyu stepped forward and addressed the group. "Whatever we're doing, we'd better do it soon," she said, a note of warning in her voice. "Me and Derrin just got back from a scout. The grog is starting to boil over out there."

"Out where?" asked Tera. "What do you mean?"

"Like, everywhere." Kuyu waved an arm. Her jumpsuit was askew, leaving the collar too tight around her neck. "It was already getting bad, the past few days. Weird shit happening, word spreading. Everybody jumpy. But now, it looks like people are just flat-out starting to panic."

"About what?"

"You know, about...Herrick."

At this, Ollie stepped forward. "Wait. Wait a sec." He cast an accusatory glare at the gathered group. "How can word be spreading when the only people who know about it are right here in this room?"

No one immediately answered, though he did see quite a few pairs of eyes drop toward the floor. Dozer, in particular, wore a decidedly sheepish expression.

"Dude," Ollie said to him. "Who did you tell?"

"No one!" Dozer answered quickly. Too quickly. Then he amended his reply. "Well, mostly no one. Just...Floyd."

"Floyd!" Tera burst out. "So then Nikki knows, too. And if Nikki knows..."

"If Nikki knows, then everybody knows," Ajanta finished soberly.

Ollie sighed. Nikki and Floyd were the husband-and-wife team behind one of the most popular shops at the Tea Party. They had their fingers on every pulse in the Neath, and their noses in every bit of back-corner business. Not that it mattered, he supposed. If Dozer had told someone, then the others probably had, too. The toothpaste was out of the tube.

"Eh, forget it," Ollie said, leaning against the wall in weary resignation. "What's done is done. What else did you guys hear?"

Derrin and Kuyu reported their findings in a breathless rush: Strange noises heard in strange places. The Warden moving ever-so-slightly in his chair at Blackstone Park, prompting concerns that he was breaking free of his curse. The crows suddenly flocking and cawing together in agitated clumps. The Novas reporting an odd sighting out on the lake: a new island, formed seemingly overnight, mostly hooded by a thick overhang of dark fog. Was that where Herrick was keeping the creatures?

"Everybody is starting to freak out," Kuyu said.

Derrin nodded in agreement. "They can feel it."

"Feel what?" Ollie asked.

The two women looked at him with dual expressions of bemusement.

"*It,*" Derrin said, and everyone in the room nodded. No further explanation needed.

It. The big "it." Ollie rubbed an ache in his shoulder. Weirdly, he knew exactly what she meant. He could feel it too, couldn't he? He'd felt it ever since he'd arrived back in the Neath. A change in the air. A thickening.

Herrick had broken out of his laboratory bubble, taking all the pent-up, caged malevolence with him. He'd cracked the shell. And in doing so, he'd upended the delicate, 360-year equilibrium of the cavern, sending shockwaves of unrest from one end to the other. The proverbial shit was hitting the proverbial fan, and somehow, everyone knew it.

Even time itself felt snippy, as though its fuse was running short. *Tick, tick, tick.*

Ollie's jaw clenched. Then he asked, "Did anyone mention...a key?"

Derrin lifted her brows. "A key? No. Why?"

"I just..." He faltered.

"What kind of a key?" Ajanta pressed.

"I...I don't know, exactly. It's nothing. Forget it." He and Laszlo shared a fleeting, nervous glance. Ollie was immediately sorry that he'd brought it up. If they knew that he was supposed to have the key, but didn't... The low-grade panic in the room would surely swell into something more apocalyptic.

Leonard, blessedly, chose that moment to weave his way to the center of the group, near the fire pit. "So, what now?" he asked Ollie. "This Herrick guy probably knows you're back. He's probably looking for you."

"We should talk to the witches," Kuyu interjected.

Ollie shook his head. "They won't help," he said glumly. "They're 'nesting,' remember? I was lucky I got them to talk to me at all."

"Maybe they're done," Dozer suggested.

Ollie opened his mouth to answer, but was interrupted by Laszlo.

"We need to do the storming of the brain," the acrobat said. When everyone turned to stare at him, he asked, "What?"

"Oh, you mean brainstorming?" Ajanta asked.

"Yes! This. This is what we need."

"What we *need* is a miracle," Kuyu grumbled in response. She dropped her butt onto one of the logs next to the fire.

"There must be some way to…I don't know, stop him," Ajanta said, though she seemed to be mostly talking to herself. "Before he causes too much trouble. Maybe…capture him, somehow?"

"Capture him?" Dozer laughed outright at the suggestion. "Ain't no way to capture a guy like that. We got to kill the sonofabitch. And the sooner, the better."

"Agreed," Derrin said, sitting down next to Kuyu.

"Dozer is right," Ellora said. She was tying her long blonde hair into a knot at the back of her head, as though prepping for action. "Herrick won't make it easy. Then again, that might be fun." Her smile was small, but wicked.

Ollie found himself repulsed by her eagerness. "What do you mean, fun?"

"I mean, I have been waiting a long time for this day. A *long* time." Ellora looked around at others, who were uniformly nodding. "That man humiliated me, stole from me, and destroyed everything that I hold dear. I did not come all this way, and make this many sacrifices, to watch him do so again." She folded her arms over her chest. "No. We will finish this, once and for all. We will finish *him*."

"Maybe throw in a little of that torture he loves so much, too," Kuyu added.

The others murmured in agreement.

"Wait a sec, here, guys," Ollie said. "Just wait. We don't need to sink down to his level to—"

"I think we do, Oll," Tera interrupted, though she didn't look happy about it. "He hasn't left us much of a choice."

"What? C'mon." Ollie looked from face to face. "There's always a choice, right?" But who was he to talk? Hadn't he just been indulging his own delicious lemon-cookie thoughts of vengeance just a few minutes before? He glanced surreptitiously over at Carmichael, who seemed normal-sized once again. Whatever Ollie had seen, or thought he had seen, it was gone.

Dozer ambled up to stand beside him. "Boy, you've been running all over hell's half-acre after this fella. You know better than anyone what he done, and what he's still gonna do. You think he's just gonna give up? Change his ways? A fox don't leave the henhouse when it's still full of hens." He adjusted his eyepatch and shrugged. "Sometimes you just got to get in there and drag that damn fox out by the feet."

"Well, no, of course I don't think he's going to *give up*. I'm just saying that—"

But the exclamations were already coming loud and fast.

"If there was a place to—"

"Y'all, we got to slap him to sleep, then slap him for sleeping."

"I know, but it's also—"

"...down at the docks?"

"Drown him!"

"...I'd like to get a hold of..."

"Maybe one of those tanks of his..."

On and on and on it went. The din of their voices, angry and scared and volatile, made Ollie take a step back. It was like watching a loaf of bread rise in the oven, too fast and too high. Burning the crust to an ugly char.

"Stop," he said.

The schemes and propositions continued to ring out, each more mercenary, more vile, than the last.

"STOP!"

All heads turned to look in Ollie's direction. The clamor came to a sudden halt.

"I get it, okay?" He held up his hands. "No mercy. I get it."

The group grumbled their assent.

He reached into his pocket for the scratchy parchment, then paused as his finger brushed the edges. This was it, then. *No mercy.* Clenching his jaw, he pulled the paper from his pocket.

Not just a paper.

A plan.

And they all knew it. The room had gone so quiet that the unfolding of the dry parchment seemed absurdly loud, like the crunch of popcorn in a hushed theater. Finally, it was open and flat. Ollie looked down at his scribbles, though he needed no reminding. The writing had been merely a formality, in the end. He knew what they had to do.

The charcoal smudges shimmered slightly in the torchlight, almost as though the glowbug had left a residue of radiance behind. Prisms danced in Ollie's vision as he centered his weight on both feet. When he began to speak, he imagined his voice leaving similar multicolored trails in the air.

"Leonard," he began, looking up at his friend. "We'll need to move all the prisoners. Can you do that?"

The big man blinked. "Like, all of them?"

"All of them, yes." Ollie used the most emotionless tone he could manage.

"Move them where?"

"I don't know. That's why I'm asking you."

Leonard paused. "We do have an island where we take them for outings, sometimes."

"*Outings?*" Dozer gaped.

"Yes," Leonard nodded. "You know, as part of the new 'happier, healthier' regimen. We're trying to give them as normal a life as possible."

Dozer stared at him. "Well, hell's bells. I didn't get no outings."

"And that's exactly why we've made changes," Ajanta said, touching his arm. "So no one else will have to suffer what you suffered."

Dozer grunted.

"Anyway, we usually only take a few at a time," Leonard continued. "All of them? I don't know, Oll. That's going to be pretty tough."

"But can you do it?"

Leonard inhaled, then pursed his lips and nodded. "If I have to, yeah. I'll figure something out."

"Good," Ollie said. He turned to Ajanta. "Can we get our hands on gardening tools?"

"I..." She blinked, seeming disoriented. "How do you mean?"

"You know, like shovels, trowels, spades. That sort of thing."

Ajanta's eyes rolled toward the fabric ceiling as she considered the question. "I could probably find some down at the tea party. Or out at the rhizer fields. How many?"

"As many as we can get. One for each of us here, and then some."

She ran a hand along her shiny braid, then nodded. "I'll take care of it."

"Thanks." Ollie's next request was directed at Ellora. "All those seedpods, on the white tree. Are they still there?" He could still picture them hanging in their multitudes, shaking and dancing at the end of each branch.

Her face betrayed her surprise. "I suppose so, yes. I don't see where they might have gone."

"And we can pick them? Like, off the tree?"

Ellora nodded, haltingly.

"Great. I'm going to need you to go gather them up. As many as you can carry. Maybe Tera can help?"

The two women looked at each other and linked arms.

"Sure," Tera said.

"What about us?" Kuyu asked, her tone sounding almost accusatory. "What are we supposed to do?"

Ollie turned toward the fire to face her. "We're going to need a tunnel dug. A wicked big one. And we'll need it fast. Can you guys manage that?" He gestured to encompass Kuyu, Derrin, Dozer, Carmichael, and Laszlo in the request. "You'll probably need to get some help. And some equipment. But I'm guessing you know a guy, right?"

Kuyu lifted one shoulder. "We know lots of guys."

Ollie had no doubt.

He could feel the atmosphere of panic and anger in the house starting to subside, though the uneasiness remained. At his feet, he heard a snort. Ollie glanced down to see Meatball looking up at him, his little beak opening and closing in sharp, quick flaps.

Ollie grinned. "Don't worry, buddy," he said. "I've got a job for you, too."

Meatball snuffled in reply, settling with a plop against Ollie's ankle.

"Ollie, my friend," Laszlo said, sidling up beside him. His face was drawn and apprehensive. "What is this plan? We will have to be careful, yes?"

"Actually, no," Ollie answered. "We're going to be the opposite of careful."

Tera and Laszlo looked at each other in bewilderment.

"What is opposite of careful?" the acrobat asked.

The opposite of careful, in this case, was returning to the scene of the crime. And facing down the devil. And listening to your bone-gut feeling at the expense of anything logical or reasonable or life-preserving. It was risking everything, and everyone, without any speck of certainty that the outcome would be anything short of total disaster. The opposite of careful was idiocy. Recklessness. Insanity.

But Ollie didn't say any of that. Instead, he said, "You guys just do your parts, and we'll be fine."

"And what about you?" Tera asked. Her eyelids lowered in suspicion. "Don't tell me you're going to rush off and try to find him."

Ollie crouched, picked up a short stick, and tossed it into the fire. *It is no accident you are here, our dear, young giant,* the witch named Bert had told him. *It is your kismet. Kizzee, kizzee, kaleidoscopee! Your divine providence!*

Bert had been nuts. "Touched," the other witches had called him.

He'd also been right. And hadn't Ollie known it all along?

He threw another stick and watched the sparks fly in all directions before answering. "I won't have to find Herrick," he told Tera. "He'll find me."

"How do you know?"

"Because I'm the one he wants."

He waited for someone to argue, or protest. But no one did. Like him, they all knew the truth: If you wanted to catch a big fish, you were going to need some big bait. And there was no plumper, juicier bait in all of the Neath than Ollie Delgato. Hell, he'd practically been training for the role his whole life.

Kizzee, kizzee, kismet.

He'd tried running. He'd tried forgetting. He'd tried pretending. And still, he had ended up here.

Now, it was time to try something else.

Twenty-Seven

Ollie was on a swing.

The world drifted past his peripheral vision in a gentle, gauzy blur: *Back, forth. Back, forth.* He pumped his legs easily, at first, then with more effort, broadening the expanse of the pendulum. Soon, he found himself ten feet off the ground at either end.

Hypnotized in flight.

The swing's seat was constructed from a single plank of wood and suspended by narrow chains that reached all the way to the top of the open courtyard. Impossibly high. As Ollie swung through the vast, open space, he thought again about the Foucault exhibit at the museum: so precise. So tenacious. Swaying from side to side in glorious, perpetual oscillation, knocking down every hapless metal peg in its path. *Bam, bam, bam, bam, bam.*

Ollie never thought he would be in this place again—at least, not voluntarily. But now that he was, he was glad to be in motion.

A wrecking ball in search of a target.

A mover of wind.

Not too long ago, Ollie had spent countless hours staring into this same, cylindrical expanse through the bars of his cell window. Watching umpteen rounds of brutal Knockdown tournaments down at ground level. Then, the next day, making his way down there with the rest of the Labor Force crew to mop up all the blood, sinew, and broken teeth spattered all over the dirt floor.

Herrick's End. His hell-away-from-home. And this courtyard had been the bleak, beating heart of it all.

In many ways, the space hadn't changed. As before, it stretched forty or fifty floors high, the hollow center of a cavernous, crumbling tower. Its curved walls were still punctuated by prison-cell windows, all unevenly sized and shaped. The windows had afforded the Herrick's End captives a view into the dim courtyard— their only view to anywhere, as it turned out. Hands, clinging to bars. Desperate faces, squashed and peering. Today, however, the windows were empty. The prisoners were gone. Leonard had ferried them all away.

The air was still thick with the stench of unwashed bodies and overflowing pisspots. The crumbly walls were riddled with cracks, black and green molds, and seeping, coppery water. End to end, top to bottom, the structure remained ominous, dreary, and crude.

And yet...some things had changed. For the better.

Someone, or many someones, had clearly tried to brighten the place up since Ollie had seen it last—all part of Leonard's "happier and healthier" regimen, if he'd had to guess. Two other swings, currently empty, hung on either side of Ollie's. Several cheery fish tanks housed mini-schools of zebra lakeslugs, hammerface eels, and indigo blennies inside their glass walls. And the majority of the courtyard's floor space had been newly devoted to gardens, most of which seemed to be sprouting rows of neon-bonnet mushrooms. The crop, he knew from experience, had a bitter taste. But the mushrooms' gleaming colors—some white, some green, some yellow, and some lilac—more than made up for it with an astonishing, bioluminescent glow.

That, and a handful of blazing torches, had combined to cast Ollie in a sort of prismatic spotlight as he swung.

And swung, and swung.

He gripped the chains and leaned back, staring up at the distant ceiling. His overgrown curls flopped on and off his forehead with each sway. *Back, and forth. Back, and forth.* Other chains had once hung from that ceiling, of course. Bigger chains. Chains that had raised and lowered a Knockdown scoreboard.

During their foolhardy escape, Ollie and his friends had grabbed hold of those chains, smashed that scoreboard, and raced up through the open air in a wild and death-defying ride to the tippety top of the massive tower. It had been a last-resort attempt, and it had worked—until they ran into even worse trouble than they had faced on the ground.

He closed his eyes, trying to recall the details. But all he saw were frantic, indistinct splotches—more like a burned-up filmstrip than a memory. Was that really just a few months ago? It hardly seemed possible. That Ollie had been a different person. That time had been a different time. Or had it? This was the Neath, after all. What had Dozer told him, when he'd first arrived? *Time moves different down here. It messes with you. Changes you.*

Maybe now was then, and then was now, and Ollie was always exactly where he was supposed to be. *Who* he was supposed to be. Maybe this swing, and this neon-mushroomy spotlight, was all there ever had been. And why not? It made almost as much sense as gravity tugging the skin on his face each time he dipped toward the ground.

Back, and forth.

Back, and forth.

He was almost fully reclined—legs outstretched, head tipped backwards—when he heard it.

A tap, tap, tapping. Then, a scritch, scritch, scritching. Then, footsteps in the gravel.

Ollie pulled himself upright on the swing.

He had suspected he would hear them before he saw them. This place—its vibrations and whispers and tangs—were as familiar to him as a recurring nightmare. He turned his head, echolocating their position like a bat.

They were approaching the doorway.

He stopped pumping his legs. The swing's momentum slowed, but continued. A little lazier, a little lower. *Back, and forth.*

Ollie felt a prickle on the back of his neck. A prickle that could mean only one thing.

Seconds later, George Herrick emerged.

———————⸎———————

The last time Ollie had seen him, the old man had been distorted by the effects of the pufferpine quill's poison, swollen up into something that looked more like a hot-air balloon than a man. But as Herrick poked his head through the doorway, he appeared to have shrunk back down into normal human size. Dark hair with a white streak. Arrowhead-shaped beard. Thick, circular glasses. Black lab coat. Slow, deliberate gait. Tapping cane.

Step, tap, lean. Step, tap, lean.

The sequence triggered an entire universe of hatred in Ollie's abdomen.

Step, tap, lean.

Herrick advanced, slowly, through the opening. He took in the sight of the swing and smiled in amusement. Their eyes locked. For just a moment, no one else existed. It was just the two of them: "The Doc," looking studious and intense, and Ollie, swinging closer and further away, closer and further away, with what little propulsion remained.

Finally, Ollie skidded his feet along the dirt floor, bringing the motion to a stop.

George Herrick nodded his acknowledgement. Then he stepped out into the open courtyard. He wasn't alone.

First, it was just the Reds. Still wearing the vividly colored jumpsuits that had given rise to their nickname, the former prison guards swarmed through the arched doorway and formed an uneven line behind their commander. Twenty or so. Maybe more. It was hard to distinguish one from another in the glut of crimson.

Ollie's neck prickled again. He kept his butt rooted on the swing.

Herrick continued to advance. *Step, tap, lean. Step, tap, lean.* The Reds followed. This made some room behind them for yet another line of minions: the rearguard. This last group, however, had a harder time fitting through the door.

Not humans. Not even animals. Ollie's skin numbed into a clammy chill as he watched each of the lab-created, tremor-inducing mutants bend, twist, claw, fight, and squeeze their way through the opening. Some, he recognized from the lab:

A five-foot wasp, yellow-and-brown striped, with a head coated in hundreds of beady eyeballs. Wings lined with actual, metal razor blades. Dangling legs. As it flew through the doorway, it emitted buzzing and clicking sounds that echoed throughout the chamber.

A creature that might have once been a wolverine. Now, it looked like a freakishly large weasel without its fur—just bulging musculature wrapped in translucent skin. It snarled as it entered the courtyard, baring overly long, blackened teeth.

A massive jellyfish, the size of a porta-potty. Blue and slimy, with tentacles reaching and sucking at the open air. No face. No eyes. The aquatic creature was somehow living—and breathing?—without benefit of water, propelling its bulbous body along the ground like a snail.

Others he had never seen, and could never have possibly imagined:

A too-big Komodo dragon, stomping hard enough against the ground to kick up clouds of dirt. Its scaly skin had been modified to include a coating of thorns. When it shot out its tongue, the prehensile organ unfurled into improbable length and ignited sparks against everything it touched.

A giant crow. Like Mrs. Paget and other others, except this one had white feathers, two heads, and multiple beaks poking out of both faces. A Salvador Dali painting brought to repulsive life. As it entered, it cawed and pecked at the walls, the ground, and the other mutants in a kind of confused automation.

An enormous, winged tarantula, hovering above the group with fuzzy, multi-sectioned, twitching legs. Pincers as long as garden shears. Unblinking, onyx eyes.

And more, and more, and more, all assembling behind the Reds in a kind of seething clump of depravity. As bad as the sight was, the sounds were almost worse: Moans. Gurgling. Growling. Drawn-out screeches. Buzzing. Hissing. Barks and grunts. Toe-curling, off-pitch intonations.

George Herrick of the Salem Village Herricks turned and surveyed his legions with obvious pleasure as they amassed. He held up a hand, as if to tell them to wait. They did. Then, he spun again and walked—*step, tap, lean...step, tap, lean*—until he reached the swing.

Ollie Delgato of the North End Delgatos stood, raising himself to his full, six-foot-six height. This enabled him to look down on the old man, which he thought would make him feel better. It didn't.

Focus, he told himself, hiding his shaking hands inside his jumpsuit pockets. But trying to ignore the restless, horrifying menagerie was like trying to avoid rocks on a New England beach. Ollie steadied his breath and concentrated on the bespectacled man in front of him. And then, finally, he spoke.

"You found me."

Herrick looked amused. Again. "Of course I found you, my boy. You are not exactly hard to find." Slowly, oh-so-casually, he reached up to rub a small scar on his neck: the remains of the pufferpine quill's entry wound. "Though I must admit, I was somewhat delayed by a minor injury. A bit dodgy, that one. But all better now, thank heavens."

Ollie studied the man's oily smile, a smile that belonged to his great-, great-, great-whatever grandfather, and searched his gut for a feeling—any feeling—of familial warmth. But all he felt was disgust. He looked over Herrick's shoulder, keeping his voice composed. "I see you brought friends."

"That I did." Herrick answered, self-satisfaction making his moustache curl.

Ollie nodded. "So did I."

At that, he sensed movement from the shadows behind him. Too far for the torchlight or mushroom glow to reach. One by one, they stepped out from the darkness: Tera. Laszlo. Dozer. Ajanta. Derrin. Kuyu. Leonard. And others, who had surprised him in the end: Nikki and Floyd. Moseby. Eduard, Alfred, Martel, Collins, Milowka, and Jumar from his old Fifth Floor Labor Force crew. Even Carmichael was there, though he was mostly hiding behind the others.

Some had folded their arms. Others had propped their hands on their hips. All of them maintained even, steely expressions. And silence.

Herrick watched the emergence with raised eyebrows. And more amusement. "Interesting choice, Oliver, to put your friends in harm's way."

"Don't call me Oliver."

Herrick ignored the comment. "Come, now. Look around you, son. Do I really need to state the obvious?" He waved a hand vaguely in the direction of the Reds and towering monsters behind him. All of them, antsy. Barely contained. Rearin' to rip off a few heads. The howling and growling accelerated. "Let us end this now, shall we? There is no need for bloodshed. Surely we can all agree on that point?"

Herrick directed the last comment to the group. No one responded. The old man sighed, as if disappointed. He opened his mouth to say more, but paused when Ollie's friends parted suddenly, making way for one more to emerge from the soupy murk.

Her golden hair shimmered as she stepped into the multi-hued, neon light. Her loose, off-white frock dragged in the dirt as she walked.

"Hello, George."

For the first time, Herrick's smug smile faltered. The old man blinked several times, hard, in rapid succession. "E...Ellora? Is that...?"

Instead of answering, the witch walked around him in a wide, languorous circle, as though appraising a horse at auction. "I wish I could say you're looking well, George, but..." She let the sentence linger, then shrugged. "I, however, am looking splendid, don't you think?"

Herrick stared at her, mute.

"I also wish I could say it was pleasure to see you again, after so long an absence." Ellora finished circling, hopped onto the wooden plank of one of the swings, and smiled brightly. "But alas, that would be a lie. And of the two of us, you are really much better at lying, are you not? One might even say you are quite expert at it."

The old man's body appeared paralyzed.

Ellora kicked her feet out slightly, setting the swing into gentle motion. "My, what is the matter, good sir? Mutant got your tongue?"

Behind him, the restless creatures stamped and spun. Some took a few lurching steps forward. Herrick, for the moment, appeared not to notice.

Ollie caught Tera's eye. She fixed him with a steady stare. *Patience,* her expression said. *Stand your ground.*

He nodded, though his mouth had gone dry.

"Well, this is..." Herrick began to stammer. "I don't... It's..." He stopped, straightened, and seemed to collect himself at last. "Ellora," he said. "It is...good to see you again."

"Do you really think so?" she smiled, tucking a bit of hair behind her ear.

"I do, yes."

She sighed. "Oh, you silly, stupid man. Lying, as ever. I wonder: Do you know of any other way to speak?" Then she shrugged, kicked out her feet, and resumed the swing's motion. "No matter. Even if you did feel gladness to see me, George, I can assure you, that feeling will soon pass."

"Ellora, darling—"

She interrupted him with a chuckle and a raised hand. "Do you remember what my sisters told you, back in Salem Village?"

His smile was forced, and tight. "I am afraid I do not."

"Oh, come now, *darling*. Surely you could not have forgotten already?" Her long hair flew through the air as she swung. "They talked to you of the irony of your very precarious situation. Of all that time you spent, searching for witches. And yet, in the end, it is the witches who find *you*." She leaned forward in the seat. "Did you think, perhaps, that you had proven them wrong?"

Herrick gripped his pointed beard but didn't reply.

"One cannot escape from one's truth, good sir," Ellora said. "No matter how deep you dig into the earth, your sins will follow. No matter how many years you steal, you cannot steal youth. No matter how many beasts you conjure and torture and corral..." She looked pointedly over his shoulder at the assembled pack. "...they will not protect you from the putrid rot inside your soul."

As she spoke, the Reds shifted and murmured in their line, glancing uneasily at the giant creatures still stomping and hissing behind them. Ollie and his friends didn't move at all.

A sharp electricity of anticipation crackled throughout the chamber, like a storm about to break. Herrick and Ellora stared each other down, neither yielding, until the two-headed crow opened its multitude of beaks and let out a fractured shriek: *Ca-ca-caw! Caw! Ca-ca-caw!*

The sound raked through the empty courtyard like fingernails on a Knockdown scoreboard. Ollie squirmed as his back convulsed.

Some of the others covered their ears or winced. Even Ellora was startled, momentarily losing her balance on the swing.

Only Herrick seemed immune to the ear-splitting caw. The sound, improbably, had snapped him back into composure. Instead of flinching, he straightened. Clutching the cane, he gave his head a sharp shake and turned away from Ellora to face Ollie once again.

"Enough of these absurd pontifications," he said. "Let us speak plainly, shall we?"

Ollie raised his eyebrows but didn't reply.

"Why not come with me, dear boy?" Herrick peered at him intently, knuckles white on the cane's knob. "We are of one blood. It is plain as rhizer flesh. Our fates are united."

Ollie guffawed in astonishment. "Go with you? To do what?"

"To take what is yours," Herrick insisted, his face flush. "Are you not tired of hiding in the shadows? Of taking only what scraps others deign to proffer? You are a Herrick, my boy! You are meant for greater things than... than... this." He flicked his fingers dismissively at Tera and the others.

Ollie's teeth clenched so tightly he could not form a reply. He cast a look in Ellora's direction. *Feel free to jump in anytime,* he thought. But the witch merely continued to swing.

Finally, Ollie fixed Herrick with what he hoped was a withering glare. "You have no power. No real power, anyway. Whatever you have, you stole. You're nothing on your own. You never were." He turned to look at the ragtag, grotesque army. "That's why you made all this, isn't it? You know it's true. You're no witch. You're nothing but a scared, weak, little man, clinging to grudges."

And Ollie would know: He'd been batted around by plenty of others just like him. On the playground. At work. In the classroom. And anywhere else he'd had to cower to avoid them. Bullies, narcissists, and entitled rich kids, bulldozing a path through life. Not caring who they hurt along the way. Taking everything. Leaving nothing but pain and destitution in their wake.

Somewhere below the thick mustache, Herrick's lip curled. "You cannot possibly be so foolish as to think me weak," he snarled. "Whatever your opinion of me, I can assure you, that would be a fatal mistake."

Ollie wavered, then heard his mother's voice in his head: *Individual reeds are always weak,* she used to tell him. *Only when they're weaved together are they made strong.* He folded his arms across his chest. "You're nothing but a liar and a thief," Ollie told him. "Whatever power you might have, whatever all this is... It doesn't belong to you."

"Do not be naïve, my boy. The world cares not how you came upon your power. It cares only that you have it. Like it or not, we are kin. Cut from the same cloth."

"I'm not *your boy!*" Ollie snapped. "Krite! I'm not your *anything.* You get that? We are *not* family." The idea was laughable. Pitiful.

"Call it what you will. For three centuries, the blood has bound us, waiting only for this moment. And now, finally, the moment has arrived! Think of it, Oliver! Think of the possibilities! All that you could possibly desire awaits just beyond that door!"

"Do *not,*" Ollie said through gritted teeth, "call me *Oliver.*"

"Leave this place," Herrick intoned, stepping so close that Ollie could smell the grog and cinder-root on his breath. "Leave this mediocrity behind."

Without thinking, Ollie reached out to grasp the old man's forearm. "It's not too late," he said. His voice had a desperate edge. "Stop this, now. *Please!* While you still can. I'm begging you. Please, please, stop this."

"I have told you how to stop this," Herrick hissed. "It is up to you alone. Make the right choice and save your friends. Save this place. Do not forget, son, I created the Neath. And I can destroy it as well. "

They stood together, eye-to-eye, like the last remaining posts of a dilapidated, barnyard fence.

Only then did Ollie realize how lost his great-, great-, great-whatever grandfather was. How lost, perhaps, he had always been. A canyon of grief and finality swelled in his chest.

"You waste your breath, George," Ellora said. She had hopped off the swing and sidled up to stand behind Ollie's shoulder. "He will not join you. Now, I ask you one last time: Will you see sense for once in your miserable life? Will you leave this folly behind?"

Herrick sneered. "It is you who wastes your breath," he told her.

The witch sighed. "Then I am afraid you leave us with no choice."

"Oooh, is this the part where I am supposed to feel a fright?" Herrick tapped his arthritic fingertips together in exaggerated dismay. Then he spat at their feet. The thick glob of phlegm landed on the tip of Ollie's sneaker. "Imbeciles. I took you as stupid, but I did not take you as blind. Do you not see what fate awaits you?" He gestured toward the fangs, claws, pincers, and weapon-toting Reds behind him. "If you will not follow me, then you will perish. I cannot stop it."

"Of course you can," Ellora pointed out. "You created it."

"They exist to protect me," Herrick told her. "If you stand against me, they will destroy you. They will tear you limb from lovely limb." He shared this as if it were pleasant news, reaching out to stroke her forearm.

"You forget your place, *thief*." Ellora yanked her arm away; her voice was dangerously cold. "Do you think I am afraid of your toys? Do you not remember whose magic created them? All that you have was once mine."

"It seems I am not the one among us with faulty memory," he retorted with a shrug. "As I recall, you gave your magic away freely to a man you barely knew. A harebrained choice, perhaps, but a choice nonetheless. It is no thievery to accept a gift that is offered."

Ellora's eyes went wide. Her skin flushed, suddenly, into a scarlet rash. Ollie could feel the rage building, radiating, between them. Clicking like a gas-stove burner ready to burst into blue flame. He placed a hand on her arm and caught her eye. When Ellora looked at him, he shook his head. *Not yet.* She held his gaze, blinked, and exhaled. The flame subsided.

Herrick rolled his eyes with a *tsk tsk*. "My dear Ellora," he said. "You may fool these humans, but you do not fool me. You are weak. Even now, I can feel it. It has been too long, and you are too drained." He looked at Ollie, then at the assembled group. "Did she tell you she would save you? That her magic was strong enough to defeat me?" He laughed, though the sound was more reedy than bold. "Alas, it is not so. She is like a fire burned down to its embers. That is what happens when you give away your gifts, I'm afraid. In the end, a spark is no equal to a mighty blaze."

Ellora's sweet smile returned. With slow, purposeful movements, she walked toward Herrick. When she reached him, she lifted a hand to brush his cheek. The gesture—surprisingly gentle—startled him; the old man shivered visibly.

"I told them no such thing," the witch said, her voice a willowy whisper. "Much as I might desire it, it is not my destiny to vanquish you." She looked back at Ollie. "It is his."

George Herrick let out a snort. "His? Oh, my dear. I doubt that very much."

"Ah, but you do not doubt it," she replied, leaning ever closer. Her lips brushed his ears. Her voice had a low, sensual quality, like a lover sharing secrets. "You already know that it is true."

Herrick stiffened. Much as he tried to hide it, fear and uncertainty flashed across his features.

Now.

Ollie had tried his best to stem this tide. To change Herrick's mind, and heart. To make the old man see reason. But he could see, finally, that it was no use. There was nothing left to do but to move forward. He felt it like the sudden onset of fever before a flu.

He swallowed past the constriction in his throat. "The time has come to plant the seeds of change," Ollie said. His voice was soft, shaky.

Herrick gave him an inquisitive look.

Nothing happened.

Shit. He had spoken too quietly.

Ollie took a step backward. "I said, THE TIME HAS COME TO PLANT THE SEEDS OF CHANGE."

At that, his friends started to scurry, disappearing once again into the dark shadows near the outer wall.

George Herrick's eyes darted. Behind him, the assembled troops jostled and buzzed. The neon mushrooms glowed. The swing, now empty, continued to sway, its vacant seat beckoning. Somewhere, someone whined.

It was the final moment of peace any of them would know before pandemonium, and ruin, descended.

Twenty-Eight

Hurry hurry hurry hurry hurry

Ollie spun in a circle, squinting. Trying to make out the shapes moving along the murky periphery of the courtyard.

There—Dozer.

There—Eduoard.

And there...wait...yes, right there—Tera.

He spun again.

There—Derrin. Just close enough to a patch of neon mushrooms to make her movements visible. She was crouched and digging a small trowel into the dirt floor, creating a hole right next to the wall. Seconds later, Derrin dropped something into the pit. Then she backfilled it with a sweep of her hands and patted the top flat.

Hurry hurry hurry hurry hurry

There—Laszlo.

And there—Kuyu. And Moseby, and Carmichael, and Floyd.

Though he could only see vague, ghostly silhouettes, they all seemed to be sticking to the plan: digging a small hole as quickly as possible, as close to the wall as possible. Then, dropping in one of the jiggling seedpods and covering it up with a protective layer of dirt.

All of which would be simple enough, if not for the inconveniently large and ferocious army of henchmen gathered nearby, just itching to squash them all flat.

Every action has an equal and opposite reaction. Ollie had learned that in tenth-grade physics. So he knew they'd only have a few seconds—at best—of uninterrupted activity. And he was right. Ollie's friends had barely dispersed before George Herrick's face twisted in confusion, then irritation, and then, anger. Lots and lots of anger.

"Ah, Oliver. You disappoint me enormously," Herrick said, his British accent dripping with disgust. "I expected this from her..." He jerked a thumb in Ellora's direction. "But you? Such a shame. So much potential, wasted. I suppose I should have known that you would prove to be no better than that father of yours."

At that, Ollie stiffened. His father? What did Matteo have to do with anything?

But Herrick was already gone. He was stalking back to his troops, all of whom were now screeching, hollering, and just generally clamoring to be set loose into the courtyard. The *step-tap-lean* sequence had sped up considerably from its earlier incarnation but was still plodding. When Herrick finally reached them, he gave an order to his assembled mercenaries that Ollie couldn't quite hear.

Whatever he had said, it caused an immediate reaction. The Reds nodded, whooped, and pumped their sparking-prod weapons over their heads. The deformed creatures behind them squealed and wailed. Dipped and buzzed. Pawed the dirt. Snapped their jaws and flicked out their tongues. Some of the Reds managed to get themselves trampled before the group had even begun its advance.

Now.

Still rooted in place, Ollie scanned the cavernous courtyard. He spotted his friends, most of whom were still digging and planting. *Hurry hurry hurry...* He kept his gaze moving in circles until he saw what he had been hoping to see:

Meatball, shuffling along the ground, his brown fur bathed in a neon-mushroom glow.

Behind him, another trog. Then another, and another. They marched beak-to-back in orderly formation, creating an unbroken fuzzball chain. When Ollie squinted, the line resembled a single organism: a giant gypsy-moth caterpillar, maybe, undulating silently through the center of the courtyard. He gaped as they passed by his feet. There had to be dozens of them: brown, black, white, tan. A trog army. Traveling faster than any web-footed, orbital creatures might be expected to move. Swift and sure. And then, faster still, until their fur colors blended into a camouflage blur.

Meatball's waddle was unwavering. His direction, clear. He was leading them all into enemy territory.

Ollie felt his stomach clench.

No! he started to shout. *Wait! I changed my mind!*

Before he could make the sounds leave his throat, Herrick's battalions sprang to life. With a roar, the Reds jumped forward. The mutants snarled and lunged. They were like a ravaging swarm of fire ants suddenly freed from an earthen mound, ready to annihilate anything and everything in their path.

But...

The trogs had gotten there first.

With speedy stealth, Meatball and his friends had surrounded the gathered legion, forming a tight circle around its perimeter. As the Reds surged forward, they tripped and fell over the trogs, yelping in pained confusion as their heads and bodies hit the ground. The mutants, in turn, stumbled over the newly toppled, red-suited men.

In seconds, the horde of fearsome aggressors had been transformed into nothing more than a mound of flailing limbs. A rat's nest of disarray. Those that could fly, did, lifting themselves above the jumble. Those that were confined to the ground—the skinless wolverine, the jellyfish blob, the thorned Komodo dragon, and others—stepped on top of each other, and the men, in a free-for-all of frantic confusion.

Ollie allowed himself a flash of relief. Meatball's trog calvary had bought them precious minutes. Would it be enough? Again, he scanned the courtyard's periphery, relieved to see that most of his friends had finished planting and had retreated back to their original positions.

Now.

"Meatball, now!" he screamed.

The trog looked up. Pinned under a crimson-suited leg, he opened his too-wide bill, bared stacked rows of chiseled teeth, and chomped. The Red screamed and yanked his leg, leaving just enough of an opening for Meatball to scurry away from the fray.

Other trogs followed, with varying levels of success. The mutants and soldiers had started to regain their footing. Ollie watched, wincing, as some kind of suction-faced, oversized toad sucked a black trog down its gullet. A few others were stabbed, one-by-one, by the giant wasp's stinger. Another met the wrong end of one of the Reds' voltaic weapons, making its fur stand on end before it collapsed into a helpless ball on the ground.

Chaos. Cacophony. Carnage.

No. No, no, no.

Ollie started to run. He would scoop up as many trogs as he could carry. He would evade the onslaught as long as he could.

He had only advanced a few steps when he heard it.

The fracturing.

Everyone, it seemed, had heard it. The riotous tumult of the courtyard stilled, suddenly, as all heads turned to look at the tower walls.

The seedpods were growing. Fast. The shoots were spreading. Moving. Widening. It was the same neck-snapping speed that Ollie remembered from the top of the Bunker Hill Monument. Hundreds of vines, snaking and reaching like hands. Thousands of leaves, swelling exponentially.

The plants had taken root at the base of the walls and forced their way, easily, inside the seeping fissures—sprouts into seedlings; seedlings into saplings; saplings into full, fat trunks of gleaming bark.

Up and up they grew. The plaster, already weak, gave way to each stem like thin ice splintering beneath a shoe.

Snap. Thwack. CRAAAACK.

The walls began to vibrate, crumble, and collapse. The courtyard, improbably, was becoming a forest. Inside was becoming outside. The decrepit tower was helpless against the rising surge.

SNAAAAP. SNAAAAP. BOOM.

Ollie gasped and jumped aside to avoid a falling rock. Then another. As the shoots and trunks cracked open the walls, hunks of mortar, stone, wood, and metal rained down on the courtyard, landing with thundering force all around.

"Look out!" Ollie yelled, pointing. One of the hungry vines had snaked its way around Laszlo's arm, pulling the acrobat toward the quaking wall. The others jumped into action to free him, stabbing and slicing the greenery with their spades and shovels.

Caaa caaaw! Caaa caaaw!

Ollie spun. The two-headed white crow was free from the tangle of bodies, along with its compatriots. Mutants, Reds, and fleeing trogs all began racing across the open courtyard. Dodging the storm of rocks. Snarling and shouting and lunging.

"Under here! Hurry!"

Ellora's voice cut through the chaos. She was standing behind him. Angry blisters covered her fair skin, sending out beams of hot, white light. She had assured them that she'd be able to conjure a temporary forcefield of sorts, strong enough to catch the falling debris and create safe passage. So far, it seemed to be working: Rocks and splintered beams were gathering in an unwieldy, hovering pile above her head, leaving a clear path below.

"Under here!" she shouted again. "Hurry!"

He could read the strain on her features. The tower walls were crumbling faster, now. Her floating pile was growing larger, and heavier, by the second.

He ran.

"Come on!" he yelled to the others. "Hurry!" He ushered them though the dust clouds, past Ellora, and into the shadows near the back stairwell. But instead of heading toward the rapidly disintegrating stairs, they veered to the right, where a tunnel was waiting. A new tunnel. A tunnel that George Herrick, hopefully, did not know about. It was their only hope now. Their only escape.

Ollie peered down into the black hole, barely wide enough for one person to fit through. One regular-sized person, not an Ollie-sized person. He could barely see past the opening—below that, total darkness.

How many for entry? he thought, grimly. *A shit-ton. A shit-ton for entry.*

The screeches and growls were getting louder. The minions were getting closer.

Now. Now, now, now.

Bracing his feet, he began to lower his friends, one at a time, into the tunnel. Kuyu. Collins. Derrin. Jumar. Ajanta. Tiny Moseby. Dozer. Leonard, who barely fit, but somehow managed to squeeze himself through. Ollie began counting them; running through their names in his head. Was everyone here? His eyes flitted through the darkness.

"Laz?" he called out.

"I am right here, my friend," the acrobat said, his Lycra-suited shape emerging from the murk. "I go now. You hurry next, yes?" When Ollie nodded, Laszlo gave his arm a hearty pat before jumping into the hole at their feet.

Tera approached his side. "Okay, ready?"

"Yeah. Wait, no—where's Meatball?"

"I don't know, but Oll, we've got to—"

"Get the others in, okay? I'll be right back."

"No, Babe, you can't—"

"I swear, I'll be right back." He kissed her, hard. "Right back."

She fixed him with a stare. "You'd better."

He tried to smile, then turned and walked back under Ellora's safety net into the foggy, booming bedlam. With mounting desperation, he scanned the ground.

Meatball should have been here by now. He should have already made it. If he didn't... *No.* Ollie didn't want to think about all the obvious ways to end that sentence. He watched from the shadows, quaking, as the mutant army advanced. The mushroom crop had already been thoroughly trampled, its phosphorescent light doused. The fish tanks had toppled to the ground in a flood of water, flopping bodies, and broken glass. The seats of the swings had been torn from their moorings, leaving the chains to dangle in the hazy, powdery air.

The trees, astonishingly, continued to grow—up, but also down into the courtyard's dirt base, where the thick roots had started to burst through the ground.

SNAAAAP. THWACK. SNAAAAP. BOOM.

One of the Reds stepped on a shard of broken fish-tank glass and went down, yowling. The Komodo dragon managed to tangle its neck in one of the hanging chains, twisting and choking as it fell. Others succumbed to the cruel, fatal crush of falling rubble. Blood spattered every surface. Howls, thuds, and shrieks filled the air.

But some of the soldiers were advancing, still. Moving toward Ollie and his friends with determined, vicious progress. Was Herrick out there, too, hiding somewhere in the mayhem? Ollie couldn't see him, and didn't care. In that moment he only cared about one thing.

Where the hell was Meatball?

There! To the right! Ollie let out a rush of breath as he spotted a moving, brown ball of fur.

"Over here, buddy! Hurry!"

The trog waddled closer. Ollie stretched out his arms.

All at once, something fell like a curtain between them. Something huge, and feathered.

A bird?

He felt himself knocked backward as the hideous apparition swooped. Moldy-green color. Massive, grimy wings. It looked like...a pelican? No, more like the bloated, rotting carcass of a pelican after days in the Florida sun. Instead of webbed feet, it had talons. And a long, serrated beak. And a colossal throat-pouch, deep and open, waiting for prey.

Trog-sized prey.

Ollie watched in helpless horror through a maelstrom of mossy feathers as the creature plunged, opened its bill, and swallowed Meatball whole.

Twenty-Nine

Ollie screamed. The sound was drowned out by something louder: a shrill, pained squawk, followed by a hiss.

He froze. The grimy pelican froze. And then the enormous bird fell over, wings crushed below its twitching body. As it landed, Ollie looked up to see Tera standing behind it. The tip of her digging trowel was dripping with blood.

"Wha—" Ollie found himself unable to speak.

He looked down, again, at the flying mutant. Saw the tool-shaped puncture wound between its pink, glassy eyes.

Tera dropped the trowel and lunged forward, grabbing the pelican's huge, serrated bill with both hands. With a grunt of effort, she plied it open. Ollie, fighting a wave of nausea, tried to read her reaction as she peered inside the bulging throat-pouch: Was it horror? Despair? When she reached inside the creature's mouth, half her body disappeared. She popped up seconds later, triumphant, holding Meatball aloft.

"Come on!" Tera shouted, tucking the trog under her arm. "Run!"

Ollie nodded, dazed, and scrambled to his feet.

She held out her free hand, and he took it. Together, they dodged the hailstorm of falling debris while trying not to trip over the escaping, scurrying trogs or the sudden explosions of root-mounds all around. The ground shook like a seismic quake.

More deformed birds, swooping. A clump of conjoined snakes, slithering. Reds, screaming themselves hoarse like ancient, marauding Vikings. All of it, barely visible in the growing clouds of detritus and dirt.

Ellora's voice, again. He felt it more than he heard it, following its siren song through the mist. Then, he saw her, still straining. Exhausted. A growing mountain of stone, wood, and rubble continued to pile atop her ethereal shield. It was too much: The weight was too great. Any second now, she would have to yield.

Ollie yanked Tera's arm. As before, they raced into Ellora's protective underpass and traveled all the way to the end.

"Go," Ollie said, giving Tera a gentle push toward the hole in the ground. "I'll get Ellora."

Tera paused, then nodded. Gripping Meatball tightly, she disappeared into the dark pit.

Ollie watched them vanish, feeling a rush of relief. Then he turned and hurried back to his great-, great-, great-whatever grandmother, who was still holding her arms in the air. Sweating. Covered in burning, raised welts.

"Everybody's in!" he called to her. "Come on, let's go!"

Ellora gave a curt, pained nod. She lowered her arms slightly, as a weightlifter might lower a barbell. Then she heaved upward, trying to fling the rocks away. Trying to give herself room to escape their crushing, inevitable weight. She was only partially successful: Some of the rocks flew outward, but others fell straight down. One landed on her leg.

Another, on her skull.

Ollie yelled something incoherent and held out his hand.

She stared at him, dazed. By the time Ollie noticed the trickle of blood on her face, it was rapidly building into a torrent.

"Krite, Ellora! Hurry!"

Still, she didn't move. He grabbed her and yanked her into the shadows. They hovered near the hole.

"Go on," he prodded. "Hop down. Hurry."

But Ellora was looking over her shoulder, not moving.

"Come on! We have to move! Now! This whole place is coming down!"

"No," she said, shaking her head slowly. "It's not." Her voice sounded oddly leaden.

"What? What are you—?" As Ollie turned, his sentence fell away. He took one cautious step, then another, peering out from the protective darkness at the chaotic courtyard beyond. "What the hell?" he breathed.

Ellora came to stand beside him. "The canopy," she said, heaving a sigh of deep disappointment. "We forgot about the canopy."

Ollie's eyes slammed shut. His fists clenched.

The plan had been wonderfully simple: Demolish the courtyard, and everything in it. The trees would do the work while Ollie and his friends escaped through the tunnel. Once they were safety out of range, the tower would collapse, crushing everything—and everyone—below its falling walls. The Reds, the mutants, and even Herrick himself: All of them taken off the board in one fell swoop, never to terrorize again.

Ollie knew it could work. He knew all too well how deteriorated the structure was, at its core, and how easily the seedpods' overpowering growth would tear it apart. And he had been right.

But he had forgotten about the canopy.

In planting the seeds, they hadn't just created a thicket. They'd created a net.

Hundreds of thousands of tons of rubble had plummeted, just as Ollie hoped it would. And some of it had, indeed, crushed the soldiers and mutant creatures below.

But the rest of the debris had not fallen to the ground at all—instead, it remained high in the air, caught in the newly sprouted canopy of white-barked trees. The mighty tangle of limbs, leaves, and shoots stretched all the way across the courtyard, forming an almost perfectly spherical, almost perfectly stable shelter above their heads. An umbrella of greenery.

A goddamn mutinous forest.

Ollie seethed at the sight. Then, he panicked. "Shit," he muttered. "Okay. Okay, we've got to move. Now." They didn't have time to reformulate the plan; they didn't even have time to *think* about reformulating the plan. All they could do was escape.

He led Ellora, still bloodied and disoriented, back to the tunnel entrance. Not giving her a chance to protest, he lowered her down. Seconds later, he followed, sucking in his stomach, fighting the claustrophobia that was rising, fast, in his chest. The others had made it through, hadn't they? Even Leonard. Surely he would fit. Either way, he had no choice. Half the mercenaries were still up there, and probably Herrick, too. Marching. Searching. Any minute now, they'd find the hole. And when they did, Ollie and his friends had to be as far away from this disaster zone as possible.

A few feet down, the tunnel blessedly widened, big enough for two people to stand side-by-side. *Thank you, Derrin and Kuyu,* he thought, letting his stomach relax and his lungs fill with air. "Right down here," he said to Ellora, quickening his steps to a jog. "It's not far. This leads out past the water trough, I think, and then we can—"

He stopped, realizing that wasn't following.

"Come on!" he said. "Look, I know you banged your head. We'll patch that up when we get out there, okay? But right now, we've really got to move."

But she didn't move.

Ollie shoved his hands into his jumpsuit pockets, summoning patience as his heart rate raced. Maybe the blow to Ellora's head was more severe than he realized. Maybe she was having trouble understanding him. Would he have to carry her? He could, of course, if he had to. She was as tall as he was, but not overly heavy. It would slow them down, sure, but if he—

"No need for all that, my boy," she said, lifting a hand. "I understand you just fine."

He startled. He had forgotten, again, that she could read his thoughts.

"O...kay," he said, cautiously. "C'mon, then. We really have to go."

She smiled.

It was the smile that did it. The sadness in her lips, and the wrinkles around her eyes, told the entire story. Ollie felt his chest tighten.

"No," he said, his tone stern. "Uh uh. Don't even think about it."

Her expression didn't change.

"Ellora, *no!*"

"The tower must fall," she answered matter-of-factly, a slight shrug at her shoulders. "And the canopy. All of it. They must be stopped."

"We'll think of something!" he blurted. "We'll...I don't know...we'll rig something. We'll come back, and we'll..."

"Ollie."

"We'll come back!"

"You know as well as I do, my dear, that we cannot," Ellora said gently. "The time is now. The sound of it rings all around. You can hear it, too. I know you can."

Tears stung the corners of his eyes, hot and sharp. "No. You can't do this."

Her smile widened. The young witch stepped forward, touching his face with a tenderness that made a whimper catch in his throat. "Aye, I can. And I must. We all have our destinies to follow, do we not? Mine leads back up there." She pointed over her shoulder at the narrowing tunnel walls. At the hole leading back out into hell.

"No. *No.* I won't let you!" A flash: his mother's deathbed. The beep and wheeze of machines. The somber smile on her weary, beautiful face. *It's time to go, Bambino,* she had told him. *You must let me go.*

Ollie smeared the tears across his face with a sleeve. *No.* He had already lost too much. He couldn't lose Ellora, too. He had only just met her. They had so much yet to do, to say. She was, he realized, the only family he had left.

The witch pinched his cheek affectionately. "It's time to go," she whispered. "You must let me go."

"You can't do this!" he begged. "Please, don't do this! We'll think of something else, I swear!"

Ellora took two steps backward. Red freckles had already arisen on her arms and neck, casting her face into a burnished glow. Blood seeped from the gash, forming a snaking river through her yellow hair, down her forehead, and onto her cheek. She did not look scared. She did not look unsure. She looked merely thoughtful, and serene.

"Go, now," she told him. "I will hold them off as long as I am able. But Ollie, I'm sorry to say that Herrick was right about one thing, at least. I am weak. He took most everything." She wobbled slightly on her feet, then lifted her chin. "I might not be what I once was, but I am still a damn sight better than most. I will do what I can, and you will do the same. Take care of Tera. Take care of your friends. Be the man I know you can be."

"Stay!" he pleaded. "Please, don't do this!"

Ellora's expression softened. "Not many people can say they've met their **great-, great-, great-, great-, great-, great-, great-, great-, great-, great-, great-, great-, great-, great-grandson**," she said. "I am a lucky woman."

He opened his mouth to protest, but she interrupted him: "You were well worth the wait, Ollie Delgato. You are the best of us."

Tears blurred his vision, turning her into a gossamer ghost.

"And when the time comes, remember your mother's words," Ellora said. "Remember the key."

Before he could reach out a hand to stop her, the young witch held up her palms. A violent force hit him like a cyclone, flinging his body down the tunnel. Ollie flailed and stumbled, struggling to regain his footing. By the time he did, he was fifteen feet away from where he had started.

And he was alone.

Thirty

Ollie lurched forward, letting out an anguished cry. He could catch her; it wasn't too late.

But Ellora had filled in the hole behind her, leaving only an impassable clog of rocks and dirt in her wake.

She was gone.

He turned, fumbled. Forced his feet to move.

Her words rang in his ears: *Take care of Tera. Take care of your friends.* That was all he could do, now. If he made it out of this tunnel alive.

His vision was still clouded by tears, but it hardly mattered: There was only one way to go. He ran and crawled and scrambled and climbed until, finally—a faint, blue-greenish light. Faces, peering through the opening.

"Ollie?"

At the sound of Tera's voice, he lurched forward with renewed intensity.

"Oll, thank God! Where the hell have you been!" Her brown eyes widened in relief; her hand reached out to pull him up.

He climbed out into the open air to find them all waiting. His friends formed a semi-circle around him as he stood, wobbly, and found his bearings.

They were standing in a scraggy, nondescript clearing, not far from the prison's former main-entrance gate. The scenery was all-too familiar... coppery stalagmite forests, the vast olive-green lake, and thousands of wormwalkers swarming on the cavern's ceiling high above. And if he turned around, he knew what he would see there, too: A still-crumbling tower. A circle of new, white trees.

His stomach clenched as he scanned the faces. He didn't see anyone from the Labor Force Crew. Or Moseby, Nikki, and Floyd.

Tera read his mind. "They're all fine, they just ran ahead," she assured him.

Laszlo, Dozer, Ajanta, Leonard, Derrin, Kuyu, and Tera had stayed behind to wait for him. Putting themselves in danger. The realization made him swell with gratitude.

"Wait...where is grandmother?" Laszlo asked, looking back down into the tunnel hole.

Ollie tried to answer, but only managed to stammer.

"Oll? What happened?" Tera asked.

"It...it didn't work. It didn't work! The trees...they caught all the...stuff...and she said...she said..." Actually, she hadn't said anything, but he had understood her intentions just the same. "Ellora... She's going to..."

They stared at him, and at each other, in perplexed concern.

Ollie stopped, collected himself. Remembered his task. *Take care of Tera. Take care of your friends. Be the man I know you can be.* He exhaled. "I'll explain later. We have to move," he said. "Now. It's going to blow."

Dozer titled his head. "What 'cha mean, bl—"

"Now!" Ollie interrupted with a shout, making them all jump. "There's no time! Let's *go!*" His hands waved in wild gesticulations. "Go, go, go!"

His friends didn't hesitate; the group turned as one and began racing away from the tunnel entrance, followed by the echoes of falling mortar and the howls of the not-too-distant creatures still circling inside the remains of the courtyard.

Ollie ran behind them, his lungs and legs burning. Meatball bounced on Tera's shoulder. Kuyu and Derrin held hands as they ran. Leonard paused to scoop up Ajanta after she tripped and fell.

Hurry hurry hurry

But when the explosion came, they were still too close. The ground bucked beneath their collective feet, tossing them like salad. Limbs flailed in all directions. The thundering boom ricocheted across the cavern with a force Ollie could barely comprehend.

He hit the dirt face-first. His ears rang with a tinny, high-pitched ping; his head throbbed. Everything spun. He waited for the quake, and the ringing, to subside, then rolled over, stiffly. He looked up just in time to see the white trees shudder. One after another, they fell—*wham, wham, wham, wham*—along with the rest of the boulders and debris, resulting in a mushroom-cloud of dust, wood splinters, and embers.

Seconds later, the fire's roar drowned out the crashes and explosions, along with something that sounded like the shrieks of dying animals. Eventually, the blast died down into a whimper of crackles and pops. The wailing sounds faded, then disappeared.

Ollie struggled to stand, coughing and shaking. The others did the same.

They watched, silent, as the powdery cloud cleared, leaving behind a smoldering pile of rubble and ash.

Ollie reeled, awestruck. Willing his brain to believe what his eyes knew to be true.

He saw...nothing.

Herrick's End was gone.

Ellora had done it! Ellora had...

A sob caught in his throat.

Laszlo was the first to speak. "Is all over?" he asked, a note of cautious optimism creeping into his voice. "They are gone? Bad men are gone?"

For a long moment, no one replied—instead, they only stared wonderingly at the empty space where the tower and trees used to be. Then Dozer answered, "Yeah, man. I think so."

The murmurs started then, followed by low-grade, wary excitement.

"Did...we do it?" Tera asked.

Ajanta shrugged and looked at Tera and Kuyu, who each shrugged in return. But their cheeks were dimpling. Their eyes, darting. All around him, Ollie's friends started to chatter and bustle.

"Krite, I think we really did it!"

"Did you see that spider thing? Damn, that was—"

"...never thought that seed would—"

"Look at that! *Look* at that! It's friggin' *gone!*"

"...four more seconds, I swear, and—"

Ollie listened and watched, feeling seasick. It was such a strange sensation, this surge of elation followed by the deep plunge of grief. He let them enjoy their victory. They deserved it.

They did not understand, yet, what it had cost.

But they would. As he stood there, nauseous, sucking in the smoke and grit, Ollie made a vow to himself: Everyone in the Neath would know what Ellora had done for them. He would make sure of it. A sign, maybe, in Blackstone Park. No, a statue. No, a carousel, like the one he had left behind on the Brickside, spinning with wonderful, whimsical creatures. *In memory of Ellora,* the carousel sign would read. *Grandmother to us all.*

"Dude, you're a genius, you know that?" Derrin called out to Ollie. She was standing with her back to the rubble, tossing her skinny arms in the air. Her normally stoic face was beaming. "You did it! Your stupid plan worked!"

Ollie opened his mouth, ready to set her straight. But a strange, loud sound—a crackle—made him stop. Then, an even stranger sight: a stain, spreading across the front of Derrin's jumpsuit.

A maroon stain.

For several seconds, nothing made sense. Derrin's face went blank. She looked at Ollie, pressing a hand against her abdomen.

He took a step toward her. His legs felt heavy, as though they were dragging through deep water. "Derrin?"

Her eyes were still on him when she dropped.

"DERRIN!" Her name left his mouth in a primal scream. Some part of him knew what that stain meant. What her collapse meant. It made no sense, and yet it did. It did, it did, it did. "DERRIN!"

As she hit the ground, a view opened up behind her. A view to an old man, squinty and filthy, his torso only half-emerged from the tunnel opening. He was pointing an outstretched palm in Derrin's direction, a lingering bolt of something yellow and electrified still visible in the air between them.

Arrowhead beard. Broken, crooked glasses. Black lab coat lightened by a layer of chalky grime.

A snarl rose in Ollie's throat.

His peripheral vision narrowed, though he could make out the rough outlines of panic all around him. He could hear Kuyu screaming Derrin's name over and over and over again, each cry like a piercing barb. He could sense the others rushing, weeping, gathering. He could hear instructions being shouted—*Apply pressure! Hold her still!* He could feel everyone's sorrow and shock. But he could not see them.

All he could see was Herrick.

The roar came from somewhere deep in Ollie's belly. It propelled him forward, past the others, across the blank expanse. He was blind with rage, yet somehow more clear-sighted than he knew it was possible to be.

As he moved, he willed Ellora's lost power to return to him. Willed the blisters and telekinesis to reenter his pores and enable him to pierce the old man's body with something terrible and sharp and deadly.

Ollie called out through the years, through the centuries, to all the ones who had come before. He was the true descendant. The last one standing. Surely, that would be enough.

It wasn't. He called, and no magic answered.

Ollie felt the absence like a smack. But he didn't slow.

Fuck magic. He didn't need it. He would do this alone. He was meant to do it, wasn't he? Isn't that what everyone said? It was his destiny to tear this man to pieces. To snap his spindly bones like breadsticks. He didn't need any alchemy for that. All he needed was two ordinary, human hands.

Blood thundered in his ears.

The sound of Derrin's moans, weaker with every passing minute, wafted into his consciousness. Then, more of Kuyu's agonized wails. Someone was lamenting, praying; someone else was calling his name.

Ollie ignored it all. He barreled forward like an F-16, locked on his target.

When the old man saw him coming, he grinned that infuriating, Cheshire-cat grin and turned his opened palm toward Ollie. Another bolt of electricity cracked through the air.

Ollie dodged it.

Another shot, and another dodge.

And another, and another, and maybe dozens more, until finally, Ollie reached him. He threw his entire, bulky, six-foot-six-inch frame against the older man's body. Together, they went down with a thud onto the rocky soil.

He made inhuman, abominable sounds as he began pummeling Herrick's face, chest, stomach. Anything he could reach. He pounded for Derrin. For Ellora. For his mother. For himself. It felt so natural, so satisfying, this discharge of force and hate. And why wouldn't it? Hadn't he learned from the experts? Didn't he come by it honestly? Maybe *this* was his birthright. His goddamn *kismet*. Maybe he'd finally found his calling. Maybe this was what he'd been looking for all along.

Ollie's vision faded to a pinprick of blue-black as he punched. He would destroy this man. He would make him writhe. He would pound a hole through his weak little body, tear out his organs, and feed them to the trogs.

Yes. Yes, yes, yes. The very thought of it was like oxygen to an inferno. Each blow and each spurt of blood made him greedy for more. Ollie had known hunger. For so long, he'd been a slave to hunger. But he'd never known hunger like this.

Herrick's face was morphing into a reddish, pulpy mush. Still, Ollie saw him clearly. He saw every sneer, every condescending wink, every spray of spittle flying from his lips as the hateful man's hateful words had poured out, time and time again.

With a moan, Ollie imagined Ellora's final, excruciating moments, somewhere back in that courtyard.

He saw other things, too. Things he wanted to forget.

All the afflicted creatures in the lab—trapped, tortured, and mutilated. Long lines of miserable and hopeless prisoners in Herrick's End. Tera and Meatball, lifeless in their tank. The spread of crimson on Derrin's jumpsuit as she slumped to the ground. And of course, all the sights that Bert, Elisha, and Lizbeth had shown him, some ancient and some not-so-ancient, of witches captured, imprisoned, and starved. Witches hung. Witches burned alive. Innocent people brought to agony and death. And for what? For *what?* With every thought, every memory, Ollie curled his fists and pounded through the pain.

Wham, wham, wham.

Herrick was coughing...choking? On his own blood? *Good.* The hunger in Ollie continued to grow.

He was so consumed with his assault that he did not, at first, notice that something else was growing, as well.

The surface of George Herrick's face, which Ollie had been so diligently pounding, seemed suddenly...larger.

And not the just the face. Herrick's whole body...bigger? Yes, bigger. Ollie had been easily straddling him just seconds ago. Now, his legs barely reached around the old man's waist. And with every punch, Herrick's girth seemed to grow bulkier still.

What the krite...?

It was the same baffling change he'd seen in Carmichael, back at Ajanta's house. Ollie had been imagining the horrible things he would do to him. Imagining delicious revenge. And as he did, Carmichael's modest frame had seemed to grow larger. But that had been just a delusion. Hadn't it?

The more Ollie pounded, the more obvious it became: George Herrick was expanding. Not like a bulbous tick, this time—more like a weakling morphing into a circus strongman.

And then, Herrick pushed back.

With a jolt, Ollie felt his own body rising. Floating. Suddenly, his fists were having trouble reaching their targets.

With a shocking whoosh, he flew up and back.

Herrick was magicking him away. The old man was healing. Despite the punishing blows, Herrick was inexplicably regaining his strength. Not just regaining...surpassing? Ollie clawed the air in helpless confusion. He could feel it in every swirling molecule around him: Herrick's power was somehow amassing into something more terrible than it had been before.

Ollie advanced again. He managed to dodge a few more bolts, then succumbed to yet another blow of force. It knocked him on his ass. Then lifted him, then dropped him. The punishing pattern continued as Herrick hoisted and smashed him like a toy—like the tattered, flopping rag doll hidden at the bottom of a box in Danvers. Soon, Ollie's eyes were nearly swollen shut, and his bones seemed cracked to their marrow. His body felt like a loose collection of rocks rattling around in a bag.

Again, Ollie rose to his feet. Again, Herrick's unseen, punishing surge knocked him down.

How long this continued, he couldn't say. Ollie knew only that he lifted himself off the ground every time until, inescapably, he couldn't. Until Herrick's power proved to be an overwhelming, unbeatable foe. Until he realized with sick clarity that his stupid human fists were no match for a man like this, in a place like this.

Until he understood, finally, that he had failed.

George Herrick was laughing.

It was a low chuckle, at first, then something louder. More mirthful. The old man reached for his cane, which had somehow survived the journey with him, and straightened. He adjusted and wiped his coat jauntily, as though the gesture would somehow cleanse the filth of the day's events.

Step, tap, lean. Step, tap, lean.

Ollie struggled to rise as Herrick approached. But his muscles, and gravity, had betrayed him. His body stayed stubbornly cemented to the ground.

Step, tap, lean.

The bearded, bespectacled man hovered over him and shook his head. He seemed normal-sized once again. Perhaps he had never changed, or grown. Perhaps Ollie had imagined that, too. Not that it mattered now.

Ollie waited for the usual speechifying. *"Oh, Ollie, you disappoint me so,"* or maybe, *"Did I not tell you what would happen? Did I not tell you all?"*

Instead, Herrick crouched down, lowered his face near Ollie's ear, and whispered. "She suffered, you know," he said, his tone as cold as February. "Your *mighty* Ellora. She suffered terribly, and then she died. And now, your poor Derrin does the same."

Herrick turned Ollie's head, forcing him to face the grisly sight: Derrin, bleeding out on the ground, with all of the rest gathered and wailing around her. They had watched Ollie's feeble attempts at battle. Witnessed his pathetic end. They knew now what was in store—for all of them.

Ollie knew it, too. He didn't want to catch Tera's eye. He couldn't bear to see the look on her face. Disappointment, probably, and regret—regret that she'd ever rescued him and took him in. Regret that she'd ever met him. Regret that she had let herself love such a miserable excuse for a man.

He heard a noise. A shuffling, on the dirt. He blinked, moaned, and turned his eyeballs to see Tera running toward him. Toward Herrick. Why? Her mouth was set in an angry, determined line. *Stay there!* he wanted to call out. *Stop!* But his lips felt misshapen. His tongue, uncooperative.

Herrick had heard her, too. The old man looked up, then casually lifted a palm in her direction.

Nooo! Ollie heard the cry inside his head, but couldn't make the sound audible.

The blast threw Tera backward, sending her sprawling. She landed and climbed back to her feet.

Herrick looked back down at Ollie, chuckling again. "Oh, don't worry, my boy," he said. "I have something very special planned for that one." He paused, shrugged. "For all of them, really. But I think I'll save your Tera for last."

Ollie found that he could only gurgle as despair clamped his heart.

Help us, he called out, if only in his thoughts. *Please, help us.* Maybe someone would hear. But he knew, as the message traveled, echoed, and bounced back into his mind, that no one did.

He heard his name; his friends were calling out to him. Why? Did they actually think he could still save them? That he could do anything else at all?

Fools. All of them, fools, for believing in him.

He had failed them. He had tried his best, and he had still failed. He was not surprised, of course. Only broken. Ollie's head throbbed with fathomless thunder. He felt his consciousness slip in and out like the tide at the North End docks, slapping dully against the wooden pilings. In, and out. In, and out.

Something was rising with the water. Words, strung together. A thought.

When the time comes, remember your mother's words. Remember the key.

Ellora. He felt himself smiling, floating in placid reverie. Then, a jolt, like a pinch.

Remember the key!

Ellora again, though less gentle. More insistent. Her voice mingled with the others, nearby. The ones who were calling his name. The black curtain in his mind fell, then rose, then fell again. What key? Where was he? What was happening?

Oh, yes: the key. He was supposed to find a key, wasn't he? But he never did. Too bad. It might have helped him...somehow. For a moment, Ollie felt regret. Then the feeling passed. He waited for the curtain to drop. For the tide to retreat. How wonderful that would be—Sleep. Rest. Peace. Each one beckoned with bended fingers.

Another pinch. Another sharp voice in his ear.

The tide began to wash back in, lifting him. *Remember your mother's words.*

His mom. Everybody loved Francie Delgato. She had made it so easy. Ollie felt his entire countenance relax as she fluttered like a Mirrormoth into his mind: her pert nose; her pink slippers; her potholdered hands lifting cheesy casseroles out of the oven.

Her words.

What will you do, when your frozen-river moment arrives? his mother had asked him. *Know who you are, before it happens. There might not be one right answer. But there will be a right answer for you.*

More recollections came, tumbling in quick succession.

A cryptic bedtime whisper in his ear, shortly after his father had disappeared: *Whatever I did, I did for you.*

A plea to the statue of a saint at the Old North Church, as Ollie's gerbil lay dying in his hands: *Pray for this small soul.*

A quiet murmur: *Sometimes, what we have already is exactly what we need.*

An off-hand comment as she studied an elderly, frail-looking woman on their block: *People look for strength on the outside. But that's not usually where it is.*

A spur to action: *Listen with more than just your ears, Bambino. Listen with all you have.*

Her voice in his head, after Ollie had fallen from a great height at Herrick's End. Then, too, the curtain had descended as he had slipped in and out consciousness.

Forgive him, she had said.

Ollie knew who she meant, of course, and he had refused. *Never.*

Forgive him, Francie had insisted. *That is your key.*

Now, the words fluttered past again, written on glistening wings.

Him. Ollie pictured his father's motionless, bony body on the bed. He remembered every awful thing Matteo had ever done—and then, he remembered the rest. All of the things he had witnessed in that strange, otherworldly place: The orange tent. The hoarded sandwich crusts. The abuse and death. The fear, and foster homes, and ominous, blocked memories.

Forgive him, Bambino. That is your key.

Ollie's stubbornness began to splinter, slowly. His anger began to melt. Why refuse her? What difference did any of it make now? It was over. Ollie had lost. He was dead already, even if his body still seemed to be clinging to its final, flimsy vestiges of life. He would do this one last thing, for her, before he left this place for good.

Ollie envisioned his father's arthritic knuckles, paralyzed limbs, and drooping face. He gathered all of his rage and pain into a tight, flat stone and imagined himself tossing it, skipping it, along the sunlit surface of Boston Harbor. And then, finally, he surrendered.

I forgive you.

The words flew like pigeons through a city square, noisy and chaotic. Ollie didn't realize how heavy they had been until they were gone.

Thirty-One

Ollie floated.

His mouth felt full of metal and marbles, though he suspected that was just blood and swelling. The pain had become fingers, poking into every mangled nerve.

He waited for the inevitable as desolation ravaged his thoughts. So much silence, and darkness. Too much. And then...noises. Confusion. Talking?

Ollie heard a deep, graveled voice.

Felt a hand pressing against the top of his chest, near his throat.

A wave of surprise passed, followed by resignation. Strangulation? Really? After all the alchemy and aberrance, it seemed almost ridiculous to meet his end in such an ordinary, brutish way. Then again, Herrick would probably relish the feel of his hands crushing Ollie's windpipe, and enjoy watching the expiration of those final, tortured breaths.

There was no fighting it. His body and will had both reached their end. At least he would see his mother soon. At least there was that.

Ollie braced himself, waiting for Herrick's meaty fingers to encircle his neck.

Instead, the hand stayed put. And...started to emit an odd, radiating warmth.

More words, mutterings. Fragments of fragments drifted to his ears; none of it made any sense.

As the curious heat spread through his body, something else seemed to be spreading with it. Something...soothing. Just a respite, or something more? The agonizing pain was starting to dissipate. Was this death? The hand pressed harder against his chest, and Ollie found that he could suddenly wiggle his fingers. Take a deep, bracing breath. Move his tongue.

He felt a tectonic skittering throughout his body. Pulverized organs... recalibrating. Torn tendons and ligaments...mending. Broken bones...snapping back into place like Lego blocks.

How was this possible?

Ollie's eyes fluttered open. He saw...shapes. A man. A large man—not Herrick? No. This man was shirtless and stippled with tattoos. His shoulders and arms were gaunt.

The image swam, still hazy.

When Ollie finally found his voice, it was hoarse. "Are you...a Sticky Wicket?" he asked. It seemed the only logical explanation. A tattooed, bellyaching Wicket, magnified into normal human size, hovering over him. But what was he doing in the Neath?

The Wicket, if that's what he was, leaned forward. "Ollie," he said with a gentle shake. "Hey. Wake up. Ollie, it's me."

Colors and shapes glided past; shards of a fractured rainbow. Ollie squinted.

"Ollie, wake up! It's me! It's..."

All at once, the blurry face snapped into focus.

If he were able, Ollie would have gasped. But the best he could manage was a feeble wheeze. He stared up, trying to blink. The features dropped together into a funnel cone of recognition: Busted-up nose. Haggard skin. Watery eyes.

"P-Papa?"

Matteo nodded, looking solemn.

"I... I don't... What are you doing here?" Was this the afterlife? No, wait—his father was still alive, in the Neath. Wasn't he?

"There's no time, kid. Can you stand up?"

"I..." Ollie's mind skipped like a scratched record as the healing warmth continued to spread through his limbs. He felt better, yes. Remarkably better. But could he stand? He didn't know. At this point, he could barely lift his head off the ground. "What are you—"

His question was interrupted by a loud, startling crack. Then another, and another. Ollie leaned onto his right side, peering into the distance at...what, exactly? What was he looking at? He could swear it was an enormous block of ice. A cube, as big as a closet. And inside this clear, frozen container... A man. It looked like George Herrick, trapped. Voice muffled. Flailing angrily and waving his cane. Making the structure crack around him.

Ollie could see, even with his barely recovered vision, that the ice was melting. Fast.

"Shit," Matteo muttered. He had followed Ollie's gaze. Then he spun back around. "Are you okay here for a sec?" the haggard man asked. "I'm going to go help your friend, but I have to hurry."

Friend? For a long, bleary beat, Ollie did not understand. And then, all at once, it came rushing back: Derrin, clutching her abdomen. A spreading, red stain on her jumpsuit. Blood. So much blood. Ollie winced, then turned his head. The group gradually came into focus: All of his friends, standing in a clump a short distance away. Wait, not all. His eyes darted. No Tera. Where was Tera?

"Ollie! Focus! You need to answer me. Are you okay?"

Derrin. Could Matteo heal Derrin, like he had—apparently—just healed Ollie? "Yeah, go!" Ollie croaked, his head barely bobbing. "Go!"

His father jumped to his feet and ran across the small clearing.

His *father?* What on God's green earth was going on?

Matteo was only halfway there when the ice-cracking culminated into a spectacular, ear-shattering burst, sending crystallized chunks in every direction. Herrick had managed to free himself from the frozen prison. Then he snarled, yanked down his coat, and lurched forward.

Matteo reacted by stopping short, lifting his chin, and holding his arms at his sides. The pose reminded Ollie of two-dimensional drawings of ancient Egyptian soldiers, standing stiffly in line beside their pharaoh.

Ollie's father began to speak. "Tiger teeth, mighty wind, bite to pain, blow to sin," he said. As he uttered the last word, a howl began to rise in the air around him.

Herrick continued to advance. *Step, tap, lean. Step, tap, lean.*

Matteo said it again, louder: "Tiger teeth! Mighty wind! Bite to pain! Blow to sin!" At that, the howl amplified. A gust of wind—so strong it was almost visible—rushed across the clearing and knocked George Herrick onto his back. His cane kept going, landing further away.

The wind continued to blow. Herrick roared in anger and frustration, still flattened on the ground.

Matteo, meanwhile, turned and resumed his rush toward Ollie's friends. They parted, plainly dumbfounded, clearing a path to Derrin's slumped and lifeless body. Matteo dropped to his knees amid a jumbled chorus of shouts and pleas; Kuyu dropped down beside him.

The shirtless man placed a hand on Derrin's chest and closed his eyes.

Herrick shouted obscenities as he fought the wind.

Ollie's friends pleaded and cried, begging Derrin to wake up. Begging this new, scrawny stranger to save her.

Matteo seemed to ignore it all. He kept his hand on her bloodied chest, concentrating. Staring down at her corpse-like form. Only his lips moved, muttering something Ollie couldn't hear—until Derrin, miraculously, started to stir.

Kuyu shouted her name; touched her face. The others let out similar exclamations of disbelief and astonished joy. Ollie felt a delirious bubble rise...then fall just as fast. His eyes jumped from face to face. Still, no Tera. Where was she? And where was Meatball?

Confusion and angst made his stomach clench. It didn't make sense. Tera wouldn't just *leave*. To make matters worse, Ollie couldn't help but notice that the mighty, uncanny wind was dying down. Herrick was back on his feet, and advancing again.

Matteo had noticed, too.

With effort, Ollie raised himself up onto his elbows. He watched in growing bewilderment as his father, yet again, adopted the strange, rigid stance and started to speak.

"Wall to wall, flame to flame, bind the rogue, snare and frame," Matteo recited, eyes shut.

Sparks jumped in the dirt, then died away.

"Wall to wall! Flame to flame! Bind the rogue! Snare and frame!" Then, again: "Wall to wall! Flame to flame! Bind the rogue! Snare and frame!"

In the next instant, the sparks grew into tall, blazing rods, like cornstalks on fire. They surrounded Herrick, who was forced to stop his progress once more.

Matteo's entire body was alight in reflected orange; Ollie stared at him, agog. Utterly speechless.

When Ellora had told him he was a half-witch, he had thought, naturally, of his angelic, enchanting mother. Anything else was unimaginable. And yet here he was, forced to do more than just imagine it. Forced to face the irrefutable proof.

His *father* was the witch? His asshole, abusive, deadbeat dad? In what kind of a world could that possibly be true?

Then Ollie remembered where he was: remembered mermaids-who-were-not-mermaids, and talkative half-crab clones, and underwater labs, and black-heart powders, and alligators with fur, and reverse chairlifts, and wormwalker urine-storms, and scratchy-tongued salt collectors, and deadly illusions, and sin Readers, and wheelbarrow captives, and a beautiful, remarkable girl who had somehow, some way, fallen in love with the likes of him.

In that kind of a world, a witchy, formerly comatose dad probably didn't even rank in the top ten on the Weirdest Stuff List. Ollie closed his eyes and slumped as his nerve endings continued their merciless assault.

And then—Matteo was at his side again, kneeling. Wiping the sweat from Ollie's brow. Peering and poking like an ER doctor.

"Knock it off!" Ollie slapped his father's hand away, feeling inexplicably frustrated. The man had just saved his life, after all. And Derrin's life. He should feel grateful. Yet all Ollie wanted to do was shove him. "What are you doing here?"

Matteo leaned back, eyes wide, his butt resting on his heels. His face betrayed his confusion. "What do you mean?" he asked.

"What do you mean, what do I mean? How did you get here? Why are you awake?"

"I'm here because...you released me," Matteo answered, haltingly, in a tone that implied that he was stating the obvious.

"What? How the hell did I—" And then, like a smack in the face, Ollie understood. *The forgiveness.* The simple act of forgiveness had somehow awakened Matteo from years of helpless torpor. "Wait. Wait a sec. Released you from what, exactly?"

Again, his father seemed surprised. "From...him." Matteo turned to look over his shoulder in George Herrick's direction.

Together, they peered at the thrashing, indignant, and spell-spewing old man, who was already well on his way to extinguishing his fiery prison.

Forgive him. That is your key.

Memories skittered like jumping-bean seeds, combining and sprouting into a sudden bonsai in Ollie's brain. He remembered a ring of keys in Herrick's End, embossed with pictures and puzzles. Unlocking Ollie's passage, one door after another, until he finally opened the portal to Elisha, Lizbeth, and Bert's lost-in-time dungeon chamber.

Then he remembered another cell, not far away—the one holding his father. His comatose father, felled by an unknown, all-powerful malady.

He remembered that same, drooling old man opening his mouth, inexplicably conveying a directive from a dead woman. *Message from your mother!* Matteo had wheezed. *Rivers do not freeze!* That one little sentence had enabled Ollie and Tera to leap the final hurdle and make their escape from the prison.

Ollie had thought his father had been nothing more than a marionette, his strings pulled by some unseen force. But now... Was he meant to believe that his dad had been there all along? He'd been aware? Watching? And, more unbelievably, *helping?*

"Herrick did this to you?" Ollie asked. It made no sense. "He made you all...?" The question withered as he spun a finger around his own face, trying, ridiculously, to indicate an unconscious state.

Matteo nodded, looking grim. "Trapped in my own body. Until you set me free."

"But...but...why?" This wasn't the time for questions. Ollie knew that. George Herrick, and all hell, was about to break loose. But he nevertheless found himself immobilized in shock and disorientation. What in God's name was going on here? He had to know.

Matteo sighed. He looked back at Herrick nervously, then continued in a tumbling rush. "When I got down here, he was expecting me. There was a prophesy, or a story...or some such bullshit. I don't know. He knew I was coming, and he got it into his head that I was going to help you take him down."

Ollie swallowed, recalling Ellora's whisper to Herrick in the courtyard: *"Much as I might desire it, it is not my destiny to vanquish you,"* she had said. Then she had pointed to Ollie. *"It is his."*

The crackling fire rods jumped and wobbled in his peripheral vision. He felt himself wobbling with them.

"He kept watch for me, I guess," Matteo continued, looking over his shoulder again. "And as soon as I got here, he tossed me into that cell, and that's where I stayed. Until..."

Ollie knew what came next: *Until* he and Leonard had interrupted their frantic Herrick's End escape to kick down Matteo's door, lift him off the floor, and carry him out.

With effort, Ollie lifted his weight off his elbows to sit fully upright. "But...he didn't kill you?"

"Oh, he tried." Matteo smiled contemptuously. "The best he could do, in the end, was drop me into that...state." His face darkened. "Not dead, not alive. Some friggin' nightmare place in between."

"Oh," Ollie said. He started to add, *"I'm sorry,"* but stopped himself. Then he started to add, snidely, *"How did it feel to be the victim, for a change?"* But he stopped himself again.

Matteo was still talking. "So...I had to find other ways to talk to you," he finished with a shrug.

Other ways. The two words hit like fingertips spinning a globe; suddenly, the world twisted around him. To steady himself, Ollie concentrated on the breath snaking through his lungs, his sinuses, his throat. *In, and out. In, and out.* He raised a shaking finger. "It was you!" he whispered. "You wrote the notes!"

Soul mates.

Weelichka the Salt Collector's words came back to him, clear as a tinkling chime. *Your soul mate is here,* she had told him, confused. *Well, was here. Then, mostly here. But not entirely? You have a very close connection. Yes. He communicates with you directly. Writing? Words? Yes. He gives you words without speaking them directly. He is gone, and he speaks to you still!*

Tera had let out a long whistle. They'd both thought, naturally, that Weelichka had been speaking about George Herrick. About the Herrick notes, which were not Herrick notes at all.

They were...Matteo Delgato notes?

Mostly here, but not entirely. He is gone, and he speaks to you still!

Ollie gaped at his father, who nodded, looking sheepish. "It was the only way I could get messages out. Through other people. And notes. And...trogs." Matteo laughed self-consciously. "Sorry if it was all a little...woo-woo." He wiggled his fingers, looking embarrassed. "Sometimes these spells get a mind of their own, you know?"

Ollie went still. "Yeah," he said. "I do."

The words echoed, as clear as the first time he'd heard them:

Hows and abouts, souls and mates. Find him his, seal your fate.

Nova red, Nova true. Fate of three rests with you.

Good is bad, beast will bite. Steer the course, bend the light.

Save the savior who is not a savior. Use the treasure that is not your treasure. Pay the man who is not a man.

Water green, three on high. Air and breath, truth and lie.

The messages had been scrawled on parchment. Voiced through dead men's mouths. Delivered to nymphs. And even transmitted to Tera in her tank: *A gift he will need, an answer he seeks. He will find both complete where the sleeping one sleeps.*

Each message had been invaluable to Ollie's survival in this underworld ordeal. Each one had guided him, directly or indirectly, to this very particular place and time.

The sleeping one—no longer asleep. Ollie struggled to conjugate his two warring realities. Was Matteo a villain, or a hero? A hindrance, or a helper? How could this man, who had done so much to destroy his life, now claim to have done so much to save it? Ollie felt, suddenly, like he was watching a show with too much static on the screen. The picture was spotty and scattered.

"Anyway..." Matteo looked over his bare, bony shoulder at the rapidly shrinking circle of fire. "We've got to move, yeah? That thing won't hold him much longer."

He was right. Herrick was holding out his palms, growling, and weakening the flames. In the past few minutes, he'd already managed to shrink them down to half their original size; soon, he'd be able to hop over them, if not douse them altogether.

Ollie scrambled, painfully, to his feet. When Matteo held out a hand to help him, he ignored it.

The others were approaching, carrying Derrin along with them. She seemed to be standing on her own two feet, with Kuyu and Leonard supporting her on either side.

Ajanta sidled up next to Ollie and touched the side of his head. "You had us worried, there, young man. Are you all right?"

"Yeah, I'm okay."

The group gathered together into a semi-circle, eyes darting. Warily watching Herrick's antics. Looking for an escape route. Ready to bolt. Finally, it was Dozer who asked what they were all thinking. "Not that we ain't grateful, friend," he began, fixing Matteo with a careful stare. "But...who in blue blazes are you?"

Ollie and Matteo threw each other glances; neither seemed to know what to say.

Leonard saved them the trouble. Stepping forward, he peered closely, thoughtfully, at the shirtless man's pockmarked face. Then he said, "I know this guy. He's from Floor Twenty. The guy we carried out, that day." He paused before adding, "You're Ollie's father."

An awkward silence followed as eyebrows lifted all around. Ollie kept his gaze firmly planted on his shoes.

Dozer glanced over at Herrick and the wall of flames. "Listen, y'all," he said. "That fella looks madder than a wet hen. Maybe we should, uh...get a move on?" He pointed toward the distant docks.

Heads bobbed in frightened agreement. Feet began to shuffle against the hard-packed dirt.

"Wait!" Ollie called out. "Where's Tera? And Meatball?"

The group stopped. One by one, each of them swiveled and peered in surprise.

"She was right here a minute ago," Leonard said.

Murmurs and nods of assent.

"A minute?" Ollie pressed. "Where could she have gone in a minute?"

At that, Leonard wavered. "Well, maybe more than a minute..."

"When did you last see her, exactly?"

The big man lifted one palm, looking unsure.

"When did you guys see her?"

They began to talk over one another:

"Well, we came out of the tunnel, and—"

"And then Derrin got hit, and—"

"And then you kept getting slammed, and—"

Matteo waved his arms, interrupting. "She'll have to catch up," he said. "C'mon, we've got to go."

She'll have to catch up? Ollie stared at his *Papa*, his so-called *father*, as a decades-old wellspring of rage and resentment boiled up to his eyelids. Now that they were standing side-by-side, he noticed with some satisfaction that he loomed over his father's hunched and withered frame. Ironic, considering how often he had once cowered in the man's shadow. Now, it was almost hard to imagine what he had been so frightened of.

"No fucking way!" Ollie snapped. "I'm not leaving here without her!"

The others threw each other nervous glances. For a long moment, the only sounds they heard were the crackle of dying flames and the broad outlines of George Herrick's raspy, shouted threats. Ollie could only make out every third word or so—something about "murder," and "crush," and "all of you,"—but the implications were clear enough.

Then Laszlo came to stand beside him. "I will stay with you, my friend." He turned to the others. "You all, go. Get to safe place. We will find Tera."

"Screw that," Derrin said, limping forward. Beside her, Kuyu nodded. The others followed, advancing together as a group.

Matteo took in their stony expressions, their folded arms, and shook his head with resignation. "Fine. Okay. I'll hold him off. I'll think of something." He began counting on his fingers, and Ollie wondered what, exactly, he was calculating. Then, Matteo began muttering mysterious phrases. Sweat covered his torso and face.

Nothing changed.

"Hurry up, man!" someone yelled. "He's almost out!"

The circle of flames now reached only as high as Herrick's waist.

"Krite, hurry up!" someone else said.

"Okay, okay!" Matteo sputtered. "It's been a while, all right? I'm *thinking*..." He tapped his fingers together, panic spreading across his emaciated face. "Ice, and wind, and fire...and...and..."

"Snowing storm?" Laszlo suggested.

Ollie shot him a look. "Dude, seriously?"

"I am only making the suggestions!" Laszlo said defensively, holding up his hands. "I do not hear anyone else making any of the better suggestions."

"No need," said a voice behind them.

They turned around to see Tera, safe and sound, wearing a trog on her shoulder and a shit-eating grin on her face. "Forget the snow," she said. "I called for reinforcements."

She pointed, and they followed her finger.

Up.

Thirty-Two

Ollie craned his neck.

At first, he saw nothing. Just a blue, wormwalkery ceiling and the precarious spikes of stalactites, high above.

Then—three black dots. Getting bigger.

Three black...crows. Mrs. Paget, and two others. They were swooping into view with startling speed. Ollie was staring for nearly a minute before he realized: They had passengers.

Mrs. Paget led the way, wings outstretched into a magnificent, mindboggling span. As she cut through the lingering clouds of smoke, Ollie studied the person riding on her back: Pointed, stern features. Frizzy hair flying in the wind.

Elisha the Witch.

His heart pattered. If Mrs. Paget had Elisha, that must mean that the other two... As they got close, his suspicions were confirmed: Elisha, Lizbeth, and Bert. The nesting witches, unnested. Unnested? He turned to beam at Tera, who merely shrugged in faux modesty.

"It was all Mrs. Paget's doing," she said.

"Like hell," he answered. In truth, he didn't care who had convinced them, or how. He was only thrilled beyond measure that they were actually here.

The witches, on the other hand, did not look thrilled. As they circled, they surveyed the still-smoldering ruins and the gathered group of bloody, battered survivors on the ground. Then, finally, they turned their attention to Herrick. And that was where it stayed.

The old man had been mid-step over the last row of fire, triumphant in his escape. His hands were outstretched, ready to advance on Ollie and his friends once again. But when he saw the approaching crows, "the Doc" had paused. And when he realized who was riding on their backs, his face had drooped instantly into a new expression.

Ollie knew that expression. He had worn it on his own face, many times—a look of bald, unmitigated fear.

Before they had even reached the ground, the three witches sent out a shock wave of color and sound. The remnants of the circle of flames around Herrick vanished. He was free. Ollie watched, holding his breath, waiting for the bearded man to sprint away. Or to resume his attacks. Yet...he didn't.

George Herrick looked down. Tried to lift his legs. They were stuck fast to the dirt. He reached down, pulling at his thighs, to no avail. Like a digital image losing its pixels, the color seemed to drain, drop by drop, from his face.

He knew what was coming.

Everyone knew what was coming. Ollie could hear the murmurs and building excitement around him as his friends watched the crows hover and land.

Whatever powers Herrick had stolen, they were no match for the ones that had just swept in from the sky.

Ollie waited for the three witches to disembark. Instead, they stayed seated on the birds' black, feathery backs. Examining their prey. Talking without speaking. Did they know what had happened to Ellora? Could they sniff out the truth in the air? Were they surprised to see the supposedly dead George Herrick? Had they pieced together the full story of his lies and machinations as soon as they had spotted him on the ground below?

Ollie couldn't guess what Elisha, Lizbeth, and Bert might be thinking, or discovering, or telepathically communicating to each other. But he did know one thing for sure about these witches, something he had learned the hard way back at their nest: Their collective memory was long. And reinforced by a sturdy foundation of grudges.

He waited for Elisha to make a pronouncement, or to lash out. But surprisingly, it was the daintier Lizbeth who acted first: She held out her hands, flat and palms-up, as though readying herself to carry a tray. Then, she began to speak.

Lizbeth's words came out as an angry hum, more of a noise than a language. The sounds grew louder, vibrating the ground. Everyone looked down at their feet, startled. Tera grabbed Ollie's arm; they clung together in tense vigilance. Around them, the others did the same.

But Herrick's reaction was the most surprising: The old man, so defiant only minutes before, had begun to openly whimper and cower.

Ollie stared, unblinking. Of all the bizarre sights he had witnessed in the Neath, this one might have been the most shocking of all.

Lizbeth's chanting grew louder still. Her hands stayed aloft. And as they all watched, a structure began appearing around Herrick's body. Just...appearing. Horizontal and vertical wooden bars. A box. No...a cage. Rectangular, and sturdy.

With a start, Ollie realized that he had seen this cage before.

A voice, a memory, hit with startling clarity. *You have imprisoned innocents! It is not too late for you to save us, and to save yourself. I beseech you now, open this cage! Stop this injustice! By your own hands, you bring us to death, George Herrick! You bring us to hell!*

It was the same cage Ollie had witnessed in his vision. Salem Village, 1692. Three prisoners, trapped in the back of a carriage. George Herrick, driving the horses. *Silence,* he had ordered, shoving one of prisoners back through the bars. *You are mad, old woman. Mad, and cursed.* He had snapped the reins without pity or pause, driving them on to their deaths.

Now, Herrick had suddenly found himself on the other side of those same cage bars. Staring through the gaps in filthy, consummate horror. Knowing what was coming and powerless to stop it.

Lizbeth surveyed her handiwork and let out a satisfied cackle. Bert and Elisha laughed along with her. The sound of their mirth made Ollie think about that odd, German word, *schadenfreude:* Taking pleasure in someone else's pain.

Ollie noticed that Tera had weakened with relief beside him, and heard his friends let out cautious expulsions of air. Was this it? Was it over, at last? The witches had arrived, and Herrick was caged.

But Ollie did not exhale. He was watching George Herrick flail around his newest enclosure and noticing something strange.

As before, Herrick's body seemed to be growing.

Was it Ollie's imagination? An illusion of the smoky haze? *No.* He felt his stomach clench in certainty as he watched Herrick's head hit the pen's wood-plank ceiling. The bearded man was suddenly more crouched. His limbs were starting to bend at awkward angles. His black-coated torso was having trouble fitting inside the cage that had easily contained him only minutes before.

Ollie recognized the terrible enlargement in the same way he recognized a spreading poison-ivy rash on his skin: with certain dread.

Lizbeth's vengeful spell, or curse, or whatever it was, wasn't hurting Herrick at all. For some ungodly reason, it was somehow making him bigger. Just like Ollie's fury had done earlier. To both Herrick *and* Carmichael. But...why? How? It made no sense.

And that wasn't all that was wrong with the unfolding scene. Just as George Herrick seemed to be growing, Lizbeth the Witch seemed, unmistakably, to be shrinking. Her legs and feet were like skinny, hand-drawn lines against the crow's obsidian feathers. Her head and shoulders were smaller than they had been when she had landed—then, suddenly, smaller still.

Ollie slammed his eyes shut. When he opened them again, he hoped to find the setting returned to normal. Instead, the warping continued. Herrick's body had grown so large that it had begun to break through the boundaries of the cage around it. And Lizbeth's already petite frame was becoming more and more doll-like on her perch.

All around him, the wary celebrations died away. The others had noticed it, too.

By the time Herrick's burgeoning body burst through the pen's roof, his look of fear had transformed into one of surprised triumph. And the witches' *schadenfreude* had skidded to a dead stop.

What was happening?

Ollie's confusion hovered, then lifted. The nuggets of truth floated around him like a circle of objects in his dreamy, empathetic netherworld. He plucked them, studied them, and understood.

Ollie knew exactly what was going on. What was going *wrong*. And he knew how to stop it.

Sailing stones in the Death Valley desert.

Every action has an equal and opposite reaction.

Forces and intentions, acting upon each other. Binding each other.

Nothing, not even a stone, exists alone in this world.

"Wait!" he called out. "Stop!"

The witches ignored him.

Ollie lurched forward. Tera tried to hold him back, but he dodged her hand.

"Wait!"

Every step was like the stab of an icepick; his body was still broken. He couldn't walk. But he *had* to walk. He had to get closer, to make them understand.

Ollie's feet staggered and shuffled. Gravity and wobbly muscles fought his progress. Still, he pressed on, inch by agonizing inch.

If the three witches noticed his advance, they made no sign. They were, instead, looking at each other in alarm—again, communicating without speaking. Bert nodded, then straightened on the crow's back. As Lizbeth had done before him, he held out his upturned hands.

"No!" Ollie called out, but his voice was weak. Too weak. "Wait! Bert, don't do it!"

They were making it worse. Couldn't they see that? Wasn't it as plain as the scorched heap behind them where a tower used to be? His eyes darted from face to face. He looked back at his friends, huddled. At the crows, stoic and stern.

Why did no one understand?

That wasn't entirely true, he realized with a start. One person understood perfectly. George Herrick had caught his eye, grinning the grin of a man with a secret. Ollie watched with dread and revulsion as the old man lowered one eyelid in a slow, self-assured wink.

The wink was infuriating. Maddening. It propelled Ollie into another painful lurch, then another. He was closing the gap, but the witches were still too far away. Too far to hear his pleas. He watched with helpless frustration as Bert began to speak:

"Watchery wizzles and buildery fizzles! Two yams in the pram and noosery snizzles!"

The now-broken cage vanished with a thundering whoosh. Almost instantly, something else had arisen in its place. More planks of wood, this time arranged into a kind of platform. An elevated floor, attached to a short set of stairs. Several framed-out wood posts. Ollie's eyes traveled to the top of the structure, where he saw something dangling. A rope.

A noose.

Bert had made a gallows.

No! No, no, no!

The witch kept up the steady stream of babble and left his hands outstretched as the structure solidified. And as they all watched in mute shock, he directed the unseen, ineffable force to lift George Herrick off the ground.

"Ever the hangman, never the hung, switcheroo necker, switcheroo strung," Bert intoned.

The old man's body floated up, up, and up, approaching ever-closer to the coiled rope.

"Stop!" Ollie screamed. The word dangled in the air, useless. He dragged himself closer, then closer still. "Stop! You're making it worse!"

Bert ignored him, repeating the strange verse again, and again, and again: "Ever the hangman, never the hung, switcheroo necker, switcheroo strung." The words sped up with each repetition.

The noose slid itself around Herrick's neck. And then—he dropped.

The old man gurgled in panic as he gasped for air. He pulled desperately, uselessly, at the tightening rope. His face reddened; his legs began to kick the air in desperation.

Ollie was ten feet away, now. Still too far. He could hear Tera and the others calling out for him, trying to stop him. He kept moving, dragging a still-useless left foot. Ignoring the ceaseless darts of pain. He knew, with sick certainty, what was going to happen. He knew what Bert's vengeance would create.

And he was right.

Herrick's body twitched and flailed. And then, once again, his body seemed to grow. Swift and strong, like a dancing-seedpod tree. Bigger, bigger, bigger. Even faster than before.

Bert, meanwhile, seemed to be shrinking—like an adult morphing into a teen, and then a teen into a child.

With effort, Ollie steadied his thoughts.

The key.

He understood, now, what had to be done. It made him nauseous and incensed, but he understood. He had to forgive George Herrick.

Impossible.

No. Nothing was impossible. Not here. If he had learned anything in this woebegone place, he had learned that.

Come on, now, Ollie told himself. *You can do this.*

He had to do this. He had no choice. Anything else meant... He wouldn't think about what it meant. Secretions rose in his throat. He searched his heart and his mind, clawing and hunting and dredging the deepest depths for forgiveness. But he found none.

Shit.

In desperation, Ollie recalled the trick he had used to forgive his father: balling up all the anger and pain into a flat, metaphorical stone, and then tossing that stone out into the metaphorical Boston Harbor. Ollie closed his eyes, smushed it all up together, and threw. The stone skipped. Once, twice, three times. He scanned the imaginary horizon for compassion, for absolution, and found...none. Again.

Goddammit!

Nearby, Herrick seemed immune to Ollie's efforts, such as they were. The old man's flailing feet reached the ground. He stood, easily, and yanked the rope from his neck.

Get it together, you idiot! Ollie berated himself. Then, unexpectedly, he heard Ellora's declaration. Saw it, actually: The words danced with a twinkle across his line of sight:

It starts with you.

Yes. Of course! It had to start with him, didn't it? He had to forgive himself, first. Okay. He could do that. Speedily, Ollie ran though the usual litany of offenses in his mind: He wasn't perfect. He wasn't physically fit. Some might even call him lazy. He'd never been a great conversationalist. He ate too much, and too often. He tended to hold grudges. He had sometimes swept crumbs off the table and onto the floor at Mr. B's caffe rather than cleaning them up properly. He'd sometimes yelled at his mother, when she was still alive. He didn't read much. Or make good eye contact with people. And there was more. So much more. Too much to catalog in that particular moment, what with George Herrick about to break out and kill them all.

Despite all that, he was a good person. He really was, right? He took care of his friends when he could, and he was even occasionally brave and mildly clever, when the situation demanded it. He was good enough for Tera to love, which was good enough for him.

Great, Ollie thought with a satisfied nod. *I forgive me. And...* He looked up at the incensed, thrashing prisoner in the gallows... *Maybe I can forgive you, too.*

He hadn't peered closely into Herrick's past. He didn't know the details of whatever pain, suffering, and raging inferiority complexes could have led to the man to do such monstrous things. Frankly, he didn't want to know. But he had to assume it was all there. If that kind of evil needed a "fertile soil" to grow, as Damira had told him, then Herrick's soil must have been chock-full of rancid manure from top to bottom. Ollie wouldn't wish that on anybody.

Not even George Herrick? He thought about that for a moment, surprised at his bone-gut answer: No. Not even him. With effort, Ollie concentrated on that part of the equation and pushed past the rest.

I forgive you, you mean, ignorant, hate-mongering bastard. God help me, I do.

And he did—mostly. He actually did. The realization came as a pleasant shock. Ollie kept his eyes on the crumbling gallows, feeling quite proud of himself as he waited for the scene to change. For Herrick to shrink back down to size. Instead, strangely, he saw more of the same. Growing, growing, growing, growing. Ollie's puffed sense of self-satisfaction began to deflate as frustration and alarm pricked like pins. What had he done wrong? Why wasn't it working?

Maybe he had to say it out loud. The words nearly choked him, but he managed to push them out: "I forgive you."

Had Herrick heard him? Did it matter? Either way, the old man's augmentation continued unabated. Herrick tossed the remains of the noose onto the ground. Fury and gratification mingled on his face while he rubbed his throat and replenished his lungs with air. He had grown to inhuman size: maybe thirteen or fourteen feet tall.

Hysteria once again ensued. From the corner of his eye, Ollie could see his friends taking panicky steps backward. Herrick was somehow snatching victory from defeat. Even now, with the full force of the nesting witches leveled against him.

Caw! Caw!

Mrs. Paget's plaintive cries echoed above the cacophony.

Too big, Ollie thought numbly.

Caw!

The crow's lament, heavy with grief, shot like an arrow through his synapses. That's when he realized: This whole damn thing was too big. Herrick hadn't only damaged Ollie. He'd damaged countless others, too. Most of all, he'd damaged the witches, in immeasurable, terrible ways. This wound was massive and profound, and Ollie's forgiveness alone would not be enough to stop the bleeding.

Caw! Caw! Caw!

But maybe something else could.

He tore his eyes away from the unfolding gallows scene and looked back at the witches. Of the three, only Elisha retained her normal stature. The other two were still shrinking.

Ollie fixed his stare on her, willing her to see the truth. From what he could tell, she was their leader. The baddest witch this side of the earth's crust. If anyone could get them all out of this mess, Elisha could.

Surely she must have figured out what was happening here? Surely she must have recognized the cause and effect?

He tried to shout as he limped closer.

Elisha was muttering, but he couldn't hear the words. Her features had hardened. She surveyed the spectacle, taking in Lizbeth's and Bert's ever-diminishing proportions, before deciding on a course of action. With a flick of her wrist, the now-useless gallows disappeared. Ollie felt a brief moment of elation: Elisha understood! The noose was gone!

Then he saw what she had created in its place.

Logs, piled into a pyramidal shape. Hay, scattered around the edges. And in the center, a single, wooden pole, standing straight and tall.

Ollie swallowed, his throat going dry as a walnut shell. He recognized that barbaric construction. He had seen dozens just like it, maybe hundreds, when Elisha had dragged him back in time to witness the atrocities perpetrated at Valais, Torsaker, and other towns and villages. It was a pyre. Created with the sole purpose of burning someone alive.

Only what you owe.

Ollie's heart dropped.

Elisha was going to make George Herrick pay. And in the process, she would end them all.

Thirty-Three

Elisha raised her palms. Her expression remained stony, and resolute.

With a ghastly surge, Herrick's body flew through the air and slammed against the pole. He remained there, helpless, as ropes rose through the air like snakes from a charmer's basket, wrapping his ankles, arms, and throat. Before long, they bound him tightly to the center post.

The witch observed her handiwork with satisfaction and began to mutter something under her breath.

A spark ignited in the hay. A small flame began to flicker.

No, no, no!

None of this was right!

Ollie felt as though he were floating outside his own body. He staggered again and again until, finally, he reached Mrs. Paget's pointy feet. Elisha sat high above him on the giant crow's back, still out of reach. Craning his neck, he cried out: "Stop!"

Only Mrs. Paget swiveled her head in his direction.

"Stop! Krite, you have to stop this now!"

But Elisha the Witch simply continued to mutter, her gaze still focused on the palms of her hands. Before long, her body began to shrink. Her robes swam. Her skin shriveled. Herrick, meanwhile, was growing. Again. With every vindictive spell she cast, with every flame she stoked, she was making her enemy bigger—and making herself smaller.

So it was, with vengeance. So it has always been.

"STOP!" Ollie called out again, his voice now hoarse with desperation. "Elisha, stop!"

He scurried around Mrs. Paget's legs as best he could, back and forth and around, agony ricocheting through every limb and muscle. There had to be a way up. He had to reach that witch! But the crow was too far off the ground, and Ollie was too injured. He couldn't climb. He couldn't—

Mrs. Paget was staring at him. She blinked her dark eyes once, then twice.

"Down!" Ollie said. "Down, girl!"

Mrs. Paget bobbed her feathered head. She seemed to be considering the request. Then, she began to lower her neck.

Caw!

Down and down and down, until she was bent forward in a genuflecting pose—and Elisha was in striking range, at last.

Ollie pounced. His barely mended body screamed in protest as he leapt over Mrs. Paget's head, straddled her long neck, propelled himself forward, and tackled Elisha, sending the both of them toppling down to the ground in a tangle of limbs.

Elisha spluttered and shoved him, hard. Then she stood and dropped her hands on her hips. "Meddlesome boy!" she spat. Then she dismissed him, immediately turning her attention back to Herrick. The muttering started again.

Ollie groaned. With effort, he climbed back to his feet. The pain was exquisite, now. Almost unbearable. He placed himself directly in front of her, gasping. Trying to impede the spell's path with his bulky body. "Elisha, you have to stop! Please, listen to me!"

Lips still moving, the elder witch slid an annoyed glare in his direction.

"You're feeding it!" Ollie rasped. "Can't you see that? You're feeding *him!*"

Her fuzzy eyebrows lowered.

"Please, I'm begging you. You have to stop this, now! You're only making it worse!"

Finally, Elisha paused her incantations long enough to fix him with an icy stare. "Do not interfere in that which you do not understand," she said.

Ollie sputtered, begged. "Look what's happening! Just *look*. Please. He's growing, and you're weakening. He's draining you! And you're falling right into his trap. We all are!"

At the base of the pyre, flames were multiplying. Herrick squirmed in his rope restraints. "She can't do it, anyway," he called out. "She can't kill me. She doesn't have the bollocks. Or the power." He began to chuckle maniacally as he writhed. "That's what happens when a witch sits in a cell for three hundred years. She gets a little clapped-out." The prisoner's demented laughter got louder.

In response, Elisha glowered and lifted her hands. "Flare and blaze, scorch and heat, skin to heart, head to feet," she intoned. And again, louder: "Flare and blaze! Scorch and heat! Skin to heart, head to feet!"

As the flames rose, Herrick's body expanded. And Elisha's contracted, again.

The old man's laughter continued. The ropes binding his wrists and ankles began to fray and snap.

"Stop!" Ollie screamed. He grabbed her arm. "He's trying to piss you off! Can't you see that? He's only getting bigger!"

Caw! Mrs. Paget echoed.

Elisha shot him another withering glance. "And what, pray tell, would you suggest I do instead?"

They locked eyes: the witch and the half-witch. She thought he was less-than, Ollie realized. Half-strong, half-weak. And she was right, sort of. One side of him *was* stronger than the other.

But she had it backwards. It was the human in him, not the witch, that made him powerful. More powerful than all of them—Elisha, Bert, Lizbeth, Weelichka, the Reader, and however many others—combined. His weaknesses, mistakes, heartaches, and defeats had given him access to something that even the most potent magical spell could not have spawned on its own.

That was the side of him that mattered, right now.

Ollie looked over at his friends. At Tera. At Meatball. They were all watching him with awed, curious stares. He straightened to his full height, towering above Elisha. The pain of his internal injuries screamed. His body was a wreck; his mind was awhirl. But when he spoke, his voice did not waver.

"You have to forgive him," Ollie said.

The witch guffawed. Up on their crow perches, Lizbeth and Bert seemed to do the same.

"You can't be serious," said Elisha.

Ollie nodded. "I am."

"Why on earth would we do that?" Lizbeth squeaked.

"Because it's the only way," Ollie said. The actual, literal, only way. He glanced behind at the pyre, where Herrick's frame had already grown taller than the pole it was strapped to.

Elisha seemed to hesitate, then flapped a hand. "This is perfectly ridiculous. Absurd. You know as well as anyone, Oliver. George Herrick does not deserve forgiveness."

Ollie took a step forward.

"But you do," he said.

She gaped at him, amused. "I believe you are befuddled, good sir. Perhaps one of those falling rocks landed on your head? I am not the one in need of absolution."

Ollie had a sudden vision of his mother, her face cast in ethereal, warm radiance. *Forgive him. That is your key.* As her smile faded from view, he was greeted by the even-more surprising sight of his flesh-and-blood father standing only a few feet away. Ollie gave him a pensive stare.

"That's the funny thing about forgiveness," he said. "It's not for the one who wronged you. It's for you."

Mrs. Paget gave a mighty, undulating shake, sending a spray of black feathers into the air. Elisha, Lizbeth, and Bert peered at each other intently as Herrick continued to struggle and grow. Ollie felt a flutter of hope. He had convinced them—he could tell. He had said exactly the right thing at exactly the right time. He had turned the tide. And now, everything was going to be all right, at last.

Then, the confident flutter stalled. Ollie could see a dark gleam spreading behind Elisha's eyes. He could feel the rage still simmering beneath the surface of her skin.

Her reply was steely: "You may be correct, young man. Perhaps in the future, we will learn if this is so. But not right now. Right now, George Herrick will pay." She paused, then added: "Only what he owes."

"Only what he owes," the other two echoed, each looking pitifully tiny on their avian perches.

Caw! Caw!

The pyre flames jumped again. Herrick thrashed—and grew. And grew, and grew. His arms had already burst free of the rope; seconds later, the old man grimaced as he reached up to yank the knots around his neck.

Ollie felt a skittering at his feet: Meatball. The trog scrambled up his legs and torso, snuffling and squealing as he landed in his usual spot on Ollie's shoulder. Ollie turned to look at his friends' faces, twisted in confusion and fear. Smoke from the ruins and the crackling pyre was making all of them cough, particularly Derrin, who was hunched over and hacking. He looked at his father, who shrugged somberly.

Then he looked at Tera.

She read the question in his eyes. She nodded, then mouthed the words: *Do it.*

The Greenway Carousel spun in his mind; as before, the falcon spread its wings and hissed: *It must be you.*

One by one, the rest whispered in his ear: The harbor seal, the swordfish, the glowbug. Myrtle the Turtle. Damira's cards. The Unnatural Wonders. Albino squid, pufferpines, and galloping lakehorses.

Yessss. It must be you.

Ollie felt the pull in his chest, instinctive and strong. Expanding his ribcage. Overflowing into every cell. When he could no longer contain it, he sent it out like a burst of song in four directions: first, to Lizbeth. Then, to Bert. Then, to Elisha. And lastly, to George Herrick of the Salem Village Herricks. Creator of the Neath. Thief, liar, and murderer.

Ollie steadied his weight, ignoring the aches and anguish, standing equidistant to them all. He imagined himself as a black hole, sucking each of them into his orbit.

Then, with a jolt, he carried all three witches into the sphere of Herrick's past. They fought, initially, with valiant effort. They didn't want to be there. Who would? But Ollie held them fast. He led them to the circle, where the floating objects beckoned. As before, the items were toy-like, small enough to fit in a hand, and hovering beside each other in a spherical orbit.

Ollie squinted at the bobbing assortment: What secrets did Herrick's subconscious hold? A ramshackle dwelling. A seventeenth-century tall ship. A bent and rusted shovel. A tarnished gold ring. A wide-brimmed hat and a leather shoe, both worn and pitted with holes.

He compelled the witches to enter the circle. They resisted, again—and again, he overpowered their defiance.

Elisha, Lizbeth, and Bert scowled. Then grumbled. Then, finally, capitulated. Ollie stepped backwards, watching as the trio began, reluctantly, to reach out and examine the objects floating all around them. They passed them to each other, talking without speaking. He observed the changes in their expressions as they stepped inside the moments of Herrick's dank, dark past, reflecting on his sorrow and struggles. Listening, witnessing, experiencing.

Ollie wondered, momentarily, what they were seeing. Then he realized that he was probably lucky not to know. Mostly he kept his distance, and tried to keep his patience, although he knew the pyre was still raging—and Herrick was no doubt nearing escape—in a place not too far from here.

When it was done, Ollie released the witches from the circle. Finally, he pulled them free of his strange, celestial world and led them back into their own.

Like boat-wreck survivors reaching the water's surface, they gasped at their return to the smoke-filled air of the cavern's clearing. Ollie's feet had not moved. Bert and Lizbeth still sat on the crow's fluttery backs. Ellora still stood across from him, swaying.

Caw! said Mrs. Paget, who was fixing him with a glare. The bird, clearly, had sensed something amiss. As had the others— Ollie's father and his friends were staring at him with perplexed and fearful expressions. They had watched him go slack, no doubt, and had probably panicked. Only Tera understood what had just transpired: She gave him a short, satisfied nod.

How long had they been gone? Maybe longer than he thought. Too long?

Herrick was enormous. As Ollie watched in horror, the old man continued to grow, cast spells, douse the flames, and sidestep the crackling logs. Any minute now, he would be free. The witches would be condensed into comical, useless size. Ollie would be pummeled once more against the hard ground, his father's magic would be overwhelmed by Herrick's much stronger wizardry, and all of his friends would suffer fates that would make Tera's time in the laboratory tank seem like a day at the Nova's beach.

The three witches looked at each other in their usual broadcast of silent communication. And then, slowly, too slowly, they looked back at Ollie.

Hurry hurry hurry

He saw Elisha's hands twitching, and he lurched toward her. "Don't!" he yelled.

Hurry hurry hurry hurry hurry

Lizbeth and Bert began to hum in harmony, reminding Ollie of the musical, oversized insects back at their nest. Elisha seemed to listen intently, but did not join in. Instead, she studied George Herrick. Truly studied him, like an archaeologist examining a damaged, ancient artifact.

This man, this monster, had taken everything. Had destroyed everything. Her face betrayed the grief of her ancestors in every line and pore.

The real witches watched it all. And they did not forget.

Ollie stepped closer. "It's not too late," he told her, his voice low. Insistent. "End this, Elisha. Take back what is yours."

With a scowl, Elisha pushed him aside and lifted her arms.

Ollie winced. It was over, then. The witch had made her choice. He covered his eyes and braced himself for the detonation.

When none came, he peeked through his fingers. Elisha's hands hovered—then dropped, falling heavily to her sides. Her expression was a woven mesh of anguish and resignation.

When she spoke, her voice rang out deep and true, blowing away the smoke. Sweeping through the centuries. Winding its way across the clearing, across the lake, and across the islands. Reverberating like a benediction inside every deep, hidden hollow of the Neath:

"We forgive you."

Ollie froze.

Herrick, too, had stilled. Elisha's declaration had made him pause his thrashing. First, he merely snickered. Then, he guffawed. The laughter roiled into the air, louder than the flames, shocking all of them with its volume.

And then...George Herrick stopped laughing. And began to shrink.

It happened fast—almost faster than Ollie's eyes could reasonably observe. As the milliseconds ticked by, Herrick was morphing from a giant into a slightly smaller giant into a normal-sized man. Not only in height, but also in weight: He was withering. Shriveling. Wasting away.

Aging?

Ollie stumbled backwards, unable to look away from the nightmarish spectacle. It took him a moment to realize what was happening. Herrick had stolen 300 years of life. And now, it seemed, the bill had come due. The ravages of each year hit one after another in a sudden, horrifying blast of sunken skin...rotted teeth...twisted knuckles...bulging eyeballs. All of it, collapsing onto itself.

Tera and the others shrieked. Meatball wheezed and circled, digging his head into Ollie's neck.

When he finally tore his gaze away, Ollie noticed another peculiar phenomenon unfolding in their little clearing. With every inch Herrick lost, the witches seemed to gain the same. Like parade balloons filling with air, Bert, Lizbeth, and Elisha were quickly returning to normal size. And as they grew, they glowed: The change had bestowed each of them with a gleam of sovereignty and magnificence... smooth, long locks. Dewy skin. Coral lips. The witches radiated vigor, resplendent in every way.

Almost as resplendent as Ellora had been.

Almost.

Ollie's heart dropped at the thought.

A bellow of anguish made him turn back toward the pyre, where the flames were nearly extinguished. In the center, unburned and untouched by all but time, sat the husk of the human that had once been George Herrick.

The old man cried out again—a serpentine wail of regret and despair that reached all the way to the cerulean ceiling. It was almost loud enough, almost strong enough, to reverse the damage of all that had been done. *Every sharp and bitter thing.*

Almost.
Herrick howled until the sound dried into wisps.
Until his body had withered into an ashen shell.
Until, like a crow boat swallowed by fog, he was gone.

Thirty-Four

One Year Later

"So, you're the guy, huh?"

"What guy is that?"

"You know, the guy who saved us. Saved this whole place."

"Nope."

"That's what they say."

"What who says?"

"What everyone says, man."

"Sorry to disappoint. That was a whole group of people. I was just one of them." Ollie shifted in his seat patiently. He and the fidgeting man were sitting across from each other in matching wooden chairs, each made slightly more comfortable by Ajanta's hand-sewn seat pads. The office was plain and rectangular. Lakestar windchimes hung in each of the two windows.

"So, how does this work? You're going to make me see stuff?" The man was clearly nervous. His jumpsuit was freshly laundered; his face was cleanshaven. His brown eyes shifted left to right.

"That's the idea, yes."

"What if I don't want to?"

"You don't have to do anything you don't want to do. But I think it will help you. A lot. So it's probably worth a try, huh?"

"Why would you want to help me?" The man snorted. "Haven't you heard? I'm a fucking criminal."

"Maybe, maybe not. In here, all that matters is the truth."

"Oh yeah? What truth is that?"

"The truth of what you did." Ollie paused. "Of what you owe."

The man straightened, defiant. "I thought we got rid of all that shit when the tower fell. Who the hell are you to tell me what I owe?"

"I'm nobody. All I can do is show you what you need to see, and then you can decide for yourself."

With a visible gulp, the man slumped again. "I don't need you to show me nothing. I was there, man. I know what I did."

Ollie nodded. "And now I can help you see it from the other side. See the effect that your actions had on other people. How it made them feel. How *exactly* it made them feel."

"Damn, dude. Why would I want to see that?"

"You probably don't. But that doesn't mean you shouldn't."

The man was sweating, twitching. Indecisive. Ollie kept his breathing steady. His eyes traveled to his desk, where the tchotchkes and gifts were starting to accumulate: A black-cat mug from Sweet Screams Ice Cream Parlor, holding pufferpine-quill pens and a miniature Italian flag. An aquarium snow globe. A glass jar filled with pink Weelichka Mountain salt. Several empty Bonfiglio's pastry boxes. His monogrammed wallet, finally recovered from Nikki & Floyd's shop. A scale model of the Greenway Carousel, complete with a crank that played tinny music. A kelp-wrapped package of "greenies" from Howerbout. A copy of *Historian's Guide to the Freedom Trail*. A seedpod, still jittering, in a tiny wooden bowl.

Absently, Ollie reached up to pat Meatball, who was snoozing on his shoulder. He let the uncomfortable silence drag on for several seconds. That usually worked.

"All right, fine," the man finally said. "Krite. Go ahead, make me see stuff." He shook his head. "I don't know why I'm doing this."

Ollie smiled. "Great. Are you ready?"

A look of panic washed the man's face. "What do I have to do?"

"Nothing at all. Just relax. It doesn't hurt. It's just like...taking a little trip in your head."

"Will you be there?" The man's voice sounded suddenly childlike. Frightened.

"Absolutely. I'll be with you the whole time. If you want to leave early, just let me know, and poof—we're gone. Right back to here. Otherwise, I'll just keep watch and bring us back when you're done. Take as long as you need. Okay?"

A hesitant nod. "Okay, yeah."

"All right, then. Let's go."

Neither of their bodies moved from the chairs. And yet, somehow, they also flew together through the nebula, feeling the bite of the wind as it rushed past their ears.

This part always made Ollie think of his mom. *My goodness, wasn't that a breath of fresh air!* she used to say, whenever she had done something she liked. Which was most things. This flight was the ultimate breath of fresh air. And Ollie felt her there, carrying him along, each time.

When they landed, Ollie led his charge toward the circle of floating objects. The man hesitated, as they all tended to do, then stepped inside and began examining each item. Ollie gave him some space, moving a respectable distance away. Then he clasped his hands and waited.

This one might take a while.

That was fine with Ollie. He had learned to be patient.

The man had once been imprisoned in Herrick's End. Floor Twenty-Seven. Now, he lived with the other former inmates on the new island the witches had created, complete with houses, huts, dining tents, and even recreation centers. Bert had even managed to conjure a few palm trees. Not Nirvana, perhaps, but not too shabby, either. They had given Ollie the honor of naming it, and so, when the sign finally went up, it was carved with two words: ELLORA'S END. Tera had used her finest brushes to encircle the name with a painted border of dainty white flowers.

Ollie offered his services to all Ellora's End residents, and many had taken him up on it. More every day. Later, if they chose, they could also visit the witch Widow Hibbins, a.k.a. the former "Reader" at Herrick's End. Back then, the Widow had laid bare each person's misdeeds, even going so far as to project them onto a wall for the world to see. These days, though, she dabbled mostly in what had come to be known as "reverse readings." With a touch of her hand, she searched each inmate's heart for two things: remorse, and benevolent intent. If she found both, the prisoner could choose to either stay at Ellora's End or start a new life elsewhere in the Neath.

Leonard had remained in his position as the population's "Superintendent of Operations," though most people had taken to calling him "Mayor." Or "Mayor Leonard." Or, once in a great while, "Mayor Mallet." In typical good-humored Leonard fashion, he would happily answer to any or all.

Ajanta was still running the Tea Party food stall, though Ollie had lately become too busy with his other duties to be much help. Dozer, fortunately, had filled in for him—initially as a temporary measure, and then as a more permanent replacement. Dozer had taken a surprising liking to the food-cart life...and to Ajanta. As the months went by, the pair worked closely together to create new recipes. Then, *more* closely. And finally, *so* closely that Dozer ditched his shack altogether and moved into Ajanta's house. Ollie suspected that the cart's name would soon be changed to Dozanta's. Or Ajazer's. Or something equally ridiculous. Just the thought of it made him smile.

Laszlo had been working in tandem with Michael Carmichael, of all people, to whip the underwater lab back into shape— specifically, into a less evil, more constructive kind of shape. The tanks, tortures, and malevolent contraptions were gone, but the lab techs had returned. Voluntarily, this time around. The Novas had even helped to reestablish the tunnel entrances, so staff and visitors no longer had to rely on riddles and dilapidated mine-shaft elevator cages to get there.

The techs were hoping to improve the effects of the pellet-gun breathing device Ollie had used, with the end goal of allowing more people the freedom to visit the Brickside. So far, they'd managed to extend the effects beyond just one week, though they were still working out the side-effect kinks. Laszlo had a dream to create a kind of Neath-Brickside travel agency, where he would escort Neathians on guided vacations to Boston and beyond. In the meantime, Laz continued to travel between the two realms, always bringing back plenty of North End and Quincy Market goodies for Ollie and his friends to sample upon each return. According to the scuttlebutt, he and his tour-guide paramour, Caroline, had become a pretty steady item, and Ollie suspected that his friend might—shockingly—be ready to leave the bachelor life behind.

Derrin had mostly recovered from her injury, though it had taken a while. In the beginning, Ollie had visited her bedside almost every day. Kuyu had tolerated his presence, then, begrudgingly, had begun to show a mild enthusiasm for his arrival. "Be careful," Ollie had told her. "People might start to think you actually like me." At that, she had punched him not-so-gently in the stomach.

His father was...his father. Nowadays, Matteo worked in the infirmary, putting his healing powers to good use and "turning over a new leaf," as he liked to say. He was also working to rehabilitate the many witches who had been trapped and depleted inside Herrick's lab tanks. Ollie remained guardedly skeptical. Often he wondered what kind of leaf, specifically, his dad was referring to, and which way it was turning. But he kept most of those questions to himself.

Matteo had made new drinking buddies over at Moseby's, where he'd become a regular. Sometimes he invited Ollie to join him, and sometimes Ollie accepted. As soon as the grog kicked in, his father would launch into lengthy, often tearful soliloquies: "You deserved better than me," was a frequent theme, as was "I was a lousy dad and husband."

It was weird. Always. But sometimes it was a good kind of weird, which was more than Ollie had ever expected to say of their relationship. Maybe, someday, they'd have a normal father-son thing going. Maybe. In the meantime, he'd settle for occasional pints at the pub.

He and Tera had expanded the crow barn out back, bringing in a few avian friends so Mrs. Paget didn't have to roost alone. She seemed to like the company. Their trog brood had grown, as well, expanding to include Meatball's mate, a whitish female they called Focaccia, and a litter of teeny, multicolored fuzzballs named Éclair, Tiramisu, Panettone, Zeppole, Florentine, and Pizzelle. Ollie didn't know which one was which, and had stopped trying to figure it out.

Tera had opened her art stall to much acclaim, as he knew she would. Her notoriety as one of the "Herrick slayers" had made business boom: People now routinely waited weeks for an appointment to get their portraits painted. Ollie loved everything she created. But his favorite, of course, was the painting she had made of the two of them, standing side-by-side. The gentle giant and the petite beauty. As unlikely and perfect a pair as there ever was. The portrait hung front-and-center in the main room of their home.

Ollie looked at it every day, reminding himself of his utterly exceptional luck. He would grow old with this remarkable woman. How crazy was that? And as the years passed, this picture would remind him of the time, place, and circumstances that had allowed them to find each other. And save each other. And follow the path that had been laid by ancestors long before.

Kizzee, kizzee, kismet.

Ollie unclasped his hands. From the corner of his eye, he noticed that his client had finished examining the floating objects and now stood, floundering, in the center of the circle.

Gently, Ollie led him away. They flew once again through the bracing air. When they opened their eyes, they were back sitting on the chair pads, as though they had never left. Which, technically, they hadn't.

The man blinked, hard, then blinked again. He was trembling. "Whoa, dude," he breathed. "That was some crazy shit!"

Ollie nodded.

"What am I supposed to do now?"

"Nothing."

"Nothing?"

"Just live with it, for a while. Think about it."

"But, she was... And then I..." The man was visibly upset. "I mean, she...!"

Ollie nodded.

"Krite! It's just.... I mean, I didn't even—" The man seemed unable to finish the sentence. Or any sentence.

"You didn't know, and now you do," Ollie said. "And that's a good place to start."

The man gave him a look of incredulity. He threaded his fingers together, then pulled them apart. He rubbed his forehead vigorously, as though trying to push around his thoughts. Then he looked back at Ollie. "And what about you, man?"

"What about me?"

"Why are you doing this?"

"Why wouldn't I?"

"Dude, you took down George frickin' *Herrick*. The witches couldn't even do it, and you did! Why are you wasting your time with...with all this?" He waved a hand to indicate the office's humble environs, and himself.

Ollie gave a soft laugh. "Don't believe everything you hear."

"So what are you going to do now?"

"What do you mean?"

"I mean, are you gonna take over the world, or what? C'mon, man. You can go into people's *minds!* You can have anything you want!"

At that, Ollie grinned. "I already do."

Then he rose to his feet, reached for his canvas knapsack, and slung it over his shoulder. "Now if you'll excuse me, I'm going to be late for dinner with a very beautiful girl. Be sure to take a cookie on your way out!" Ollie pointed to a nearby tray of chocolate-dipped macaroons from Bonfiglio's. Mr. B's favorite. He was halfway to the door when the man called out.

"Hey, Mister Delgato?"

"Please, I told you: Call me Ollie."

"Mister...Ollie?"

"Yes?"

"Can I come again next week?"

Ollie nodded and winked. "Same time, same place." He turned to leave, then paused and reached for the cookies. "Maybe just one," he said, waggling his eyebrows.

He walked through the doorway into the faint blue light of the cavern, descending a series of stone steps. The wormwalkers had entered into a dim cycle and the fog was thick, making navigation difficult. He squinted into the murk, seeing nothing. And then...a glint. Growing brighter as it buzzed into clear view.

A glowbug.

A delicate, rainbow-hued glowbug, just like the one that had helped to illuminate his plans on that fateful day. Maybe the very same one? Could that be possible?

Ollie went still, holding his breath as the tiny creature landed on his fingertip.

"Well, hello there," he murmured, trying not to startle it. His heart pattered unexpectedly. Something about the insect's sudden

345

appearance in the gloom felt so...comforting. So miraculous and strange. As though someone, somewhere, was trying to send him a beaming, multicolored message. The creature was so frail, yet so bright, like a little harbinger of—

A snapping tongue interrupted his musings. Meatball slurped, then swallowed.

Ollie's fingertip was empty. The glowbug was gone.

He turned to stare, incredulous. "Dude! What the hell?"

The trog on his shoulder ignored him, spinning and resettling with a satisfied grunt.

Ollie shook his head. Then he hardened his expression and held up the cookie. "Fine. But don't think I'm sharing this with you. Because I'm not. Not one single bite."

Meatball didn't seem worried.

"I mean it!"

Five minutes later, the trog was licking macaroon crumbs off his beak. And the well-worn, winding path had, as ever, led them home.

Acknowledgements

Thank you to the incomparable Galen Surlak-Ramsey and the entire team at Tiny Fox Press, including Natalie Day, Maya Sherlick, Elizabeth Young, Wahid Sarwar, Celena Nimmo, and Jennifer Ayala, for your support, advice, and brilliant edits. You make me look good, and more importantly, you make this fun. As Ollie would say: I am the luckiest person in the room. The very luckiest.

Thank you to Dan Gagnon, Lead Park Ranger at Boston National Historical Park, for sharing your knowledge (time and again) about the Bunker Hill Monument.

Thank you to Paula Ricci for the fascinating behind-the-scenes peek at the Salem ghost tours. Your generosity and time are much appreciated.

Thank you to Suzanne Taylor at the Freedom Trail Foundation for patiently answering pesky questions from a pesky writer about Boston's coolest magical portal... I mean, historic attraction.

Thank you to Doug Drake for your incomparable proofreading prowess. (Something tells me you and Laszlo would get along famously.)

Thank you to the incredible humans and canines at Operation Delta Dog: Service Dogs for Veterans (OperationDeltaDog.org). We will always be family, no matter where we roam.

Thank you to Ann Garvin and all of the wonderful Tall Poppy Writers: I'm honored, still, to count myself among your ranks.

Thank you to my audacious colleagues at A Mighty Blaze, where we've all teetered outside of our comfort zones long enough to learn a thing or two—and make a friend or two. George Herrick (shockingly) said it best: A spark is no equal to a mighty blaze.

Thank you to my writing-workshop crew, who cheered me on throughout this series, read innumerable drafts, and didn't let me quit until Ollie's story was complete: Jenna Blum, Hillary Casavant, Mark Cecil, Tom Champoux, Jennifer De Leon, Catherine Elcik, Chuck Garabedian, Julie Gerstenblatt, Kimberly Hensle Lowrance, Edwin Hill, Sonya Larson, Joseph Moldover, Jenna Paone, Kris Paull, Jane Roper, Whitney Scharer, Adam Stumacher, and Alexandra Sunshine. Damn, you people are special.

Thank you to Susan Arapoff and Tricia Chamberlin for braving the heat and hills of Charlestown (and the pasta and pastry of the North End), all in the name of very important research.

Thank you to Martha and Dan Voner, parents extraordinaire. Your kids never have to wonder what true love looks like.

Thank you to Ian, for solving my magic-rock problem, and to Lucy, for solving my magic-tree problem. You're the Sweetest Screams a mom could ask for.

And thank you, always, to Scott. I love you to the Neath and back.

About The Author

 T.M. Blanchet is a former reporter, editor, and award-winning humor columnist, as well as the founder of the nonprofit organization Operation Delta Dog: Service Dogs for Veterans. She's also the producer and host of A Mighty Blaze Podcast, which features weekly interviews with bestselling and debut authors. T.M. is a proud member of the Tall Poppy Writers, the Science Fiction & Fantasy Writers Association (SFWA), and GrubStreet in Boston.

Website: tmblanchet.com

Instagram: t.m.blanchet
Tiktok: @tmblanchet
Facebook: Facebook.com/tmblanchet

About the Publisher

Tiny Fox Press LLC
11782 Little River Way
Parrish, FL 34219

www.tinyfoxpress.com